CRUELTY

EDWARD LORN

CRUELTY

Also by Edward Lorn

Bay's End
Dastardly Bastard
Hope for the Wicked
Fog Warning
Pennies for the Damned
Fairy Lights
The Sound of Broken Ribs
The Bedding of Boys
Everything is Horrible How
No Home for Boys

Collections

What the Dark Brings
Others & Oddities
Word

CRUELTY

CRUELTY

WILL

The deaf man and the prostitute moseyed on down the road.

Sounds like the beginning of a joke, William Longmire thought. Only he didn't know the punch line. He supposed the kicker was the blown head gasket in his '89 Pontiac Bonneville, which was now a good two miles behind them. A laugh track played in his head. His life— sitcom material if ever there was such a thing. His feet hurt. They'd been walking for hours. He'd started counting steps as soon as they left his broken down car. Each step equaled one yard. So far they had travelled two miles. Trees bracketed them on both sides—nothing but dark, hopeless woods wherein Will would surely lose his bearings if he tried to escape into their waiting branches.

The whore's name was Jennifer. "She's a country pro," his father would've said. You didn't drop by a street corner to pick up a country pro. Oh, no. You knocked on her door. But you had to come recommended. His buddy Kirk had put in a good word for Will, and Jennifer had invited Will over. Kirk had slapped him playfully on the back and wished him luck. Will, blushing, had thanked his friend and taken the Bonneville out to Kerrville. Hopes of scoring had filled Will's mind—bedroom shenanigans only fitting the nastiest of porno movies. But when he knocked on Jennifer's door, she'd had other plans.

The pistol was still jammed in his side. As they moved briskly down Highway 16, out in the middle of nowhere—Will's butt cheeks clenching and relaxing, seizing and abating—Jennifer seemed intent on shoving that small caliber weapon *into* him instead of shooting him with it. She kept twitching. Will watched her from the corner of his eye. A full moon made the country pro look washed out, gray and emaciated. Her lips were moving, but of course, he couldn't hear her. Back at her trailer—a shoddy, run-down relic from the '50s—he'd been able to read her lips: something about money, and then another thing about breath. Since he'd had a good bit of time with her under his belt—four hours, to be exact—he'd come to the realization that Jennifer hadn't been saying "breath" at all.

Her teeth looked like wasted pilings; cylinders of rotted wood worn down by the constant battery of oceanic waves. The knee-length jean skirt and yellow Abercrombie & Fitch tee fluttered about her, as if draped over clothesline. Sores stood out on her flesh—red splotches on gunmetal skin. Will was reminded of an anorexic elephant with necrotizing fasciitis. Moreover, he recalled a PSA he'd seen in his senior year in high school. *The Effects of Meth*, the program had been called.

So, no, Jennifer hadn't been saying "breath."

Will had lost his hearing in junior high after swimming in bacteria-infected water. Skinny-dipping with friends in a rural neighbor's pond had sounded like a great idea at the time. The murky fluid settled in the bottom of his ear canal, festered, bred, and almost turned septic. There had been pain. Even more agony when his mother had examined him with an invasive procedure involving a Q-tip. She'd said he needed his ears drained. He hadn't liked the sound of that. Before the procedure, everything had sounded thick, distant and full of echoes. The doctor was a burly lumberjack type. Even wore the requisite shaggy beard. The physician lingered in Will's ear, making heavy groaning noises, as if Will's condition was just the sorriest sight he'd ever seen. There was a *pop* then a flood of warm fluid. A smell akin to moss and cinnamon. Sick to his stomach. Retching into a pink basin while Mommy patted him on the back. He remembered craning his neck to look up at her. Mom was talking, but he couldn't hear a thing. Either ear. He threw up some more and passed out.

As he moved down Highway 16, Jennifer's handgun stuck deep into his ribs, he was glad he couldn't hear her. That might have seemed backward to some people, but to Will it made perfect sense. He didn't want to know what she was saying; her lunatic rambling would be sure to drive him mad. The car breaking down had done something to her, shattered her already cracked mind. Withdrawal, Will guessed. She needed a fix, and it was nowhere in sight. She scratched absently yet viciously at a glistening wound on her forearm. It opened up and black blood snaked from the hole. It glistened in the moonlight like a slick, fat worm laid out on a gray beach. He felt sick to his stomach.

Will had the ability to speak, but he never did. Not being able to hear himself, he was constantly concerned with how he would sound. Would he be too loud? Would he unknowingly make weird noises? He was forever aware of the status of his vocal cords, whether or not they vibrated with activity or remained dormant. Kirk never mentioned anything of the sort, and neither did Will's mother, but that could be nothing more than a courtesy. How rude would they sound if all of a sudden they said something to the tune of, "Stop that god-awful noise! You're not a pig"? Of course, Will only had his own experience to rely on. When he was seven, Will and his mom had passed a man in the grocery store. The stranger was stocking shelves, squealing and grunting like a rutting hog. Being the social child that he was, Will said hello. The man didn't respond. Mom dragged Will away by his wrist.

"He's deaf and dumb," Mom had said.

"What makes him dumb?" Will understood deaf. That meant the man couldn't hear. But what made him dumb? It wasn't a word Mom used often.

"He doesn't know how to speak. It's a... it's a turn of phrase."

In the years since Will had lost his hearing—all seven of them—he'd tried his damnedest not to be the second half of that turn of phrase. He could be deaf. He could allow that much. But he would not be seen as dumb. So he focused on not making a peep. He felt the decision had served him well.

Reading lips came almost naturally—God's way of making up the difference, Will supposed. It helped that he knew what words should sound like, which movements of the lips created what inflection, and so on. He counted his blessings that he'd been able to hear for the twelve years he'd been granted the sense. After it was snatched away, there was sadness, but Will was stronger and smarter than even he knew. Instead of crawling into a corner and bawling on a daily basis, he'd taken sign language courses and read books on the subject of being deaf. He'd even gone as far as reading everything he could on Helen Keller. He wouldn't admit this to anyone else, but he felt comforted by stories of the deaf and blind girl. At least he could see.

The gun dug into him further, and his vocal cords thrummed with life. Will was pretty sure he'd shrieked. Fear, he'd forgotten all about the fear. Just as he'd forgotten his cell phone.

He saw his phone then, an eternity removed, sitting on the bookshelf at home, mocking him. A common misconception was that deaf people had no need for such devices. But in the age of texting and social media and wireless communication, phone calls were not one's only option of reaching out to touch someone. He'd first noticed the absence of his phone while on the way to Jennifer's. He was lost, wanting to use his cell to text Kirk for clearer directions, but hadn't been able to find it. He pulled over into a closed gas station—a mom-and-pop called Bob's Bait and Fuel—and dug through his pockets before rummaging around in the Bonneville's center console. He even checked the glove box. Nothing. He beat his fists against the steering wheel. He'd come four miles on Highway 16, was another ten miles from home, and didn't want to turn around. Being a typical nineteen-year-old male, he'd been thinking with the wrong head. He should have turned around then, headed on home to a cold shower or a rigorous coupling with Sally Palmer and her five sisters, but he hadn't.

The state trooper had pulled in behind him while Will was still debating what to do about his current predicament. Will's heart leapt into his throat. He couldn't breathe. He tried to swallow and he felt his throat click. Spinning roof lights turned the evening into a Kmart special. *Half off stupid, horny teenagers*, Will thought.

Two minutes later, the trooper exited the cruiser and came to Will's side of the car. The man was tall, maybe six-two, but no less than six foot. Will was only five-five. The trooper's chubby cheeks belied his thin frame. The man looked like a walking lollipop, all thick on the top and stick-thin on the bottom. Will already had the window down. The trooper's lips moved at a rapid clip. Will didn't catch a word. He lifted his hands from his lap very slowly, so as not to raise the trooper's suspicions, and placed a palm over each ear, shaking his head in the process. The trooper nodded. From somewhere behind him, the trooper removed a notepad and, pulling a pen from the spiral binding, began to write.

License and registration. Proof of insurance.

Will produced the documents, but the trooper didn't return to his car. The man looked over Will's ID and Progressive card. He kept nodding, as if something was abundantly clear to him. After a full minute the trooper gave him back his information. Will didn't think the man had even so much as glanced at his registration.

The trooper wrote: *What are you doing out here? This place is closed.*

I'm lost. Stopped 2 txt friend for dir X but 4got phone.

Where are you heading?

Will began to jot down the address, but decided to leave off the house number. He was, after all, going to see a woman who rented out her vagina for a living. It occurred to Will that the authorities around these parts might know of her. He handed the tablet with the street name written on it back to the trooper.

Two more miles down. Only street on the left. Be safe.

And with that, the trooper was gone. Will felt giddy with relief, almost stoned with gratitude. He shoved his arm out of the open window and waved back at the cop.

In hindsight, Will felt like an idiot for being so joyous and thankful back at that gas station.

Beside him now, Jennifer tripped and went sprawling on hands and knees. Will had a brief thought, one that involved running into the woods. But before the idea had fully formed, Jennifer had the gun up and pointed at him in a sideways fashion. He didn't have to read her lips to know she was saying, "Don't even think about it."

It occurred to Will then that Jennifer might not know he was deaf. Not that that information would have changed anything. But he was starting to put some things together. For instance, she kept talking even when she wasn't facing him. He could see the cords in her neck throbbing and stretching while her jaw jacked up and down. This new info did absolutely nothing for Will's state of mind, but it was something else to think about other than getting himself shot by some psychotic tweaker bitch.

Jennifer collected herself and stood up. She wiped her free hand on her yellow tee, leaving a dark smudge the size of a football smeared across her midsection.

She'd torn her hand up pretty good on the asphalt. Her palm probably looked like a topographical map of the Rockies.

She roared at Will, the muscles in her neck straining, veins bulging in her temples, as she thrust the gun into his face. Her lips formed the same unintelligible word over and over again. Three syllables, Will thought, because of the way her jaw jerked open and closed thrice before shutting completely. Then she would start again. Mouth working three times, tongue flicking at those shit-colored teeth, spraying rancid spittle over the barrel of the gun and into his face.

Will clapped his hands over his ears. She stopped screaming. Her head tilted to the side, comically, like a dog with a query. She made a duck-face. Will almost laughed. He slapped a palm to his mouth then covered his ears again and shook his head.

Realization bled over her face, and the comical expression disappeared. She waved the gun around in front of him, the barrel looking big enough to drive a tractor through, her mouth forming a word that he could understand. The thin lips pressed together, blossomed out, spread into a grin, and then died in a frown.

She'd said, "Mute."

He nodded, feeling himself deflate with relief.

She started to laugh, hard. Her free hand clutched her concave stomach while the rest of her twitched and jerked like a marionette controlled by a drunken puppeteer.

Losing one sense enhances the remaining four. The world had seemed brighter, higher in definition, after he'd lost his hearing. Tastes didn't just play over his tongue any more; they popped, exploded, crackled like live wires. He could smell dog shit from a mile away; always knew when Kirk had been on a protein shake binge, the smell of his expulsions skunky and goatish. Along with all that, his sense of touch—the receptors in his skin that dealt with nuances such as wind on bare skin, hot and cold sensations, and vibrations—had become so keen that he imagined he could kneel beside a railroad track and feel the very earth vibrate with the violent trundling of an approaching locomotive.

He stood there before Jennifer, watching her cackle at his deafness, and felt the briefest shift in the air, a displacement of sorts; an invisible hand gently nudging at his right hip.

When it was gone, so was Jennifer.

It took him half a minute to realize that what he'd felt was the rush of air being pushed into him by a speeding car. The vehicle was going so fast that it was nothing more than a flash in his vision. Jennifer was there, and then she wasn't. In fact, all he'd really seen of the car was a streak of moon in the windows as it flew past. The sight was not unlike seeing a comet speed by right in front of your eyes.

He jerked his head to the right as the night went bloody with brake lights. The smell of burning rubber crashed into him, knocking him back a step. Something was rolling across the road in the glow of the headlights, tumbling like a carpet dropped from the back of a van. It came to rest twenty feet away from the car, bent and twisted like a pretzel.

The car had fishtailed, its trunk ending up in the oncoming lane, and the front bumper hanging over the dividing line. The driver's side door was thrust open, but no one got out.

Will took a hesitant step forward, chest hitching with breath, the smell of scalded tires making it hard to find an ounce of fresh oxygen. He reeked, as if he'd dove into a vat of melted Barbie dolls. The aroma clung to him like a lover.

Still, no one emerged from the car. Will squinted into the compartment; saw no one at the wheel. He drew his attention back to the crumpled mass in the road. Jennifer's right foot was flush with her right cheek. The left leg jutted from her side, making her look like a check mark. Her arms were above her head, as if she were a ref at a football game and someone had just successfully kicked a field goal. And there was so much blood. Blood on the front of the car. Five feet of blood painted in one long brush stroke, starting somewhere between the car and Jennifer, and ending where she'd come to rest. A puddle of the stuff beneath and around her, spreading outward.

Will took a step back, bent over, and blew the remnants of two McDoubles all over the pavement. What came out of him was pink.

Movement to his left. A hunched over figure moved away from the side of the car and into the headlights.

Long, curly black hair covered the face of the stooped figure. The body was ambiguous; Will had no idea whether he was looking at a man or a woman. All he knew was the person had a weight problem. Morbidly obese would have been an understatement. Will guessed maybe five-, no, six hundred pounds. It didn't walk, it waddled—lurching forward like a fattened Frankenstein's monster. A chubby hand came up and brushed away the tight black curls.

A baby doll smiled back at Will. The cheeks were red circles, mimicking blush. The rest of the face was pink, but cracked. The paint had flaked off in places and the black underneath showed through, which was somehow scarier than anything else about the thing. Dressed in black from neck to boot, the thing seemed nothing more than a head floating in the night. Will's heart trip-hammered, a thundering *ker-thud*, *ker-thud*, *ker-thud,* in his head.

The baby doll observed Will, seemed to study him. Then, it rolled—that was the best way he could describe it; the thing didn't turn, it *rolled*—to the side, tilting into the turn so deeply that Will thought it would surely topple over, before it shuffled off in the direction of Jennifer's broken corpse.

Insanely, Will was no longer in the moment. Something bounded around his head, punching at the surface of thought, begging to be heard. As distressing as the obese baby doll was, another thought was more pressing.

Will had not seen headlights. For some reason, that fact alone set his teeth on edge and brought him around to the appropriate level of terror. Merely seeing that god-awful face hadn't been enough, but knowing the intent, the purpose of the thing now approaching Jennifer in a slow, shuddering gait, struck home the urgency of his situation.

No headlights. It hadn't wanted them to see it coming.

But there had been headlights afterward, after Jennifer had been smashed to hell upon the cold, hard asphalt of Highway 16. *Of course there was*, thought Will. *It wanted to see its handiwork*.

The baby doll didn't seem interested in Will, and for that he was glad. Positively overjoyed. He could escape. But how?

A tiny, tinny voice, like one through a distant loudspeaker, spoke up in his head.

You have a perfectly good car right in front of you.

Will didn't want to. He wanted to run away, actually run, no matter how insane that sounded. He didn't want to set foot in that thing's car. But he had no other choice.

That's crazy, another, deeper voice said. *You don't even know that this thing means you harm.*

It was that second voice—the insane thought that this thing of nightmares could want anything other than to rip him asunder, bit by bit—which thrust him into action.

Will ran. He sprinted around the back of the car, only then noticing the vehicle was old, really old, and that it reminded him of his grandfather's Studebaker Hawk. In fact, he thought that was the exact make and model of the car. He'd helped Pop work on the Studebaker during the summer while Will had been in high school. When Pop died of a stroke last year, Mom had sold the car to pay for the funeral. Baby Doll's ride was a two-door coupe with foot-tall wings in the back and a trunk almost as long as the engine compartment. Add in the signature low roof and yes, sir, a Studebaker Hawk, sure enough.

The driver's side door was still open, and he slid inside with little difficulty. When he hit the seat, he felt the rumble of the engine through the springs under the upholstery and knew it was running. The dash glowed faintly, giving everything a dark, greenish-yellow glow. A thick air of Juicy Fruit gum hung on the air, sickeningly sweet. The Hawk was an automatic with a bench seat.

Outside, Baby Doll was coming. The thing was dragging Jennifer by her ankle. It would step forward, pause, jerk her forward, then take another step. It was slow going. Will had plenty of time.

Will grabbed the shifter, wrenched it toward him, then up, and shoved his foot so hard into the gas pedal that his ankle went wonky, sending bolts of lightning up his leg and into his hip.

Some darker version of Will wanted to run the nightmare down, crush it beneath the steel undercarriage of the Studebaker, but at the last moment he wrenched the steering wheel to the left, missing the hulking monster by mere inches.

He was gone, safe. The nightmare was over, behind him.

Will began to cry.

CRUELTY

INNIS

Nefarious cocksucker, Innis Blake thought. *Lying, cheating, nefarious little cocksucker!*

She'd never used "nefarious" or "cocksucker" in a sentence before. Yet she felt that the situation called for a specific type of vulgarity. Bruce was a criminal. He'd stolen her heart. He was also a cocksucker. She'd caught him, mouth full and eyes wide, servicing his boy toy. How could she have been so stupid? How could he have been so evil? It wasn't the gay part. That she could almost live with. It was the betrayal, the running around behind her back; the lies. "Going to the gym, babe," and "The boys and I are hanging out," all turned out to be code for "I'm off to swallow some dick, be home soon!"

In the passenger seat, Merlo chuffed. The beagle didn't like to see her angry. He kept trying to scoot over onto her thighs to comfort her, and she'd have to shove him back by his nose. None of this was Merlo's fault, but she couldn't have his forty pounds nestled in her lap while she was trying to drive.

"I bet he even tried to suck *your* dick!" she said.

Merlo whined.

She slapped the steering wheel. "Bruce, you nefarious cocksucker!" It was the first time she'd said it aloud and it felt good that it was out there now, spoken for both her and Merlo to appreciate. She started to calm down, to think.

She'd have to call Whitney in the morning, see about buying out of the lease she had on the apartment. Let Bruce have the place, but she didn't want to be responsible for the rent if he suddenly decided to move in with his new man. How much would Whitney charge her? Three, maybe four grand? She wasn't sure, but tomorrow was a new day, so full of promise and so wonderfully devoid of nefarious cocksuckers.

"Just you and me, boy," she told Merlo.

The beagle looked up at her with those puppy dog eyes, circled three times atop the seat cushion, and curled up into a ball.

"I see how it is. Your momma's hurting and you wanna take a nap. No, no, go on. Go to sleep. See if you get Alpo in the morning. Walmart bargain bin for you from now on. Uh huh. Don't look at me like that."

Merlo exhaled at length.

Innis did the same. "I need to find a hotel. Should we live it up, pup? The Hilton, maybe? Or should we slum?" She growled low, a mischievous tone to her voice. Merlo's ears perked up and his eyes widened. "You know," she cackled, "a Motel Eight or Best Eastern?"

Merlo tucked his nose under his paws.

"Right. We deserve something nice. I think there's a Drury Inn in Kerrville. We'll see. Nothing under a hundred dollars a night though, right?"

Merlo was asleep.

"Some companion you are."

Innis judged herself in the rearview mirror, her green eyes looking black in the dark car. Was she so perfect that she could lambaste Bruce to such a degree? Had she not also faltered on their journey together?

"I didn't blow anyone in our living room, if that's what you're getting at," she told her reflection.

She tossed her brown hair over her shoulder, her almond skin flushing pink in the glow of the Audi's red dash lights, and wondered if Bruce had ever really meant it when he'd called her beautiful or gorgeous or stunning. Probably. As a gay man, he was probably even jealous of her more feminine features, something he would only be able to achieve with the help of surgery and hormones. Who was she kidding? She didn't even know if he was that kind of gay. He might love his man parts just as much as the next guy.

A nasty, insidious thought crossed her mind. It burrowed frighteningly deep. Would she ever be able to trust another man again? All the fight went out of her and she slumped in her seat a bit. Would she become some old maid, incapable of trusting or loving another person? That was nonsense, she assured herself. Of course she wouldn't devolve into some prudish biddy. She had her whole life ahead of her. Thirty wasn't old. Her own mother had been thirty-three when she'd become pregnant with Innis, and forty when she gave birth to Innis's brother, Gerald. Gerald was five years in the ground, but he'd lived a good life up until some white asshole shot him dead in the middle of the street.

"Just what I need, thoughts of Gerry."

It seemed her brain was working against her, trying to dig up the most unsettling and displeasing thoughts it could muster. She hated herself for not wanting to think about Gerald, but she hated Bruce even more. In the end, she thought about her dead brother.

Eighteen was much too young to die. Given the circumstances, though, eighty would have been a bad age to die. Gerald had been walking home from band practice—he'd played the flute, and had been quite good, too—when he was approached by an off-duty security guard, Grover Duchamp. Duchamp had been snorting coke all day and had convinced himself it was time for him to kill somebody. Simple as that, Duchamp said during the trial. He pulled out a Ruger P95 and shot Gerald in the neck. When the cops came, Duchamp was kneeling beside Gerald, his finger plugging the hole in her brother's larynx. He told the responding officer, "I'm sorry," before aiming his gun at the policeman. Officer Bart Pleats shot Duchamp four times, paralyzing but not killing Gerald's murderer. Duchamp was sent to prison for life without the possibility of parole.

Caitlyn Blake, their mother, cried for nine days straight. Innis knew because she'd been there, had counted. Caitlyn refused to go to the trial, said that nothing could ever replace Gerald, so what was the point? So Innis had gone. And Innis had watched her brother's murderer frown when they passed down his sentence. Duchamp didn't cry or make a scene. Duchamp just frowned, as if someone had stolen his candy bar. Innis had never known hate so strong, so acidic, as when she had looked upon that man's sulking face.

At least the nefarious cocksucker was better than Grover Duchamp, she thought.

"Here we are," she told her reflection, "right back where we started. Fuck you, Bruce."

Nine months wasn't a long time, she knew that now. All her friends had warned her about jumping into the relationship with both feet, but she hadn't listened. When her mother said three months was far too soon to be moving in with a man, Innis had balked and strutted out the door; again, not listening. When she'd called her dad out in North Carolina to give him the news about moving in with Bruce, Dad had said, "White men are nothing but trouble." She'd responded by saying she loved Bruce. Dad hung up on her. She didn't think Bruce being Caucasian had anything to do with him being trouble, but once again, she should have listened. Everything seemed so clear now. As if all her friends and family had been psychics on a par with James Van Praag and Sylvia Browne, which was to say, not real psychics at all but damn good judges of character.

She asked the rearview, "Was it P.T. Barnum who said, 'A sucker's born every minute'?"

Her reflection didn't answer.

The car hit something. Innis was tossed in the air, banging her head on the ceiling, as the tires bounced over something far too big to be human. Merlo slid off the seat, yipped, and came to a thudding halt on the floorboard. Again, the car bounded upward as the rear wheels met whatever animal she'd hit. At least she hoped it was an animal. She stomped the brake, thanking God for anti-lock, and came to a stop at the scrub on the side of the road.

Merlo whined from under the glove box.

"It's okay, boy." Fact was, she had no idea if everything was okay, but felt obligated to comfort the canine.

In the rearview, her brake lights turned the world a dark crimson. She tilted the mirror to get a better look, but couldn't see much: the broken yellow line in the middle of the road, darkness not entirely defeated by her rear lights, a section of asphalt darker than all the rest. Could that darkness be someone? She didn't know. Couldn't tell. She tried to tell herself it was some*thing* not some*one*; that she had simply run over some poor woodland creature. It would be sad, a real Disney tragedy, but not cause to worry about jail time.

It moved.

"Oh, God." She gasped, slapping a palm to her mouth.

It rolled over.

"Oh, yes, yes, yes—" she chanted, over and over again like some kind of rite, as if she could will away this person's injuries simply by repeating that mantra.

It stood.

"Oh, thank you, Jesus!" She wasn't a terribly religious person, but seeing that person standing made her believe in miracles. After all, she had run them over. With both wheels.

And they had gotten up.

Her stomach twisted into knots. Something was wrong.

The mystery person did not approach the car but turned, leaned down, and grabbed something from the road.

Automatically, she snatched her iPhone from the cubbyhole under the stereo and unlocked it with a swipe of her thumb. Merlo whined from the floorboards, and didn't seem to want to get back in the seat. Innis resolved to check if he was hurt from his tumble once she'd made the required call. The person in her rearview was drawing closer now, allowing her to see the sheer size of it. She dialed 9-1-1. The figure was dragging something, and by the looks of it, something heavy. Innis engaged the speakerphone. The stranger staggered forward, drunkenly. There was something about its gait that didn't seem right, but she couldn't put her finger on it.

The dispatcher answered, "Emergency services, how may I direct your call?"

Innis whispered, "I hit someone with my car."

"Ma'am?"

A little louder, "I hit. Someone. With. My car."

The dispatcher came back with a far more serious tone, "What is your name and location?"

"Innis Blake. Highway 16, between Fredericksburg and Kerrville." Innis paused, breathing hard, every exhalation caustic. She squinted to get a better look at the approaching figure. "Is that a mask?"

"What, ma'am?"

"He's... *huge*." At least she assumed it was a he. If it were a woman, she was the biggest lady Innis had ever seen.

"Ma'am, can you see a mile marker?"

"I—I think I should leave."

"You shouldn't abandon the scene of an accident, ma'am."

"This person doesn't look right, lady."

"Leaving the scene of an accident is against—"

The figure was only a couple of feet from the rear of the Audi. Innis could see its face quite clearly now.

Innis shuddered. "He looks like a baby doll."

She put the car into drive.

"Is this the person you hit? Are they up, walking around?"

"Oh yeah," was all Innis could think to say. She eased her foot off the brake and the Audi rolled forward two feet before she stopped it again.

The dispatcher said, "You need to have them lay down until the paramedics arrive."

Innis laughed. It was a nervous thing. "I'm not getting out of my car, lady."

The person in the baby doll mask shifted course and began walking toward the driver's side of the car. Innis removed her foot from the brake again and the car idled forward. The masked individual lurched forward, hobbling quicker, matching the speed of the Audi's slow roll.

That's when Innis saw the shoe. She'd been so intent on watching the lumbering man-thing that she'd taken her attention off whatever he'd been dragging. In his right hand, clenched firmly in a black fist, was someone's sneaker. Their body, half-hidden by the baby doll man's immense form, slid into view.

Innis screamed. She stomped on the accelerator and the car responded. The tires spun in the grass and the Audi fishtailed, swinging the rear of the sports coupe back out onto the asphalt. When the rear tires screeched up onto the pavement, the Audi shot forward into the tree line, where it met the resistance of a sturdy oak. Innis was thrown forward. Her forehead rapped sharply against the steering wheel. Her hairline split and warm blood spilled into her eyes.

Merlo barked twice, then fell silent.

A voice drifted on the air as the world spun in her vision. Someone was asking her if she was all right. Hadn't she been talking to someone? Wasn't there something important she needed to focus on?

That something landed on the hood, shoving the car down on its springs. In the backsplash from the headlights, the woman was an ugly sight, face like a busted watermelon; her gender only evident by the bra strap dangling from the sleeve of a yellow tee. Slowly, the woman slid off the side of the car.

Innis looked left, saw the lumbering baby doll pulling the woman back behind him. He swung the woman's corpse up and over his head as if he were at one of those carnival attractions with a sledgehammer in his hands, vying for a prize. The woman crashed down on the windshield, shattering it, and landed on the dash. Innis was covered in safety glass and sticky blood.

The baby doll ripped the woman off the dashboard, swinging her back behind him. He pivoted to the side, reared back, and slammed the body into the driver's side window.

During all of this, Innis continued to scream. She couldn't stop herself. One night-cleaving wail after another tore out of her until madness seemed inevitable. Merlo growled low in his throat, sensing danger. Innis scurried across the center console, grabbed the passenger side door handle, pulled with her hand and thrust with her shoulder. Merlo studied her with sad eyes from under the glove box. There was a click just as her shoulder slammed into the padded-leather door. Pain exploded in her neck, raced across her collarbone, and down her arm. She struggled to find the lock. When she found it, she pressed it. But the lock immediately snicked back down. She shoved her finger into the power lock control again, and once more it reengaged.

Merlo snaked up and out of his hiding spot. He quickly climbed up onto the dash and bolted out of the car through the busted window.

I should have adopted a Rottweiler, Innis thought.

Timidly, she glanced back over her shoulder.

The baby doll had leaned into the shattered window on the driver's side, head tilted, grinning at her. The small cracks in the pink paint showed black underneath. The cheeks were fat, red and round—horribly cheery, considering the circumstances. Within the holes above the cheeks, two jaundiced eyes studied her. One thick arm dangled inside the car, a black-gloved hand fingering the door controls.

Innis tried unlocking the door again, but it was no use. As soon as she disengaged the lock on her side, the baby doll locked it again.

Innis drew her legs up to her chin, sobbing. The baby doll leaned out, and for a moment Innis thought he was leaving, but the thick arm never went away. The baby doll flipped the door lock, the one that controlled the driver's side, and pulled the door open.

The doll flooded in, like evening being poured into the world, and Innis hit the lock one more time. Even as seeking hands fell upon her, she shoved the door open and spilled out onto the damp grass of the roadside.

She tried to crawl away, but he had her ankle. She saw the dead woman being dragged behind the hulking baby doll and Innis's fight or flight instinct roared into action. She rolled onto her back and kicked at her trapped leg with her free one, intent on breaking the fingers that held her. She saw the way he'd bludgeoned the car using that poor woman's body, saw herself in that woman's place, and kicked harder. Her left leg was on fire from the kicks she dealt with her right. She was hurting herself as much as she hoped she was hurting the masked maniac. It was no use. He wouldn't let go.

With the passenger side door wide open, the dome light had come on. In its glow, the baby doll emerged, climbing down her leg and on top of her.

A mechanical voice said, "Mah-mah."

Innis thought she could hear cooing.

CRUELTY

WILL

The Studebaker ran out of fuel twenty feet from the gas station where Will had run into the trooper.

Will, sobbing uncontrollably, beat the devil out of the dash and steering wheel. His vocal cords strained and vibrated. The pads of his hands stung, as if on fire, yet he continued pounding away. Curses flew from him untethered. The last time he'd spoken had been to try to hear himself, over seven years prior. His throat was raw. On and on he screamed.

Get it together, that tinny voice said. *Maybe there's a pay phone.*

He gazed out the windshield, wiping his eyes one at a time with the back of his hand. The square building seemed so close, yet so far away. He didn't want to get out of the car. His desire to stay inside the comfort of the Studebaker was inane. The baby-doll-thing couldn't be anywhere near him. It was slow. And on foot. Will had stolen its car. He was safe. Nothing to be concerned about. Yet his hand hovered over the door handle, shaking. He glanced around with all the furtive caution of a child checking for his parents before trying to steal a cookie from atop the fridge. To his left, the tree line ended ten feet before the gas station's parking area and pumps. To his right, more trees. Trees for years. Decades. Endless trees, stretching off into a blackness so thick that Will believed it a tangible entity. He was all alone.

If only he'd stayed home. Had he simply hung out with Kirk, or just gone to bed alone, this nightmare would never have happened. He kept seeing Jennifer's lifeless body being dragged behind that monster's tremendous girth, and that baby doll's face, framed in tight black curls, hovering in the night like the moon itself. He blamed Kirk and the trooper because blaming himself hurt too much. Placing blame on them meant he hadn't been as stupid as he really was. Who goes out in the middle of nowhere to get laid? Not him. It was Kirk's fault; all Kirk's *goddamn* fault. Kirk should have talked him out of it. Or, at the very least, shouldn't have given him directions to a meth whore's place. He blamed the trooper, as well. Of course he did. The trooper, with his lollipop body and blue uniform, should have taken him in for questioning. Yeah, that was it.

Would've, could've, should've, the tinny voice mocked. *Get out of the car.*

Will pulled the handle and stepped out into the night. He left the key in the ignition and the headlights blazing. Absently he wondered how long the battery would last; how long before he'd be thrust into darkness.

Bob's Bait and Fuel wasn't like most gas stations. There were no security lights around the perimeter of the building. Not a single light left on inside, either. The interior of the mom and pop was inky, the darkness thick and foreboding. He jogged around the entire building, praying for a phone booth. Nothing. Of course not. Not in this day and age. Not when everyone had cell phones and computers were the size of paperbacks.

He had no other choice but to break a window. On the left side of the building he found a cracked section of curb. It looked as if someone had rolled too far forward and scraped the undercarriage of their vehicle, leaving behind a fist-sized chunk of concrete. He snatched it up and went back up front. He stood by the pumps, a good ten feet from the front doors, reared back, and threw the piece of concrete as hard as he could at the frontage. The chunk bounded off the glass as if it were made of rubber, ricocheting off to the right and landing at the corner of the Igloo ice fridges.

Will roared his frustration to the heavens. He stalked over to the chunk of concrete, picked it up, and tried again. The glass cracked, just slightly, leaving an indentation about the size of a dime with four fissures extending from it. The rock rebounded at him. He hopped to the side as it whizzed by his left knee.

Will rinsed and repeated, until the rock finally crashed through the safety glass and landed on the tile on the other side of the door. He stuck his arm through the hole and found the no-turn bolt for the lock. A key was needed for either side of the door. Groaning and grumbling, making more noise than he had in seven years, he fought to remain calm.

He had to get inside. He had no other option. He turned to face the pumps. Maybe he could use one of the nozzles to pry away more glass so he could get inside. He judged the length of the hose in his mind. He'd be over five feet short, so that was a no-go. He spotted a squeegee sticking out from a compartment on the side of the middle pump. He grabbed it and returned to the window. Sliding the handle in at an angle, he shoved on the wet end. The aluminum handle gave way, bending in the middle, and Will bonked his head on the glass.

Had his mother been around, she would have poured tabasco sauce down his gullet or scrubbed his tongue with Irish Spring. Such foul language he'd never used in his lifetime.

Not thinking, using only brute force and fiery frustration, he began slamming the handle of the squeegee against the glass.

The glass gave, showering gummy particles inward. Will backed away in a state of dumbfounded glee; a grin spread so wide on his face that his cheeks hurt. Though there was a push bar in the middle of the door, the glass was a single pane. He kicked at the bottom, loosing the last bit of safety glass from the frame. Ducking under the pull bar, he was in.

Flood lights kicked on as he entered the store, no doubt a motion sensitive security measure. The inside of Bob's Bait and Fuel smelled like the ocean, salty and fishy. Though Will saw nothing that would give off that kind of aroma, it was all around him, reminding him of summers spent on a boat with his father in the Gulf of Mexico. That was before Mom divorced the old man and Dad moved to North Carolina.

In the center of the store sat three rows of shelving, dual-sided and loaded down with fishing equipment, bait tubs, canned goods, toiletries, bags of chips, motor oil, and anti-freeze, along with other miscellany. The left and rear walls were banks of coolers, which stored beer, soda, microwavable burritos, and prepackaged sandwiches. On the right, stretching the entire depth of the store, was the cashier's area. Pickled eggs and Slim Jims, a lottery machine and cash register, all sat atop a long section of counter. Candy bars and gum slept in boxes on shelves hanging from the front of the checkout station. On the wall behind the register, cigarette packs by the hundreds were stuffed into compartments, and in between one bank of smokes and another was a black phone on a beige base. He strode toward the entrance to the cashier's area, which was located at the far end, near an alcove where a **Restrooms** sign hung above the opening, and on down the cramped confines to the phone. He snatched the receiver off the base and screwed it to the side of his face. A low vibration and a push of displaced air across his temple indicated a dial tone. He jabbed at the nine then the one, twice, and the vibrations on the side of his face waxed and waned, telling him the call was going through. The low thrum ceased. Sporadic hisses ran ghostly fingers across his temple—hopefully the telltale sign that someone was answering his call.

He swallowed hard and his throat clicked. He had no time to test his voice. Digging up ingrained memories of speech from some far-off continent of his brain, he said, "Help. Someone's dead."

He recalled being twelve again, *CSI* on the TV in the living room, one of his father's favorite shows, trying to remember how interaction with a dispatcher was supposed to go. They'd be asking him who, what, where, why, and how. The when of the situation was *now*. All he had to do was fill in the blanks. First, he needed to tell them a why.

"I'm deaf. I won't be able to hear your responses." He paused to give them time to accept this fact. "Someone got hit by a car on Highway 16. That same person tried to kill me. I stole... borrowed the car they used to run Jen...the girl over." He was talking too fast, felt sure his words were running together though he had no way of knowing for certain. "I broke into... I'm at Bob's Bait and Tackle...no, Bait and Fuel! On 16. Please help. Please!"

A soft burst of air tickled his temple. Were they actually trying to respond?

"I'll leave the phone off the hook. I think you can trace it."

Lights swept across the rows of cigarettes, making his shadow look as if it were running away from him. He cocked his head to the right and glanced out the front of the store. Someone was pulling up next to the pumps. What time was it? After midnight, he assumed. The store was obviously closed. No way it was someone pulling in to fill up. It couldn't be the cops already, could it? Even though that question played though his mind, he still thought, *Damn, that was fast.*

He couldn't see whether or not the vehicle was a police car. It had parked behind the pumps farthest from the front door. He moved down the checkout station to the glass. He leaned left, trying to get a better look around the pumps. He could see the headlights for only a second before they blinked out. His eyes adjusted quickly. In a matter of seconds, he could see the grill of the car in the moonlight. What seemed like Olympic rings were set into the grill. But that wasn't quite right. The Olympic rings were three on top and four on the bottom. This one was only a row of four interlocking circles. What kind of car had that emblem? For the life of him, he couldn't remember.

He started to turn, intent on going around to the doors to try and get the driver's attention, when he saw the massive shape move around the end of the pumps. Will's heart froze, sending icicles into his limbs. He dropped to a catcher's stance behind the counter. Even as he did so, he knew he was damned. Whether or not the baby-doll-thing had seen him or not, he had no line of sight on it, and wouldn't be able to hear the thing coming. He crouch-walked back toward the restrooms, careful to stay low. Halfway down the aisle, he dropped to his hands and knees and crawled the rest of the way. The restrooms would have a lock. He could wait the thing out. The cops were coming. They had to be coming. If nothing else, he'd admitted to breaking into the store. That should be enough to bring at least one cruiser.

The end of the counter blocked his view of the front doors. That was good. If he couldn't see the baby doll, the thing wouldn't be able to see him either. A water fountain sat by the wall at the end of the alcove. A unisex restroom lay to the right, and a door marked **Employees Only** to the left, probably granting access to the space behind the coolers.

Will wondered, *Where's the back door?*

The exit could be back there behind the coolers. It was a very good possibility, at least. He quickly weighed his options. He bypassed the restrooms and pushed into the door marked **Employees Only**.

A row of doors used for stocking the coolers were to his left. On his right was a walk-in. Next door to the walk-in was the back door.

But he had to know where the baby doll was. The feeling was so strong, so controlling, that he found himself gazing through rows of Pepsi and Mountain Dew bottles without even thinking. Nothing stirred in the store. He stood on his tiptoes and glanced over the top of a dozen Red Bulls. At that angle he could see the trunk of the car, but only about six inches or so of it. Still, no sign of movement.

Where did you go? Will thought.

A sudden rush of wind on the backs of his arms and neck caused him to spin around. The back door was open. The doll filled the space.

Two arms came up, and for a second time, Will was reminded of Dr. Frankenstein's stitched-together creation. He threw himself back and bumped into the coolers then hopped to the right, sidestepping toward the restrooms. He crashed through the door to the coolers, into the alcove, and his momentum carried him into the restroom. He slid on something wet and went sprawling. He rolled over, pushed himself up and back on the palms of his hands, his feet slipping and sliding in whatever wetness lay underneath him. The restroom door swung closed.

Will whipped his head left to right, right to left, then craned his neck to look behind him. The only window in the small one-stall, single-sink room was set high in the wall. The glass had what looked like chicken wire woven into it. Will didn't think he was going out that way. Even if he managed to break the glass, the frame was only a foot wide and half as tall.

Fear overtook him. He backed into the corner of the restroom, bawling. At any moment the baby doll would burst through into his hiding spot and tear him to shreds. He was sure of it. The idea wasn't an *if* but a *when*.

His heart no longer went *ker-thud*. It went boom, *boom, BOOM!*

CRUELTY

How long had it been since he'd called 911? How far away was help? Was there any chance in hell that he'd get out of this nightmare alive? He didn't think so.

So, you're just going to sit here and wait to die? that tinny voice asked.

At least a full minute had gone by and there was still no sign of his pursuer. Maybe it didn't know he was in the restroom. No one with any sense would have voluntarily trapped themselves in a dead end. He hadn't *meant* to come in here. His inertia had *carried* him in. The baby doll could be out in the main section of the store, looking for him. If so, maybe he could simply sneak out the back as he'd initially intended.

Will composed himself as best he could and stood. He slid forward through glistening wetness he couldn't explain. Maybe the restroom ceiling had a leak. His overactive imagination made the moisture on the floor into blood and he shook his head to clear the image. *No reason for the floor to be covered in blood.* He looked down at his hands. Though the restroom was dark, he could tell they weren't covered in blood. They were pink and pale, not a bit dark.

As he came to the door, it began to swing inward. He slid to the left, ending up behind the door out of sheer luck.

The baby doll lumbered inside, walking in jerking, mechanical movements. Will thought that if he could have heard, he'd have found his ears tortured by the shrieking of metallic joints. That sickly sweet aroma of Juicy Fruit filled the small bathroom. Will thought of dead things and shuddered.

The baby doll went to the one and only stall and pulled the door open. Will, once again acting out of survival instinct and nothing else, stepped out of the corner. He shoved both of his hands into the baby doll's back, hoping to knock it into the stall. Will found a resistance unlike anything else he'd ever encountered.

Under the black garb, the back was smooth and cold, hard.

Like that of a porcelain doll, that tinny voice offered.

The baby doll was immovable, solid and rooted in place. He hadn't budged it an inch.

The head turned, ever so slowly, until yellowed sclera met his own eyes.

It winked at him.

Will moved. He wrenched the door open just enough to squeeze through and tore off into the main floor of the store, slowing only to drop down under the pull bar of the shattered door. He squatted and monkey-walked out into the space between the store front and the pumps.

As he sprinted to the car behind the pumps, the make of the car became glaringly obvious—some kind of Audi sports coupe; a black two-door with a broken front headlight he hadn't been able to make out from inside the store. The right front corner of the car was bent in, as if someone had driven into a telephone pole. He ripped the driver's door open and slid inside. As his hands played over the ignition box, his eyes strayed toward Bob's Bait and Fuel. The fuel pumps blocked his view of the store.

His hand came up empty. In horror, he glanced down at the ignition box. No keys.

Fine; if he couldn't escape, he'd arm himself. The trunk was certain to have a crowbar or crossbar for tire changing. He used the dome light to find the trunk release—a circular button on the dashboard beside the steering wheel. When he pressed it, he saw the trunk pop up in the rearview.

Will got out and ran around to the back of the car.

Of everything he might have expected to encounter at the rear of the Audi, a black woman flopping like a fish from the trunk was not one of them.

CRUELTY

INNIS

The smell of shit and blood clogged her nose. She gasped several times, letting cool night air clear her passages. She'd been in the trunk with the dead woman for only a short period of time, but the wretched stench seemed to have filled her completely. She retched onto the tarmac beneath her, but only bile came up. Acid laced her mouth, gagging her once more.

The man in the baby doll mask had stuffed her into the trunk as if she were just so much luggage. She'd tried to crawl back out before he could close it, but the lid had come down hard, braining her. She rolled backward into the deep trunk and came to a rest at the back. When the trunk had opened a second time, she didn't move, expecting him to reach in and snatch her out so he could finish the job he'd started. Instead, the monster had shoved in the husk of the dead woman, right on top of Innis. The lady was nothing more than a bag of flesh from having been pummeled against the car repeatedly. The dead woman had crapped herself, as well; the smell was so powerful Innis could feel the stench on her tongue. She didn't just *taste* it—she *felt* it.

Now, her prison was open and she was out. She dry-heaved, coughing with her spasms.

She became aware of a high-pitched sound, like a tornado siren, but shriller. It went off three bursts at a time: *skree, skree, skree*. At first she thought it was her car alarm, but the Audi's security system wasn't quite the same octave. Had it been going the whole time? She thought so, but the trunk's interior lining had muffled the cacophony. Now that she was out, the sound became deafening.

Something grabbed her shoulder and she shrieked. Rolling out of its grasp and onto her back, she found a scared-looking white boy gazing down at her. He spoke in puzzles and she was missing some of the pieces; his words—if she could even call them words—were all jumbled up together.

She didn't really care what he was saying, though. The only thing she could focus on was the fact that he wasn't the masked maniac.

"Is he dead? Did you kill him?" she asked.

The young man fell silent. He shook his head.

New fear sprouted. She pushed herself up, approached the stranger and grabbed his shoulders. She shook him. "Then where is he?"

The boy kept shaking his head.

"Talk, damn it!"

He laid his hands over his ears and continued to shake his head.

"You're... what? Deaf? You can't hear me?"

He nodded in quick jerks.

"Heeeeee com' in."

Not deaf *and* dumb, so that was a plus. She looked around, trying to get a bead on their location: medium-sized gas station named Bob's Bait and Fuel; two rows of six gas pumps; the Audi was parked near the road; the baby doll was nowhere to be seen.

"Weeee gotta go." His words emerged like a movie's dialogue track in slow motion. He spoke fine when he didn't rush, simply languidly.

"Come on." She grabbed his wrist and started for the front of the car.

He tugged back at her. When she turned back around, he was shaking his head again. "No keeeeeys."

"He took the keys?"

"Uh huh." His voice cracked between uh and huh.

"God damn it!"

While she cursed, the young man dug in the trunk. He came out with a crossbar—the multi-tool used for changing the Audi's tires. He seemed pleased with his find.

"Weeee gotta go." He began pulling her by the wrist toward the tree line on the left side of the station.

"I'm not going in there," she said, but her words were wasted on him. His back was turned. He couldn't see her lips to read them.

He was adamant about the woods, and strong, too. He tugged her along until she finally gave in. They had come within five feet of the line where the asphalt ended and the woods started when she saw the figure rounding the back of the store.

Her fear of the baby doll man was counteracted by another, more pleasing thought.

"My phone," she said to the deaf man. "My phone's somewhere in the car."

Even as she said it, she knew it didn't matter. That pleasing thought melted beneath a sea of terror. They had run out of time. The man-doll was coming.

CRUELTY

TOM

Texas State Trooper Tom Morgan was parked on Interstate 10, fifteen miles north of Bob's Bait and Fuel, when the call came in that someone had broken into Robert Hunt's out-of-the-way gas station, courtesy of Shirley from Kerr County Sheriff's Department. Tom pulled out from behind the Hardee's billboard where he'd been resting his eyes—not sleeping, as he would tell his wife; just resting his eyes—hit the roof lights, and headed back toward Highway 16.

Four minutes later, Shirley came back over the band to tell him that the person who had broken in had called. As odd as that sounded, what the caller—a deaf man?—had said was even stranger. Someone had been killed—a girl, by the information Shirley was able to attain—and the caller had stolen the driver's ride. Or something like that. On top of all that, she'd sent available Kerr County Sheriff's Deputy Nick Wuncell out to a separate accident involving a pedestrian only ten minutes before, to the same general area, but didn't have an exact location. Nick was approaching from Fredericksburg on 16, but hadn't yet found any signs of the accident, which explained why she'd called the trooper in on the break-in.

Tom didn't bother trying to wrap his head around the garbled info. Instead, he shoved a little harder on the accelerator and the speedometer rose from eighty to ninety-five. Outside, trees rushed by on both sides as his halogens sliced through the black before him.

He thought about the teenager he'd found lingering outside of Bob's earlier that night. How long had it been since then? He glanced at the time display on his computer. It was quarter to one in the morning. Four hours had passed. Had William Longmire been waiting for someone? Fellow hoodlums with whom to pillage Bob's wares? Tom didn't know, but he was bound to find out. Using what little detective skills he'd been graced with, he figured something must have gone wrong during the break-in. Someone not happy with their share, perhaps, someone who'd run down one of their comrades in the hopes of stealing more than their cut.

Cold wind whistled through a one-inch crack in the driver's side window of the cruiser. Old habits died hard. Tom had once been a two-pack-a-day smoker. Nell—his wife of nine years—had tricked him into quitting. She'd gone to the doctor and had lied about being a smoker since the age of fifteen. Chantix was prescribed. She filled the script, brought it home, and forced the tiny blue Pfizer tablets on him. He balked, as surely as a child denied their favorite blankie, but in the end, Nell had outlasted Tom's protestations. To this day, he couldn't ride without the window cracked, every now and then his fingers rising to the opening to flick at an imaginary butt. He could even smell the smoke on the air, thick and inviting.

Nell was a good woman, stubborn as a brush fire, but full of love for her man. The two had never had children. Tom shot blanks, something which he constantly worried about. Both of them were approaching forty—he thirty-nine and she a year younger—and surely her biological clock was coming unwound. Concern that she would leave him for a man with a sack full of able soldiers had waned over the years but still niggled at him from time to time. He could still see the sadness in her eyes when they passed a school or daycare, and the wistful gaze she gave families while they were out at dinner together. Yes, Nell was a good woman.

The road drew into an S-curve and Tom slowed to fifty to take it. At the end of the S, he accelerated again, pressing the gas to the floorboard. A mile from Bob's, he cut the roof lights, not wanting to give the perps fair warning of his arrival.

The Audi sports coupe parked at the roadside pumps perplexed him. The high-end automobile didn't fit the profile of a bunch of kids who got their kicks from breaking into small businesses. The trunk was open, the driver's door ajar, and he could see no one inside. He pulled up flush with the passenger side of the sports coupe, yanked his flashlight from the console, and shone the light into the car next to him. The windshield was busted, as was the driver's side window. The top of the hood looked smashed to hell, too.

Snakes coiled in his gut. He reversed. The Audi had been in some kind of accident. The front right corner was bent in, as if it'd been wrapped around a telephone pole. The headlight was ruined; not a shard of glass remained in the frame. He continued backing up. After parking nose to nose with the Audi, leaving only enough room for him to squeeze between the cars, he got out.

The grille held the telltale Audi emblem—four interlocking circles. He crouched down and shone his flash over the bumper. The underside of the bumper was bent upward, as if the vehicle had run over something big, like a deer, or maybe a feral hog. The indentation stretched the entire length of the bumper, and was a good eight- to ten-inches deep. Shirley had said someone had been hit, hadn't she? A girl, if Shirley had her facts straight. The Audi was higher off the ground than most sports coupes, with a good foot of clearance underneath. There wasn't anything wrong with the grille of the car; no sign to indicate that the victim had been standing when struck. But, if the victim had gone over the top of the car, smashing the hood and shattering the windshield, where had the damage to the undercarriage come from?

Tom walked around to the trunk. He played his flashlight over the contents. When he saw the crumpled mess of the girl inside, he immediately drew his gun. Training took over. Safety off and finger over the trigger guard. He no longer played the role of the inquisitive state trooper; he was now Tom Morgan, Texan.

Something about the pile of flesh turned his skull into a blender, making a daiquiri out of his gray matter. The woman had been slender. He could tell as much from her thin ankles and wrist, which were, for the most part, the only solid things about her. Her hands were oddly shaped, broken things, but the fingers were skinny. Fluids seeped from every busted open section of flesh. Her face reminded him of a kicked-in jack-o'-lantern. If this girl had been run over, the driver had repeated the process over and over again. Tom had seen hit and runs. She was not one of them.

That could also explain the damage to the undercarriage as well as to the top of the car, Tom thought. What kind of sicko was he dealing with?

Urgency taking over, heart beating a drum solo in his chest, Tom backed away from the Audi and directed his flashlight at the front of the store. Since he'd arrived, he hadn't heard anything other than the soft ticking of his cruiser's engine as it cooled. Now, he could hear the eerie cry of a loon. Crickets chirped and cicadas thrummed; power lines above him buzzed with life. Adrenaline had heightened his senses. He could smell the girl in the trunk. In death, she'd messed herself.

He spoke into the radio on his shoulder, "Shirley, come in."

Her soft Mexican accent answered, "I gotcha, Morgan. Wuss up?"

"I'm gonna need Kerr County out here at Bob's, possibly every deputy you can give me. Hell, even call Randy." Randy Miser was Kerrville's appointed sheriff; a good, God-fearing man, with a presence as big as his god. "Send an ambulance, too. I found... a body in a trunk."

The radio crackled with static for what seemed like a full thirty seconds. Tom was about to ask Shirley if she'd heard him when she came back, "*Que*? Sorry, what did you say?"

He repeated himself then added, "I don't know what the hell is going on out here. Just send me some backup, please?"

"Okay, Morgan, callin' it in now. But... I don't know how long it will be. Nick's chasing ghosts trying to find that other accident, and Baker—" Emmanuel Baker was one of the other graveyard shift deputies who worked for Kerr County—"—is off tonight. Did you at least find the caller?"

Good question. Where was the caller? The thought went crashing through his mind like the Kool-Aid man assaulting a brick wall. *Oh yeah!*

"Found a car that's obviously been in an accident. That's where I found the body. Checking for the caller now. I'll update you with whatever I find. Oh, and Shirley?"

"Yeah?"

"Let it be on the record that I don't like this. You guys need to hire more deputies."

"Noted. Be safe, Tom."

"Right. Over."

He moved toward the front of the store. Inside, the place was dark. In the glow of the flashlight, Tom found the front door had been the criminal's point of ingress. He dipped under the pull bar and stepped into a pile of shattered safety glass. Service piece out in front of him, the flashlight flush with its side, he moved through the small convenience store/bait shop, sweeping the area from left to right. In the far corner he found a busted flood light, then another one in the opposite corner. *Someone didn't want the light drawing attention*, Tom thought. He cleared the space behind the register then went to the restroom. He backed inside, pushing the door open with his butt, not wanting to leave his rear unprotected. His right foot came down in something wet. He heard the splash and felt the give of his sole on the slick surface. He aimed the beam down and found water sloshing into a drain set in the middle of the floor. The water had come from under the stall door. He could still see the faint trail it had left. He stepped into the stall and shone the flashlight into the commode.

An arm stuck up out of the bowl, as if someone were inside the pipes, trying to climb out. Tom flinched, disgusted. The stump had clogged the toilet. Water as still as glass came level with the rim of the commode. The ends of the fingers were raw and red, devoid of finger nails. All sorts of wicked imagery played through Tom's mind—someone having their nails ripped off, one by one; a captive prisoner scrabbling at a stone wall, seeking purchase and escape. More visions came, but he pushed them aside and turned to leave the stall.

Standing in the doorway was a figure so large its presence made Tom's knees weak. Instinctively, he swung his gun upward and the individual slapped it away with a backhand. Tom's gun went off, the bullet smashing into the doorframe. The same hand that had batted away his gun clapped down on his arm. With a quick jerk, Tom's forearm snapped. The gun clattered to the ground. He stared dumbly down at his shattered appendage, the lower part of his arm now a capital L. The pain was excruciating, and the world seemed to tilt in his vision. Another hand found his neck. With crushing force he was hauled up and shoved back against the outer wall of the stall. Tom's good arm came up, brandishing the flashlight, which he used to beat the figure about the head and shoulder. In the swinging beam of the torch, he could see the ghastly aspect of his attacker: cracked pink paint over inky blackness; sickly yellow eyes shining with malevolent intent; tight, black curls framing a grinning face.

The doll snapped its head forward. Tom's nose disintegrated. He realized he wasn't breathing, couldn't breathe—the hand on his neck was impeding his flow of oxygen. Blood from his destroyed nasal canal pooled in the back of his throat. The thing's free hand brushed down Tom's chest. Then it was on his stomach, his crotch. He wanted to thrash and fight, but the grip on his neck was so tight he felt that if he risked any sudden movement his spine would snap. The doll leaned to its right, dipping down as its hand roamed over Tom's calf, then to his knee. Icy fingers—solid, not fleshy—wrapped around his left ankle.

Tom's lungs burned with pent-up carbon monoxide. The world became a starry night.

I'm dying, he thought quite calmly.

The baby doll brought Tom's leg up and out to the side, like a ballerina stretching on a banister. With ungodly force, Tom's leg was shoved back. His knee stopped at the corner of the stall wall, but his calf and foot kept right on going. He heard his knee shatter, felt the ligaments and muscle ripping away from their moorings.

Tom didn't scream. He gasped, sucking in air as he was let go, sounding not unlike a *Velociraptor* from one of his all-time favorite movies, *Jurassic Park*. He crashed down onto the damp floor, rolling this way and that, groping at his ravaged leg. He could feel pieces protruding, sharp daggers of bone that had torn through the skin. Suddenly, dying wasn't such a horrible concept.

The flashlight had landed in the alcove that allowed access to the restrooms and the **Employees Only** door. In its glow, he could see his service piece between the black boots of the looming baby doll. His right arm was useless, but his left was reaching for the gun, that lizard brain trying to lengthen his longevity.

A boot came up. A boot came down. His phalanges smashed like china tossed against a cinderblock wall. The baby doll made mashed potatoes on his hand then lifted its leg. Tom snatched his limp hand back, tucking it painfully under his right armpit. He tried to push himself back, wanting to escape, but only managed to ram himself up against the stall wall. He began to blubber and mumble incoherently, pain and imminent madness rendering him a toddler.

The baby doll turned and left.

Tom's breath exploded from him in confused snatches of crazy laughter. Over his maniacal cackling, he could hear a soft metallic ticking accompanied by the cooing of an infant.

Tom passed out.

CRUELTY

WILL & INNIS

They'd gone about a hundred yards into the dark wood when light flooded in behind them. Will slowed, turning to look behind them. The illumination grew brighter, framing the frantic woman in an almost heavenly glow. She'd turned as well, was looking back the way they'd come. Her shoulders rose and fell in quick, sporadic movements. She was obviously out of breath. His own breathing wasn't so bad. He'd run track in high school and jogged every morning even though he had graduated last year.

"Cops?" he asked. He saw her jaw working in profile. He tugged on her arm. She turned to face him.

He repeated himself, and she shrugged.

Will leaned to the left then to the right, trying to look around her, but all he could see through the trees was the unmistakable bluish-white glow of halogens. The fact that he couldn't see anyone moving in the cone of light comforted him. The baby doll was nowhere to be seen and the trees weren't wide enough to hide the monster's tremendous girth.

"What do we do?" he asked.

She jerked her head toward the lights. They began walking back in the direction of the gas station. Will felt a burning fear spoiling his stomach.

This is crazy, Innis thought. *I'm going to get myself killed.*

But Innis was of the mindset that whoever had arrived, whether civilian or officer of the law, had a vehicle. A ride was better than the Shoelace Express any day of the week, especially when you were being chased by a homicidal man dressed as a little girl's plaything.

She wished Merlo had been braver. She could use some canine comfort. Damn cowardly dog. She tried to think better of Merlo, to reassure herself that if he'd remained in the car, he'd more than likely be dead now, but it did nothing to assuage her anger at the dog. First Bruce had betrayed her, and then Merlo. Fuck them both. It was a selfish thought, but one she found difficult to shake.

They moved slowly, noiselessly, through the woods. Somewhere far off, a loon tittered and cried. She heard the soft crackle of radio static accompanied by distant voices. The headlights—if that's what they really were—dimmed. Innis's heartbeat escalated.

The deaf man came alongside her, and they walked in parallel. They'd entered the trees running for their lives, and now that they were walking, the way seemed ten times longer. The gas station came into view between the trees, more than fifty feet from where they stood. The Audi was surrounded by a halo of brilliant light. She grabbed Will's hand and sidestepped through the trees, with him in tow. She found a better angle and saw that the headlights had dimmed because the responding officer had parked his car nose to nose with the Audi.

But where was the responding officer?

Innis kept moving sideways, tugging the deaf man along, scanning the area, and hunting for the immense black figure with the baby doll mask. Those jaundiced-eyes flitted into her mind and she shuddered.

Swirling red and white lights on the road, approaching from the highway, made Innis's heart beat even faster. Help was here. The nightmare was over.

A sound like a screeching crow shattered the silence around them. Though the woods could play tricks on a person's hearing, Innis thought the sound had come from inside the gas station. Had someone choked on a scream? She couldn't be sure.

She could hear the approaching vehicle's engine. An ambulance came rolling into the parking lot of the station. The emergency vehicle stopped, but no one got out. Innis dropped the deaf man's hand and bolted for salvation.

Will ran after the woman, close on her heels. He hadn't known she was going to take off like that, so he'd been late to start. Soon enough, he passed her, coming to the driver's side door of the ambulance a good five seconds before she arrived. Will slapped his palms against the glass, startling the Hispanic-looking driver. The EMT had a pencil-thin beard and mustache, was well-tanned and muscular. His eyes were as big as moons in his head. He made a shooing motion with a loose wrist at Will. Will stepped back and allowed the medic to exit.

Another EMT rounded the front of the ambulance. She was thin, almost wiry, with chestnut hair and a scar on her cupid's bow from an apparent soft palate repair. She was saying something, but Will couldn't read her; the harelip twitched and moved weirdly, making it difficult for him to judge her words.

"He's deaf," Innis told the female medic.

"Ah," was all the woman with the scarred lip said.

"What happened? Where's the trooper?" The male EMT jerked his chin in the direction of the cruiser.

"We don't know," Innis said. Everything else just fell out of her. She relayed the night's events as she knew them as quickly as she could. When she touched upon the man in the baby doll mask, both EMTs raised their eyebrows questioningly, but she pressed on. When she got to the bit about being stuffed into the trunk with a dead woman, the same woman the baby doll had used to pummel her car with, both medics seemed to finally get it.

The radio upon the EMT's shoulders squawked and a tiny voice came over the air, too low for Innis to make out what was being said.

"Sheriff's department is on the way. Is the body in the other car?" The male medic asked, once again hitching his chin at the pumps.

Innis nodded.

"I got this. Stay with them, Ben," the woman told her partner, moving across the lot toward the roadside pumps.

"He's still out here, somewhere," Innis told the remaining EMT. "It might not be safe."

Ben, seemingly ignoring Innis's comment, said, "Come around here and let me look at that head wound."

Innis had forgotten about the gash at her hairline, the one the steering wheel had given her when she drove the car into the tree. She followed the EMT around to the back of the ambulance, where he pulled the doors open and climbed in. She went in after him. Inside, she turned around to face the rear doors then sat down on the awaiting gurney. The medic tooled around in what looked like a tackle box until he found the supplies he needed to clean her up. All the while, the deaf man stood at the doors, looking in at her with a puzzled expression on his face.

Will felt uneasy. Everyone—the black woman, the two EMTs—seemed to have forgotten that there was still a clear and present danger. None of them had any idea where the doll was, not to mention the responding officer.

Maybe the woman from the trunk was traumatized, not thinking properly. He knew that he wasn't so sure of what was going on, his mental faculties all jumbled up and synapses misfiring. Still, he couldn't be the only one concerned that the murderer remained uncaught.

He stopped watching the medic cleaning up the woman's bloodied face and went back to the front of the ambulance. He surveyed the area, scanning the lot and checking for moving shadows. He saw none. Maybe the killer really was gone, had been scared off by all the new arrivals.

His gut told him differently.

The security lights were off, Will realized. Did they shut down of their own accord now that no one was inside to trigger them? He thought that could be it, but once again that ball of lava spread in his gut, acid boiling away at the soft lining of his stomach.

It suddenly occurred to him that he was all alone out here. He wanted another body to occupy the night with him. He made his way over to the pumps, walking through the glow from the brake lights of the trooper's cruiser. He wondered if it could be the same guy who'd approached him while he'd been lost earlier in the night, and actually laughed.

How things come full circle, huh?

The trunk of the Audi was closed, he could see as much by the cruiser's headlights.

Where the hell is that medic?

He came around the rear fender of the Audi and stepped right into her. Or, what was left of her. Entrails stretched from the trunk, dangling between the woman's lower half and the Audi's rear bumper like a suspension bridge. He saw what had happened so clearly that he wished, for the first time in his life, that he was an ignorant man, blissfully lacking deductive skills above a toddler's level.

She'd been leaning into the trunk. Someone had come along and slammed the lid down, probably repeatedly, cleaving her in two.

The night became brighter. Will turned and saw the cruiser racing backward, headed directly for the ambulance and the unknowing victims inside.

Innis heard the screeching tires at the same time Ben the EMT did. She could tell by the expression on his face. He was up before her, heading for the rear doors, when the world went topsy-turvy. She could hear herself screaming as she tumbled inside the ambulance. Across the bank of medical equipment she went, rolled onto the roof, then down the other wall. She crashed down into the space between the gurney and the medic's bench where Ben had been sitting a second before, and then she was falling onto the roof again. Something let go in her shoulder. Pain exploded—a canon's blast, bright and violent. She cracked her temple on the overhead light.

The world went away.

Will reached out with both hands, as if he could intervene by a simple effort of the mind. The cruiser slammed into the side of the ambulance at a good thirty miles per hour. The emergency vehicle, top heavy as it was, went rolling away as if it weighed no more than a child's toy. Someone was ejected from the open rear doors, went rolling across the paved lot and out onto the highway. When that person came to a stop and didn't move, Will recognized the male EMT.

The ambulance rolled twice before colliding with the trees. Will took an automatic step forward then stopped. What was he going to do? What *could* he do? He looked down at the crossbar in his hand, glanced back to the dark woods behind him, down at the half-woman bloodying the tarmac, then ahead just in time to see the baby doll exiting the cruiser. It seemed to be considering its options. It looked from the wrecked ambulance now lying on its roof at the tree line to the still-unmoving form of the EMT in the road, then back at Will.

The baby doll moved for the ambulance. It was going after the woman. The EMT wasn't a present threat and it was obviously not worried about Will and his poor choice of weaponry.

Will froze, indecisive and terrified, watching the baby doll awkwardly duck into the rear compartment of the ambulance.

He could run, just run away and never look back. He could flee like the coward his mind was telling him he needed to be. *Save your own skin*, that tiny, tinny voice said.

Will turned his back on the woman and headed for the road, running back toward where he'd abandoned the Studebaker. He would keep running. Eventually someone would come along and save him. This was America, and his country was full to the brim with people. He couldn't go on forever and not find help. He wouldn't tell them that he'd left a woman to her death. No, he couldn't; didn't even think he could live with such a secret, so why bring someone else in on his weakness?

Will escaped into the night, feet pounding asphalt, mind compressing itself into a ball of shame. Still, he was alive. His head was loud with failures.

CRUELTY

Cruelty knelt before the dark woman, playing with the hair of its prey. *So bloody and innocent*, it thought. Its body ticked and whirred as it dragged her from the wreckage of the ambulance. Above the click and hum of its inner workings, Cruelty could hear a wailing far off in the night. More would come, it knew. But Cruelty had had its fair share of fun for the night. It thought about the body in the gas station's cooler, the one whose arm it had torn off like a mean kid does a daddy longlegs. Cruelty considered taking the crippled trooper along as well, but decided against it. Forgiveness didn't have room for two captives. Cruelty's master was quite clear about that.

"Only one at a time, Cruelty. Only one. That's a good Cruelty," Forgiveness had said more than once. It seemed a spell which Cruelty could not break. It wanted more. One was not enough. Never was. Cruelty demanded satiation. Seemed the more people it hurt, the greater its need became. But it would listen to Forgiveness, had no other choice. If it didn't play by the rules, Forgiveness would turn Cruelty off. Forgiveness was its master's namesake, but its master shared no other qualities with the word. No, Cruelty would not be forgiven any transgressions, so it would only take the dark woman. She would have to do.

It stuffed the dark woman in the trunk of the trooper's cruiser, closed the lid, and got in behind the wheel. The seat was pushed back as far as it would go to allow for Cruelty's thick body, but its bulging gut still touched the wheel. It put the cruiser into gear and pulled around the gas station to the dirt road behind the store. The cruiser bounced along the rutted road, doing no more than twenty, until it came to the junction of Ranchero Road. Cruelty pulled out onto the pavement and headed in the direction of home.

They'd find the Studebaker and the boy who had escaped, and that was fine. Let the boy tell his wild stories. Let the trooper—if he lived, that was—back the kid's tale. Cruelty didn't mind. Ninety long years it had been playing the same game, and would continue for ninety more. Maybe even an eternity. Forgiveness had allowed it life eternal. Cruelty knew no fear, welcomed no worry.

It would have fun with the dark woman. She'd run Cruelty over. She deserved to pay. Though it did not know death, it knew pain. Its body was cracked, and the joint in one knee no longer worked. It couldn't move its neck, had to turn its whole body if it wanted to look around. Forgiveness would fix everything though. Forgiveness always did. Cruelty assumed it was partially its own fault. It had been cuddling with the sick girl in the road when the dark woman came along.

Cruelty made a left onto Forgiveness's long, dirt drive. A quarter of a mile later, it parked in front of the cabin, the cruiser's headlights showcasing the iron and steel artwork with which Forgiveness had populated the front yard over the years. There was the Angel of Death, in steelwork, its metal cloak billowing around it in an unfelt breeze, forever in a state of static movement. The aluminum skull peeked out from under the hood, gazing at Cruelty and smiling, as if to say, "Another night of fun over, huh, Cruelty?" At the corner of the porch stood Regret, Cruelty's sullen sister. She had been made into the Mother Mary. Though Forgiveness kept no god above himself, he'd dreamt of the virgin one night, and the next morning, had begun work on her likeness. She wore iron robes, and held in her hands a babe. Not Jesus, but a horned demon made from coffee cans and barbed wire. Standing watch over the porch, perched upon the lip of the roof, a pewter gargoyle snarled: in its mouth, a snake; in the snake's maw, an apple; in the apple, a worm. There was a meaning to the piece that Cruelty did not understand. Forgiveness could be obtuse in his creations, and Cruelty did not question him. Other ironwork lay about the yard, unfinished; Forgiveness's work seemingly never done. One of Cruelty's favorite pieces—the bust of a man with a bull's head—needed facial detail. Cruelty liked the piece as it was: the nose without holes; the grinning mouth devoid of teeth; the eyes blank, needing irises; no ears to be found.

Cruelty cooed, thinking pleasant thoughts.

The front door of the cabin swung open and Forgiveness strode down the old porch steps.

"Dah-Dah," Cruelty said, without thought.

Forgiveness, black of hair, blue of eye, thin of build, and forever young, came to the car, shaking his head. He pushed the sleeves of his gray cardigan up his arms then crossed them on his chest. Cruelty got out and went to its master.

Forgiveness said, "They'll be looking for that car, Cruelty."

It hung its head in shame.

"Cheer up. You did no wrong. I'll just have to be hiding it soon. Less playtime, is all. Have you brought home a new friend?"

Cruelty pointed back to the trunk. "Mah-mah," it said.

"Very well. Bring her inside. You, uh... *did* dispose of the last one as I wished?"

"Dah-dah," Cruelty cooed.

"You're a good child, Cruelty, I don't care what they say about you." Forgiveness winked at it before going back inside.

When Cruelty opened the trunk, it saw that the dark woman still slumbered. It watched her breathe to make sure she still lived. Blood had coagulated and congealed on the woman's temple. It grabbed the woman up and slung her over its shoulder. Around the cabin they went, Cruelty bouncing joyously along, until it reached the back of the structure. It pulled the cellar doors open and descended.

Forgiveness had left the bare bulb, which hung in the center of the cellar, shining dimly. Below the light lay an aged wooden table with iron restraints built into each corner. Cruelty laid the dark woman down atop the table, shackled her with her arms above her head and her legs spread-eagled, making her look like a giant X. Then he took the inner stairs up into the cabin, where Forgiveness sat on his bed, oiling a tinker toy. The object shared Cruelty's likeness, was indeed the scaled down version of itself, which Forgiveness had used to create Cruelty—a test subject, and nothing more.

Cruelty didn't like the miniature version of itself. There was no reason to be jealous. The toy didn't share Cruelty's ticking, living heart. Yet envy filled Cruelty, spilling over, turning Cruelty's cooing into a whining of sorts.

Forgiveness looked up and smiled. "This old thing still gets to you, huh, kid? All right, then. Away it goes." Forgiveness dropped the doll and kicked it backward with his heel. The tinker toy disappeared under the bed.

"Dah-Dah," said Cruelty. Had it been able to grin, it would have.

"Who's a good child?"

"Dah-Dah."

Forgiveness raised the can of WD-40. "Do you want some oil?"

"Dah-Dah."

"Good," Forgiveness said, patting the section of bed to his right. "Come 'ere and siddown, then. That's a good Cruelty."

Cruelty sat beside its master. Forgiveness oiled its joints, but stopped when he reached Cruelty's neck.

"Why, child, you're hurt."
"Dah-Dah."
"Lemme get my tool kit."
"Dah-Dah."
Forgiveness disappeared down into the cellar.

CRUELTY

TURTLE

T urtle needed a fix. The ants were crawling, had been since Jennifer ran off with the mark. *Where is she? How long has she been gone?* All these thoughts tracked heavy boots through Turtle's thoughts, leaving depressions in his mind; caverns too dark and confusing to navigate.

Twon had called four times so far. The cook wanted his money. Turtle didn't blame his supplier. If Turtle had fronted two grams of primo crank to two layabout tweakers with a promise from said addicts to sell the goods, Turtle would expect his money as well. Twon didn't play. Turtle was scared. And in the crushing fist of a rather vicious case of withdrawals.

Naked, Turtle sat upon the leather sofa in the living room, picking at his already bleeding foreskin. His real name was Simon Allison, but that name was so far removed from him that even he referred to himself as Turtle. The nickname had come from the boys in the locker room, back when he was in high school. Those boys had said his cock looked like a frightened turtle, one with its head tucked inside its shell. Turtle had a rare condition. Basically, his manhood didn't look like manhood at all—rather, a second belly button with a set of balls dangling beneath. His condition wasn't what made him itch, though; the jonesing did. His fingernails came away smelling of rust and man-musk. Crank. He needed some crank.

For the umpteenth time tonight, Turtle sprung from the sofa, turned, and headed to the trailer's open

57

kitchen. Whining like a hungry pup, he grimaced at the empty cabinets. He'd checked the cupboards so many times that nothing remained inside; their contents were scattered across the peeling linoleum under his feet. He climbed onto the counter, feeling the faux-wood flex and crack under his hundred pounds of skin and bones. He stood spread-eagled over the sink. Blood from his scratched foreskin dripped into the basin as Turtle reached into the upper cabinet and ran his hands over the bottom of the cupboard.

Nothing. Of course there was nothing. He and Jennifer had smoked it all. And when his Bic ran out of fluid, they'd crushed up the remaining shake with the butt of the lighter and snorted the dust. Even the drips were gone; that lovely meth-laced mucus that slid down the back of his throat like sour syrup.

Why is it so fucking hot? Turtle thought as his hand found its way back to his gouged foreskin.

Pick, pickpick, pickpickpickpick...

Someone knocked on the front door. Turtle started, spinning his arms at his sides in an attempt to regain his balance. His fix-deprived brain acted in reverse, sending a foot backward over the edge of the counter. He went down hard, his right hip taking the full brunt of the impact. Turtle trundled across the small kitchen like a child learning how to stop, drop, and roll.

The knock came again followed by, "Open tha door, muddahfuckah!"

Even through his pain, Turtle recognized Twon's accent. The cook was from the Caribbean. Where exactly, Turtle didn't know or care.

Twon called again, his words punctuated by the rap of his fist upon the door, "Imma come in, Turt', and if I do, you be hurtin', seen?"

"I'm comin'!" Turtle squealed as he pushed himself to his knees. His right hip protested, locked up, and he collapsed onto his side.

Outside, the rusty hinges on the screen door screeched seconds before the frame crashed against the side of the trailer. The front door came down like a drawbridge, landing with a thump on the carpet in the living room. Turtle stared in amazement at the fallen door, wondering how in the hell Twon had managed to knock it down in such a fashion. Turtle had only seen such a thing in cartoons. He found it almost comical.

Twon strode across the downed door, looking forever tall from Turtle's kitchen floor vantage point. The cook wore a solid blue tracksuit with a Nike swoosh over his left breast. When he set eyes upon Turtle, Twon's chocolate-colored features creased with confusion.

"The fuck you naked for, Turt'?"

"It's hot in here," was all Turtle could think to say.

"Git some air conditionin', seen?" Twon looked around the small trailer then leaned back and craned his neck to glance down the short hallway leading to the single bedroom. "Where yo bitch?"

"I t-t-told you on the phone, man, she's off tryin' t' score your cash." Turtle grasped his sore hip and whimpered. "I fell off the fuckin' counter!"

"Does I give a fuck? Lookit me," Twon said as he pointed to his nose. "Not one fuck given. Nar' bit. Now, git up, you fuck. Up!"

"I can't stand!"

"Oh, you muddahfuckin' bitch, you. I said—" Twon rushed Turtle, dipped down, and scooped the tweaker under the arms, "—git up!"

Turtle's hip popped as he was lifted from the floor. Strangely enough, the joint felt better. Then Twon shoved Turtle back into the lip of the sink and an all-new pain shot from his coccyx to his neck.

When Turtle could focus on the surrounding world again, Twon had a nine-inch butcher knife clutched in one hand. Turtle didn't know at what point Twon had grabbed the shiny piece of cutlery, but he recognized the crimson handle. The knife had come in a Paula Deen gift set that Turtle had bought Jennifer three Christmases ago, back before she hooked him on crank. Before the scratching and the weight loss. Before some angry meth-producing islander seemed intent on carving Turtle from his shell.

"Imma fuck you up, kid. I won' me money, and me won' it now, seen?" Twon's eyes twinkled with menace.

"I ain't got it. I'm sor—"

Twon slashed with the Paula Deen Special and Turtle's left bicep split like a rotten tomato. Turtle's knees disappeared. It wasn't the pain that made him collapse; it was the blood. All that glistening red flowing from his arm. As he fell, he cracked his head on the lip of the counter. He should've blacked out, but the Twon situation alongside a shattering case of the DTs had his adrenaline going. He clutched his lacerated arm, sobbing. He could see muscle between his fingers. There was something white in there, under the blood.

That's your bone, Turtle, he thought. He cried louder.

Twon didn't approach him. Instead, the cook turned on his heel and moved toward the hall. He vanished into the corridor.

Fight or flight was not a question Turtle bothered himself with. Only one verb popped into his head. *Flee*. Still clutching his gushing bicep, Turtle slid himself up the cabinets at his back, inch by inch, until he was standing. He could hear Twon making a fuss in the bedroom, tossing what sounded like dresser drawers this way and that. The cook was busy. Turtle could escape.

Turtle hobbled toward the busted-down front door. His limping gait slowly became a jog as he rushed through the empty frame and down the four wooden steps to the gravel dooryard.

A beastly, wall of a man looked at Turtle over the barrel of a shotgun. The bore seemed to smile at him. This new guy was just as white as Turtle, but twice as big; corn-fed and blond to boot. Turtle came to an unsteady stop two feet in front of the stranger.

"Yo, Twon!" the stranger called as he racked the slide. "Your bird's leavin' his nest!"

Turtle craned his head back in time to see Twon coming down the steps. The cook shook his head as he went.

"The fuck you t'ink you doin'?" Twon pointed the tip of the Paula Deen Special at Turtle's chin. Gingerly, Twon touched the blade to the underside of Turtle's jaw and rotated it, as one does with a screwdriver. "You wan' die tonigh', Turt'?"

Turtle shook his head. The knife cut into him. Warm blood slid down his neck. He froze. Snot ran from his cupid's bow, across his lips, and over his chin. He didn't dare suck it back up. Any more movement would surely be greeted with death.

"Ollie," Twon hitched his chin at the stranger, "git tha duct tape outta tha trunk. Make a mummy outta `im, seen?"

"Yup," Ollie said.

Gravel crunched under the stranger's feet as he went about his duties. The trunk popped open. Things banged around inside. Ollie returned. A slow rip sounded as the heavy adhesive tape was unwound.

Turtle didn't take his eyes off Twon as Ollie rounded him with the duct tape, securing Turtle's arms to his sides. The pressure would stop the bleeding in his arm; at least, Turtle hoped it would. When Ollie was done, Turtle couldn't feel his hands. His circulation had been cut off. *Gotta take the good with the bad*, he thought. Though he was currently doing his best impression of King Tut, Twon had yet to kill him.

"Now," said Twon, "we go'n go back inside t' talk. Ollie, bring `im."

As Twon walked back up the steps, Ollie shoved the shotgun in between Turtle's shoulder blades and dug in.

Turtle took the steps one at a time, trying to prolong what little time he had left in this world.

Back inside, Ollie directed Turtle to the worn leather sofa. Ollie pushed him down on top of the cushions. Turtle landed on his side. Twon helped him sit up then dragged the glass-topped coffee table flush with Turtle's shins. Atop the glass sat Jennifer's Scooby Doo pipe, a fund-less Green Dot prepaid card, a thin coat of powder leftover from the last of Twon's meth, and the empty Bic lighter. Twon brushed the drug paraphernalia onto the floor and sat down on the glass.

"Where yo bitch?" Twon asked.

"She went off with some trick to try and score your money. The dude only had enough to pay for a lay, so she made him take her to an ATM. But that... that was hours ago."

"Wha' time?"

"I don't know, man!"

The Paula Deen Special slid into Turtle's bare thigh, as if Twon were doing nothing more than placing it back in its sheath. Turtle bucked in pain. The knife jerked and the incision grew longer. Turtle could feel the tip of the knife scraping against his femur.

Turtle exploded, "For fuck's sake, maybe three hours ago! Four... I don't know!"

Ollie said, "Might should ask him who the guy is that she went off with."

Twon nodded in agreement. "Who she run off wit'?"

"Some guy my buddy Kirk put her on to." Turtle tried not to squirm, for fear that the butcher's knife would open his leg further, but he couldn't help it. Not only had the pain become dizzying but the ants were back, too. And he couldn't scratch. Somehow, that was the worst thing of all.

"You don' got a name?" Twon asked.

"Fuck naw, man. He's... he's just some teen out t' score some pussy."

"You whore out your old lady?" Ollie grimaced. "You balls deep in secondhand materials. Yuck."

"How your buddy know this guy?" Twon asked.

"They room together." Turtle's breaths were coming easier now, and the pain in his leg had subsided. He'd heard somewhere that the body shuts off receptors to alleviate the agony of death. God damn, he hoped that wasn't the case here.

"Where this?"

Turtle saw a light at the end of the tunnel—a little beacon of hope. Words fell out of him. "In Fredericksburg. Nancy Lane Apartments. Corner of North Brundidge and Ridgeon. Kirk Something-or-other. He lives in 10C."

"I know the place," Ollie said. "Nice digs. What's this Kirk guy do?"

"I don't know. He spends most his time working out. Why the fuck does it matter?"

"So he's a big guy?" Ollie asked.

Turtle shrugged. "You got a street-sweeper tucked under your arm, man. Ain't nobody bigger 'n that."

"What we do wit 'im?" Twon asked Ollie.

Turtle's brain misfired and he hiccupped, as if the two actions were connected somehow. Things were coming together. It no longer seemed as if Twon was the boss and Ollie the lackey. Turtle doubted that Ollie was in charge, though, as Twon had ordered him to bring Turtle inside. Partners, maybe, but not boss and subordinate.

"You got a knife. Handle it." Ollie glanced down at his shotgun before heading for the door. "Ammo's expensive these days."

Turtle deflated. "No."

Twon gave him a soft, almost kind face. "I trusted you, Turt'. I don' trust lightly, seen? Goodnigh', muddahfuckah."

The knife came out of Turtle's thigh. The addict didn't feel it. There were no shouts or pleas for his life.

The ants stopped marching. He laid his head on the back of the sofa.

Twon slit his throat.

Turtle took a long time dying.

CRUELTY

RANDY

Sheriff Randy Miser prayed, "My Lord, which art in heaven, hallowed be thy name, what kind of clustermug have I gotten myself into tonight?"

The slumped-over man sitting on a throne of soft drink pallets had had his arm ripped off. The man's appendage—along with Randy's night—was circling the drain. The image of the nail-less hand reaching up out of the toilet bowl still flickered through Randy's mind. Not to mention the state of poor Tom Morgan, the unlucky state trooper who had first responded to this nightmare.

Randy twirled the platinum wedding band on his finger, trying to piece together—no pun intended—what had happened to the armless individual. The flesh around the wound was raw and jagged, but hadn't spilled blood onto the cans of soft drinks and beer surrounding the deceased. Randy assumed the arm had been taken off postmortem. The remaining arm was draped over a stack of Righteous Cola in twelve-pack boxes. To the right, a tower of Pepsi framed the decedent. The body had been leaned back against the stainless steel wall of the cooler, its butt on a flat of Budweiser suitcases and its chin resting on its chest. Randy felt an urge to reach under the corpse and pull out a cold one—just a little something to calm his frazzled nerves—but he was twenty years sober in the eyes of the Lord, and would do nothing to spoil all his hard work.

He stopped playing with his wedding band. Florence had died four months ago, but he hadn't been strong enough to take off his ring. Didn't think there was that much strength in all of God's creation. They'd had thirty solid-gold years together before the diabetes took her. She'd lost one foot and three toes on the other before she went. Randy had been a good husband: bathing her in bed, helping her in and out of her wheel chair, cooking, cleaning, and everything else his lovely wife had done before noncompliance took her ability to walk. Flo had always loved her sweets. "Gimme some sugar, Sugar," he recalled her saying. But she hadn't meant a kiss. In AA they called people like Randy "enablers". He didn't see himself like that, though. He had simply tried to make his wife happy toward the end, had given her what she wanted.

He shook thoughts of Flo out of his head and focused on the present circumstances. State Trooper Tom Morgan—not really a friend of Randy's but a long time acquaintance—had been smashed to bits in the restroom. Randy hadn't seen damage like that since 'Nam, and hadn't thought he would ever see it again. Tom was alive, though. The women hadn't been so lucky. Out by the pumps, a woman and a half resided in the trunk of an Audi; one cut in two and the other nothing more than a rag doll. The car—registered to one Innis Blake—was a wreck; dents and shattered glass everywhere, and the driver was nowhere to be found. Deputy Nick Wuncell had run the Blake woman's tag. Her race had come back African American. Randy knew who the bisected woman was—Paramedic Georgia Jackson of Kerrville. She'd brought Randy cookies when Florence died. The other woman was most assuredly Caucasian, and completely unknown to the sheriff. So, yes, the driver was not on scene.

Tom Morgan was currently en route to Kerr County Medical to be assessed and, hopefully, put back together. In a different ambulance—one borrowed from Fredericksburg—Benjamin Geiger followed. Nick, upon arriving at the scene, had found the paramedic in the road. Half Ben's face was gone, torn off by road rash.

But things got stranger.

Randy knew what had happened to the ambulance. The kid Nick had picked up said "the killer"—the boy's words, not Randy's—had used Tom's cruiser to ram it before stealing the trooper's car. That wasn't such a bad thing, though, as all state vehicles had tracking devices installed. What confused Randy was the Studebaker Hawk sitting thirty feet back on Highway 16. Who in Hades did *that* belong to?

Behind Randy, the cooler door had been propped open with a plastic pallet of two-liter Sierra Mist. In came Nick Wuncell, all of twenty-five years old, with less hair on his face than a newborn's backside. The kid looked far more put together than Randy felt. Come to think of it, Nick never showed much emotion, period. Randy hadn't noticed until that moment.

Nodding toward the corpse, Nick said, "The antique belongs to him."

"Sorry?" Randy heard him perfectly well; he just hadn't expected that information to be the case.

"The guy's name is John Landover. There's a picture of him with his wife in the glove box of the Studebaker."

"How'd they fit in the glove box?"

Nick quirked an eyebrow. It was his turn to say, "Sorry?"

"The way you said it sounded like they were in the glove box when someone snapped a photo of... never mind. I was kiddin'." Randy suddenly felt very old and out of touch.

"Not really the time for jokes, is it, Sheriff?"

"Stop calling me *Sheriff*. It's too darn formal. Randy, kid, my name's Randy."

"Force of habit, Sir."

So's that Sir *crap*, thought Randy. Nick had applied for the Kerr County Deputy's position two months after coming home from Afghanistan. Nick was tough, had that thousand-yard stare the youngbucks get when they watch their friends being turned into roadside pâté on a weekly basis, and Randy didn't envy the kid the nightmares that must surely plague his slumber. Randy had his own war scars, mostly of the mental variety. Maybe one day he'd sit down with Nick over a cup of coffee and shoot the kid advice on how to deal with the shakes and sweats. There was no cure for PTSD—or whatever in Hades headshrinkers were calling shell shock these days—but there was attrition; a gradual decrease in the number of breaks a vet had. Once upon a time, Randy had used alcohol to kill the memories the smell of napalm created when mixed with rice paddies and jungle moss, or the odor of dead children in mud holes that moonlighted as sewers.

"John Landover, you say?" Randy asked.

"Yes, Sir. He's out of Beaumont. My guess is he was passing through when all this—whatever this is—happened."

"Don't tell anyone this, Nick, but I'm sorta glad you're just as confused by tonight as I am." Randy gave the kid a wink. Nick's face remained flat and unmoved.

"Do you like the deaf kid for all this?" Nick asked.

"I don't *like* anyone for this. I doubt that boy could've taken Tom down by himself. Besides, didja see how busted up Tom was? What'd the boy use, a sledgehammer? Naw, don't seem right. Something's missing. Call it a gut feeling."

Nick glanced down to where Randy's sizable midsection draped over his belt buckle then averted his gaze.

Randy laughed. "Go on and look. I kinda welcomed it, didn't I?"

Nick didn't so much as smile.

Randy sighed. "Lighten up, youngbuck. It's going to be a long night."

"I... I just... " Nick trailed off.

"Go on. Say your piece."

"I just don't... find you funny, Sir. No offense."

This made Randy laugh again. "Neither did my wife. Sometimes I think she only stayed with me because of my millions."

"You have millions, Sir?"

"You know what, Nick? You're a lost cause. Let's go talk to that deaf boy of yours. What's his name?"

"William Longmire, Sir."

"Of course it is. Tell Moxie he can take old John Landover to the mortician's office, too. Oh, and don't forget his arm. It's in the toilet."

CRUELTY

WILL

In the back of Nick Wuncell's patrol car, Will shook. He couldn't help it. Did they think he'd done all this? Why else would they have him handcuffed to a bar in the backseat of a sheriff's car? Cops didn't handcuff witnesses, did they? He shouldn't have waved down the deputy, should have kept right on walking. But the man doll was out there somewhere. When it was done with the black woman, it would be back after him. Of this, Will was certain.

The time on the deputy's dashboard computer read fifteen after four in the morning. Outside, the parking lot of Bob's Bait and Fuel bustled with life. Two unmarked gray sedans sat at the pumps, nose to nose. Another three Kerr County Sheriff's vehicles were parked by the road, blocking the entrance to the gas station. Will had seen two ambulances come and go; one taking the EMT from the road, and the other escorting the body of the trooper who'd stopped to check on Will earlier that night. Even though the trooper's face was covered in gore, Will had no problem recognizing the thick, round head and thin torso as the gurney rolled by. The Lollipop Man had seen better days.

A blue Ford Ranger was parked at the front doors of the store. In its headlights, an elderly man in golf shorts and a Bermuda tee argued with a Hispanic man in a suit—one of four neatly dressed individuals who'd exited the unmarked sedans. Will thought them Feds, or perhaps state investigators. For the second time that night he tried to remember Dad's favorite crime dramas, and how the chain of command worked in a situation like this. Will settled on state investigators, as the FBI might have taken longer to get out here at this time of night. The old man was of no importance. Will figured he was the owner, maybe even the titular Bob of Bob's Bait and Fuel, because the octogenarian had been the one who'd unlocked the front doors so the paramedics could get the trooper out.

The deputy who had introduced himself as Nick rounded the back of the Ranger, the sheriff a few steps behind him. Will had yet to speak with the balding man with the gray beard, but he recognized the sheriff from his reelection campaign the year prior. Signs that read *Vote Randy Miser for Sheriff* had been placed in more front yards in Fredericksburg and Kerrville than not, not to mention all the television commercials with Sheriff Miser's grinning face all over them.

Nick came to the cruiser, opened the rear door on the driver's side, unlocked Will's cuffs, and pulled him out. The deputy put Will's hands behind his back, cuffing him once more. Will leaned back against the rear fender of the cruiser.

Old Spice hung thick on the air, but underneath the cologne hid another scent—urine. Had the sheriff or Nick wet themselves?

The sheriff gave him a curious glare. "Can you read my lips?"

Will nodded.

"Good. Do you know who did—" the officer made a wide, sweeping gesture with his hand "—all this?"

"Yes." Will wanted to keep his answers short. Oddly, he still worried about how he sounded.

Randy Miser crossed his arms over his keg of a gut. "I'm waiting."

"The guy was big. *Huge.*"

"Big how?"

"Fat. Maybe six hundred pounds. His skin was hard."

"Hard?"

"Like metal… "

Or porcelain, Will added internally.

"So he coulda been wearin' something under his clothes, is what you're sayin'?" The sheriff's Texan accent was so thick that Will had problems with that last statement. He asked Miser to repeat himself and the sheriff obliged.

Will nodded. "Something like that."

Nick said, "Body armor, maybe?"

Sheriff Miser shrugged. "Who knows?"

They spoke as if Will wasn't there. He felt like a child in the presence of adults. He wondered if they realized he could still read their lips from profile.

"Go tell the tasties what our boy here said," Sheriff Miser told Nick. Will tried to figure out who the "tasties" were, but when Nick approached the lone suited man standing by the unmarked sedan, Will figured Sheriff Miser had actually said "staties." So, Will had been right. They *were* state investigators. Not that that information did him a fat lot of good, though.

"Did you see who was driving the Audi?" asked Sheriff Miser.

Will shook his head.

"We're still missing the driver. Did you see anyone else out here tonight?"

"A woman. A black woman. She was in the ambulance when the killer rolled it."

"There's no one in there now."

"The killer must've took her."

"You keep saying that—*the killer*." Miser scratched his silver beard. "Start at the beginning and tell me what happened."

Will mixed lies and truth like a seasoned bartender. His roommate, Kirk, had sent him on an errand. See, Kirk didn't drive, and he wanted Will to run out to this one girl's house to pick up some money she owed Kirk. Kirk hadn't come because he had to work. He'd needed the money before tomorrow, though, because he had to make the light bill payment before the power company knocked them back to the dark ages. On the way, Will had come across a hitchhiker. Her name was Jennifer, and her current residence was the trunk of the Audi, tucked in tight with the upper half of the medic with the harelip. Will's car—an '89 Pontiac Bonneville—had blown a head gasket. Will and Jennifer were walking along—

(*The deaf man and the prostitute moseyed on down the road*)

—when the killer in the Studebaker Hawk ran Jennifer down. How did he know the make and model of the antique vehicle? Will had helped his grandfather restore one just like it. Everything else that came out of Will's mouth was the truth.

Will had never considered himself a good fibber, mainly because he rarely had to lie, but Sheriff Miser looked convinced of the night's happenings. It wasn't until Will remembered Jennifer's gun that the anxiety came. Had they found the country pro's gun? Was Sheriff Miser feigning belief while Will made a fool of himself?

And why the fuck does the sheriff smell like piss?

"You've had one helluva night, boy." Sheriff Miser placed a hand on Will's shoulder and squeezed. "We'll find this guy, don't worry."

Sheriff Miser might've taken Will's sigh of relief to mean that he appreciated the reassurance, but Sheriff Miser would've been wrong. That Miser believed his story made Will happier than a fat kid at a buffet.

Should've told him the truth, that tiny, tinny voice said. *Who cares if you were out trying to get laid? All that really matters is that the hooker tried to rob you.*

Will wished he knew where the off switch that controlled his inner thoughts was located. That tinny asshole was beginning to get on his nerves.

Oh, and don't forget about the woman you abandoned, chump. Whatever happens to her is your fault.

The voice was right. But Will could live with being a coward. Because the operative word there was *live*. Unlike the woman he'd left for dead, Will would most certainly *live*.

INNIS

Innis Blake slept.

Somewhere far off, a clock ticked. Not your average clock, though. This one tick-tocked like a beating heart.

She could see nothing, was in a total blackness—cave dark. Heavy straps lay across her upper arms, pinning her to a seatback. Though she could move her mouth, no sound would issue from her. She tried to scream several times, but it was as if someone had run off with her vocal cords. A rusty odor snaked up her nostrils.

A scuffing sound presented itself, like that of a chair being pulled across hardwood. Innis looked up and down, left then right, but couldn't lock onto the direction of the noise. A whine accompanied the scuffing now, and Innis felt sure she would go mad from the clamor.

A light flickered on, cast by a single lamp on the floor in the corner of a concrete room. The lamp was old, shadeless, Victorian, maybe porcelain, with ivy and purple flowers creeping up the body. The bare bulb didn't bother Innis's eyes. She was only vaguely aware that she hadn't needed to adjust to the light at all. With the room illuminated, Innis hunted the source of the scuffing. She found an odd sight above her: a rollaway door being pulled across the ceiling. Innis was reminded of opening a sardine can. When it was three-quarters of the way across, the door stopped.

In the open space lay midnight.

A small, pink object fell out of the darkness, flopping to the ground just a few feet in front of her. Innis leaned forward to get a better look then lurched back in revulsion. A hand—a *human* hand—twitched on the concrete. A leg, removed at the knee, flopped down next to the hand. The toes splayed, waving at her. Though she had no voice, Innis tried to scream. Her throat hurt.

She pinched her eyes closed, willing the recurring nightmare away. Many a night, the dream had tortured her. An internet site on dream theory had told her the nightmare meant she was afraid of losing something vital to her existence. Innis didn't care what it meant; she simply didn't want to have the dream any longer. The World Wide Web had been unable to help her with that.

Innis willed herself awake, but her mind was having none of the strong-arm routine. A door had been locked and secured, and Innis had misplaced the key. It was like trying to surface from a winter lake after your swimming hole had frozen over.

Instead of waking, Innis's eyes fluttered open to yet another queer sight. She was in the middle of a street, arms unencumbered, freed from their previous bindings. Night had fallen in this part of town. She could hear distant, muffled voices from the surrounding tract homes: the soft calls of excited children, one crying babe, a TV show's laugh track, and an enraged man wanting to know where his mother*fucking* dinner was. A man walked past Innis on her right; blue shirt, black slacks, short cropped brown hair. He was snuffling, as if he was in the throes of a rather nasty cold. A pistol swung at his side from one white-knuckled fist. Farther up the road, rounding the curve onto this street, was Innis's brother, Gerry. He wore his marching band uniform, and his flute case hung from his left hand. Gerry didn't stride, he bounced; he looked so damned happy. One month away from graduation and he looked so terribly happy. Innis reached out for her brother, wanted to go to him, but could not move her feet.

Grover Duchamp, the coke-addled security guard who'd decided it was time for him to kill someone, raised his Ruger P95 and shot Gerry in the neck.

But Gerry didn't go down. Rather, Gerry offered his sister a worn smile that weighed more than lips and teeth. His mouth moved but no sound issued forth; perhaps she had gone deaf, like... like who?

But, no, she wasn't deaf.

Gerry stuck his index finger to the bullet hole on his neck. When he spoke again, his words were clear.

"Fancy seeing you here, Innie."

Innis slapped a hand that didn't exist to her mouth and gasped.

Gerry dropped to one knee. He pulled the flute's case onto his raised knee and went about undoing the clasps. Now that both of his hands worked on the case, his wound was free flowing. Blood ran down and over Gerry's prized brass flute as he pulled it from the case's confines. He wiped it off, looking not unlike a samurai swiping clean his blade after having killed hundreds on the battlefield.

The mouthpiece did not go into Gerry's mouth. He placed the reed to the hole in his neck and began to play the *Super Mario Bros.* theme song. Innis's heart ached. She recalled how Caitlyn and Gerry had sat in the great room for hours on end; Mom trying to teach him how to play Tchaikovsky's "Swan Theme," or Leontovych's "Carol of the Bells," and Gerry having none of it. He kept calling Innis in, bragging about how he'd finally learned the theme song to their favorite video game. Once Mom gave up for the day, Innis would power on the floor set, unravel the controllers, and blow out their copy of *Super Mario Bros. 3*. They'd both grown out of part one some time ago, and part two was nothing more than some insane Japanese port Nintendo had released to keep people interested in the series until Shigeru Miyamoto finished the next installment.

The *Super Mario Bros.* theme ended and Gerry went into "Habanera" from *Carmen*. A symphony of unseen players joined in. The night came alive with the sounds of music. Gerry serenaded his sister, playing his instrument with that ghastly, leaking hole in his neck. His murderer, Duchamp, pirouetted out into the street, tippy-toes flitting across the asphalt, as if he were an experienced ballerina.

Their mother, Caitlyn, sat in a rocking chair beside Innis, weeping. Nine days Mother had wept. Innis knew because Innis had counted. Like a child tallying sheep, waiting on the sandman to come, Innis had counted. She'd counted because she hadn't known what else to do.

To her left, Bruce the Nefarious Cocksucker was on his knees before his unnamed boy toy. Bruce pulled his mouth away, spat onto the street, and smiled. A bubble burst at the corner of his mouth.

Everyone began singing—Duchamp, Caitlyn, Bruce, the faceless boy toy—and the symphony peaked, the cellos and Spanish guitars falling into a steady, haunting rhythm. Gerry no longer played. He wept.

Gerry pressed a thumb over his wound and said, "I will make you regret."

That terrible ticking timepiece was back, playing metronome to the clamoring choir. So loud. So god*damned* loud. So....

Innis Blake woke from one nightmare and stepped into another. Above her, a bare bulb swung lazily from an orange extension cord which had been draped over a two-by-two in the ceiling. She smelled blood, and hoped it wasn't hers. Yet somehow she knew the odor came from her. She remembered knocking her head on the steering wheel. Saw Merlo the Cowardly Beagle run out of the shattered windshield. Felt the ambulance rolling. Her head throbbed like a hammer-smashed thumb.

CRUELTY

In TV medical dramas, Innis had seen plenty of folks waking up on gurneys. Usually, it was a POV shot, one from the person who had been under for one reason or another. She felt like that now as a young man came into view, leaning over her from above her head. He looked upside down, and clean-shaven—and as odd as those two things sounded when placed in the same sentence, that was exactly how he appeared to her. The young man's jet-black hair was slicked back; all but a Superman swoosh at the front. *He's a greaser*, Innis thought inanely. His blue eyes bore into hers. He grinned—a Cheshire cat with sinister intent.

"Oh," he said, his voice very soft and serene. "She's woke cruelty."

"Rrrrr... " Innis was trying to ask "What?" but clarity was still miles away. She attempted to drag herself from yet another level of this odd dream. What else could this be? The man wasn't making any sense. *She's woke cruelty*? What could that even mean?

"Are you with us, ma'am?"

"Rrrrr... "

"Oh, that's all right. Better you miss this part. Cruelty, do your thing, dearest."

There, he'd done it again, speaking to someone off camera, almost as if that someone was *named* Cruelty. Cruelty wasn't a name, though. Half-drunk with sleep, she laughed.

The dark-haired, blue-eyed man-child disappeared. Innis could hear that clock-like heartbeat once more—

(Had it ever stopped?)

—and felt her own heart beat a little faster. She recognized it now. And as realization brought Innis up and out of slumber's fog, the doll stepped in, stage right.

It cooed, "Mah-Mah."

Innis found that, unlike in her dreams, she could scream. She could scream very loudly.

CRUELTY

RANDY & WILL

Randy's testicles were swimming. His incontinence pants had failed him. He wasn't even aware of it until he saw the deaf man's nose twitching. Then, Randy could smell himself; that acidic ammonia aroma, sickeningly thick, as if he'd been set upon by a band of window washers, their spray bottles on full-auto. Randy turned away from the deaf man and brushed his hand almost imperceptibly across his fly. Damp. It couldn't be denied. Surrounded by the peers he worked with on a daily basis, along with four state investigators he didn't know from Adam, Sheriff Randy Miser had leaked about a gallon into his Pampers.

God only knew, he wasn't a cussing man, but at that moment a foul string of words rushed across his tongue and out his lips. The deaf man—what was his name again?—gave Randy a cautious glare.

"Looks like—" Randy paused, carefully assessing what he said next before sticking his foot in his mouth. "Looks like I'm gonna have to take you in for questioning. I hope you didn't have a ball to get to."

"I did... ent do... any... thing."

Randy thought, *He sounds retarded every time he talks.*

Straight away, another thought leapt into his mind, *That wasn't very Christian-like.*

I've got three bodies, two people en route to the hospital in critical condition, one hearing-impaired eyewitness, and a missing woman. Excuse me if I'm a wee bit on edge, oh All-Knowing Nitwit of my Mind.

The voice went silent. Randy felt a modicum of victory until he realized he'd essentially told himself to shut up. His pride melted away.

Will didn't want to get in the car with the pissy sheriff. Nonetheless, he followed Sheriff Miser to the cruiser. Will's options were limited. In fact, he thought there was only one option available—obedience.

He was placed in the rear section of the sheriff's cruiser and, once again, handcuffed to the bar under the steel grate that kept criminals from getting to know the driver on an intimate level.

The car smelled of baby powder. The man doll flashed before his eyes. Will flinched. He tried to raise his hands in self-defense but the cuffs stopped them a good two feet from his nose. Will had read somewhere that one's olfactory system was tied closely to memory, but on this go around, Will found his nose off by quite a lot. The doll hadn't smelled like talcum powder. It smelled of death and Juicy Fruit. Of decay. With that thought, the cogs in Will's brain clicked into place, warming up his mental engine. Was the man doll dying? Did the person under the mask have some kind of disease? Gangrene, or something equally deadly and disgusting? Was its body shutting down? Could its jaundiced eyes mean that the thing was on its last legs? How about the way it rolled instead of walked, tilting all cattywampus as it shuffled along like an old man without a cane? Will didn't know how he'd use any of that information even if he was right. The only thing he knew for certain was, if the doll came again, Will wouldn't mistake its odor for thirty-five cent gum that—juicy, or not—tasted nothing like fruit.

After briefly speaking with the man in the suit who'd previously been talking with the owner of the store—Bob of Bob's Bait and Fuel, Will assumed—Sheriff Miser returned to his car. As the sheriff slid in, Will wished urine didn't overcome baby powder in the Game of Scents.

As Randy adjusted the mirror to look upon the deaf man, he asked, "Can ya read my lips from this angle?"

The boy nodded.

"I'll keep the dome light on so's I can ask questions on the way. Ain't really supposed to, but it'll save us some time interrogating you back at the station."

"I did... ent do... anything," the boy said, for the second time that night.

"That's all yet to be seen. Just settle back. We got ourselves a thirty minute drive ahead of us."

Randy reversed out of Bob's Bait and Fuel, minding the other four cruisers lined up at the road, barely squeezing between a rear bumper and a Yaupon bush. The shrubbery scrubbed along the cruiser's side panel, sounding like diamonds cutting glass.

"What's your name again, son?"

"William Long... mire. Call me... Will." The boy looked sad in the rearview, despondent. Randy wanted to ask him who'd stolen his puppy, but every one of his jokes had struck out on Nick, so he kept his buffoonery to himself. Randy wasn't truly in the mood for joviality, anyway. It was more of a nervous reaction. Bad happenstance turned him into a clown, after a fashion. The puddle he currently sat in wasn't conducive to hysterics, either.

Unlike him, the excuse he'd given State Investigator Markum would hold water.

"I need to get the boy into protective custody ASAP," Randy had said.

"You do that," Markum responded, crinkling his brow and looking laughably serious.

"When you finish up around here, I'll have him ready for your round of questioning, deal?"

"Sounds good."

Randy had turned to leave.

"Sheriff Miser?" the suit called.

"Yuh?" Randy said, turning back.

"Spilt coffee or something on the front o' ya. Might wanna change. People'll think you wet yourself." State Investigator Markum winked.

Some darn investigator you are, Randy thought. *Can't even see this old man's pissed his Depends.*

Or maybe Markum had been trying to be polite. Oh well, didn't really matter anyway. While it was on his mind, Randy pulled up the texting function on his cell phone. Randy took Highway 16's S-curves one-handed as he jotted down a simple message to himself.

Talk to doc about Ditropan not working.

He sent the text to his own number and exited the application.

His doctor had placed him on Ditropan—oxybutynin to those in the pharmacological field—two months after Flo's death. When Randy asked if the death of his wife could be blamed, psychologically, for his leaky pipes, the doctor had said, "No. You're bladder's tired, Randy. All's there is to it. You've stretched it out, and there isn't any going back."

"What about a transplant?" Randy had asked.

The doctor laughed; the sound so full of book-learning and crappy bedside manners that Randy believed the doc had forgotten who he was speaking to. Where was the respect nowadays? Certain positions used to *mean* something; being a county sheriff didn't even command respect as it once had. Randy had seen the subtle shift in societal thinking after coming home from Vietnam—people looked at you differently. As if *you* owed *them* something, and not the other way around. As the years went by, and America stuck its nose into varying different pies, Randy watched civvies' appreciation hit an all-time low. Sure, you got the occasional, "Thank you for all you do/did for our country." But all those people really meant was, "Thank you for going so I didn't have to."

"We don't do bladder transplants, Randy." The doctor continued to chortle. "Incontinence isn't—no offense—but it isn't exactly *life* threatening."

Randy hadn't liked the way the doctor had said "life." The way the young sawbones hung that word out there (*life*), elongating it (*liiife*), emphasizing every bit of its single syllable until it seemed the four letter word would snap like an over-capacity suspension bridge. *Ly (SNAP!) fuh.*

"Are... you look... king for... the woman?" Will asked, breaking Randy out of his recollections.

"We will, yes. Did you say you knew her?"

Will shook his head.

"When was the last time you saw her?"

"We... got lost... in the... woods. I *lost* her... in the... woods." It seemed the more the boy spoke the stretchier his words got.

Just like your bladder, Randy thought.

Lies, all lies, Will thought. What did it matter if this man knew the truth? Will had escaped, left the black lady to fend for herself. So what? Being a coward wasn't a crime. Who was he hiding from?

Myself, that's who.

There had been a time in Will's life when he had been strong, unshakable. Where had that time been secreted away? He was no longer the boy who'd had his ears lanced. The person he was now would have run screaming from the tip of that needle. He wasn't the same kid who'd dove into textbooks about the hearing-impaired, needing to know his condition as a fish needs water to breathe. He was a scared little boy, now; one who would rather curl up in a corner than seek enlightenment. Because enlightenment meant seeing the world for what it really was; all big and nasty and full of stinky, scary men dressed as dolls.

Will wanted to blame someone else for the events of the evening, like he had earlier tonight, but couldn't. That tiny, tinny voice would no longer allow it. It didn't matter to Will that Jennifer was dead—what was one less meth whore in the world?—but that poor woman in the back of the ambulance...

Will cleared his throat. He had Sheriff Miser's attention. Will said, "I... I lied. I did... ent lose her... in the... woods."

CRUELTY

KIRK

Lifting weights was like sex. You shouldn't let your partner know you're hurting. Also, you should give it your all. Don't be a pussy. Pound it.

Kirk Babbitt had a way with words. At least he thought so. On more than one occasion, he thought he'd like to be a poet. Yeah, that'd be nice. Poets got all the bitches. The right words in the right sequence, all rhyming and shit, could drop panties faster than a trip to the gynecologist. In fact, maybe being a gyno wasn't a bad idea, either. Or, better yet, a Gyno Poet. Imagine the play he'd get. Surrounded by vagina, he'd be King Inumdeep, from the Land of Humpaho!

The random dude Kirk had snagged from the free weights glowered down at him. Kirk had promised the man that he'd spot him after Kirk got his pump on. That was over an hour ago. Now Kirk was so vascular that he looked like an engorged penis, glistening and veiny.

Kirk pressed another three-fifty, blurted, "Hun'red!" and let the bar slam back home on the bench's poles. His spotter scrambled backward, seemingly scared the bar would bounce free and crush him under its weight.

Bitch ass, Kirk thought.

Kirk laughed as he sat up. "Sorry, man. My bad."

"You still got time to spot me?"

Kirk glanced around the empty twenty-four hour gym. "Might have to find someone else. I think I mighta pulled something. Sorry 'bout that."

"Right." The guy walked off without another word.

If it hadn't been for the bicep tear he'd suffered a year ago, Kirk wouldn't have bothered with a spotter. But after snapping the muscle from its moorings, and that bar coming down on his neck, Kirk had learned his lesson. Never pump without a chump. Six months without lifting with his right arm had him looking a bit lopsided. To counteract his unbalanced physique, he'd had to stop working out all together. The only thing he allowed himself was cardio. But that shit wasn't enough. He didn't know how the bitches did it. Run, run, run, and what did you get? Sore legs and a sweaty ass crack. No wonder gym girl vagina smelled like old socks filled with mackerel. It was one of the main reasons he didn't eat out at the Y anymore.

Kirk headed for the showers. He took off his black wifebeater, spandex shorts, and boxer briefs, and stuffed them inside his duffel. He pulled out the washcloth he'd brought from home, along with his Irish Spring body wash. Leaving the bag on the benches in front of the lockers, he chose the corner stall, locked himself in, and masturbated under the lukewarm spray. No good workout was complete without a final release. He shot his seed into the drain, turned off the cold water, then the hot to full blast, and sterilized himself. He scrubbed every inch of his body. Feeling brand new, he cut the water, collected his things, and exited the stall.

The guy with the knife was black. Not brown/black like Kirk, but black/black, like charcoal hidden up midnight's asshole. The guy's too-white eyes glowered at Kirk; his smile as bright as sunlight in a tanning bed.

"Whaddup, my *neegah*?"

Knife or no knife, Kirk couldn't help it. "Only nigga I see here is the one holding a blade to an unarmed man. Be 'bout it, or drop the piece."

"What's this *be 'bout it* nonsense, Ollie?"

A new voice came from Kirk's left. "I'm guessing he wants you to face him like a man." The as-yet-unseen man was chewing something. Maybe gum, but Kirk wasn't taking his eyes off the knife to check. Kirk wished the locker rooms were more like the weight area, with floor-to-ceiling mirrors. Instead of being able to see the second man in the wall across from him, all Kirk saw was a bank of lockers, his duffel bag atop the changing bench, and an angry fucker with a red-handled butcher knife.

The tip of the blade met with the tip of Kirk's nose. Despite his mass, Kirk could move fast when needed. He saw himself slapping away the blade, tackling the brother, and tea-bagging him to death before the man named Ollie could intervene. Only problem was, Kirk didn't know if this Ollie character was packing fire. A knife wasn't shit, but a bullet in the head could ruin your day.

Kirk slapped on a faux smile. "What do you want? Money? I'm broke, so gimme a break."

"Mucho attitude for a man with a knife in his face, eh, Twon?" asked the unseen man.

"He not nar' bit scared, Ollie. Maybe I start dissecting this muddahfuckah and he starts being scared."

"Sounds good to me."

There were two things in life Kirk couldn't stand: Clingy-type bitches, and being spoken about as if he wasn't standing right there. So, when the Twon guy dropped the knife's tip from Kirk's nose, Kirk kicked as hard as he could. Twon's nuts felt about as sturdy as cotton batting against his shin. The overly dark, knife-wielding asshole hit the floor like a bag of laundry dropped from a chute. His knife clattered across the floor, slid under the stall door, and was gone.

Snick-snick

Kirk froze. His dad used to work at a gun range, cleaning up all the nice white men's discharged rounds, and putting up fresh pictures of Clinton and Bono for the Republican crackers to blast holes into. Some days, Dad would bring a much younger version of Kirk along with him to work, where Kiddy Kirk would listen to skeet being blasted from the sky, or handguns being emptied inside the claustrophobic confines of the shooting stalls. There was absolutely no other sound on Earth like the racking of a shotgun's slide. Abso-fuckin'-lutely nothing.

Kirk deflated. "God damn it."

"What made you go and do something stupid like that, Kirk?" asked the unseen man.

Kirk lifted his hands, feeling weaker by the second. Was he really going to go out like a chump? Was he just going to stand there and be a bitch about it?

Finally, Kirk looked at the unseen man. This Ollie guy wasn't chubby but he was nowhere near as fit as the tracksuit-adorned man rolling around on the ground, clutching his bait and tackle. Ollie didn't look a bit bemused or upset, either. If there was any emotion bubbling through the man, Kirk couldn't read it. At least this Twon person had seemed excited. Shaking his head ever so slightly, Ollie stared at Kirk blankly.

Holding his gut and groaning, Twon pushed to his feet. He stumbled into Kirk, shoved Kirk off to the right, and shuffled into the shower stall. A moment later, Twon reappeared, once more brandishing his red-handled butcher knife.

"You muddahfuckah, you. Imma cut you, muddahfuckah. Imma—"

"Twon?" said Ollie, like a parent speaking to a child.

"What?" asked Twon.

"We need information first."

Twon shook. Cords stood out in his neck. A vein at Twon's temple looked about ready to burst. Beads of sweat rolled between his eyes, down the length of his nose, and plummeted from the tip. Twon poked the knife at Kirk, stopping only centimeters away from Kirk's pecs each time.

"What do you want?" Kirk asked.

"Where's your roommate, is all?" said Ollie with a jolly old smile. "Tell me where he is, and all this goes away."

That little motherfucker, Kirk thought. *I get him laid and this is how he repays me? I'm gonna—*

Wait...

Kirk hitched his chin at the man made of night. "You say your name was Twon?"

"Actually," Ollie raised his hand and waved it, "that was me that said his name."

"You know me?" asked Twon.

"You sell speed, right?"

"No bid'ness of yours, muddahfuckah. Not good speculatin', seen?"

"Ain't nobody speculating, Twon. If you want to know where Will is, you gotta pay the ferryman."

"You wordy for a muscle head, blood."

"And you ugly for someone who resembles a Hershey bar... *seen*?" Kirk grinned.

Ollie laughed. "He sounds just like your ass, Twon."

Twon ignored his partner. "Where is he?"

"Who? Will?"

"Yea, muddahfuckah, who else?"

"I don't know. I set him out to score some pussy and—"

Twon growled. "God damn it."

The cook moved quicker than Kirk expected. One moment, Kirk was standing there, staring at the pitch black surrounding Twon's eyes, and the next he was staring down at the butcher's knife buried to the hilt in his left shoulder. He hadn't even seen the asshole move, much less stab him. Then he was on his knees, crying like a little bitch; his hands splayed out in front of him as he screamed toward his widely spaced fingers.

The door to the locker room creaked open. Kirk's spotter stuck his head in and said, "What the fu—" before realization painted his features.

"Help!" Kirk pleaded with the man in the door.

"Next time," the spotter said, "maybe you spot someone when you say you will. You guys clean up when you're done, okay?"

"Will do," said Ollie.

Ollie waved at the man as the door swung closed. He laughed. "Guy thinks I'm really going to mop up your blood, Kirk. Thinks just 'cause I paid him to keep his mouth shut that I should follow his orders, I guess."

Kirk grasped the handle and began sliding the knife out. With a sharp kick, Twon shoved it back in. Kirk was thrown to the tile, the tip of the knife protruding from his back clinking on the floor and echoing off the rows of lockers.

"You one stu-peed muddahfuckah."

"You do the honors this time." Ollie tossed Twon a roll of duct tape. "The guy said this place gets busy around five in the mornin', and we're quickly coming up on that. Wrap him up so he don't bleed in the car then meet me out back." Ollie skirted the blood spattered on the tile as he left the locker room.

"You're... " Kirk stared up at Twon, struggling for breath. "You're not gonna... not gonna kill me?"

"You done killed yourself, blood. Now, me gotta keep you 'live." Twon stretched his arms out to his sides, unrolling the tape as he did so. "Now, be careful, seen? Wouldn' want'cha meetin' tha ferr'man before ya time."

Twon tore the knife out of Kirk's shoulder and proceeded to circle him with the tape. After ten passes, Kirk felt like a water balloon, all tight and sloshy. He thought, *So this is what internal bleeding feels like*. The world spun. Before Kirk could pass out, Twon lifted him off his knees and threw Kirk over his shoulder. Twon grabbed the duffel, and left the locker room.

As they passed the free weights, Twon patted Kirk on his bare ass. "We go'n stop by ya place 'fore we drop you at hospital, blood. Hope ya dunt mind."

CRUELTY

NATALIE

Trooper Natalie Holden found Tom Morgan's cruiser with little trouble. The GPS on the state vehicle marked the location within a hundred feet. Further hunting had been unnecessary, though, as whoever had dumped the car had left the roof lights on. She'd seen them clear as day from Ranchero Road. Swirling blue gave an eerie cast to the dry bed of Camp Meeting Creek. While Crime Scene Analysts Michaels and Demuth searched the car for clues, Natalie remained at her car and radioed in to dispatch.

"Trooper Holden here. No sign of the missing woman. Over."

Shirley's slight Mexican accent came back forlorn. "Keep searching, yeah."

"Don't really have much choice, do we?"

The unspoken bond all law enforcement individuals shared resounded in Natalie's head. She hadn't seen the state Tom was in, but she'd eavesdropped on the radio band conversation between Kerry County Medical Center and the paramedics who were bringing Tom in for treatment. One shattered hand, a broken arm, and a compound fracture of the left leg sounded like something out of a horror film. She'd find whoever laid the beating down on her fellow officer. And when she did, she might just see that individual draw a gun on her, whether they actually held a firearm or not. In her mind, she went all Harry Callahan on the sicko. The perp wouldn't feel lucky in the slightest.

Analyst Dwight Michaels climbed the embankment of Camp Meeting Creek and approached Natalie, dusting off his gloved hands on his brown slacks. His gray, shoulder-length hair stuck to the sweat on his forehead and cheeks. *He needs a ponytail holder*, Natalie thought. A lab kit hung from his right hand.

"There's a little blood in the trunk, but not much else. The last thing on Morgan's computer is a game of Solitaire." Michaels sighed, his face drawn up in a grimace in the glow of the cruiser's headlights. "Whoever ditched the car wiped down the steering wheel. There *are* prints, ma'am, but they're smudged as hell. I ain't getting a thing off 'em, I can tell you that much."

"The blood fresh?" Natalie asked.

Michaels nodded.

"Any way of telling—?"

"I can't tell shit until I get back to the lab. This ain't *CSI Miami*, ma'am. Shit takes time."

Natalie chuffed. "Thanks."

Michaels retreated to his van, which was parked across the street in front of a field with a barbed wire fence segmenting the land from Ranchero Road. Off in the distance, a pair of headlights bounced in the early morning haze. Natalie had seen the dirt road on the right as she was coming in. The beams seemed to be coming toward her from that direction. She rounded the rear of her cruiser and stepped out into the road.

On the other side of the street, Michaels put his lab kit in the rear of the van, closed the doors and leaned against them. He lit a cigarette and exhaled blue smoke into the oncoming headlights.

A newer model Dodge Ram pickup came to a stop behind the crime scene van. The transmission shuddered as it was thrown into park. The headlights went out. A dark, hunched figure got out and walked toward Natalie. When the man walked into the glow of her brake lights, Natalie could see just how old he was. He wore white coveralls over a blue, sleeveless t-shirt.

"Can I help you?" Natalie asked.

The elderly man's voice was gruff. "Name's Burt Waters, officer. Might have some information fer ya regarding that car ya'll so fascinated with."

This piqued Natalie's interest. "Really? What's that?"

"Dat car right there weren't dropped off too long 'go."

"Did you see who dropped it off?"

"Naw, didn't. Only seen their outline. Wife seen the roof lights come on while she were makin' coffee in the kitch'. She drug me in from the livin' room, where I were watching the early bird news in my long johns. I thought it were funny the way the person just left the car and runned off into the woods. I knew then that it weren't no officer or whatnot. Besides, he weren't no taller than my mailbox. You pulled up 'fore I could even get dressed proper."

Natalie asked, "You saw all that from your house? I can't even see your house from here."

"'Noculars, honey. My Rangefinders are good fer two hun'red yards if they're good fer an inch. Son-in-law runs an army surplus store in San Antoine. Got 'em for a pinch and a song."

"And how did you come by the individual's height. You said he was what... no taller than your mailbox?"

The old man nodded. "I come to that conclusion simple like. The person runned by my mailbox on their way into the woods." He pointed to a single bricked-in mailbox about twenty feet down on Camp Meeting Creek's side of the road. About four feet tall, Natalie estimated. Either she was dealing with a child, or someone who was vertically-impaired.

Could someone that small have gotten the best of Tom Morgan? Maybe she was looking for more than one individual.

Something else the old man had said drew her attention. "You said you saw the person run off into the woods, but we arrived before you had a chance to fully dress yourself?"

"Yep. That's what I said."

"How long does it normally take you to get dressed?"

He laughed. "I'm eighty-three in four months, darlin'. It takes me a coon's age to put myself together nowadays."

"How long's a coon's age, Mr. Waters?"

"Call me Burt. 'Bout thirty- to forty-five minutes."

Natalie did the math in her head. The first call had come in three hours ago when Kerr County Sheriff's Deputy Nick Wuncell ran up on the scene at Bob's Bait and Fuel. He'd found Tom Morgan half-dead in the restrooms. Backup was called in. Natalie was assigned the duty of locating Morgan's cruiser using GPS. She'd been on scene here for no more than twenty minutes. Bob's Bait and Fuel was only fifteen minutes away from where she now stood. If Burt Waters was right, and the car had been dumped only a little more than an hour before, that meant someone had taken a joyride before dumping the cruiser.

"Could you hang around while I make a call, Burt?"

"Been retired for 'bout as long as you been alive, honey. I ain't got nothin' but time."

Natalie smiled at that. Leaving Burt on the side of the road, she walked around to the front of her cruiser. She pulled her cell from her breast pocket and speed dialed Frank Markum.

The state investigator answered on the third ring. "Markum."

"Hey, Frank, it's Natalie. I'm out here on Ranchero Road. I have a possible lead on the person who took off with Morgan's cruiser but I need some help."

"What can I do for you, Natalie?"

"I think whoever stole his car might've went somewhere else before ditching the ride. I have a witness here that says he saw a person run off into the woods about forty-five minutes before we arrived." She relayed the timeline, and Markum concurred.

She continued, "What I want to know is, is there any way I can pull up a history on Morgan's GPS? Like, every place the cruiser stopped before being dumped?"

"Sure. You by your computer?"

Elated, Natalie said, "Gimme a minute."

She dipped into her car and logged into her station. She followed Markum's directions to a T, and after about twenty keystrokes stared at a detailed map of the injured trooper's vehicle's last whereabouts.

"Can I pinpoint time stamps?" she asked.

"Come again?"

"Can I pull up a certain time? You know, single out the past two hours?"

"Yeah, yeah. Hold Alt+F4. In the new window, type in the starting and ending times you want to check."

Natalie did so. The blood in her ears sounded as if she were head-deep in a marching band's bass drum.

"I got it. Do you have a pen and paper?"

"Way ahead of you." Natalie could actually hear Markum smiling.

"It's actually not too far from here. I think I passed it on my way to Camp Meeting Creek. It's... " She trailed off.

"Natalie? Nat, you there?" Markum sounded concerned. Natalie thought he should be.

"You aren't going to believe this, Frank. Not in a million years."

CRUELTY

Oh, Cruelty wanted to play. It wanted to play so bad.

The dark woman stared up at it with eyes so wide that Cruelty believed he could see her very soul cowering before it. Beneath her screams of terror, Cruelty could hear its own heart tick, tick, ticking away. It shuddered in glorious anticipation.

Forgiveness leaned against the boarded walls of the cellar, chomping an apple. He'd made Cruelty wait. Cruelty didn't like waiting; patience not being a virtue Forgiveness had installed in his creation. Still, it knew better than to be disobedient. Besides, Forgiveness had allowed Cruelty a plaything so close behind the last one that Cruelty really should be grateful. So what if it had to wait until Forgiveness returned from dumping the trooper's car? It had had the wonderful joy of watching the dark woman beg for her life. Now, she'd given up her pleas. Only tasty terror-laced wailings now came from her. Cruelty sucked them up.

"Start with her fingers. She won't need them," Forgiveness said. "That's a good Cruelty."

The dark woman balled her fists, denying Cruelty its prize. Had it been able to laugh, it would have. Cruelty clamped one stiff hand on the dark woman's wrist and squeezed. The bones turned to dust in its grasp. The dark woman erupted in agony.

"Now, Cruelty, how are you supposed to play with her fingers if she can't feel them?"

"Mah-Mah," it cooed, disappointed. Cruelty seemed at an impasse. What was it to do now?

"You know… she has another hand." Forgiveness was so smart. Cruelty could live many generations and never be so knowing.

Cruelty rolled around the table, gliding to the sobbing protests of the dark woman. She made such lovely music. It wanted to dance.

The fingers on her other hand were splayed; the nails biting into the wood of the table. Cruelty pinched the tip of her middle finger ever so slightly. Sometimes, it didn't know its own strength. It had to be careful, precise, or risk flubbing this as well. Slowly, Cruelty bent her finger toward her wrist. The knuckle shattered and the digit went limp. He continued to push back until the bone poked through the skin. Then, Cruelty twisted the finger off, as one scoops ice cream from a tub.

The dark woman sang with agony. Notes of sheer anguish soothed Cruelty.

"That's a good Cruelty," its master said. "Now, the knife."

CRUELTY

INNIS

When Innis was thirteen, her friend Monique had dared her to take Baxter Avenue—aka Thrill Hill—on Gerry's skateboard. Baxter Avenue was a forty-five degree angle that ended in an open field. No curb to worry about. Nothing but soft green grass to soften the end of the ride. Not being one to back down on a dare, Innis had taken her best friend's challenge. She bellied-down on the skateboard while Monique complained that that hadn't been the deal. Innis was supposed to ride it down like a skater, on her feet, not like a coward, on her belly. Innis had said that Monique should have been more exact with her dare, before shoving herself off with the tips of her tennis shoes.

Everything went fine until she hit the fist-sized pothole. The right wheel caught and Innis was sent sailing, chest first, across the asphalt. Her blouse had provided about two seconds worth of protection before shearing off. Her training bra went next, torn in two by nothing more than friction. As Innis's bare chest met pavement, her chin arrived as well. She recalled the deep gouges in her flesh feeling hot and cold at the same time. She remembered the brilliant pain quite well.

Still, that pain was nothing like what she was going through now.

Luckily, she could no longer feel her right hand. Her wrist had been shattered and the nerves were dead. She was rather glad she had a strap at her neck that kept her from looking down at her useless hand.

The middle finger on her left hand was another thing all together. It was everything; a pain so all encompassing that Innis felt faint, on the verge of drifting off. Maybe that was best. She'd just close her eyes and go away. She pinched her lids closed. Tears and sweat stung her eyes. Keeping them closed was like trying to flatten a stainless steel ball bearing in the palm of your hand.

"Nuh, uh, uh, child," a soft, faintly masculine voice said. "Open up."

Seeking fingers pulled one eyelid open. A star shone in her vision. No, not a star. A sunburst of bright light. The bulb above her was glinting off something.

She focused, then wished she hadn't.

The hand held a safety pin. Up close like it was, the pin looked forever large, like a prop from *Honey, I Shrunk the Kids*. Fingers pinched the metal. The needle point released.

Innis could not see the face of the person whose fingers held her eye open, but she could hear them breathing in her right ear. For the first time since she was a child in church, she prayed. Prayed that this would be over quick. Begged to die quickly.

She would not be so lucky.

The safety pin entered her eyelid, slid into her eyebrow, and was clicked closed. Innis blubbered, all out of screams now, as the process was repeated with her other eye. Blood pooled in her vision. She tried to blink. Fresh pain shot across her brow and into her temple.

There was silence for a while. Innis had no way of knowing how long. Blood, sweat, and tears stung her eyes, but there was nothing she could do about it. Cold water splashed Innis's face, washing away the acidic mixture of fluid.

She stared upward, unable to do much else. It was like gazing up through the surface of a pool and seeing the sun in linear patterns on the surface. A cloth was draped over her face. The wash rag soaked up the water and she could see again. She didn't want to, but she did.

The doll held a scalpel in one hand. It clicked the blade against its face. The surgeon's instrument descended to Innis's hairline and bit into her scalp.

That soft, vaguely masculine voice said, "Cruelty will make you regret."

"Dah-Dah."

"That's a good Cruelty."

CRUELTY

MERLO

As dawn brightened and the world turned lavender, Merlo crept through the woods. The beagle was hungry, lonely, and missing the Lady. Insects and birds cried all around him. His ears twitched, but otherwise he ignored the woodland clamor.

A squirrel raced past and up a tree. He snorted, uninterested. Tree rats did nothing for him. A little Alpo would be nice, though. He licked his lips.

Ahead, through a thicket, was a house. Smoke rose from the chimney, caught the air and twisted away. Merlo could smell bacon. The Mister had loved smoked meats, would secret some to Merlo when the Lady wasn't looking. Merlo missed him. Maybe even more than he missed the Lady.

A fat man came out of the house, bouncing down the steps of the high porch two at a time. The wood creaked in protest under his weight. The sound hurt Merlo's ears. The dog whined. This drew the fat man's attention. He stared, looking as if he wanted to sniff Merlo's butt. Merlo would let him. He was a friendly dog.

"There's a good boy. Who you belong to, eh?"

These words were lost on Merlo. He knew only a few human words: bacon, down, sit, hungry, and lovins. The Mister, not the Lady, used the former. Usually *lovins* came before and after the bacon. This Merlo liked more than naps under warm sun.

The fat man came to Merlo, smiled, and held his hand out, palm down. Merlo sniffed him. He smelled flowers. Merlo sneezed. The man snatched his hand away, laughing. The fat man wiped his fist on his jeans.

Merlo popped up and put his forepaws on the man's hip. The fat guy scratched Merlo behind the ear then stopped. Merlo didn't like stopping. He nudged the man's hand, whining a little for added effect. Merlo felt him playing with the collar Merlo didn't like so much. He enjoyed the collar as much as he enjoyed "sit" and "down."

"Say, boy, you're chipped."

Merlo didn't know what these words meant, but he hoped they translated to something akin to bacon.

"How 'bout we go into town, pal? Wanna ride?"

Ride? Did Merlo know this word? Hadn't the Lady used it on occasion? Hadn't he been riding when the scary thing happened? The scary thing hadn't smelled right, hadn't smelled of bacon in the least. Merlo once found a squirrel in the park. Something else had killed it. Merlo didn't chase tree rats. He had his pride. But that decaying rodent had smelled something like the scary thing. And anything that smelled of death was worth running from.

Wait. What had he been thinking? Something about a familiar word. Now it was gone. Merlo smiled up at the fat man.

"You're a good boy," the guy said, as he dug his fingers around under Merlo's collar. "Let's find out who you belong to. Whataya say?"

Merlo barked. He was happy again, had forgotten all about the scary thing and the smell of dead tree rat.

A minute later, Merlo's face hung over the side of a pickup's bed, wind buffeting his loose jowls. The Lady never let Merlo do this. A small window lent access to the inside of the truck. When Merlo was tired of the wind in his face, he stuck his head through the space. The fat man reached up and scratched him under the chin. Merlo liked that very much.

CRUELTY

CRUELTY

JOHN

Twelve hours earlier...

John Landover pulled into Bob's Bait and Fuel and parked his Studebaker around back. It was eleven o'clock in the evening, and the store was already closed. No matter. He only needed to piss and then he could be on his way.

John drained his bladder against the side of a green dumpster, which was pressed against one corner of the store. A fat rat scurried out from under John's golden shower and scampered toward the tree line. John tilted his head back and roared with laughter. The rat wasn't all that funny, but John was five snorts into his personal stash of crushed crystal and he might as well have been in a Jim Carrey movie. John sucked a trail of snot up his nose and sneezed. The convulsion snapped his head forward and his hands up. Unfortunately, he still held his noodle in those hands. A final spritz of urine, pushed out by the concussive sneeze, splashed against his chin.

John snickered as he used the back of his sports coat to wipe the piss from his bottom lip. He zipped up and slid behind the wheel of the Studebaker. Adjusting the rearview, he smiled back at himself. He pulled the baggie from the inside pocket of his sports coat and used his overlong pinkie nail to dip out a healthy helping of crushed powder. Finger to nostril, John made like a Hoover. The fiberglass-like substance stung, as if he were huffing fire ants, but the wave of pleasure that came on the tail end of the pain was forever worth it. He glanced into the rearview. The green dashboard lights made him look like a demonically-possessed leprechaun.

He sneered, completing the image, and screamed with laughter. He pushed the mirror back into place. Started the car, pressed the brake, put it in gear.

Something walked through his brake lights.

He started, wheeling around in his seat to get a better look behind him. It was the cops. He was sure of it. The fucking piggies had been watching him since he left Beaumont and now they were making their move. He shouldn't have snorted the goods in plain view. That was about the stupidest stupid thing he could've done. The last five toots John had done in bathroom stalls at gas stations along his route to Kerrville. He hadn't had that option at Bob's Bait and Fuel. The damned place was locked up tighter than a chastity belt.

"Well, I'll be a fist-fucked koala bear," John said, breathing hard. "What I'm s'pose to do now?"

His concern didn't rest solely with the piggies seeing him pinkie diving but with the four gallons of methylamine hidden behind the backseat. If he got caught with that shit in his possession he'd spend at least three days in county before being seen by the judge. It was Thursday night going into Friday morning. He doubted he'd get same day service in a Podunk place like Kerr County. That meant the courts would be out of session until at least Monday. Hell, not to mention what Twon and Ollie would do to him once he was released.

What to do, what to do...

John jerked the gearshift back into park and yanked his foot off the brake. The red glow behind the car dimmed. He supposed all he could do was wait for them to approach the car. He wondered if it would be local or state piggies this time. He recalled the seventies, when Texas State Troopers used to bust up the rest area acid parties he'd attended from time to time. Those were the good old days. Ladies for miles. All he had to do was trip and land in some decent poon. They were all stoned out of their minds. None of them remembered anything. He rolled off many a gash only to have the very chick he'd just diddled ask him who he was or if he fancied a dip in her pool, completely unaware he'd already chlorinated her waters.

John tapped his long pinkie nail against the leather steering wheel cover and hummed a song he didn't know the name of—some recent Top 40 tune about things to do on the weekend. His inner thigh itched like hell but he refused to scratch it. The last thing he needed was to reach down between his legs and get lit up by a bunch of troopers with sensitive trigger fingers. He imagined hundreds of Smokies secreted out in the woods, all watching him through the scopes of high-powered rifles as he sweated.

John realized two things at the same time. First, not a single officer had made themselves known. With all the experience John had with law enforcement over his almost sixty years on this revolving rock, he'd never known a piggy to be quiet. In fact, the asshats couldn't keep their mouths shut. This bothered him, but not as much as his second revelation, which was: There was someone standing in the passenger side window. They were big—big enough to blot out the entire window with their girth. The only reason he knew they were there at all was because John could hear them breathing.

When did you roll that window down...?

They were just standing there. Waiting. Like Death hunting a soul.

You done way too much tweak, Johnny boy.

John grasped the keys hanging from the ignition box. He wondered how quickly he could turn over the engine, switch gears, and race away from whoever lurked outside his window. He was about to enact his plan when the person dropped down and revealed their horrifyingly pale face.

John Landover screamed.

Ollie screamed back at him, half-laughing as he shrieked through the open passenger side window.

CRUELTY

"Goddamn it, Ollie!" John hollered, his heart pounding in his ears. He clutched a hand to his chest. "You know how fucking old I am? How many drugs I gotta take just to keep this ticker ticking? Fucking dammit!"

"Calm down, you old fuck," Ollie said, as he yanked the door open and flopped in. "Lay off the speed and you won't have to worry about that beat up muscle you got resting 'tween your tits." Ollie slapped John across his man boobs, making them jiggle.

After taking a minute to catch his breath, John asked, "Where the hell you come from?"

"I'm coming from Fredericksburg. Had a drop I needed to make. I was riding behind you the whole time and didn't know it was you in front of me. Go figure. When I saw you pull in here, I pulled in after you. By the way, you got a tiny dick."

"Your mother don't mind it none. What're you doing watching an old man piss, anyhow?"

"I wanted to sneak up on you, give you a heart attack, and steal all that methylamine you got hidden in this clunker of yours." Ollie smiled. His teeth were so white John could see them in the dark.

"Where's Twon?"

"I'm meeting him at his lady's house, then we're going to see Turtle and Jennifer. Which brings me to you. You're late."

"I've had to drive the speed limit all the way here. Can't be bookin' it when you got... *substances* onboard." That was only half of the truth. The other side of the story was that John had made more stops than necessary so he could shove more crystal up his sniffer. But Ollie didn't need to know all that.

"*Substances*," Ollie said, chuckling softly. "That's one way of putting it. All right, old-timer, get a move on. Drop the shit off in the shed and get gone. 'Kay?"

"Bye—" John waited until Ollie was out of the Studebaker before finishing his sentence, "—asshole."

It was bad enough John had to call in every two hours to let Twon know where he was while carrying the methylamine, but to have this Ollie guy on his case was a little much. John didn't believe for a moment that Ollie had simply been following him. Twon had sent his partner to keep track of John. Hell, John didn't even know who was in charge. He knew that if Twon didn't cook the product, Ollie, clever or not, would have to find another job. And John didn't take Ollie for the nine-to-five kind. If the meth business went south, Ollie would take up an equally profitable position somewhere else. Perhaps as a hitman. John had once watched Ollie kneecap a teenage girl who'd had her hair done up in pigtails. She looked like one of those dolled up Catholic schoolgirls pervs liked to hound. Ollie had turned both her kneecaps into ground pork, all because she hadn't made with the funds after Twon had given her a brick to sell in good faith. John had thought the girl had been a brilliant idea. Who'd expect a sweet, innocent-looking gash like her to be slinging crystal? No one. Because it had been Ollie's idea to use her, he'd been the one who had to handle her. John could still hear her screaming.

John tried to recall who'd hired *him*: Twon or Ollie? Probably Ollie. Ever since he'd started sucking down nose candy, John had trouble even remembering his name. Catch John on the wrong day and ask him his full name and you were bound to be there a while. But as with the girl with the pigtails, who'd suspect someone like John? Hell, he was old enough to be Ollie's grandpa.

John pulled onto the dirt road behind Bob's Bait and Fuel, drove down to the end, and made a left. After a while, he came to Ranchero Road, where he turned off onto a rain-rutted stretch of dirt road. He passed the cabin with the freaky statues out front, shuddering at the sight of them. The steelwork Angel of Death glowered at him. The ironwork rendition of the Mother Mary always turned his blood to ice. Tonight, a young man in a gray cardigan sat on the steps, picking his teeth with something. The young man waved at John, and John waved back. There was someone else on the porch: a fat fuck whose face John couldn't see because their back was to him. It looked female, what with the long, curly black hair, but John knew length-of-hair didn't mean shit when it came to guessing gender. Hell, he'd only cut all his locks off five or so years ago. And only then because he'd finally grown tired of washing it.

As John rolled on by, the big bastard with the long, curly black hair twisted to look at him. John shook his head, attempting to clear the hallucination. John assured himself that he couldn't have seen what he thought he'd seen. If he had, that young man on the porch had some creepy-ass friends.

It's not Halloween. What the hell's up with that mask?

The behemoth with the curly hair rolled forward, like a fisherman casting line, as if it had to throw its shoulder out first before the rest of its body would follow. It had just started down the steps of the front porch as John trundled away from the cabin.

"Odd motherfucker." John laughed, although he found nothing funny about the fat fuck in the baby doll mask. Truth was, the guy/girl had unsettled him, and even though he'd emptied his tank back at Bob's Bait and Fuel, the urge to piss niggled him.

Around a short bend, Twon and Ollie's house came into view. He parked in front of the eighties relic and got out. He pulled the driver's seat toward the wheel, reached down between the backseat and the wall, found the pull cord secreted there and tugged on it. The backseat flopped forward. With modifications funded by Twon and Ollie, the Studebaker's trunk had been shortened by a foot to allow for smuggling methylamine from John's job at Bollock-Nancy Chem in Beaumont to Twon's kitchen on the outskirts of Kerrville. John's employers would notice an entire barrel missing, so he never stole much at one time. Usually only a couple ounces off the top of several different barrels over the course of the month. Twon and Ollie's operation was profitable, but not huge. Four gallon jugs of methylamine went a long way, was a month's supply for the cook and his partner.

John grabbed two jugs full of white powder in each hand. He sat them behind the car, opened the trunk, and snagged his miner's helmet with the flashlight attached to the brow. He clicked on the light and made for the woods behind Twon's house.

He stepped gingerly into the woods. Twon was nuts, that couldn't be argued. Being in his employ meant having to be trained to skirt the booby traps—twelve landmines, one spiked log trussed up in the trees à la *Predator*, and a shotgun rigged to go off if someone hit a tripwire stretched between two trees, made for one hell of an obstacle course. John walked to the right of the tree with **TWON HEARTS MARY JANE** then ambled left in front of the Campbell's tomato soup can nailed to a tree trunk. He advanced along a length of orange-dusted construction twine on the ground and made a hard right at a white pickle bucket.

He stopped in front a *Playboy* magazine, which had been made to look like it'd been discarded in a bush, and admired the tits of the gash on the cover. Farah Fawcett had better nipples than this whore, but John felt his old friend twitch all the same. Sixty years old and his power drill still worked. Viagra didn't hold a candle to meth.

John faced the cooking shed. Walking in a straight line from where he currently stood would see him in thirty or more pieces thanks to the final landmine. He veered right, on the diagonal, and strode between two trees with laminated snowmen stapled to the bark. He cut back, hard left, and approached the shed. Nothing exploded. He was still in one piece; all in all, a successful hike.

He laid the jugs on the steps, unlocked the shed, and then stepped inside to complete his drop. The cone of light from his helmet illuminated the forty-by-forty space. Vats and beakers and other scientific bullshit he'd never understand slept on work tables. The dormant lab looked like something out of a Mary Shelley book. He couldn't believe his fountain of youth was created here. It never ceased to amaze him; such a beautiful drug made by such ugly equipment. John offloaded the milk jugs on a table by the room's only window, which had been foiled over. He locked the shed and navigated the booby traps in reverse.

Humming absentmindedly, John rounded the side of the house.

Standing by the mailbox, looking sinister in light of the moon, was the fat fuck in the baby doll mask.

John started, hopping up on one foot, as if someone had thrown a firecracker at his shoes.

"The hell are you?" John barked.

The fat fuck tilted his head to the right and stared. Nothing more.

"Speak up, asshat!" John called, as he began to back away. Then he added, "I got a gun, fucker!"

The doll-faced tub of lard took a single step forward.

No, John thought. *It didn't step. It rolled, just like it did on that porch as I drove by. It rolled down the porch steps because it was coming after you.*

"Mah-Mah," the fat fuck cooed.

"Fuh-uh-uh-uck you, man!"

John's intention was to turn around and run. And if it weren't for the sudden cramping pain in his chest, he might have made it into the booby-trapped woods. He might have hidden out in the shed until Twon and Ollie returned and rescued him. He might have lived.

Alas, none of that happened. He collapsed to his knees in Twon's driveway, clutching his left man boob. He glanced down at his cock pressing at the front of his slacks—still at attention from his run-in with the porno mag. He cussed that swollen thing, and blamed it for using up too much blood. What else could it have been?

John was a perfect specimen of health. After all, meth did a body good.

Hey! You can't hear your heart beating? How about that.

It was the oddest thing. Living with the steady thrum of a pulse as soundtrack to one's life made the world a quiet place without the beat of your main drum.

So goddamn quiet.

John remained only vaguely aware of the fat fuck's approach. It cooed, like a real-life, honest-to-God baby doll. One of those Kewpie Dolls John's grandmother used to collect. Only this doll's face was old. Cracked and peeling. And such darkness underneath. An inky... oily... black...

"Make love, not war," were John's final words. He flipped the fat fuck baby doll the bird.

The doll ripped his arm off.

CRUELTY

NATALIE

Twelve hours later...

Trooper Natalie Holden was leaning against the hood of her cruiser when State Investigator Frank Markum pulled up in his unmarked black sedan. Burt Waters waited on the other side of the road, in the cab of his Dodge pickup, warming his hands in front of the vents. Natalie wasn't a bit cold, but she wasn't an old man, either.

Dawn had broken over an hour ago, but the sun still hid behind the trees in the distance. Crime Scene Analysts Michaels and Demuth were on a smoke break behind their van. When they saw Markum's arrival, they flicked their butts into Burt's property and disappeared inside the rear compartment of the van. *Good,* Natalie thought, *they have plenty of work to do.* She thought about poor busted-up Tom Morgan in surgery, fighting for his life, and hoped those science geeks came up with something, and soon.

Markum parked and got out. He wore a black suit and a charcoal fedora, as if he'd just stepped out of a Raymond Chandler novel. Like most men in any position of power, the half-Panamanian, half-black state investigator walked with a certain swagger. His shoulders swiveled opposite his hips, and Natalie was reminded of the actor Timothy Olyphant in his role as Raylan Givens on *Justified*. Only Olyphant was hot, while Markum reminded her of Tony Montana after snorting a deskfull of blow.

"Mornin', trooper," Markum said.

She nodded at him. "Nice of you to come all the way out here to give me the bad news."

"We can't do anything about it, Natalie. That operation has been going for nine months. If we barge in on them now, the DEA will have our asses."

"But Tom—"

Markum held out his hand, palm facing her. "I want to find who did this to Tom just as much as you do, but not even Tom would want you to ruin an investigation that would have this entire area's supply of crystal off the streets."

"Such bullshit," Natalie groaned, thumping the hood of her cruiser with the ball of her fist. "I suppose I gotta tell Nell that we're not following the only lead we have on the person who crumpled up her husband like a breakup letter?"

"You"—he pointed a crooked finger at her—"aren't going to say anything to anyone about this. If Tom's cruiser stopped on that drug dealer's road, the surveillance team will have seen it. Once they check in, the DEA will get word back to me. It will all be added to their list of charges when they eventually raid this guy."

"So we like Twon and his crew for this?"

Markum nodded. "I don't know what kinda shit Tom stumbled on, but whatever it was, Twon Chatham wanted it kept secret. Badly. To hit a state trooper, even in an out-of-the-way place like that gas station, is unlike him. The guy usually doesn't fuck with authorities. It's not his style. But who else can we look at? Twon—or one of his goons—must've driven Tom's cruiser back to the house then realized what a piss-poor idea that was, so they dumped the car out here." Markum gestured to Tom's cruiser down by the creek bed. "The techs find anything?"

"A little blood in the trunk. They're done collecting. Just waiting on a go ahead from me to take everything back to the lab."

"What're you waiting on? Give them the go."

"I was waiting to ask you if there's anything special they should be looking for?"

"No. It's not like we're gonna find a kilo of speed tucked under Tom's seat. Let 'em take off."

Natalie glanced at the van's driver's side window. Michaels sat behind the wheel, staring out at her. She gave him the thumbs-up and he responded with a nod. The van started and, a second later, drove away.

"I have to tell Nell something, Frank." Natalie knuckled back a tear. The sudden emotional dump was unlike her. She dreaded facing Tom's wife. Didn't think she could keep the truth from her.

Hey, Nell, how you holding up? Oh, yeah, I guess it does suck not to know whether your husband is going to live or die. Look, we're doing everything we can. Only we're not. You see, there's definitely not a stakeout going on that's halting our progress on finding Tom's attacker/attackers. No way *is some crystal-meth-slinging fuckwad running around after possibly ordering a hit, or enacting the hit, on your hubby. By the way, how are your azaleas? They coming in all right? I* so *need to plant my rose bushes...*

"Tell her we're doing everything in our power to make this right. Okay?" Markum said. "And that's all. You're the only one who knows about this. That's why I came all the way out here. We have to keep the band quiet, or risk screwing everything up."

"Whatever."

"You okay?" Markum asked, with what seemed like genuine concern. He reached out and patted her elbow.

"Perfect." She nodded curtly. "Thanks for asking." She attempted to keep the sarcasm from her tone but failed.

Markum withdrew his hand. "Don't say anything, Natalie. That's the last time I'm telling you."

She flashed back to the conversation they'd had on the phone, the one Markum had instigated after Natalie had put two and two together regarding the stakeout's general whereabouts and the last known location of

Tom's cruiser before it was dumped in Camp Meeting Creek.

"I'm coming out there to talk to you," Markum had said. "Don't say a damn thing to anyone. Not a single person. Maintain radio silence until I tell you otherwise. I don't care if rapture starts; do not pick up that radio until I get out there."

She'd thought his tone odd, overly forced. Now she knew why.

Markum hoped to gain something by working in the background, off the books, for the DEA. She didn't have hard proof, but she could see the devil in his eyes, plotting. Markum was up to something. Something more than what he let on.

For one, why couldn't she tell her fellow troopers about this whole thing? Secondly, why couldn't she tell Nell Morgan? What was Tom's wife going to do? Hunt down Twon and slaughter the cook along with his entire crew. Call a news station and blab, ruining all hopes of the perpetrators ever being caught? Highly unlikely. She thought about the peace of mind it would give Nell to know that Tom would eventually see justice served, and wanted to spit in Markum's face. Then there was the driver of the Audi. With the news that Tom's cruiser had been out at Twon's house, all mention of the missing woman was gone. Markum no longer seemed to care about the rest of the details of the case.

"We'll let the DEA have it from here. Once I get a chance, I'll interview this Longmire kid, the one they found walking the highway, and I'll pass whatever info I glean from him on to drug enforcement agents. You're done here, Natalie. Go see Nell. Give her a hug from me."

"Sure thing," Natalie said dispassionately.

She shook her head languidly as Markum strode back to his cruiser, that same pompous swagger to his step.

He's walking like a man on the verge of promotion, she thought. *Cocky dickhead.*

Natalie walked across the street to where Burt Waters waited in his Ram. She rapped her knuckles on his window, and he rolled it down.

"Say, Burt, you said this guy, the one who dumped the car... he was short?"

Burt nodded, the skin of his neck trembling like a turkey's wattle. "Tall as my mailbox, I would say. Why?"

"Just double checking."

"That your boss pulling off?" Burt pointed back to the black sedan, as Markum drove away.

"Not really. He's above me, but I don't really answer to him. Look, Burt, you've been a big help. Thanks for everything. You can head back home, if you want."

"Think I'll hit the Huddle House in Kerrville. Being interviewed by pretty young women makes me a sight peckish, if you don't mind me saying so."

Natalie laughed. "Mind you saying what? That you're hungry?"

"That you're—aw, hell, you know what I meant. Bye, pretty lady."

"Bye, Burt."

As the old man drove away, Natalie used the radio on her shoulder to call for a tow truck to remove Tom's cruiser. In the back of her mind, she replayed Burt's description of the suspect who'd ditched the state vehicle out here at Camp Meeting Creek.

> *"Naw, didn't. Only seen their outline. Wife seen the roof lights come on while she were makin' coffee in the kitch'. She drug me in from the livin' room, where I were watching the early bird news in my long johns. I thought it were funny the way the person just left the car and runned off into the woods. I knew then that it weren't no officer or whatnot. Besides, he weren't no taller than my mailbox..."*

Natalie glanced at the mailbox at the corner of Burt's long drive. The post wasn't much more than three feet tall, and the box atop it no more than a foot. Had Twon enlisted the help of a kid, or was one of his goons a little person? She doubted either. Twon wouldn't have left such a task to an amateur or someone who couldn't hold their own in a scuffle, should one arise. Twon himself was a good six-foot. Natalie had never had a run-in with the cook, but she'd seen his mug shot, the one hanging back at headquarters, more than once. Whether Twon knew it or not, he was quite popular with local and state law enforcement. And now that the cook had put one of their own in the hospital, he was going to pay.

"Besides, he weren't no taller than my mailbox..."

After she spoke with Nell at the hospital she'd have to finger through the mug shots for every known association of Twon's. A man no taller than a mailbox shouldn't be too hard to find. This was Texas. Things were bigger in Texas. Something little would stand out.

CRUELTY

NELL

They were supposed to be okay. Tom had quit smoking. She'd started therapy for her obsessive–compulsive disorder, and things were getting better. They were about to look into artificial insemination because she wanted (*needed*) children. Now their future was filled with helium, floating away like some balloon in the clutches of a distracted toddler.

The doctor came out just after nine o'clock that morning to give Nell Morgan the news; some good, some bad. Tom would walk again, but not without the use of a prosthetic. His shattered leg had to be removed, along with his crushed right hand. They simply couldn't save it. The bones had been reduced to powder. The doctor was ever so sorry. During this news (*some good, some bad*) Nell sobbed quietly. What was this nonsense? A lost hand? The need of a prosthetic leg? What sort of trickery was this practitioner on about? She wanted to see Tom. Why couldn't she see Tom?

Because Tom wasn't fully out of the woods, yet. He was in a shock-induced coma. He might never wake up.

"This is common," the doctor had said, "with victims of trauma the likes of what Thomas has been through."

Thomas. Did this lout have to be so damn professional? Would it hurt for him to use "Tom" instead of "Thomas" and give his patient a little more humanity? Everyone knew Trooper Tom Morgan. No one had ever heard of this Thomas person.

Nell wept by a floor-to-ceiling window. She gazed out from Surgery's waiting room, off into the distant horizon. The sun burned lonesome above the trees. Down below, cars scrolled by on Douglas Street in downtown Kerrville like ticker tape. All those ants marching. All those unknown individuals going about their day-to-day activities, knowing nothing of Nell Morgan's plight—the Reconstruction of Tom.

If not for the churning dread in her stomach, she might've been hungry. In fact, she could have mistaken a looming foreshadowing for hunger pains. What she was certain of was that she wouldn't leave this waiting room until she was able to see her husband. The vending machines lurked just outside, in the hallway, but she didn't risk grabbing a Snickers and missing the—

(some good, some bad)

—news. The only refreshments in the waiting room was a pot of hours-old coffee that looked to be the consistency of wet cement, and a pencil keeper full of saltine crackers. The crackers would settle her stomach, but she hated to discard the feeling. With that bubbling terror gone, would she lapse into complacency? Nell refused to chance it. She needed to be on her toes; sour stomach or not.

Hovering in the back of her mind was the crushing idea that, when she finally did leave Kerrville Medical Complex, she'd be going home alone.

The waiting room doors whooshed open. Nell gazed numbly at the approaching trooper. The woman was quite pretty, perhaps Native American, with a ball of black hair perched upon the back of her scalp, smoky gray eyes, and an olive complexion. She offered Nell a small, crooked smile. Nell had the sudden urge to scream. To grab this woman by the lapels and thrust her against a wall. To ask her, *"Why the hell are you smiling?"*

"Nell?" the woman asked. She stood three feet away from Nell, hands and arms moving around without obvious direction, as if their owner didn't know what she wanted to do with them.

"Yeah," Nell breathed. Had the woman not responded, Nell might have thought the word nothing more than a thought.

"How, uh... how is he?"

Nell shrugged. "Don't know."

Everything came crashing down, blotting out the sun, and, just like that, Nell passed into dark territory. She collapsed into the waiting embrace of a stranger; some sad-eyed doll of a woman, one who petted the back of Nell's head with tender strokes. One who allowed Nell her weakness.

Hysterical breakdowns are odd things. They can come on without instigation, out of nowhere; viciously cruel in their voracity, devouring the bleak-hearted. Nell had never known such hopeless desperation. Her eyes drained, soaking the woman's uniform top. Nell screamed her indignation into the woman's chest. Deep, soul-evacuating howls escaped her. She was on her knees, not knowing how she got there, her head resting in this stranger's crotch. Slowly, the woman knelt and embraced Nell. Her arms were strong, almost manly, like Tom's, and another wave of screams exploded from her.

One word kept resounding in Nell's mind: coma. She'd watched documentaries on TLC about coma states, either chemically- or trauma-induced, and knew the expectancy of someone coming out of such a thing the same person as when they went in was a cold, fifty-fifty shot in the dark. She'd read *The Dead Zone*, and, though she doubted Tom would awake with psychic powers like Johnny Smith, Nell remembered the heartbreak she'd felt at Johnny's lost time—a part of his life gone like water into steam.

Coma.

Would Tom wake up? *Could* he wake up? Would around-the-clock care be needed to sustain him? She saw diligent home health professionals slinking through her house, needing to do their duties but not wanting to impose. Awkward situations where she'd need to clean

Tom in between rotating shifts of help. All these improbabilities rocketed through her mind, like a shuttle taking off from Cape Canaveral through a morning's mist.

"Why?" Nell sobbed. "Why him? Why my Tom? Why...?"

"It could have been anyone," the woman said. "We don't think it was planned. Tom was in the wrong place at the wrong time."

Nell looked up through blurry eyes and into the eyes of this lady trooper. The woman suddenly seemed familiar. Nell imagined her with eye shadow, muted lipstick, and hair down, cascading across her shoulders.

"Natalie? Is that you?"

Natalie offered Nell that crooked smile. "Yeah, Nell, it's me."

Nell glanced down at the face-sized wet patch on the trooper's shoulder and sucked snot. "I made a mess of you."

"It'll all come out in the wash," Natalie told her.

"Will it?" Nell asked. She bit her lips to hold back the flood of emotions threatening to break through again.

"I'll do everything I can to make sure it does. Tom's a strong man. I'm sure—"

"He's in a coma." The word came out in a rush of hot, pent-up breath, more of a grunting, breathy sound than actual words.

"I'm so sorry, Nell," Natalie said. A tear pooled in the corner of one eye. Natalie blinked and it tracked a rivulet in her foundation.

"Yeah, well..." But the rest of her comment, if she'd meant to make a full statement in the first place, died on her tongue.

"Is there anything I can do for you? Do you need something to drink? Something to eat?"

Nell shook her head. "I only need answers. I need to know if Tom's making it out of this. I need to know if I'm going to be sleeping alone. Because I hate sleeping alone.

My feet get cold... and... and... what the fuck am I even saying?" Nell splashed down against Natalie's shoulder again. Nell's body hitched against that of Tom's coworker, but Natalie felt like stone under her, unbendable.

"I'm sorry, Nell," Natalie repeated. "I'm so damn sorry."

CRUELTY

KIRK

Kirk Babbitt stared at the blood transfusion bag with distaste. *They're pumping someone else's insides into me.* He couldn't get the thought out of his mind. Did they even sanitize that stuff? Boil it? *Something*?

He reached under his gown and grazed his hand over the dressing on his shoulder. Doc said there'd be some nerve damage, that Kirk's pectoral muscles would probably twitch from now on if he reached for something over his head, but he'd live.

The past four hours were a bit of a blur. He remembered the meeting with the cook and his white-bread boyfriend at the gym. He recalled being stuffed into a backseat, then having a shotgun rammed into his ribs as they rode to the apartment Kirk shared with Will. Twon had parked at the curb, and run inside. The cook had returned several minutes later. Then they dropped Kirk off at Kerrville Medical Complex. Literally *dropped* him off. Ollie used the knife they'd stabbed Kirk with to slice his arms free of the duct tape. Ollie popped opened the back door and, with a set of boots in Kirk's ribs, shoved Kirk onto the pavement. Tires squealed and the bodybuilder was enveloped by a cloud of spent rubber. Kirk, not realizing just how close to death he was but having a damn good idea this was turning out to be one shitstorm of a day, dragged himself into the emergency room by way of the ambulance dock.

Duct tape still covered his chest and shoulder, but with his new movement, blood finally leaked through. He made quite the mess.

CRUELTY

The triage area was strangely devoid of bustling bodies. Kirk could hear voices calling excitedly behind one door or another. Feeling neglected and weak, Kirk hollered, *"Somebody wanna see 'bout a motherfucker?"*

A cinnamon-skinned beauty with a thick ass and mosquito bites for boobs hidden by neon scrubs rushed out of the noisy room. She saw Kirk's trail of blood before she saw him; this was evident by the way she looked past him, all wide-mouthed and googly-eyed, as if she were impersonating that kid from the first two *Home Alone* movies.

"Hey, bitch!" Kirk had cried out. "Down here!"

Then came the blur; a hard shift in the veil of reality. He vaguely remembered her instructing him to lie down, that he needed to relax. It seemed he recalled calling her a cum-guzzling gutter-slut, but he couldn't be sure. He'd liked to have thought he was a classy guy who respected women. The bitch didn't deserve to be called a *cum-guzzler*. He had no idea if she gargled man-juice. But one could hope.

On the next level of his memory storage unit was him atop a gurney and screaming something about a conspiracy involving white bread and Caribbean jerk chicken, but this must've been a dream, because Kirk Babbitt was no nutjob. He knew wackos. His mother had been one. That's why'd she killed Dad with one of guns he'd stolen from the shooting gallery. His father, the thief, and his mother, the cold-blooded murderer. No wonder Kirk was such a valuable member of society.

They'd given him something at some point that had made Kirk feel as if he'd just guzzled a gallon of tequila and then taken a rafting trip on Lake Placid. A warmth covered him like paint poured over a bronze statue. Darkness soon swallowed him like a greedy lover.

He woke with a start sometime after ten a.m. Confusion stole over him, and it took several minutes for Kirk to digest that he was in a hospital, that he was alive and all right, and that the midnight man wasn't creeping in the shadows.

The midnight man...

Something surfaced in Kirk's mind, of being a young boy tucked in bed snug as a bug, and peeking over his comforter as the midnight man with the foggy eyes slunk out of the shadows in the corner and toward the bed. The midnight man was darker than shadow, a kind of deeper blackness, filled with moving things. Those smoky eyes, like fog with high beams splashed across it, drilled into cowering Kirk Babbitt and infected him.

Kirk had run screaming out of his room, wanting Mommy, needing Daddy, but preferring the National Guard. Daddy couldn't be risen from his slumber, so Mommy had had to do. She groggily ushered little Kirk Babbitt back down the hall and into his room. The midnight man was still there, but Mommy didn't see him. Mommy assured Kirk there was nothing to worry about, that nothing lurked in the shadows waiting to snack on slumbering children.

But Kirk had watched the midnight man pour himself into Mommy. Mommy had gone slack-jawed and dull-eyed. Mommy tucked Kirk back into bed, kissed him on the cheek with cold lips, and shuffled back down the hall. She whispered as she went.

Whispered a word that lingered on the air like cigarette smoke. An archaic word lost on children.

Dastardly...

"Can I get you something for the pain?" The smiling nurse standing in the door to Kirk's hospital room was heavy-chested with lips as wide as her hips. Kirk's penis stirred beneath his gown.

"What's on the menu, chick?"

Her smile melted away. "My name's Katisha. Doctor Patel ordered Percocet every four hours and Dilaudid for breakthrough pain. Which one do you want?"

"Which one ain't gonna make me drool on myself?"

"I'll be back with the Percocet." She eased the door closed.

Kirk's eyes drifted from the door to the shadows in the alcove below the television. Was there something there, swirling?

"Fucking drugs, man," Kirk said, and laughed it off. There was no other excuse for all the bullshit running helter-skelter through his mind. Swirling shadows? Midnight men? What the fuck was wrong with him?

He wondered where Will was. The last thing Kirk wanted to see was his buddy being set upon by the two heavies responsible for his current vacation. Kirk lifted the phone with the spool of twirling cable off the nightstand. He dialed Turtle's number, hoping the dealer was sober and with it. The phone rang, unanswered. After the twentieth ring or so, Kirk disconnected. He rubbed his palm over the new stubble on his chin. The growth popped and crackled, like embers in a fire.

Twon and Ollie had been after Will. But why? Slowly, like the mercury dropping in a snowstorm, he remembered. Because Will was with Jennifer. But if Will was with the meth whore, where was Turtle? The dealer wouldn't have dipped out without turning on his answering machine. Maybe Turtle had simply been on a bathroom break. Kirk picked the phone off his lap and dialed again.

Another twenty rings.

Kirk hung up.

To keep his mind off the swirling shadows below the TV, Kirk considered a chasm's worth of possibilities. Will had gone to score some tail. Jennifer had left with Will. Turtle was left home alone. Twon and Ollie would have gone there first. And, having not received suitable answers from Turtle, they'd hunted down Kirk. Things did not bode well for Turtle. Being a junkie and a dealer always came with the danger that you might dip into your own stash. Had Turtle partaken of his own supply?

Had he not been able to pay? Was that why the cook and his whitebread boyfriend were screwing with Kirk?

But why stab Kirk and drop him off at the hospital, half bled to death?

Kirk rewound to the moment just before Twon had jumped out the car to run inside the apartment Kirk shared with Will. Had Kirk seen a pen and notepad in Twon's hand? What could the cook possibly need to jot down? A note? But what would that note say?

Hey, Will, we're meth producers looking for our drug money. Seems you ran off with our dealer's live-in whore. Please return her so we won't have to feed you your balls.

Sincerely,
The cook and his whitebread boyfriend.

Kirk shoved his head back into his pillow and his shoulder twitched in protest. "Ain't nobody got time for you, asshole," he told his bandages. Pain had always been something Kirk could overcome, a bodily function he could control. Like hunger or taking a shit, he'd worry about it when he had time.

The nurse returned with his pain pill. Kirk dry-swallowed it, leaving the nurse holding the tiny cup of water. When she seemed to realize he wasn't going to take the water, she left. He watched her ass float her out. Nice cans. He thought maybe he had just the right size can opener for the job.

No matter how hard he tried to focus on the whys and why nots of this mess Will and he had been thrust into, there was a more pressing need straining between his legs. The nurse's ass swiveled in his mind's eyes. He saw himself peeling her cheeks apart (either set) and filling the void. He lay his head on the pillow, squeezed his eyes closed, envisioned taking the Percocet-delivery-system in the mouth, then the ass, and finally twirling her around so he could glaze her face like a doughnut. Will stared back at him.

Though Kirk pumped with furious abandon, trying to ignore his friend's face on the nurse's body, nothing happened. His wrist soon became tight and sore, and Kirk stopped, defeated. Precum dampened his hand, but a full load had not been dropped. He grunted his dissatisfaction.

"Fucking drugs, man," he assured himself. "It's just the drugs."

Was it? Or could it be that he'd glimpsed Will's face on the nurse's body. His friend mouthing two words in a cycling mantra.

"Help me," the deaf man said. "Help me..."

"How'm I supposed to nut with you watching, dude?" Kirk ran a hand down his face in frustration, realizing all too late that he'd chosen the wrong hand to do it with.

WILL

William Longmire let himself into a feet-funky apartment. After spending the better part of four hours waiting to be interviewed by some state investigator that never showed, Will was almost glad to have the odor of Kirk's shoes to come home to. He breathed a sigh of relief, tossing his keys into the Dixie Cup Kirk had stapled to the table in the short foyer. He ambled over to the bookshelf and snatched up his cell phone.

Oh, what trouble you could have saved me last night, Will thought, pressing the cold device to his warm cheek.

The face of the baby-doll-thing flittered behind his eyes and Will shivered. Whether or not the authorities ever caught up with that sick fuck, Will doubted he'd get the image of its aged countenance out of his mind. Cracked, peeling paint. Long, curly black hair. Jaundiced eyes...

"Nope," he said aloud. His voice popped in his ears. It was good to speak again. He'd gone so long without uttering a single word, simply to keep from sounding foolish, and all that had disappeared thanks to some psychopathic killer. Will was going to have to get used to being a Chatty Cathy.

He threw open the curtains behind the television, letting the light of the day wash over the room. Dust motes stirred up by the movement of the drapes sky-dived through the beams of light coming in through the venetian blinds. Will flopped down in his worn recliner—he and Kirk had skipped the typical couch and loveseat upon moving in, and went instead for a twin recliner deal. It gave more room for the Xbox 360 they'd bought off some tweaker for fifty bucks. The console had come with a Kinect motion sensor, and it was much easier to play between the recliners than having to move a sofa all the time because the room wasn't deep enough.

Will snagged the remote off the glass-topped coffee table and powered on the television. Taped to the center of the TV was a note written in scratchy script; he got up and tore it off.

Kirk was not the best read of Will's friends, but Will had imagined Kirk to be a sight more literate than the document proved.

Think I riped sumthin at the jim. My cars actin funny. Pik me up wen u git home?

Kurt

Kurt? Will had always assumed his roommate's name was Kirk. All this time and he didn't even know how to spell his friend's name? That was a shame. He crumpled up the note and tossed it into the wastebin next to the fridge. He was turning around to head for the door when something occurred to him.

Will moved briskly down the hallway, toward his bedroom. In his closet, he pulled a Reebok shoebox from the top shelf and laid it on his bed. He ruffled through the few papers that were in there: his passport, birth certificate, Blockbuster Video contract, a photocopy of the first application he'd ever filled out, and the lease to their apartment. He yanked out the lease and flipped through it.

There, on the last page, was Kirk's full name, printed on one line and signed on the other. Kirk's name was printed clearly as K-I-R-K, not K-U-R-T.

Okay, Inspector Poirot, what do you make of that note up front?

The letter was obviously a fake. But why would someone forge—*rather shittily,* Will thought—a note telling him to pick up his roommate at the hospital? Was Kirk actually at the hospital?

Will had one course of action.

He returned to the living room and booted up his laptop where it lay sleeping upon the bar that segmented the kitchen from the area with the recliners. He navigated to his default text-to-talk app and dialed Kerrville Medical Complex. On the other end, an electronic voice would tell the person who answered the phone that they were speaking to someone who was hearing-impaired. Once the call was connected, the virtual operator would give the call over to Will. He'd type and it would convert his text to speech, and vice versa for the person on the other end.

The screen flashed: CALL ESTABLISHED.

Will typed: *Hello, I'm looking for a friend of mine named Kirk Babbitt. He would have been brought in today.*

After almost a full two minutes, the response came: PERK RABBIT IS THIS A JOKE

Those computer voices were not always the easiest things to understand. Same with the speech-to-text program.

No. The patient's name is K-I-R-K... B-A-B-B-I-T-T.

Another pause; this one almost five minutes in length. Will kept looking down at the call connection, expecting the person on the other end to hang up, thinking he was screwing around.

KIRK BABBITT IS IN ROOM 438.

Thank you.

So Kirk was in the hospital. Had he actually hurt himself at the gym? Maybe it was worse than a pulled muscle. Could the spelling of the note have resulted from some kind of stroke brought on by lifting too much weight? Will doubted it.

Will had spent half the night running from some nutcase in a baby doll mask, someone that could still be out there, and now he had to worry about Kirk? Will dropped down into his recliner, extended the footrest, and dredged up his memories of the previous night.

I wouldn't have been out there had Kirk not sent me there. The previous evening's events flickered before him. The images played as if he'd been a spectator and not a participant.

Will had been on the computer, watching a young girl fellating a guy who owned roughly a yard of penis, when Kirk burst through the front door, bragging about how well he was doing at the gym now that his torn bicep had healed. Will tried his best to cover himself up but he was caught and he knew it.

"You need to do something about that, virgin boy. Here," Kirk brought out his cell phone, "you gonna get your dick wet tonight if it kills you."

Present Will frowned at Kirk's rather fitting prediction. Trying to get laid *had* almost killed him. Well, a girl named Jennifer almost had, anyway. He could still see that gun, with its huge barrel bouncing around in his vision. Her laughing, showing off those wasted pilings she had for teeth.

Will had shaken his head fervently at Kirk, but to no avail. The call had been made. Kirk jotted down the instructions, and shoved Will out the front door. Will could have argued more, but there was something oddly arousing about meeting a woman with the sole intentions of fucking her, paying her, and forgetting she ever existed. The thought left him cold inside, yet he couldn't ignore it. His lizard brain showing through, he supposed—that part of him that would have clubbed some cavewoman over the head and dragged her away by the ponytail. He had to laugh at that imagine. Then there was the modern-day equivalent, which had a woman in a business suit dragging a dirty caveman away by his testicles. This image he found even funnier, if not a bit more accurate.

Jennifer had dragged Will away, into the dark fantastic. Into a realm polluted by six-hundred-pound baby dolls with murderous intent. Had started a chain of events wherein Will had failed someone because he was a coward. Where he had been reduced to a yellow dog, running away with his tail firmly tucked between his legs, protecting his nuts.

Now, Will leaned forward and let his arms fall between his legs. He sat like that for some time, wondering what he should do about Kirk. His roommate, in his own weird way, had only been attempting to help a friend. Will doubted Kirk knew what awaited him behind the door of Jennifer's trailer. Why send half your rent away to be robbed in the night? Didn't make sense.

He called a taxi. He told the driver to take him to Kerrville Medical Complex. He'd worry about having his broken down Bonneville towed some other day. Right now, Will wanted a friend's company, even if that friend was bedridden in a hospital. It sure as hell beat thinking about country pros and giant psychotic baby dolls.

TWON & OLLIE

Twon watched as the young man stepped out of 10C. The cook tapped Kirk's house key against the steering wheel while changing radio stations with his other hand. He wasn't paying attention to the keys or the tunes. Twon thirsted for blood. *Jennifer's* blood. And if he had to go through this kid to get it, so be it. The Caribbean was a dark place if you didn't mind the shadows, and Twon knew the truth behind the old saying, "There is more than one way to skin a cat."

Ollie saw the impatience written all over his brother's face.

"Calm down, Twon. We'll get her."

"I's tired of calming down, seen!" Twon barked. His breath smelled of garlic and Lysol.

"Not here. Not now. His neighbors will remember someone running off with him."

"They don' see me."

"You're not half as invisible as you think you are. Be patient. We'll snatch him at the hospital, and then we can work on him back at the shed, undisturbed. Cool?"

Twon gripped the steering wheel so hard it made a sound akin to corn popping.

"Twon? Are we cool?"

"Yuh, we cool. I won' me money, Ollie. That muddahfuckah know where it tis."

"It's not just your money."

Across the parking lot, the young man copped a squat on the curb. He snatched up some loose gravel and threw the pebbles at nothing in particular. A few minutes later, a cab pulled up and the young man hopped inside.

"He don' got no car?" Twon asked, a bewildered look etched all over his face.

"Doesn't seem that way." Ollie craned his neck to watch the cab pull out of the apartment complex. "Go on. Follow them."

"How'd he get out to Turt's if he ain't got no car?"

"I don't know. Pull him over and let's ask."

"Don't fuckin' mock me, seen? Don't care what Momma say, I'll still cut you, muddahfuckah."

"Duly noted. Drive."

CRUELTY

MARKUM

State Investigator Frank Markum parked just outside of the KOA campgrounds and got out. He nodded at the acne-ridden teen behind the glass of the booth. Pimple Face grinned back, flashing green-banded braces. Markum sympathized with the kid; during his own high school years, he'd looked just like the teenager. With that complexion and all that hardware in his mouth, the teenager looked like a walking birth control advert.

Markum wove through permanent and temporary RV hookups, waving at residents and vacationers alike. This time of year, the grounds were bustling with life. Kids were out of school for winter break, and KOA was currently running a FAMILIES HALF-OFF promotion. Because of all this, and the fact that Twon Chatham's house was only a mile north as the bird flies, the area was a perfect spot to secret away the DEA's surveillance trailer.

In the rear corner of the campground, a fifth-wheel trailer had been set up against the tree line. A chubby agent with a horseshoe of black hair sat outside, smoking a cigar and drinking a Mountain Dew on the steps that led up to the front door. He eyed Markum with a curious stare as the state investigator approached. The agent stood and shook Markum's hand.

"Howdy, chum," Chubby said from around the cigar tucked into the corner of his mouth. "What can I do for you?"

"Hi, Paul. Dennis inside?"

"He might be. But what can *I* do for you?" Paul chewed at his stogie.

"I can talk to Dennis about it," Markum said.

"Nah." Paul shoved his hands into the pockets of his jeans and rocked back on his heels. "Like I told you last time you come out here, I know your kind, Frankie. Be a good lil boy and head on home. This ain't no place for your shenanigans."

"No need to be a jerk abou—"

"Frank?" Dennis called from behind the screen door of the trailer. "Ignore Paulie. Come on in."

Frank waved to Dennis. He asked Paul, "You ever get tired of being an asshole?"

"Nah." Paul smiled. His cigar titled upward like an erection. "Can't give people shit if you're not an asshole."

"Classy, Paul. Real classy."

"Ah, fuck off." Paul stepped aside to allow Markum entrance.

Markum joined Dennis inside.

Dennis seemed even skinnier than the last time Markum had seen him, two days earlier. Even his hair looked thinner. Long hours and late nights, Markum assumed. Dennis eased the door closed. Once the lock snicked, Markum grabbed the thin man by the forearm and yanked him close. They kissed.

Dennis moaned against him. Markum caressed his lover's back; ran his hands through Dennis's hair. Dennis tasted of cinnamon gum, or maybe Tic Tacs. For some reason, the flavor stoked Markum's fire, and he could feel himself straining against the front of his briefs. Then Dennis's hand was there, rubbing through the fabric. Markum mewled into Dennis's mouth.

Dennis pulled his mouth away. His lips were flushed, and he was smiling. "Down, boy." He squeezed Markum's crotch tenderly. "Tonight. I promise."

"Tease." Markum ran a hand down his lover's front, grabbed his belt, and tugged him close again. He bit playfully at Dennis's lip. "What did I tell you about being a tease?"

"You have to be patient. Tantric, even."

"Fuck your Zen bullshit. I want you. Now." Markum leaned in and nibbled Dennis's neck.

"Oh... you..." Dennis whispered into his ear.

Markum felt Dennis relax. Markum led him to the bathroom.

Fifteen minutes later, Dennis showered while Markum waited at the control console. The bank of monitors displayed the video feed from six cameras, three of which were set up around Twon's house. Two had been secreted inside the house, in the main traffic areas, while the last one had been installed facing the tree line behind the two-story Victorian. Somewhere in that forest was the kitchen where the cook created his poison. Markum hoped he would be there when they raided the operation. He wanted to see Twon's face when forty or so DEA and local officials stuffed a boot up the cook's ass.

Dennis, shirtless and drying his hair one-handed, appeared in the doorway to the bedroom, which had been converted into the surveillance area.

"You don't have any cameras facing the street?" Markum asked.

"Nope. Best thing we have is the one above the front door. Why?"

Markum sighed and relaxed back in the office chair. "Somebody almost killed a trooper out at Bob's Bait and Fuel last night. Stomped his ass real good. We're thinking Twon had a hand in it. The person who did it stole Tom Morgan's car and drove out to Twon's road. If Twon's not involved, it's one hell of a coincidence."

"Oh, somebody came by the house last night. Older guy made a drop out in the woods. Several gallons of a substance we have yet to identify." Dennis typed in a command and opened the monitor controls. He used the mouse to navigate through the time signature until he hit eleven o'clock the previous evening. In the bottom right corner of the screen, which showed the backyard of Twon's house, a man of average build walked into view carrying four one-gallon milk jugs. He disappeared into the tree line. Dennis fast-forwarded until the man exited the woods.

"Pause that," Markum said excitedly. He leaned in to get a better look at the display.

"Hang on," Dennis said. He clicked a few buttons and the backyard camera image filled the entire display.

Markum stared at the now empty-handed individual. There was no mistaking him.

Markum tapped his index finger on the screen. "This guy's dead."

Dennis shook his head in quick snaps. "Huh?"

"He was found in the cooler of the gas station where Tom Morgan was attacked. Someone ripped his arm off."

"They did wha—?"

"It's a long story. Any idea who this cat is?"

"John—"

"I know his name."

"Would you *please* stop cutting me off? You know I hate—"

"Do you know what he does for Twon, or not?" Markum asked sternly.

Dennis sighed. "He's a delivery guy. He runs whatever's in those jugs—probably pseudoephedrine— from his job in Beaumont to Twon's house, here. He does it once a month. Every month. Like clockwork."

"Wait... why would Twon kill his delivery guy?"

"Don't look at me. I just watch the cameras. I need to find a new shirt. You need to watch where you're aiming that thing of yours when you—"

"Is he Twon's only delivery guy?" Markum asked.

"As far as I know, yes."

"But you're not the only one who watches the cameras, right? What about Paul?"

"He covers them when I sleep, yeah, but we mark all comings and goings in our log. He hasn't made note of anyone else. There's Twon and the new guy, this delivery guy, and the old woman."

"The new guy?" Markum asked.

"Some white guy came in about a month ago. Seems all buddy-buddy with Twon. Carries a shotgun with him everywhere he goes."

Markum studied the still image of the old man coming out of the woods. He looked different with his arm still attached, but there was no doubting that he was the same guy Moxie had taken back to the coroner's office. Markum could see him quite clearly, propped up against those stacks of soda pallets. Sheriff Randy Miser had told Markum that his deputy, Nick Wuncell, had identified the man as John Landover, a resident of Beaumont, Texas. That information matched the information he'd received from Dennis. Now, as to the mystery of why Twon would murder his only delivery guy, Markum was stumped.

"Maybe Twon didn't kill him," Dennis said, as if he'd read Markum's thoughts.

"If he didn't, who did?"

"That's your job, hon, not mine." Dennis pulled a plain white tee from a duffel bag in the corner of the room and yanked it on.

"Did you have video of him leaving?" Markum asked.

"Don't know. Here," Dennis said, as he made a few key strokes, "this is the feed from above the front of the house, around the same time."

The screen reverted to its previous three-by-two display.

"Weren't you watching it?" Markum asked.

"Why? Landover makes the same delivery every month. He comes. He goes. Nothing special happens. How was I supposed to know he ended up dead last night?"

The camera angle from above the front door of Twon's house showed the entirety of the front yard in lime-green night vision, along with a sliver of the driveway where the concrete met the asphalt of the road. Markum could see the front fender of the Studebaker they'd found out on Highway 16, a few feet from Bob's Bait and Fuel, parked at the edge of the driveway. So the man coming out of the woods had been John Landover. That much was a certainty.

Something moved behind the Studebaker. Markum squinted at the bank of monitors.

"Whoa, hold up. Who's that?" Markum tapped the neon green orb hovering behind Landover's car. It looked like a face.

"Lemme enlarge it." Dennis tapped furiously at the keys. The image full-screened.

"The fuck is that?" Markum erupted.

The image, now completely taking over the sixteen-inch monitor, stared back at him. Markum's blood dropped several degrees and he shivered.

A huge baby doll glowered at him from over the hood of the Studebaker. It just stood there, its body a darker green than the bright lime surrounding it.

"That's fucked up," Dennis said, then laughed nervously.

The giant baby doll rolled around the front of the car and disappeared up the driveway. A few minutes later, the passenger side door of the Studebaker opened. The car bounced on its shocks. The door closed. The baby doll rounded the car once more and got in behind the wheel. The Studebaker drove off.

Markum wanted to know what had happened just off camera. If only the gate of the shot had been wider. All he needed was another two inches and he would have seen everything he needed.

Still, his mind filled in the blanks. The person in the baby doll mask had snatched John Landover and tossed him inside the Studebaker. Whether or not Landover was still alive when he was thrown inside, Markum didn't know, but he doubted it.

One question resounded in Markum's head: Did the masked person work for Twon, or were they a private contractor? If Twon wasn't involved in the death of Landover, that left the investigation open to Markum to delve into. But if he found Twon had ordered the hit after all, he'd be interfering with the DEA's investigation. Not to mention, he'd upset Dennis.

"Well, that was weird," Dennis said, as he scratched the top of his scalp.

"Yeah," Markum said. "Can you make this live again?"

"Sure," Dennis leaned in and punched in a new command on the keyboard. The display flashed from night vision to the current sun bleached view of Twon's front yard. All seemed copacetic.

"When was the last time you saw Twon?" Markum asked.

"It's been almost twenty-four hours since he's been home. He left around one o'clock yesterday afternoon. No other activity around the house since then, other than Landover, of course."

"I think I want to check it out."

Dennis went wide-eyed. "Check what out? You can't go out there, Frank. You'd jeopardize—"

"No one has to know who I am. I go out there with a Book of Mormon tucked under my arm and no one can say I'm not some elder looking to convert the local drug dealer. Right?"

"I still don't like it. That's a pretty secluded area out there, Frank. It's not like Twon gets visitors all the time. He'll know something is up."

"I don't think he will." Markum stood. He laid his hands gingerly atop Dennis's shoulders. "It'll be okay. I promise. Besides, I might not even bump into him. You said he's been gone since yesterday afternoon. Maybe he's out of town."

"I don't want you going. I'll pull my DEA status if I have to, Frank. Consider it an order. I order you not to go out there."

Markum shrugged. "I don't work for the DEA. You're not the boss of me, sweet'ums."

"Damn it, Frank, *please*."

"Is this about the case, or are you worried I won't come home."

"Both." Dennis looked terrified. Markum thought him sweet.

"Listen." Markum petted Dennis's cheek. "I'll take someone out there with me. I know just the person, too. She was itching to run out there earlier but I stopped her. The attack on Tom Morgan really got to her. We'll be careful, I promise."

"You're going either way, huh?"

Markum nodded.

"Then get the fuck out of here. What does it matter if I say no? But if you screw up this case, I will leave you. I'll go home to my father's and you'll never see me again. And if you get yourself killed, I will fucking kill you, you hear me?"

"No one's going to kill anyone. I'm a big man with a big gun, remember?" Markum said, patting the lump where his jacket hid his shoulder holster.

"You're an asshole."

"And you love every inch of me."

Dennis rolled his eyes. "Get out of here. I better see you tonight."

"Yes, dear." Markum turned to leave.

He'd made it all the way to the front door of the trailer before Dennis called, "I love you."

Markum stepped outside, pretending he didn't hear him.

CRUELTY

INNIS

Back in the concrete room with the Victorian lamp in the corner, Innis Blake, still strapped to her chair, opened her eyes. The disembodied hand and leg lay in the middle of the floor, two feet away, as if she'd never woken. As if the baby doll with the scalpel had been the dream and *this* the reality. She crinkled her nose at the sight of them and felt white-hot fire spread from her forehead to her chin, as if someone had poured molten lead over her head. There was something wrong with her face. Very wrong. Even in this dream inside a dream, Innis could feel the pain of the real world seeping through the cracks. But, to feel pain in a dream... Wouldn't that wake her?

Only if she were capable of waking.

In this nightmare room, this twenty-by-twenty cinderblock prison with the rollaway roof, Innis thought that maybe this was what being in a coma must feel like.

A warm narcotic feeling pulsed through her. Her face only hurt when she moved it, so she tried to remain still in that regard.

Another body part fell from the ceiling; this one, a foot. Another slapped the concrete next to it, making a pair. Both feet were rights; definitely not from the same person.

Of course not, Innis thought. *They don't belong to anyone. You're dreaming.*

The drop rate increased. Three more appendages flopped down onto the floor: a hand and two arms, all lefties. Another six pieces fell from the darkness above.

Innis lost track of which body parts were new and which were old. A pile of them now resided in the middle of the cinderblock cell. Above, the black maw vomited a waterfall of extremities. The hands, arms, feet, and legs came so rapidly and in such numbers that soon Innis was buried up to the waist in body parts.

She could feel the cold flesh against her bare legs. It made her skin crawl. This was all too much for her to take, much less understand. Knowing that she was stuck in a recurring nightmare wherein she could feel pain was jarring enough, but feeling the icy sensation of dead things pressing against her caused Innis to shiver with fear as well as revulsion.

The avalanche of appendages ceased. Innis breathed hard, could hear her own ragged gasps and exhalations. That warm narcotic feeling vanished. Her skin prickled as she hyperventilated. She kept trying to reassure herself that this wasn't possible, that all this craziness was only a dream, that she was stuck *in a dream*, and she couldn't wake up.

The sea of people pieces undulated, as if someone had dropped a stone in a pond. The ripples weren't moving outward, though. Rather, they moved inward. Concentric waves rolled over her, one after another, as soft as tides lapping at a river's edge. The tide came and went, covering her chest then drawing back out level with her waistline. All this was new. Though the nightmare was one that had haunted her slumber for as long as she could remember, Innis had never been trapped in an ebbing and flowing ocean of body parts. She wondered if she could drown here. Was it that insane of a thought? She had yet to awaken, even though she could feel everything happening to her.

With a kind of cool resignation, Innis Blake wondered if she were in hell.

As if in answer to her thoughts, a voice crooned, *"I have always wanted to have a neighbor... just... like... you..."*

"Who's there?" Innis's voice echoed dully.

"I've always wanted to live in a neighborhood... with you..."

"Please... please, help me?" Innis sobbed.

"Let's make the most of this be-ooooo-tiful day... Since we're together... we might as well say..."

"Who *are* you?"

"Would'ja be mine... Could'ja be mine... won't'cha be mine, m'neighbor..."

A few feet ahead of Innis, an arm with its hand attached reached out of a swell of pieces. The hand waved at Innis.

Her dead brother rose from the rolling tide of body parts. When he had revealed himself up to the knees, he stepped out of the mass of appendages like a man striding ashore. He dusted off his bloodied band uniform, cocked his head to the side, and gave Innis the saddest smile. Through her tears, she saw him mouth several words. She didn't understand him. Gerry shook his head, stomped his foot on the undulating sea of flesh and bone beneath him, and snapped his fingers, as if to say, "Oh, yeah, I forgot!"

Gerald shoved his thumb into the bullet wound in his throat. "That's better."

Innis screamed.

"Shhhh..." Gerald hissed. "You'll wake the neighbors."

Innis blinked. The extremity-flooded cinderblock prison was gone. She now stood on the street where Gerald had been gunned down by coke-addled security guard Grover Duchamp. Gerald lay in the center of a chalk outline, in the middle of the road, his right leg bent back at an odd angle behind his butt. His other leg jutted out to the side. Arms at his sides. He had a look of surprise on his face. He stared upward with glassy eyes. His arm creaked, like Dracula's coffin in the old Universal film, and Gerald stuck a thumb in his neck hole.

"I'll make you regret." He tugged his thumb from the wound with a pop.

"What?" Innis asked meekly. "What are you talking about? Where am I? What is all this?"

"It's what they do," said a different voice. This new voice wasn't really male and not completely female; somewhere in the middle, like Mary Martin's voice when she played Peter Pan.

Fog seeped into the world from all around Innis. Thick, roiling mist that smelled of swamp and dead things. Innis had given up questioning how real everything had become. She was here. That was a fact. And whether or not this was some insanely realistic dream world or hell itself, she didn't think knowing her location would help her cope with whatever was going on.

That Peter Pan voice came again. "They will make you regret."

"Regret what?" Innis asked, her voice sounding muted in the encroaching fog. "I don't... I don't understand!"

"You're not meant to understand. You haven't been brought here to... *understand*. They'll get'cha, girl. Now, shhhh... the doll's coming."

Innis expected to wake up. She expected to snap her eyes wide to see the freakish doll-thing staring down at her. But none of that happened.

In front of Innis, a vein carved into the fog, as if a snowplow had driven through. Stuttering toward her was a baby doll. It was a foot tall, and dressed in a black gown. The movements were mechanical, but there was something eerily organic about the way it moved its head back and forth, as if looking for something. Innis could hear a soft ticking, like that of a grandfather clock, and she was reminded of the life-size version of the tinker toy. In comparison, the scaled-down version seemed newer, brighter, happier.

The toy shuttered to a stop. It raised its head to meet Innis's eyes. It cooed. "I'm sorry."

"Fuck you." Innis took a step back.

"If you're here," the baby doll said without moving its lips, "you're not out there."

"What do you want?"

"Mah-Mah." The doll sounded just like its life-sized counterpart. Rage gunned Innis's accelerator, and she rushed forward. She punted the tinker toy down the street, where it was swallowed by fog.

"Feel better?" the Peter Pan imposter asked, giggling. "It's just a toy, lady. What you want is out there. Not in here."

"In here?" Innis's voice trailed off. "What do you mean in here? Where am I?"

"In here... with me, of course."

A boy of no more than ten stepped out of the fog to Innis's right. One twinkling eye gazed upon her, while the other hid behind an eye patch.

He smiled. "Won't'cha be my neighbor?"

CRUELTY

Cruelty peeled the dark woman's face off. Her blood made the process difficult, but at least she wasn't struggling anymore. Though Cruelty loved the sweet agony that had poured from the woman while she was awake, Forgiveness had work that needed to be done. Cruelty was to have a sister.

Regret stood in the corner, looking down at her future self. The Mother Mary statue frowned perpetually. Cruelty could only image how happy Regret would be when the dark woman's essence brought her out of the fog. Cruelty could almost remember the fog. Could almost remember *before*. That was silly though. There was no *before*. Cruelty was all it had ever been. Ninety years of perfection. Nine decades of Cruelty.

The last of the dark woman's face came off with little resistance. Cruelty set the scalpel down and lumbered from the table toward Regret, her prize held out in front like a peace offering. It *was* kind of a *piece* offering, Cruelty mused.

Forgiveness had been gone for some time, and Cruelty, who had no need for clocks and other such time-keeping devices, had barely noticed. Forgiveness had ordered Cruelty to complete the transfer before nightfall. They'd be moving soon. Cruelty didn't know how it felt about that. It liked the cabin. It liked finding drifters that came to see the bad men. It liked to play. There was no guarantee they'd find playthings just anywhere they traveled. They'd stopped in Ohio for a time, back in the fifties, and had found no one. Then there was New York, which had been plentiful. California and South Dakota had been dry, while Arizona and Montana fruitful. Utah had been a veritable gold mine of anguish. Texas had been a massive triumph. A successful harvest was hit or miss, though, and Cruelty hated misses.

Cruelty laid the dark woman's face upon Regret's countenance. It pressed the warm flesh down with tender pats, making sure not to tear the skin. Sometimes, Cruelty didn't know its own strength. It had to be oh so careful. *Pat, pat, patpatptat... pat...* It had tried to convert the old man whose arm it had torn off last night, but the man died by the time Cruelty returned to the cabin with him. Forgiveness hadn't been happy about that, but had allowed Cruelty another hunt. Now they had the dark woman.

The dark woman gazed at Cruelty with Regret's eyes.

Cruelty cooed. "Dah-Dah."

Regret's frown slowly pulled upward. She smiled.

On the table, Innis twitched.

MOMMA

Momma stirred.

A purple tongue painted gray lips black. One rheum-encrusted eyelid creaked open. The eyeball flickered left, then right. Up, then down. Cool blue walls surrounded her, awash in pale yellow light, which emanated from a bare bulb in the ceiling. Ever so slowly, a gnarled hand, cracked and wrinkled with age, snaked from under the covers. Another feeble hand followed, and together they slid the quilt and top sheet down her body's length, toward her feet.

As she sat up, her back popped like rollercoaster cars being dragged to the track's apex. A pink silk nightie covered her emaciated form. She could see her hip bones jutting against the fabric. Her legs resembled railroad tracks without crossties: wasted, concave on the sides, and seemingly too weak to carry her weight.

One calf at a time, she slid her legs off the edge of the bed. Her feet landed in fluffy softness, as if by habit. Her toes crept into a pair of pink bunny slippers. Not until she took a step toward the room's sole window did she truly believe the floor would not claim her. Rocking forward and backward, she maintained her balance. Three more steps and she was at the window.

The view overlooked a cracked driveway with what looked to be a dark oil spot in the dead center. A dark smear led toward the road, but stopped before the street began. Beyond that, the street wound into the woods and disappeared around a bend.

Momma laid a warm palm against the chilled glass and exhaled. Her breath frosted the pane. In the mist, she drew a clover.

Darkness had yet to swallow her. A new day had dawned and she was safe. For now, it was a good time to be alive.

Momma shuffled across the carpet toward the door. As she passed the closed closet she caught sight of her reflection, life-sized and depressing, in the mirror hanging from the door. She traced blue veins from her feet and up her thighs, lifted her nightie and cringed at the dangling flesh of her womanhood. She pulled the gown up and over her head to reveal her concave stomach bracketed by bulging ribs. Her deflated breasts showcased erect nipples the color of eggplant.

The boys hadn't been home in several nights, and she'd run out of food. How long did they believe she could go without nourishment? If she could find one, a rat roasted in the fireplace would serve her well. She'd eaten worse than that in her many years on Union Island: cat, dog, human. Nothing was too taboo. Man didn't taste of chicken; he tasted of man. Nasty, greasy meat that reminded her of hog thighs drenched in lard. As the memory of her cannibalistic endeavors surfaced, Momma spat onto the carpet. She'd never eat human again; she preferred four-legged rats.

She grasped the closet's knob and pulled toward her. The door swung outward without the protest of its hinges. Inside, she found a blue sundress that must have been four sizes too big for her now, but it would have to do. She slipped on the dress and zipped up the back. Every movement of her appendages felt as if she were the Tin Man deprived of oil. She snickered at the image of rubbing cooking grease into her joints to make them cooperate.

Dressed, and hungrier than ever before, Momma shambled out into the hallway of the second floor. She lingered at the banister, looking down at the bare home they'd made for themselves. None but the bedrooms were furnished, and only those because she and the boys refused to sleep on the floor. She clicked a long, cracked fingernail against the oak railing, thinking on why they'd chosen this place to begin with. The rent was low, but the utilities were high. She froze in the winter and boiled in the summer. The back door didn't lock, and the window over the flowerbed whistled when the wind blew. Still, it was her home, and her boys were happier here than they had been on Union Island. Twon had finally found a woman with whom to procreate. For the longest of ages, Momma had been worried that her youngest didn't like females. He'd not been like Ollie, who was ravenous in his need for women. Ollie had fancied a bitch in pigtails until the sprite had come up short on her sales. Ollie had crippled the girl. Momma had liked the sprite. Sad about her. So very, *very* sad.

Momma eased her way down the stairs one step at a time, making sure both feet were firmly planted before moving on to the next. Some time later, she laid a foot down on cold hardwood. She ambled into the kitchen, where she came across a note stapled to the tabletop. There was a vent in the ceiling, and if papers weren't secured, they'd blow off and away. Momma wasn't able to bend like she once had, so the boys made sure to keep her in mind when leaving messages.

She snapped the paper away from its anchor, and in a gravely voice, began to read.

"Momma. We gunna be a bit longer. Turtle and Jennifer's been bad. There's ham in the icebox. Collards and beans behind that. Milk was fresh when we bought it. Love, Ollie."

She choked on the last word, stumbled to the sink and ran herself a glass of tap water. She drank greedily, rivulets of cool liquid skating through the wrinkles on her chin. She let the glass fall into the sink, where it shattered. She held firm to the lip of the basin. Her body quaked as coughs continued to throttle her.

"God"—she screeched—"damn it!"

She gripped the edge of the counter so hard that her fingernails bent back. One more forceful hack threw her forward, and the nail on the middle finger of her right hand shot off, to go swirling down the drain along with the water she had yet to turn off.

"*Bondye èd tanpri,*" she prayed, asking in her native Haitian Creole for God to have mercy on her.

Knowing that her death had not been foreseen this way, she only needed to ride out the painful expulsions. Her body would soon understand it wasn't in any real danger and would breathe normally.

"*Respire,*" she coughed, willing breath into her body. "*Respire... respire... respire...*"

Attempting to catch her breath, she craned her neck, seeking the ceiling. Instead, her eyes landed on something a sight more interesting.

"What's you?" she asked the lipstick-shaped thing that had been secreted on the underside of the cabinets over the fridge.

The thing's pupil dilated. Having not been born yesterday, Momma kept reaching, right on past the one-eyed device and up into the cabinet overhead. She shook her head, pretending to be angry at the lack of food in the cupboards.

"You's got ears, *bèl ti fi*? Eh?" She had no idea why she'd called the cyclopean device a "pretty girl" but she did all the same.

If the camera could hear her, it was already too late, so Momma prayed that a plague would befall the person watching on the other end: a nasty flaking of the skin; unprotected, enflamed muscles locking up until tendon ripped from bone; teeth dropping from a death's head grimace; hair raining down like tinsel from a shaken Christmas tree; nothing left but a bloody skeleton grinning at a television monitor.

In her native tongue, she said, "I curse you, *stranger*. I own you." She stretched out "own" for almost a full five seconds.

Feeling content that the malediction would find and ravage its prey, Momma turned from the camera's gaze and left the kitchen.

It was only then that she realized she no longer coughed. Mind over matter, she thought. She didn't mind matter and it didn't mind her.

"God's pretty thing," she sang, as she passed from the hallway and into the empty living room. "May life be given to you! *Devil*, you naughty one, let no light cleave the dark ahead of you!"

The water had cleared her throat, and she found her high falsetto quite beautiful as it resounded from the bare walls. When she was but a girl, she'd been a member of the Christian man's choir. That was before Huxley had planted Twon in her belly, and twenty years ahead of Twon sharing blood with Ollie, making the older boy part of their brood. Oh, how those boys used to fight when they'd first met. But when the white men came with their dogs, Ollie had saved Momma's life. Those men had shown up, crying and calling, screaming utterances of "witch!" and "devil woman!" as they hunted her. She'd been fleet of foot and sharp of mind in those days, and had evaded the Christian men, those bastards who believed an invisible man had nailed his son to a cross to save mankind from a lake of fire. *Such rubbish.*

Now she remembered why they'd come to this house. She and the boys had traveled across water because of those men, had escaped to Ollie's father's home. The older boy was still much of a mystery to her, even a decade and a half later...

My, how time flies when you aren't being hunted day in and day out.

Even now, standing in her own living room, thousands of miles away from that dark hunt, she spat onto the floor. If she could be present while horses raped the Christian men's mothers, and witness their children cooked on spits, Momma could very nearly die a happy woman. Alas, those times were gone like the wind and tossed into the chasm of memories. It was time to move on. Almost time for recompense.

She curtsied and sat cross-legged in the middle of the floor, facing the window. Linear shadows and bars of light from the venetian blinds played over her as she rolled her torso in wide circles, meditating. She hummed quietly, working her mind away from the thoughts of the ham and collards and beans Ollie had tucked away in the icebox. Not knowing when her boys would return to her, she would save the meal until her mortality was further threatened.

Behind her eyelids, a motion picture built of memories played out: Twon born bloodied, long as a fish, to the crowing of a rooster. How her baby boy would love his mother. Even now he sold poison to sustain her. He'd kill the entirety of the world to make sure she could have but one more breath, and for that her love of him was everlasting. Ollie the same. She cared for that chubby, pale face as much as she cared for her dark son. For blood they were, and as blood they would die. It had been foretold.

But she would perish first.

In fire.

Her exhalation exploded from her, bending her over until her forehead all but smacked the hardwood. Could she somehow sidestep the coming obstacles? Could she deny the Bastard his prize? If an answer was to be had, she knew not where to find it. He'd been bested before, but how? The more she lingered on the thought, the more frustrated she became.

The Bastard would be drawn to this place as she and her boys had been. The Father would bring about the End, and the Bastard would be fed. Over a thousand miles away, the chasm yawned wide. Inside, He slept.

CRUELTY

Here, on the outskirts of Kerrville's hill country, Momma fumed. Eyes closed to the horrors yet to be seen, she shook with rage. Angry or not, she knew the End, like a jilted lover, had come for her. She would not go without a fight.

FORGIVENESS

Forgiveness, smiling under the noonday sun, sauntered across Guadalupe River and into downtown Kerrville. He admired the old Arcadia Theater, and remembered a time before moving pictures. A time when life was simpler.

Nevada in the summer. Men with guns on their hips, and dreams of prosperity in their minds. When Native Americans were considered savages, and white men brought gifts of sickness and death wherever they settled.

Now, blurred images of trucks and cars and people strolling down sidewalks accompanied him during his journey. Unlike Cruelty, he didn't need a ton of steel and wires and rubber to get around. He walked in the early days, and he could walk now. Down the middle of Main Street he strolled, whistling a merry tune, while many around him, either on foot or inside their fancy machinery, completely ignored his existence. A slight few, no more than a handful really, acknowledged the young man in the gray cardigan but did not see the real him.

A guy in a blue pickup thought Forgiveness looked like a young man wearing a beat-up leather jacket who had his hair slathered in pomade. The driver of the truck frowned but waved. Forgiveness responded in kind.

A gray-haired lady pushing a walker in front of Pompeii Café saw Forgiveness as a young woman of twenty-three skipping down the middle of the road in a golden sundress, with a cherry-red bow resting in her chestnut hair. She convinced herself that senility (or perhaps dementia, the thought!) was to blame.

A blond teenager, driving illegally (having only a permit and not an actual license), crumpled the hood of his canary-yellow Toyota Corolla against the rear end of the blue pickup because, for the shortest instance, the teen could have sworn his baby brother was walking down the center of Main Street, arms swinging at his sides as if he hadn't a care in the world. As if little Dougie hadn't been lost to the raging waters of the Guadalupe River during the flood that had swept through the hill country of Kerrville in 2004.

Forgiveness bathed in their projections; welcomed them, really. Whistling, he continued on.

Ten minutes later, he sauntered through the ambulance bay of Kerr Medical Complex, strode out into the emergency room waiting area, stepped aboard the elevator, and rode it up to the third floor. The conveyance—such devices he'd never get used to—opened, dropping him off in the antiseptic-smelling confines of another waiting room. He passed a weeping woman who seemed on the verge of hysterics. Forgiveness wondered who the grieving lady would project upon him. Perhaps a younger, healthier version of the comatose husband bounding around in her head? Mayhap indeed.

Forgiveness moved across the waiting area unimpeded by the twenty-odd chairs placed therein and passed through the double doors into the recovery area. He lingered beside a nurse's station manned by a black woman with silver hair and a sallow-faced technician who was bragging about his proficiency at drawing blood with a Vacutainer.

The nurse thought that if she were a few decades younger she'd ride every inch of what the young lab tech had hiding under his pink scrubs, and that it was a good thing menopause had come, or else she'd probably be sitting in a puddle. White or not, *Tony was cuh-uh-ute!*

The young phlebotomist wondered if this nurse—Ms. Diana Kidd—thought he was gay. And, if Ms. Kidd did, was it because of his salmon-colored uniform? Should he bring up his nonexistent girlfriend, or somehow toss in that he loved sex with girls? *Well, not girls,* stupid, *but women...* Why was he so concerned with people thinking he was gay? Was he gay? Holy shit, was he... *bisexual*?

Forgiveness silently drummed his fingers against the counter top as he gleefully absorbed the thoughts of these two individuals—their innermost fears and desires swirled around him like bored butterflies.

Nurse Diana Kidd caught Forgiveness in her peripheral vision, but instead of the young man in the gray cardigan, or Forgiveness's true form, the nurse thought she saw one of her old girlfriends from college: Monique DeBardeleben—absentminded chick with insulin-dependent diabetes. But no, that couldn't be possible because Diana Kidd had been to the funeral, had seen Monique (who'd been found stiff with rigor on her dorm room floor—cause of death: ketoacidosis) lowered into the ground. Nope. Monique was definitely, quite completely, most assuredly, stone-cold dead. The nurse went back to her conversation with Tony the Lab Tech, and Forgiveness moved on.

So many memories, so little time, he mused.

Forgiveness slid away a curtain to reveal a man covered in wires and bandages sleeping atop a hospital bed. Monitoring equipment beeped and hummed and clicked. A bag of fluid dripped into a clear cylinder, down a length of tubing, through an intravenous cannula and into the man's forearm. Forgiveness focused on the slumbering man's thoughts. Or rather, the lack thereof. Without being able to read the coma victim's thoughts, he would have to guess at a name. Forgiveness was only privy to such if they were allowed through undisturbed thought. Because of this, the man on the bed was nothing more than a nameless length of flesh and bone encased in blankets and propped up on pillows.

"Who are you, my friend?" Forgiveness asked, wondering why he'd been drawn to this empty shell.

He couldn't find a single recollection.

No memories meant no reaping.

No reaping, no harvest.

Simple as that.

Forgiveness drifted back out into the hallway and returned to the nurse's station. He briefly cursed the fact that hospitals no longer put patient names on doors or the front of charts. Privacy standards, and all that nonsense. No worry, room ten's chart was numbered clearly, and currently sat on the desk to Diana Kidd's right. He hesitated. If he reached down and picked up the chart he'd surely scare the bejeebus out of the nurse and her pink-clad friend.

He needed to push.

"You forgot"—Forgiveness whispered—"to chart something."

Forgiveness waited patiently as the nurse's face crinkled in confusion. Her mind raced, alive with undone duties, bustling with thoughts of forgotten tasks. One clear image stood out above the rest: A red neon sign, larger than life, pulsing behind a crowd of exploding synapses. THE CHART!

Forgiveness rounded the desk and stood behind Diana Kidd as she lifted room ten's chart and flipped it open.

Atop the first page, jotted beside **PATIENT NAME** was last name first, first name last: Morgan, Thomas. Forgiveness, on his tiptoes, was about to turn away when his gaze settled on the notes regarding Morgan's arrival.

Patient recovered from restroom of Bob's Bait and Fuel...

"Oh, Cruelty." Forgiveness shook his head ruefully. "Oh, that's a bad, *bad* Cruelty."

Forgiveness figured the man on the gurney must have been the Trooper whose cruiser he'd dumped out by Burt's house. Before now, Forgiveness had assumed Cruelty had simply stolen the state vehicle. Forgiveness had no idea there was an untended body. He shook his head again, inwardly damning his creation. No wonder he'd been pulled here. The trooper shouldn't have lived in the first place, was unfinished business.

Forgiveness hated a messy situation. There were enough distractions these days without piling on more drama. Oh well, Forgiveness would fix things, like always, and when he returned home he'd punish Cruelty accordingly.

The bright glory of such a pleasant day melted away and Forgiveness was left with his thoughts, as no man, woman, child, or spirit should be. A heavy blackness spoiled his mood. Kerrville had been a wellspring of pain, even if it was almost used up, and they'd need to move on in a matter of days, but leaving behind a mess like this... Well, there was absolutely no excuse.

Leaning over the comatose man, Forgiveness peeled back one slack eyelid.

He jumped back in horror, clutching his chest.

"No..." he breathed. He fought for words. Struggled to wrap his mind around the emptiness lurking behind Tom Morgan's eyes. It wasn't possible. Couldn't be. The boy was dead, destroyed by a dark woman not unlike the one he'd chosen to become Regret.

"Dastardly..."

The voice came from nowhere and everywhere all at once, was followed by a childlike tittering—the subtlest laughter.

Then it was gone.

Forgiveness found he'd pressed himself up against a crash cart. Luckily, the wheels were locked, or he might have rolled it into the next curtain-walled stall. The nurse and her lab tech buddy would have thought that rather odd indeed.

A terrible thought coursed through Forgiveness's shell-shocked mind.

Without intending to, he spoke three words: "I'm not alone."

The curtain to Thomas Morgan's alcove jerked back and a doctor, nose deep in a chart, stepped up next to the trooper's bed. Forgiveness didn't wait to hear what the medicine man in the white coat would say, had seen and figured enough for one day. Forgiveness, feeling drawn to another corner of town, took his leave of the doctor and his patient.

The weeping woman perched by the window in recovery's waiting area would be far worse for wear in a moment or two.

Forgiveness only wished he could be there to suckle her pain.

CRUELTY

TWON

Twon parked on the third floor of the parking deck, facing the hospital. He killed the engine, yanked his door handle, and kicked open his door. He peered over the edge of the low concrete wall as the taxi deposited William Longmire at the front of the main building, less than five feet away from the sliding glass doors.

From the passenger side, Ollie called, "For fuck's sake, you're going to land the both of us in the slammer. Calm the hell down!"

Twon glanced back and found Ollie half in, half out of his door, yelling at him over the roof of the car.

Twon pointed over the concrete barrier. "Imma get dis muddahfuckah, seen. Gonna feed 'em his nuts 'til he pukes up where Jennifer."

Twon sprinted across the parking deck, his feet shooting out in front of him in long-jumper strides. Rage and impatience boiled inside him. He wanted their money, or he'd have blood. This William's blood, or whoever's. Waiting be damned. Momma was hungry.

Fingers locked around his bicep and Ollie twirled Twon around to face him. Ollie's cheeks were flushed with exertion. Twon kept telling his brother he should lose some of that weight before they had to bury him in a plus-sized coffin.

"The fuck you wan'?" Twon growled.

"You can't run up in this bitch wit' your dick in your hand, man. You know better 'n that. We get locked up, and where does that leave Momma? Huh? Just think, you stupid—"

Twon ripped the red-handled butcher's knife from the belt of his pants and stuck the blade to his brother's throat. "Finish that sentence, muddahfuckah. Go on. Finish it!"

Spittle showered Ollie's face, but he remained silent.

Twon continued. "I 'bout had 'nough of you shit, seen? Boombaclot *cryin'*, day in, day out, bitch and bitch *and bitch*, while I do the man duties. Fuck you, seen?" He shoved Ollie away with his free hand. "I get this money, blood, and we be *gone*. No more bullsheet, hidin', waitin' for Him to come creepin' in the nigh'. It be better than this, I swears it, Ollie. I goddamn, muddahfuckin' swears it!"

"Not this way, man. Not like this. Even if you grab this kid up and have him take us to wherever Jennifer's hiding, that won't mean fuck-all if the cops is huntin' us. Bitch prolly ain't even got the money. Why else would she be hidin' this long? So... calm... the fuck... down..."

Ollie took a step toward Twon, and Twon growled.

"Muddahfuckah!" Twon raged into his brother's face. "*MUDDAHFUCKAH*!"

Ollie ignored him. "We'll make it before they get Momma. I promise you, man. Just... just calm down, a'ight?"

"You don' know shit, Ollie. I be her son, seen? Her *son!* She birth me, seen? *Seen*? And He... He can't have her."

"Like I don't know none of this, right? Like I ain't been having supper and sleepin' in the same goddamn house with y'all for nigh-on fifteen years? Like... like you didn't promise me that, no matter where we went, what we did, we'd be tight? Tight-as-fuck brothers? I saved both of you... *been* saving both of you... You remember, Twon, huh? Or didja forget that shit, too?"

Twon made weak circles with the butcher's knife, the tip pointed at Ollie. "Fuck you, muddahfuckah. I don' forget shit."

"You go in there waving that pigsticker, and all this is over, man. All the drugs, all the runnin', all of it ain't for shit if you get hauled in because you weren't thinkin' right."

Twon sighed long and hard before saying, "What you tink we should do?"

"He's gonna go in there to see his buddy." Ollie smiled. "And so are we."

Both Twon and Ollie noticed the pretty Latino woman trembling by the door to the parking deck's stairwell at same time. She wore green surgical scrubs, and had her brown hair tucked into a ball behind her head. Chubby in the cheeks and heavy about the hips, she resembled a cherub.

Twon made eye contact.

She dropped her keys.

"The fuck you lookin' at, bitch? Ain't'cha got somethin' better t'do than stare at a muddahfuckah?"

She blathered, rambling off some Hispanic-sounding nonsense.

"You don' speak English too good, huh?"

Ollie erupted in guffaws.

"What the fuck you laughin' at, Ollie?"

"She's doesn't..." Ollie slapped his leg, melting into further hysterics. "Oh... that's funny as shit! She doesn't speak good English... Oh, that's fuckin' *rich*!"

Twon shook his head. "You tink you funny."

"I don't '*tink*' nothin', you sorry sumbitch." Ollie threw his arm around Twon's shoulder and both men headed for the elevator.

The woman sidestepped past them, still mumbling in something other than English.

Twon pressed the call button and glanced back at the lady.

When she arrived at her car, she stood bolt straight. Eyes closed, she whispered something that Twon figured was a prayer. She opened her eyes and turned to find Twon glaring at her. He casually walked over to the stairwell, dipped, grabbed her keys, and swung back to standing.

He tossed her that which she prayed for. They bounced off her breasts and into her cupped hands.

Twon lifted a finger to his lips. "*Shhhhhh...*"

The woman, stumbling on her high heels, threw herself inside her little red Miata. Just before Twon stepped onto the lift, he could hear, as well as smell, the woman's escape as she peeled rubber in an attempt to be far, far away from the scary black man and his redneck partner.

As the doors slid closed, Twon's mind shuffled between thinking about the money Jennifer owed him, making sure Momma was safe, and his own dark-haired beauty—the love of his life. But cupid's kiss would have to wait.

The bait had been gobbled up.

It was time to reel in the catch of the day.

CRUELTY

WILL

Will checked with the volunteers stationed in the lobby before riding the elevator up to the fourth floor. Stepping off the lift, he approached the nurses' station. A red-haired can named Billie (as garnered by her name badge) pointed him in the right direction.

Kerrville Medical Complex, when viewed from above, is a ginormous X. Rooms one through thirty were located on the north-facing side of the hospital, while rooms thirty and above were housed in the south end. He pivoted away from the nurses' station and made his way toward Kirk's room. He slid his hand along the fat plastic banister that ran along the pastel blue wall. His feet slapped pea-soup-green and eggshell-white checkered flooring.

Room 438 was four doors down on the left. Will rapped his knuckles three times against the hollow wooden door, feeling the vibrations travel up his arm, pressed the handle, and entered Kirk's room.

Kirk—head back on several pillows, eyes closed, hands resting in his lap—looked like shit. Will was reminded of Dave Chappelle in his role as Tyrone Biggums—ashy complexion and all. First off: Kirk needed a haircut. Secondly: someone needed to reintroduce him to the joys of shaving. If Will didn't know any better, he'd have thought Kirk was a street bum. Only thing missing was a wrinkled fast food cup half full of jangling coinage.

"Wake... up." It felt good to talk. He no longer felt odd about vocalizing. After last night's run-in with the psychotic baby doll, people mocking his slow speech was, for William Longmire, a fear diminished by contrast.

Kirk's eyes rolled under their lids like beach balls draped in brown satin sheets. Will repeated himself, but Kirk didn't stir. Finally, Will approached the bed and kicked its CPR release—the handle with the red plastic tip that served to flatten the bed so that life-saving measures could be taken at a decent height.

Will slid behind the privacy curtain.

Kirk's bed slammed down and leveled out. He scrambled awake. His hands gripped the bedrails and he yanked into a sitting position. Broad, muscular shoulders rose and fell with frantic breath. Kirk glanced around the room.

His lips flapped rapidly as he wiped his brow. Will didn't catch a word of what his roommate said.

Will burst from the curtain, doing his best impression of a howler monkey. His mother had taken him to the zoo a week before he'd lost his hearing, and Will could vividly recall the dual-chinned primate's garbage-disposal-like call.

Kirk's eyes went wide and he clutched his chest.

"You wouldn't believe the night I had," Will said, slower than was probably necessary.

Already calming down, Kirk made a concise movement with his mouth so Will could read his lips.

"You're a fucking asshole, dude." Though Kirk did look glad to see Will, the bodybuilder also seemed standoffish. His eyes continuously darted to a space just above Will's right shoulder. Will turned to see what he was looking at, but only found the room's door, which was slightly ajar from his entrance.

When he faced Kirk again, he caught his roomie in mid-sentence. Will rolled his fists over one another, as if doing the cha-cha.

Kirk said, "What are you doing here?"

"Damn it," Will sighed. "You didn't leave the note."

Kirk shook his head. "What note?"

The bodybuilder's eye flickered back to above Will's right shoulder then immediately returned to Will. "You have to"—he jabbed a stiff finger into Will's sternum—"get out of here."

Will ignored him. "What happened to you?"

"Tell you later." Kirk made the universal sign for OK with his index finger and thumb while raising his eyebrows. Redundantly, he said, "Okay?"

"I come all the way out here… and you want me to leave?" Though Will felt as if he were speaking at a normal speed, Kirk seemed impatient—like Will was taking forever to spit out what he was trying to say.

Kirk shooed him away. "Leave. Now."

"What's wrong with you?"

"I was attacked. If you stay, they're going to chew your food."

"Chew my food?"

Kirk dropped his face into his hands.

"What?" Will asked.

Kirk looked up. "They. Are go-ing. To get. You too."

"Oh."

Kirk raised his eyebrows. "Oh?"

Kirk sent a volley of harmless slaps at Will, like a father leaning in to tickle his son's stomach. Will shoved his flailing hands away and said, "I'm not leaving until you tell me what's going on."

The bodybuilder met his eyes then glanced over Will's shoulder. Kirk visibly deflated, shaking his head sorrowfully.

"Too late."

A cold hand gripped Will's collarbone and spun him around.

The man was black. Not brown. Not dark-skinned, but several shades deeper that Wesley Snipes on the color palate. Will hated to realize this first, but something told him it had nothing to do with race, that even this man's mother would mistake him for a lump of charcoal. In spite of the situation (whatever that might be) Will snickered.

The black man slapped the shit out of him.

Will flew over Kirk's lap as if he were diving off a high board at the Olympics. He crashed down on the opposite side of the bed, his shoulder screaming, his cheek instantly throbbing, and his heart trip-hammering with confusion. He had enough time to wonder what the hell had just occurred before the black man was looming over him, big and bad and blowing noxious breath down over Will's delicate sense of smell.

Will backpedaled on his palms until his back smacked into something solid—quite possibly Kirk's nightstand. He tried to stand but the black man shoved his foot so hard into Will's crotch that Will thought he felt one testicle pop like a stomped grape. Had he possessed the gift of hearing, Will would have heard with horror the keening noise escaping his underutilized throat. He collapsed to the side, hitching with uncontrollable breaths that didn't seem to want to journey all the way down his throat and into his deprived lungs. Black-and-white spots danced in his vision like waltzing panda bears.

Then he was being lifted. He didn't want be, it was just the fact of the matter. He was thrown—not shoved, not pushed, not ushered, but tossed—into the wall beside the window overlooking the parking deck. Will slammed arm first into the corner where the wall pushed in to allow for a bay-window type of seat. Something cracked in his upper arm and lightning scorched a trail up into his shoulder. He dropped to his knees, blubbering, begging for his life, but what came out of him was not any language humankind had ever created. Some people called it gibberish.

Will flopped back onto his haunches. He held his broken arm to him with his good one.

The black man approached, dropped into a catcher's stance before Will, and actually smiled. Smiled as if he and Will were the oldest of chums, the bestest of buds, Broseph and Bromax reunited.

Words poured from the man, but Will couldn't decipher a single one. The black man spoke funny, with weird inflection and sloppy oration. Oddly, Will wondered if this guy was mentally retarded.

The guy paused, eyebrows arched, as if waiting for Will to answer. No more than a count of two passed before he reared back and knocked the taste out of Will's mouth—close-fisted this time, and with enough force to make Will see Jesus.

The crucified son of God, butter-slathered yeast rolls nailed to the bottom of his feet, skated by, winking at Will. In the distance, at the base of Golgotha, John Travolta reprised his role in *Saturday Night Fever*. Homer Simpson popped out of a burning bush and waggled a large yellow penis at Will. Fireworks erupted from Homie's urethra in brilliant reds and blues and greens before everything went dark.

He was shaken awake. Instinct took over and Will jerked his hands up to protect his face. His shattered arm didn't cooperate, protested enough that tears flooded his already sleep-murky vision. A hand clamped over his mouth. Snot bubbles burst as he was forced to breathe through his nose. A coughing fit took him over. The black man snatched his hand away and wiped it on his shirt.

The black man pressed a thickly callused finger to his lips, telling Will to hush. While he'd been out, someone had dragged him into the restroom. The black man, shaking his head from side to side, as if to warn Will that any sound issuance would result in his untimely and brutal end, put a hand to Will's chest and gently pushed him in between the wall and the toilet.

Will didn't think he'd taken his beating in silence. Someone must have come to see about his assault.

He thought that surely this nurse or doctor or tech or whoever might be on the other side of the restroom's door must be able to hear him down here, breathing heavily and crying like he was. He was sure that at any moment the door would be flung open and droves of knights in shining armor would flood in to save his ass. Superman would be nice, but he'd settle for Aquaman popping out of the toilet water like some bare-chested orange-and-green jack-in-a-box. Hell, right now, he'd take that weird fucker from *SpongeBob*, the obese superhero who needed a starfish slapped to his face to breath under water.

Will wasn't able to estimate how long he sat there, scared into silence, his own frightened breaths rumbling in his dead ears, before the restroom door swung outward and a chubby white man stepped in.

Will read his lips quite easily. "All clear."

For the second time in twenty-four hours, Will was certain he was going to die.

Strangely enough, he found himself wishing he'd died back there with the poor woman he'd left behind, hidden inside her ambulance tomb, awaiting the afterlife. Then he recalled what Sheriff Randy Miser had told him, that they'd not found the owner of the Audi. She could still be alive, after all.

Will laughed breathlessly, mirthlessly, as the black man scooped him off the floor and ushered him to his doom.

How fitting, how *astronomically* karmic, that he should pass from this world not knowing whether or not the woman had lived or died.

Life's a bitch, and then you die a deaf man.

The chubby bastard helped the black man carry Will, one of them under each of his arms, from the facilities. He grimaced and ground his teeth in an attempt to ward off the painful throbbing and sharp bolts of agony emanating from his broken arm. Will hung his head low, sobbing. His canvas shoes, toes down, glided across the vomit-green-and-off-white tile.

CRUELTY

Will glanced up to find Kirk in a wheelchair, parked at the door. His roommate's face was slack, utterly devoid of emotion. Will surmised the bodybuilder had resigned himself to their shared fate as well. Kirk's cold stare sent blades of ice cutting into Will's stomach.

CRUELTY

RANDY

Sheriff Randy Miser sat at his desk, his cell phone pinched between his shoulder and cheek. On the other end, Moxie—Kerr County's Medical Examiner—burped epically.

"Excuse me," Moxie said. "Where were we?"

Randy scratched his forehead as he reread the notes he'd taken during the first five minutes of the call: Two bodies, one cut in two by the trunk of a car, and the other pulverized. Dental records might be used to identify the unknown female, but the bisected woman was obviously EMT Georgia Jackson. Georgia's family had been notified, thanks to Deputy Nick Wuncell, and for that Randy was glad. Things were bad, but God was in His heaven, and Randy felt he'd come out the end of this thing half-sane because of it.

He'd had to let the deaf boy go on home, and he still didn't know if that had been the best decision. State Investigator Markum had called an hour after Randy had secured the boy in the drunk tank. Randy had just changed into a fresh pair of Depends and dry uniform pants (both of which he always kept on hand in his locker) when the phone had rang.

"We aren't gonna need to talk to the boy, Randy," Markum had said. "We have a lock on who worked up Morgan. Thanks for all your help, but we got it from here."

Randy had wanted to cuss the soft-voiced man for everything he was worth, but decided that wouldn't have been very Christian of him. He'd let William

Longmire loose, wished him luck, and told him to stay far away from Bob's Bait and Fuel in the future. The boy said thank you in that slow, half-retarded way of his.

"What did you call me?" Moxie asked.

"Huh? What?" Randy said, coming out of his reverie. "Say what? I dint say nothin', Mox."

"You called me—or someone—retarded. You feelin' like yourself, sheriff?"

"Yeah... naw... Hell, Mox, I don't know what I feel like. Still trying to get last night out my head, ya know? Anyway, I was just talking out my tailpipe... thinkin' too hard 'bout that boy I had to let go, is all."

"He's retarded? The boy, I mean?"

"Naw. Just deaf."

"They don't like being called that." Something clinked on Moxie's end of the line—metal on metal.

"What don't they like being called? Retarded?"

"No. Deaf. They prefer hearing-impaired. It's a PC thing. Not my cuppa tea. I don't mind being offended. Adds a lil spice to life, like tying up your wife every once and a whi—" Moxie cut off. Randy was about to ask him what was wrong when Moxie started up again. "Sorry about that, Randy. I didn't even... I didn't think about Florence."

Randy burst out laughing. "Is that all? Heck, brother, that dint even cross my mind. She been dead some months now, Mox. I ain't harpin' on her like that. She's with the Lord, and that makes me a happy man."

"You sure?"

"Lemme ask you somethin', Mox."

"Shoot."

"If you were in prison, being beat on every day and feeling just Godawful miserable, then you got pardoned and released, and you found out someone had bought you a mansion in the mountains where you could do and live how you wanted, would you want your loved ones feeling sorry for you?"

"Do what?"

Randy sighed. "She wasn't happy here, Mox, is what I'm sayin'. The diabetes stole her foot and made a mess of her physically as well as emotionally. She ate herself into the ground, and I didn't stop her." He wanted to add that, in a way, he'd helped Florence into the ground, but didn't think Moxie would appreciate that, no matter how well Randy explained himself. "Now, I know she's up in heaven running through green fields and having coffee with her kinfolk. She's better off, is all I'm saying."

"Jennifer Pillsbury," Moxie said.

"Excuse me?" Randy asked, not sure he'd heard the ME correctly.

"The lady what resembles a bag of crushed marbles? She's Jennifer Pillsbury, from here in Kerrville."

"Heck, that was quick." Randy had to admit, he was impressed. He knew most of those crime shows on television were full of crap, what with how quickly they got results on labs and other such science-type things, and figured Moxie had an ace hidden up his sleeve. "How'd you get that done so fast?"

"First thing I do when I get a Jane Doe—"

"'Cause you get so many of 'em that your table's overflowin', right?" Randy chuckled.

"Funny, joke boy. Listen, first thing I do is get an X-ray of the teeth. This girl didn't have many left in her head to begin with, so I figured it was going to be something the dental offices around town or the ER had seen before. You see, she's got meth mouth."

"Yuck," Randy cut in.

"Exactly. So I sent off the X-rays of her jaw, and Joey Cummings—he's the ER doc at the hospital three days outta seven—just emailed me back. Says that she comes in all the time looking for pain meds, he assumes when she runs out of meth. Said in the email that he'd know those dead trees pretending to be teeth anywhere."

"Hang on. Lemme get to a computer so I can run this girl's name."

Randy didn't really have to go anywhere to get to his desktop PC. He simply twirled in his chair so that he was facing the left wing of his desk. He searched for a Jennifer Pillsbury in Kerr County. Moxie started up a conversation about his wife's beef stew and how you could cover dog droppings with the stuff to make it edible. Randy pretended to listen as he watched the program process his request by way of a slowly filling red bar in the bottom right corner of the screen.

Five minutes into Moxie's diatribe on how celebrating Columbus Day was like throwing a party for Hitler's birthday, an emaciated blonde woman, whose smile looked to have been constructed out of tiny vertical Lincoln logs, appeared on Randy's screen. Though the picture was a mug shot, the sallow-faced broad was smiling. Randy didn't remember ever having her in custody. He looked at the date of her arrest and found that Nick had pulled her in while he, Miser, had been on leave because of Florence's death. Nick had her up on charges of possession with intent to sell, and prostitution. She'd been bailed out two hours later by Simon Allison, who'd put down the same address as the one on Jennifer's license in his contact info. Probably her boyfriend, Randy thought, or a brother with a different daddy. Either way, she was currently wanted for jumping bail. Randy would have to call Eunice over at Flattery Bonds to let her know one of her clients had met judgment.

"She's a pretty 'un," Randy chortled.

"Most meth heads are." Moxie yawned. "Anyway, Randy, buddy, I gotta go. I need to get these girls on ice before they start smelling like roadkill, then I have to take a nap before the wife drags me out to Friday dinner. Catch you tomorrow?"

"Sure thing. Have a good 'un, Mox."

Randy disconnected the call and faced the screen once again. Haunted-eyed, sunken-cheeked Jennifer Pillsbury gave him the chills. She looked like a zombie from a Romero flick, decayed flesh and all. She had a wet-looking sore under right eye that seemed infected, and another one on the lobe of her left ear, as if she'd tried to widen the hole for her earring with a belt sander. Randy clicked off the monitor and swiveled around to check his stationery. He'd be in the office by himself today, but Nick would be in at three to relieve him, which was a little over two hours from now. He glanced up to where his cruiser's keys hung on the wall beside the entrance to his office and wondered if he should go out on patrol to kill time until Nick came in.

Outside, he heard the arrival of a loud motor. The engine died shuddering; a door popped open and slammed closed. Randy stood, adjusting his belt and making sure his fly was up before stepping out.

As he left his office and walked down the short hallway into the lobby of the station, he heard the front entrance squeak open and the chime of bells tolling above the door. He rounded the corner to find a tall, heavy-set man with jowls as big and flabby as Randy's butt cheeks, hitching up his pants in the foyer. At the man's side was a young beagle on a leash.

"Help you?" Randy asked.

"Name's Cafferty. Chuck Cafferty. Nice to meet you...?"

"Miser." Randy held out his hand and the large man shook it. "Sheriff Randy Miser."

"Ah, right. I recognize you now." The man smiled. He managed mouth care better than he did his weight. The guy's teeth shone brighter than a halogen spotlight, and Randy chided himself inwardly when he realized he was squinting.

Cafferty added, "Got one of your reelection signs in my front yard."

"Thank you for your support, Mr. Cafferty. What can I do ya for?"

"Look, I know you ain't the humane shelter or whatever, but I gotta give this pooch to someone. I can barely feed myself, much less a dog. I been to all the vets in town, and I ain't got the gas money to be hunting outside of town, if you get what I'm sayin', so can you take him?"

"Me? What am I going to do with him?"

"What am *I* supposed to do him? He wandered up outta the woods at me this morning, and I've been trying to find someone to take him ever since. He's chipped. Got the tags on his collar to prove it. Maybe you can call someone about him?"

"I don't have access to that network. Speaking of which, why haven't you checked the pound?"

"They closed on Fridays. Ain't that somethin'? You'd think it'd be only the weekend, but they closed on Monday, Friday, and both Saturday *and* Sunday. Hope nobody in this town needs animal control 'cause of some wild animal attack. They'd have to wait until Tuesday through Thursday to be saved."

Randy chuckled. He liked the big guy's sense of humor. "What happens if I don't take him off your hands, Mr. Cafferty."

"Well, he ain't my legal responsibility, so I don't guess you could stop me from just dumpin' him on the side of the road somewhere."

Randy smiled. "You ain't gonna do that, though."

Cafferty quirked an eyebrow. "How you know that?"

"I like dogs, too, Mr. Cafferty. I'm guessing you—like me—had a dog when you were a kid, and it chaps your backside that he or she ain't part of your life anymore. But, like you said, you can barely feed yourself. Now, I ain't no Angela Lansbury, but if you didn't care about what happened to this dog, you wouldn't have gone through all the trouble of running him all over town trying to find him a temporary home. So, no, I don't think you'll drop him off on the side of the road."

Cafferty's heavy shoulders slumped. "You ain't gonna take him, then?"

"Sure I will. I just wanted to let you know I was on to you."

The big man brightened. "Thank you."

He handed Randy the leash.

The dog observed Randy with wet eyes. Its tongue lolled from the side of its mouth, panting. It'd been months since Randy had something—or some*one*—to care for, and even though there was no law saying he had to dog-sit until the pound reopened on Tuesday, Randy felt strangely obligated to see after the beagle.

"His name's Merlo. Like the wine, but without the T. I don't think his owners knew how to spell," Cafferty said, as he pulled at the front of his shirt. Randy had seen many an obese person perform the same action, and most of them didn't even realize they were doing it. Seemed to be a fat-person tic, as if they were always concerned their bellies were eating their shirts.

You're one to talk, he thought. Although Randy's arms and legs were thin, he'd acquired a beer gut during his rambling days between 'Nam and taking on the badge.

"People name their pets all kinds of weird things," Randy said. He leaned down to scratch Merlo behind the ear. "Look at that one horse movie—*Seabiscuit*. I mean, what's a sea biscuit in the first place, and what's it got to do with horses?"

Cafferty jiggled when he laughed. "Ya got a point, sheriff. Do I need to sign something, like a drop slip or something?"

"Nope. Like you said, he wasn't your responsibility in the first place. Anything else I can help you with, Mr. Cafferty?"

"Naw, sir. You have a good day."

"You too."

Cafferty left and Randy followed him out. The big man poured himself behind the wheel of his truck and drove away. Merlo nudged Randy's leg, and the sheriff scratched the dog atop the head.

"Now what, pup?"

Merlo only slobbered. Thick ropes of drool slid off his tongue and polka-dotted the concrete pad in front of the entrance.

"Wanna see my office, boy?"

Merlo barked once and returned to panting.

"Don't get too attached to me, you hear?" Randy said as he led Merlo back inside. "Come Tuesday mornin', we're gonna find out who you belong to and get you home, okay?"

The dog chose the right to remain silent.

"You're right." Randy nodded. "If you never make any promises, you ain't gotta worry about breaking them."

CRUELTY

NATALIE

Natalie Holden, seated alongside the front windows of Pompeii Café, sipped a caramel frap while waiting on Markum to show. Outside, lunchtime traffic had dwindled to a minimum, and people were headed back to work. Inside the café, two people stood in line— a fiftyish Hispanic woman in a pantsuit and a young black girl in skinny jeans and a black tank top. The tanned barista—a man in his early twenties, and possibly a college student—shuffled from side to side, shifting his weight and drumming his fingers on the counter, as he waited for the older woman to make up her mind. The five glass-topped, aluminum-legged tables in the small shop's lobby were unattended.

Having changed from her trooper uniform to street clothes after Markum had phoned about meeting her to discuss important details regarding Tom Morgan's assault, Natalie now wore a pale yellow blouse, blue jeans, white Reeboks, and a Smith & Wesson .38 Special on her hip, allowed by the concealed carry permit presently tucked in her back pocket. Her long black hair was pulled back in a ponytail, which reached all the way to her tailbone. She kept her car keys on a carabiner clipped to a belt loop on her left side and a small pouch that contained her coins, paper money, and American Express card in her front right pocket—the credit card was reserved for retail therapy emergencies only. Purses never were her thing. Having been a tomboy most her life, she found that many girlie things were lost on her.

She wished Markum would hurry the hell up. She still had to go shopping for her grandmother, and then deliver Kaku—Comanche for grandmother—her monthly package out to the reservation, west of Fredericksburg. It was an hour-and-a-half drive, and she wanted to make it before sundown. As the day wore on, now pressing almost two o'clock, Natalie didn't think that was going to be possible. Kaku would be disappointed, but she wouldn't starve if her granddaughter's visit was delayed until tomorrow.

Markum's black sedan swerved into a spot at the curb in front of Pompeii Café, and Natalie blew out a sigh of relief. The statie, carrying a leather satchel over one shoulder, hopped out the car. Once again, she noted the way he walked: the swivel of his shoulders opposite his hips, the swagger, the air of confidence he exuded. She felt oddly jealous of the way he seemed to float instead of walk. There were women that would kill to move with such grace.

Markum shoved the door inward, met her eyes, nodded, and strode briskly in behind the girl in the skinny jeans. Natalie waited patiently as the older woman was served her order, then the black girl, and finally Markum, who placed his order and waited at the bar while the tanned barista did his thing behind the counter.

A bagel in one hand and a coffee in the other, Markum dropped into the seat opposite Natalie and threw on a bright smile.

"Trooper," he said.

"Investigator," she returned. "Wanna tell me what all this is about? I have things to do today."

He sat his purchases on the tabletop, unslung the satchel, laid it in his lap and unzipped the top. He pulled out a manila folder and placed it in front of Natalie, beside her now-cold beverage. "You requested these, I believe."

Natalie flipped the folder open to find mug shots of all Twon Chatham's known associates. "Thanks."

"Least I can do since I'm making you keep your trap shut on this whole matter." He blew steam from the sippy hole in his coffee cup's lid and took a long pull from it. "Nobody under five-foot in there, though. You sure your source is correct?"

"Burt Waters said the person who ditched Tom's cruiser was shorter than his mailbox. I'm apt to believe him."

"Isn't that the old man who was out there when I came to see you at Camp Meeting Creek this morning?"

She nodded.

"And you think that geriatric's eyesight has remained twenty-twenty over the years?"

She shrugged. "It's worth a go. If we can place a finger on who Twon's got running errands for him, we can make you look even better to your DEA pals."

She looked up from the folder to judge whether or not Markum knew how hard she'd just baited him.

He didn't seem to mind the implication that he had something to gain from working with drug enforcement officials. In fact, he looked the exact opposite of nonplussed. "So you've decided to help instead of hinder. That's good, trooper. Very good. You might see yourself with a commendation before all's said and done." Markum took a petite bite of his plain bagel, chewed, swallowed, and partook once more of his coffee.

"What if—?" Natalie stopped, not quite sure she wanted to speak aloud the idea suddenly bounding around in her head just yet.

"Yes?" Markum asked.

She drank her own coffee, which was now the exact temperature of the room around her, and shook her head almost imperceptibly. "What if," she began again, "Twon had nothing to do with Tom's attack?"

Markum clasped his hands together and leaned back. "Go on."

"What if this is someone who's after Twon and his crew? Someone with their own agenda? Maybe they sent this person out to Twon's house in Tom's cruiser knowing that we'd be able to track it. Knowing that we'd come down even harder on the cook after Tom was found all beat to hell and back."

"Ah, she's a bright one, folks." Markum laid his hands palms down on the tabletop. "What else has been running through that brilliant mind of yours?"

"I don't like being patronized." She sat bolt straight in her chair and threw her shoulders back. "If you're fucking with me—"

"Now, now, calm down. I am truly impressed at your deductive skills. I myself have come to the same conclusion. You might think that I'm working with the DEA to further my career, but my motives are very much of the ulterior variety. I have someone on the inside, yes, but my relationship with them is... personal, I promise you. I have been privy to some classified information only because my contact needs to vent after work. Whether or not you choose to believe this is beside the point. But, I assure you, I'm telling the truth. Now, what neither the DEA nor my superiors know at this time is that I am taking up an investigation into exactly what you've been talking about. I firmly believe, with every ounce of my gut instinct, that Twon's in trouble. That someone's after him, and that someone is quite the... character." Markum's eyes gleamed, like a bond villain monologuing his evil plan.

Natalie eyed the investigator suspiciously, but found not a single tell in his countenance. If he were lying, he was damn good at misdirection. "So... what now?"

"That's why I called you. I plan to visit Twon's house tonight. I gleaned a bit of information from my... contact. The man Randy Miser's deputy found in the cooler of that gas station last night isn't the innocent victim we once thought. He was Twon's supplier of pseudoephedrine, or something like it. The old man's name is John Landover; he's out of Beaumont. He worked for a chemical factory before his untimely death at the hands of... someone. I saw part of it transpire through video procured by my person with the DEA."

"And you have no idea who this person is? The one who killed Landover?"

"Nope." Markum frowned dejectedly. "He was wearing a mask. A rather creepy one."

"A mask?"

"The feed was night vision, so it was hard to see properly, but it looked like a baby doll face, from what I could make out, at least."

Something went icy in her guts—frigid nightcrawlers burrowing. "A... baby doll?"

"Trust me, I'm just as confused as you are. Out of all the shit I've seen in my decade-and-a-half on the force— ski masks, presidential faces, nylons, burlap sacks—I've never seen anyone commit a crime dressed up like a doll. Things these days just get weirder and weirder. Anyway, I'm going out there this afternoon. You said you had something to do, an appointment? Can it be postponed?"

Natalie thought about Kaku, fridge almost empty, and awaiting a visit from her *peta (daughter)*, and sighed heavily. "I might can work something out."

"How long before you can get back to me?"

Natalie stood. "Gimme two minutes."

She left Markum sitting where he was and walked outside. She used the fob on her key ring to unlock her Daytona, and slid into the passenger's side door. Snatching up her cell from the center console, she pressed *send*, scrolled down to the last call she'd made to Kaku, and instigated the call.

Kaku, sounding frail, answered on the fifth ring, saying hello in her native tongue. "*Ma ruawe?*"

"Kaku, it's your *peta*. How are you?"

"Fine, lovely. Are you still coming today?" Kaku asked, as if she already knew the purpose of Natalie's call.

"Do you have enough food in the house until I can make it out there tomorrow?"

"*Peta*, what wrong?"

Natalie was taken aback by her *kaku*'s off-subject question. "Huh? Why do you think something's wrong?"

"You no sound yourself, girl. I'm old, and these bones work less and less, but mind still able to cut like knife. So, you tell me, what wrong? Man trouble?"

"No, Kaku, I just… I feel like I'm letting you down all the time. I don't get a chance to visit so much these days, and when I do, our time together is short. Mom would kill me if she were still alive."

"Donna was good woman, a good *peta*, like you, and she would have loved the just and strong woman you become. I know this. No worry, girl. You worry too much. Make you infertile."

Natalie laughed boisterously. "Kids are the least of my worries, Kaku, but I'll take that into consideration."

"You consider it much, girl, 'cause whether or not you want baby, I want great grandchildren. Still, you need to find strong man before you make baby. Strong like you. Pretty man wouldn't hurt either."

Although Natalie laughed, she found tears welling in her eyes. "Love you, Kaku."

"Many loves for you, *peta*. Now, you run and do what you must, and I'll eat with Running with Rabbits."

Natalie raised her eyebrows, shocked. "Who's this Running with Rabbits character."

Kaku snickered. "He's pretty and strong… but he's mine, girl. Get your own man. Listen, Natalie, Branch of My Heart"—it had been ages since Kaku had called Natalie that, and because of it, Natalie no longer cried softly, but openly wept—"I have survived many years, longer than my husband, your *toku*, and I will continue to survive until I am dragged away by my hair to the Great Prairie in the Sky."

"You don't really believe wild horses are going to run off with you when you die, do you?"

"No, but it makes good story for grandbaby." Kaku giggled. "You go now, girl. Stop worrying. Especially about me."

"Okay. Have fun with Running with Rabbits."

"Oh, he'll be the one having fun, *peta*, bet your ass he will. Tomorrow, girl."

Natalie wished Kaku goodbye in Comanche and hung up.

When she turned around, Markum was less than two feet away from her, smiling.

"What tribe?" he asked.

"Shoshone. I'm full-blooded, *and* the only member of my tribe to ever go to school off the reservation. You should have heard my parents." Natalie, smiling, shook her head. Her hair flapped from shoulder blade to shoulder blade. "They said the outside world had corrupted me, like some kinda demon had crept up my ass in the night to possess me, and that's why I chose to live and work away from home. It didn't matter to them that I wanted to be a state trooper or how renting an apartment was cheaper than driving back and forth from the reservation to work everyday."

"Parents can be stubborn. Especially when they get it stuck in their heads that you didn't become the person they expected you to be." Markum's face took on a dark cast. Troubles unspoken were at war on his face. Natalie chose not to probe for explanations to his suddenly dour mood.

After a few second's silence between the two, Markum looked up, feigning a smile.

"The woman on the phone... she's your mother?" he asked.

"*Grand*mother. After my parents died—my junior year of college—I took over helping my *kaku*—sorry, my *grandmother*—with grocery shopping and other stuff."

"That's respectable. How'd your folks die?"

"They were ripped apart. Are you ready to go?"

MERLO & RANDY

Merlo lay on his side, licking himself next to the man with the big gut. Big Gut knew all about lovins, and Merlo thought the guy would do for now. If bacon came, Merlo would like Big Gut even more. He'd enjoyed his time with the fat man in the truck, but somehow Merlo had known that situation was temporary. Still, he'd gotten a cheeseburger out of the deal, had scarfed it down while the fat man ate three of them by himself.

Merlo, sadly, found that he was thinking less and less about the Lady. Her face had disappeared from his eye. Absently, Merlo lapped at his balls and tried to recall what she looked like. The Mister was but a distant memory now, one that consisted of olfactory triggers: stinky stuff from a bottle that had made Merlo sneeze, armpits and hair that smelled of flowers, which Merlo had not minded so much. It reminded him of going for walks and peeing on roses. Oh, and bacon. The Mister had been famous for bacon.

Big Gut sneezed forcibly, causing Merlo to hop onto his feet, growling.

"Excuse me, pup," Big Gut said.

Merlo had no idea what these words meant. Instead of pondering their deeper meaning, he nudged Big Gut's hand. The man responded kindly, digging his fingers in under Merlo's chin. Merlo liked this more than basking in the sun's warmth whenever he was let out on the balcony the Lady and the Mister shared together.

A twinge Randy hadn't felt in nigh on two years lanced his bladder. It was only vaguely familiar at first, but then his brain caught up with his body.

God is good—I have to piss!

Not minding whether or not the Lord would consider his language appropriate, Randy shot from his chair to standing. He skipped over Merlo, apologizing, and rushed out of his office, down the hallway, and into the public restroom by the entrance. He pushed through the door with one hand while the other worked at his zipper. He was halfway to the urinal when he realized his incontinence briefs didn't have a hole from which he could draw his gun. Grumbling gibberish under his breath, sounding not unlike Yosemite Sam in a fit of stuttering rage, he dropped pants and all around his ankles. He penguin walked the rest of the way to the stall, his penis spitting and sputtering in his fist.

"Ah, hell, come on," he yelled, as urine dribbled from his knuckles.

Finally he thrust his pelvis into the urinal and shuddered with glee as he voided forcibly against the porcelain.

Randy, thanking God for this miracle, did not hear the bells above the door, nor the visitor's voice calling out to whoever was there.

But Merlo did.

The dog paused, head cocked, ears lifted, as the stranger called, "Anyone here?"

The voice was much different than normal humans, and Merlo first thought there was more than one person in the lobby. He hopped up, like the capable dog that he was, and padded down the hall. Merlo halted halfway down. There was something familiar on the air. His nose twitched as he attempted to catch a better scent. His tongue dripped, dangled over the edge of his chin, tasting everything around him. Merlo began to back away.

Dead tree rat. No doubt about it.

A monster made of darkness rounded the corner into the hallway.

Merlo, hackles raised, loosed a volley of what he hoped were adequately intimidating barks and growls as he continued to reverse toward the office.

"Good doggy?" the creature said in multiple voices. Merlo was unaware that what now bristled under his coat was called goose flesh. He was a dog, and dogs did not concern themselves with inane responses like the prickling of one's skin. What Merlo did concern himself with, however, was the very real possibility that he was about to die.

Dead tree rat filled his nose. Not wanting to but needing to all the same, Merlo sneezed once, twice, and then a third time—blowing snot a good ten feet ahead of him onto the monster's undulating feet. He needed that horrible stench gone from him. He'd give anything to smell bacon or armpit flowers or bottled musk. Anything but decaying squirrel. Absolutely *anything*.

Not again, Merlo thought in his dog brain, though not exactly with those human words.

First he'd been taken from the Mister and his endless supply of bacon. Then he'd been forced to leave the Lady to fend for herself against the dead-tree-rat-smelling thing in the hopes that he would live to once again feel the joy of lovins. Then the fat man in the truck had abandoned him.

Merlo was all alone again.

"You see me, don't you?" the thing said.

Echoing voices surrounded Merlo. He yapped and bit at nothing.

"You belong to the dark woman, don't you?" It pretended to sound cheerful, friendly, but Merlo was not a stupid dog. He could smell the badness coming off this creature, could see the shadows leaping off the roiling blackness that were its shoulders.

Where was Big Gut? Why had he left Merlo?

"Come here, now. That's a good doggy."

Merlo didn't think he could bark any louder, but he did. He hurt his own ears with this one. The monster seemed unimpressed, though. It continued to swirl toward him, shifting and re-forming with every step it took.

Merlo backed into a corner and yelped. When had he left the hallway? How had he gotten back inside the office? He didn't recall backing through the door, but he must have.

There was no place left to go. Nowhere to run.

Merlo wished for lovins and bacon and help. Mostly help, though. He was scared and lonely and had no way to protect himself.

A voice said, "What the fuck?" and Merlo was glad to hear that it was only one voice, and that it belonged to Big Gut.

Merlo was saved.

Randy stalled in the hallway, his chest hitching with breath, as he watched his dead wife reach for the cowering dog in the corner.

"What the fuck?"

He couldn't help himself. The foul language had just fallen from him, and he hoped God would forgive him, considering the circumstances. After all, it wasn't everyday that your deceased better half strolled into the office for a visit.

Randy shook his head in an attempt to clear his vision. This was crazy—flipping bonkers. Florence had been in the ground for six months; he'd watched her take the final breaths that led her to that two-thousand-dollar casket—the one he'd had custom-built to hold her immense body because the stock caskets the funeral home offered were about two sizes too small. Because, by the end, his Florence had really let herself go, but Randy had not loved her any less. Mainly because he'd helped her on her road to immobility.

She looked lovely, though: healthy and vibrant and luminous and, God in Heaven, all too real. Her skin shone with the light of life, and her short-cropped brown hair seemed to have been freshly curled. He could even smell the hairspray. Randy wondered if Florence had seen Debbie down at the salon before dropping in to see him.

"What the fuck?" Randy repeated, as Florence turned and beamed at him. "Who... what the... *who are you*?"

"I'm whatever you see... Randy, is it? Yes, *my* Randy. My loving food delivery system, how I've missed you so."

"Flo? It... it just can't be. You're—"

"No, honey. I'm right here, aren't I? I mean, you can see me, right? And seeing, as they say, is believing."

Tears streamed down Randy's cheeks. He hadn't even noticed he'd begun crying.

"Flo?" he sobbed. "That really you, baby?"

"I'm right here, honey. Your beautiful Flo, come back to you."

"I... I'm, uh... I'm sorry, Flo. I, uh... I shouldn't have kept giving you them sweets. *I shouldn't have! WASN'T RIGHT OF ME!*" he blubbered and wailed.

"Oh, honey," Florence cooed. "That's why I'm here, then. I can show you forgiveness. Do you want to know forgiveness? Is that what you want? Come, honey. Come to forgiveness."

Randy felt himself drifting forward without wanting to. Although the love of his life stood more than five feet from him, something about the mute expression on her face terrified him. His heart slammed against his ribs, and there didn't seem enough air in this hallway to feed his lungs.

Florence trailed her fingertips across the wallpaper as she progressed.

Soon, they would meet in the middle.

Four feet away.

Three feet.

Two...

Randy swiped his forearm across his leaking eyes. His foot lifted to step forward, but he willed it down. Instead, he took three quick steps back and drew his revolver, drawing a bead on Florence's right eye.

It was the way this Florence was dressed that finally caused Randy to retreat. He remembered the gown she now wore vividly, because he'd picked it out. Florence's wedding dress had been the last thing he'd seen her in, because he'd chosen to bury her in it.

Over his gun, Randy barked, "Don't take another step, you... whatever you are."

"Randy?" She cocked her head to the side and the smile on her face seemed to slide off onto the floor. Something swam under her right cheek, like a cockroach under a napkin, and her eyes gleamed at him malevolently. "Randy, put down the gun."

"Put your hands up on the wall, damn it! *NOW!*" Randy fumbled with his cuffs, but they seemed rooted in place on his belt. "I said, *NOW!*" he bellowed.

"*Tsk, tsk, tsk,* Randy. That's not very welcoming of you, now is it? That's a bad Randy, yes it is."

The Florence-thing yawned wide. Her eyes rolled back and fell into her skull, disappearing from view. Two dark chasms glared at Randy. His guts roiled, on the verge of dumping everything he'd eaten today into the seat of his Depends. The Florence thing exhaled and frigid, fetid breath washed over him.

Randy squeezed the trigger three times. The hallway boomed with gunfire. The .357 shells passed through her, leaving ragged holes in her dress over unmarred flesh.

"I only offered forgiveness, an escape from your memories. But, *no*," it mocked, "you had to be stubborn. I will swallow you whole, sheriff. Devour everything that once was Randy Miser. And you will simply be no more. Do you hear me, old man? *I AM FUCKING HUNGRY!*"

The revolver fell from Randy's trembling hand. Willing his heart not to give out on him, he spun on his heels and sprinted for the front door. Behind him, the Florence-thing roared with laughter. He wasn't stopping to ask what was so funny, that was for sure. He wouldn't stop until he reached his cruiser. Even then, he might drive forever until he keeled over behind the wheel, because he knew, in his heart of hearts—down to his very core—that the Florence thing was far from done with him.

Merlo saw his chance. He raced past the pillar of shadow as it roared. Down the hallway he shot, legs shoving him faster and faster forward. He tilted into the turn and his nails caught carpet. He propelled himself through the entrance to the sheriff's department just before it swung closed.

Big Gut booked toward a silver and brown car. Merlo followed, shortening the twenty feet between them with long strides. Big Gut tossed the car door open, and Merlo threaded through his legs and up into the cruiser. He hopped into the footwell, where he cowered, shaking.

Big Gut was saying something, something about how much of a good dog Merlo was, but Merlo didn't care. He wanted the man to hurry up, to get in the car and run them away from monsters made of darkness.

The man played with a few things Merlo didn't understand and the engine roared to life, sounding so much like the growling creature they'd left behind them that Merlo peed all over the floor of the car. He jumped from the puddle up into the passenger seat, where he pressed himself into the upholstery in an attempt to become one with the leather.

"Damn, damn, damn," Big Gut said, and though Merlo had no idea what those words meant, he agreed with the sound of them. That sound said they weren't going away fast enough.

With a squeal of tires, the car rocked forward, screeched to a halt a second later, and then flung Merlo back into the seat.

The dog settled into a ball and pressed his nose flush with his butt. At least it didn't smell like dead tree rat.

Merlo liked that very, very much.

CRUELTY

NELL

Nell Morgan, breathless and weeping, stumbled through sliding glass doors into dull sunlight. She moved like a spent windup toy across the hospital's turnabout. She brushed past an old man pushing a walker along the sidewalk. He called after her, begging her pardon, but she ignored him.

Her future unsure and mind unsound, she shambled toward downtown in a fit of crushing depression. Gravity bore down—a new enemy hell-bent on driving her into the concrete and crushing her under its uncaring weight. Walking required the utmost concentration. One foot in front of the other. Step by step. Slow and steady wins the race, and all that nonsense.

The doctor's words resounded in her head, bounded off the walls of her skull, flittered through her synapses, killed logical thought, murdered sanity, and throttled certainty.

Did she have someone she could call? She really shouldn't be alone right now. The hospital could provide a counselor, someone to talk to in her time of need. Was she all right? She looked unstable.

Brain death.

No, she wouldn't accept it. Tom would be all right. He'd pull out of this. Be a stronger man than ever before. He'd learn to walk again once he received his new space-age leg. Tides would be rough for a while, but he'd navigate through like the experienced sailor he was. Nell would still love him, even if he was missing a few parts, glad that she still had her man to wake up to every morning.

We're going to pull the plug.

What? Like he was a cell phone with a fully recharged battery? Like he was an alarm clock with a broken snooze button? *Pull the plug*? They couldn't make her do it, so they were going to proceed without her. She'd be damned if she were going to stand by and watch them kill him. Tom would do the same thing in her shoes. He'd laugh in the face of any doctor that diagnosed his Nell with "brain death." "I'll make you brain-dead, asshole," is what Tom Morgan would have said. "I beat smoking, and she'll beat this!"

It's what he wanted, Nell.

Did Tom have a living will? Of course he did; he was an officer of the law, a Texas State Trooper, and his job was fraught with danger. Anything could have (and had) happened. Tom was what medical professionals called a DNR. *Do not resuscitate.* In case of emergency, do not break glass. Do not pass GO. Do not collect two hundred dollars. Game over. His mother had suffered for months after a massive stroke ended her brain activity. Mama Morgan had been kept alive by chemicals and respirators, until finally even modern science couldn't hold the matriarch of the Morgan Clan in this world. Tom always said if something bad happened to him, he didn't want to linger like his mother. But if he was truly brain-dead, he wasn't really lingering. Logic dictated that she wasn't keeping him from some celestial appointment because he'd already moved on. His body was simply being stubborn. The big man in the sky would have to wait. Nell Morgan was infamous for having things her way. She'd lived with both OCD and Tom, during his withdrawals from those blasted cancer sticks, and if there was anything she obsessed over it was her compulsion to be with her husband.

I'm sorry, Nell, but the choice isn't yours.

You knew, you son of a bitch, Nell thought, as she shuffled into traffic. A Dodge Ram blew its horn at her. The driver of a Honda Civic asked her if she had a "fucking death wish."

This time, she spoke aloud: "You knew I wouldn't be able to let you go, you selfish asshole."

You don't have to leave, Nell... Mrs. Morgan? Nell? He'd want you here for this!

"You selfish... *selfish*... asshole," Nell stammered, as she stepped up onto the sidewalk and dropped to her knees. She buried her face in her palms and bawled.

"How... how could you... *leave* me? How... *could you*?"

"Nell?" a voice asked.

Slowly, Nell Morgan tilted her head. Sun spiked through tiny holes in the weathered awning over the front door of Pompeii Café. How had she gotten downtown? Why was the sun so high? What damn time was it? Had they already murdered him?

"Is he dead yet?" she asked of no one.

"Nell, it's me." Nell glanced at the soft face which kept saying her name. Natalie, wasn't it? The nice Native American girl who worked with Tom and had come to see about Nell before the brain death diagnosis. "Nell? Oh God, honey, are you all right?"

"Is he dead yet?" she repeated. Suddenly cold all over, she wanted to be out in the sun. Needed the heat. She shoved to her feet and wobbled off the curb. More car horns, which she didn't bother herself with. Nell shambled down the middle of the road, screaming repeatedly, "Is he dead yet? *IS HE FUCKING DEAD YET*?"

A hand gripped her shoulder and she spun, flailing, to face her attacker. She punched in downward motions, striking her assailant with the ball of her fist.

"*IS HE DEAD YET? HUH? IS HE?*"

"Nell? Nell, it's me, Natalie. I need to get you out of the street. Okay? We're gonna get you—"

CRUELTY

"*I DON'T WANT HIM DEAD! GIVE ME BACK MY TOM!*" Nell melted to the street, body hitching, eyes dry and aching because the well of her soul had run dry. Shuddering, Nell whipped her head back and wailed to heaven itself, hoping God was listening, that he felt bad, that he felt some inkling of remorse for stealing Tom from her. God. Tom. Selfish bastards, the lot of them. What was she supposed to do now? Who was she without Tom? Who was Tom without her?

"Nell, I need you to stand up? Please, honey, I don't want to have to drag you out of the road."

Disembodied voices enveloped her. She seemed surrounded by ghosts intent on conversation. Couldn't these specters see her writhing in her anguish? Couldn't they mind their own goddamn business?

Nell popped to her feet. She swiped at the apparitions, parting the sea of ethereal onlookers, and dashed away.

"Nell!" someone—or many someones—called.

Reeling, she ran through the sparkling light of a Texas midday sun, looking as if she were being riddled with bullets as she went. Her whole body bucked and twisted with fruitless sobs.

Her and Tom at home, sitting in front of the big screen, *The Walking Dead* plodding along because the series finale was still four episodes away. Tom shoveling her lasagna into his smiling mouth. Him winking at her. Her grinning back. These were the things relationships were made of: a small nod, subtle eye contact, a knowing gaze, a brush of a hand across your back, a massaging of the shoulders, nuzzling her neck, melding and becoming one another. Walking upstairs, hand in hand. That was the last time they were together, not more than two nights ago. Had it really been that recent? She fancied she could still taste his mouth on hers. Then, yesterday afternoon, her waving goodbye from the front door as he backed down the driveway. He'd called around midnight and told her about the kid he'd found outside Bob's Bait and Fuel. Groggy and wanting to go back to sleep, she told him, "That's nice," and had fallen asleep on him. Later, she'd thought the conversation a dream, but it was real. That was the saddest thing, really, that her last contact with Tom hadn't been her wishing him goodbye, but that she'd blown off something he thought was important with a complacent "That's nice," before he'd shattered like fine china on concrete.

Nell Morgan raced through now-stalled traffic, past the Amoco on the corner and the Walgreens across the street, crossed onto the bridge spanning the gap of the Guadalupe, and wove between a Mack truck carrying oxygen tanks and an avocado-green hatchback. She rushed to the low wall overlooking the river. Panting, she braced on the edge. Her soft fingers ground into the abrasive stone as if she meant to leave her fingerprints in the concrete, therefore proving she'd once been here, that this day had happened, and that everyone should remember. God... Tom... all of them. That this was the price of being selfish. Hearts broke with finality, akin to atoms splitting. She pushed to her tiptoes.

Tom had been all she'd ever known, her complete universe. Her problem with his smoking had had nothing to do with the smell of his shirts or the taste of licking an ashtray when they kissed. She'd instigated his quitting, lied to her doctor to get those antidepressants that moonlit as smoking cessation drugs, so that she could have her husband forever. How could she, in good conscience, have sat around and watched him kill himself? And now what? What did she get for all her trouble?

Brain death.

"No..." she sobbed, fresh tears of the kind she thought no longer possible spilling down her cheeks. Warm runnels washed into the part of her lips, where they crossed the verge and dropped to her chin. "No. No. *No*..."

She felt in her core that if she denied his death she could somehow heal him. But, as she watched the brown water swirling beneath her, she came to the truth of it. Somewhere down there, under the mud and silt, was a place devoid of pain and suffering. She lifted one knee and straddled the low barrier. In the distance, an island no larger than an SUV parted the dirty water. In the center of the island, a single tree. The tree was bare. As bare as Nell. Naked to the world. She swung her other leg over while behind her people screamed and begged and pleaded with her to "just turn back around!" Someone told someone else to go after her until someone talked them out of it, saying Nell would take them down with her. How cold was that? Even now, as she sat at the precipice of oblivion, people were more concerned with themselves than they were her.

Selfish bastards.

Selfish bastards, the lot of them.

Well, she had (*some good, some bad*) news for them. It was her turn to be selfish. She would make the decision, snatch control away from all the selfish bastards in the world. Nothing else mattered. Not anymore. Tom was gone. Dead of brain. She was gone. Dead of heart. Neither of their bodies had caught on to the fact, so someone needed to step in and pull the plug.

Step in...

Step...

St—

"Nell?"

Tom's voice.

She looked down, up, side to side, then out across the mild river, wondering where his voice had come from.

"Nell, baby?"

"Tom?"

"Hey, baby. You're gonna be all right, right?"

"Where are you? *I want to see you!*"

Into her right ear, Tom whispered, "I'm right here."

She snapped her head around and found Tom standing there in his trooper uniform, the same clothing she'd last seen him in. It even had the minuscule mustard stain on the left lapel. She hadn't been able to get it out completely. She'd nagged him for days over that one, how he needed to respect his work clothes because no one would respect a man with mustard on his collar, it didn't matter if he'd caught them speeding or what kind of fancy car he drove. Cleanliness meant you were serious about the details. A mustard stain said you might take a bribe, if for nothing else to pay for dry cleaning. She reached out and pinched his lapel with her thumb and index finger, hiding the spot. If she were going to remember him like this, she didn't want that damn yellow anomaly standing out later.

Later?

Would there be a later?

Once again she gazed out over the rushing muddy water, the green rows of trees lining the Guadalupe, to the blue sky, all but cloudless—a shimmering, crystal-blue ocean dotted with fluffy white caps.

"Tom?" she asked, in a hushed tone.

"Yeah, baby?"

"How're you here?" Nell turned back to the frowning countenance of her hubby and caressed his cheek with one trembling hand. He felt so goddamned real. She bit back a sob, but still managed: "You're supposed to be—"

"I know. It's all right." He smiled the same smile that he had when he'd proposed to her. That goofy grin that said, "I'm not sure what I'm doing, but screw it."

"Did I already jump? Is this"—she motioned to the amassed crowd stuffed together against the line of stalled traffic—"heaven?"

"Heaven doesn't exist, baby, you know that."

She nodded sullenly. "Somehow, I knew. I mean, I always went to church—"

"Nell, do you want me to forgive you for something? Is that why I'm here?"

Nell whimpered, "Yes. I'm... I'm so sorry I made you quit smoking. I know how much you enjoyed it. I know you only did it for me. Here I am, complaining about how selfish you've been, and all I've been is selfish. Tom, I'm sorry. I should've let you—"

"Got her!"

The sudden shift of point of view was jarring. First there had been Tom's beaming face. Next she was on her back. Moonlike faces bore down on her, backlit by the blinding afternoon sun—day and night lingering in the same space. Her wrists were smashed together and restraints snapped on. They scooped her up under her arms and dragged her away. To where, she didn't currently know.

Tom still stood by the low wall. He faced the Guadalupe, as she had, but his eyes were closed. He smelled the air, as a chef samples the aroma of soup.

"Do you forgive me, Tom? Tom, do you?"

A blackness—thicker than smoke but not as substantial as water—poured off her and drifted to her sniffing husband. Tom drew the dark aura into his mouth and nose. He shivered.

"Please forgive me! Tom! Tom, forgive me." But they kept pulling her away. Down the road, into the back of a car, where a woman she recognized joined her in the backseat. Nell twisted and sat on her haunches, screaming at the rear window and, beyond that, her husband.

"*DO YOU FORGIVE ME? TOM, DO YOU FORGIVE ME?*"

Tom skipped like a broken film reel. One moment he was at the low wall, the next he was within fifteen feet of the cruiser. Then he was beside her window.

"Who is that, Nell? He kinda looks like my—"

But Nell had stopped listening because she was trying to hear what Tom was saying. He mumbled, and she couldn't decipher his words through the glass.

"Roll the window down!" she screamed to no one in particular. "*ROLL THE GODDAMN WINDOW DOWN!*"

The woman said, "Nell, is that—"

"Roll the window down!" demanded Nell.

"Daddy?" said the woman beside her.

Something in the woman's question struck Nell in the chest, and Nell yanked her legs out from under her so she could sit down and look at the black-haired woman.

"*Daddy?*" Natalie repeated. Eyes gleaming. The off-duty trooper looked starstruck. "Daddy, is that you?"

"No," Nell whispered. She glanced at Tom, then back to Natalie. "No, no, no..."

"You look so good," Natalie said. She clasped her hands together at her breasts. Tears streamed freely down her face.

"No," Nell said again, and looked over Natalie's right shoulder into the reflection of the swirling darkness behind her, hovering on the other side of the window. "That's... that's not your daddy."

"Yes, yes it is." Natalie pointed, like a child trying to inform everyone of exactly what bike she wanted for her birthday. "He's right there!"

Nell shook, but she refused to break eye contact with the undulating darkness over her own shoulder. She swallowed hard, steeled herself, and slapped the everloving shit out of the trooper. Natalie's jaw jerked left. Nell's right hand stung, but she pushed through the pain. She grabbed the woman by the cheeks and wrenched her around to look at what Nell herself could see, that what was outside the rear passenger side door glaring in at them wasn't Tom Morgan, and it sure as hell wasn't this woman's *daddy*.

Natalie screamed. Nell didn't blame her.

Sanity flooded in and Nell Morgan saw everything very clearly. Aside from the freak made of nighttime standing beside her window, there was a dark-haired man with clean features standing by the front of the cruiser. He wore a blue suit, was possibly FBI, maybe statie—which one, Nell wasn't sure, but she knew a company man when she saw one. What she hadn't seen before was the look of terrified confusion plastered all over his face. She had no idea who or what he was seeing, but she knew in her heart it was neither Natalie's father nor Tom Morgan.

"What is that?" Natalie asked, trembling.

"I don't know," Nell answered.

"I mean, what in *the actual fuck* is that thing?"

"Do you know the man standing outside, in front of the car? Him?" Nell pointed.

Natalie, without taking her eyes off the nighttime man, nodded. "Markum. His name's Frank Markum."

Nell was shocked at how much better she felt, how clear her mind was. Still, the image of that darkness coming off her, and Tom (or whatever that thing was) sucking it up like spaghetti good enough to make you orgasm from taste alone, was stamped on her psyche.

"Do you have his number?" Nell asked her backseat companion.

"Yeah," Natalie said, quite flippantly, as she continued to watch the mercurial darkness.

"Call him and tell him to get in the car." When Natalie didn't move directly, Nell added, "Now, please."

Natalie shook her head as if she were disagreeing with Nell's request, yet reached into her pocket and pulled out her cell phone.

CRUELTY

MARKUM

"Did you hear me, faggot?" Papa Markum asked him. Frank Markum willed his mind to clear, begged that he wasn't right here, right now. Papa Markum took a single step forward before glancing at the cruiser then back to Frank.

"Wha... what do you want me to say? Haven't I said enough?" Frank shook his head for the umpteenth time. He was a man of sound mind, and considered himself more than just sane. Frank considered himself well-put-together, on-his-shit, composed, and overly perceptive. The antithesis of the Mad Hatter—the Sensible Haberdasher. Still, Papa Markum was here, in the flesh, giving him that same cross-eyed stare he'd given him every day for all his life. The left eye was lazy, perpetually studying the lumps and bumps of a nose that'd been broken several times during Papa Markum's fifty years of street fighting and illegal cage matches. He was such a tough man, simply bursting with machismo, and Frank had known that coming out of the closet would destroy his old man. He'd been wrong, though. Destroy hadn't been a strong enough word. Annihilated, perhaps. Eradicated, maybe.

People milled about, walking past the parked cruiser and the standoff between Papa and Junior Markum, seemingly unaware that anything was awry. Most passed in a daze, as if the entire population of Kerrville had been drugged and corralled like sheep waiting to be shorn of their wool. Frank saw all this because he didn't want to look at his enraged father. He didn't want to peer into those red-rimmed, bloodshot eyes. Didn't want to smell the aroma of tequila and cigars on Papa Markum's breath. The pieces of dinner stuck in his front teeth.

Frank remembered it like it was yesterday. He'd just been promoted to investigator, and the world was his oyster. He wouldn't have to worry about bills or other related monetary bullshit. He could pay the old man off and never set foot in his dusty-ass house again. (Ever since Mom had left Papa for a carpenter in New Mexico the sink stayed filled with slimy dishes; moldering carpet teemed with roaches; the upholstery and every bed in the house had been infested with swarming bedbugs; you could even hear rats in the walls.) Yet Frank was the supposed failure.

He'd come through the front door with steel in his spine and four grand in his fist, the last of the ten-thousand-dollar loan Papa Markum had given him to put down on Frank's house (a house he shared with his lover, Dennis), back when Papa still had enough cash hidden in the floor vents to buy cleaning products.

Papa Markum had been watching a fight on his antique floor set when Frank let himself in. There seemed to be more than enough space between the two men—an acre if a yard. Dad scratched himself through his basketball shorts with his pinkie while the other four fingers managed not to spill an ounce of the Pabst Blue Ribbon they held; Frank lingered by the door, shivering with icy fear, as he stuck out the cash and said, "I'm gay."

"The fuck you mean you're gay?" Papa Markum barked laughter. "Get the fuck in here and stop fucking around. You're letting more fucking bugs in the fucking house. As if I didn't have enough friendly fuckers running around 'neath my feet." Papa Markum had the vocabulary of a teenage boy who'd been raised on the hard streets of the Bronx, and Frank wondered how he'd ever considered this man someone to look up to.

Frank took on an authoritative tone in an attempt to hide any emotions that threatened to bubble over his defenses. He waggled the banded bills at his father. "The state promoted me. I'm an investigator now. This is the last of the money I owe you, all right? I don't need any more loans. I don't have to hide anymore, and you don't have to like it. We can go our separate ways, like you and M—"

"That *guerro* you been shacking up with ain't your goddamn roommate, is he?" Papa said, still seemingly enthralled by the TV. He still hadn't looked at Frank.

"He's you're fucking butt buddy, I s'pose? Ya fuck him in the fucking ass while you reach around and yank his crank, huh? Go on, tell Papa all about how you diddle your fucking boyfriend, you fucking queer-bait douchebag. I didn't fucking whack Big Bart Baskins 'cross that glass jaw of his so I could raise no fucking cream puff. My papa didn't come over here on a boat from Panama so you could get shit on your fucking dick. Get the fuck outta my house."

Papa Markum's words stung, but Frank had expected them. Still, somewhere inside—perhaps buried deep in the darkness where he'd sheltered his inner child—he was in agony. He wouldn't show his papa any weakness, would not give him the joy of seeing how his words lanced and lacerated like tangible blades.

Frank had knuckled back a tear before it betrayed him, laid the cash atop the television (where Floyd Mayweather Jr. was currently remodeling someone's face), and marched for the front door.

As Frank pulled the door inward, Papa Markum said, "You make me fucking sick, you fucking faggot."

Frank, foot ready to step out from his father's life and away from his sharp words, faced his father once more. He shook his head imperceptibly.

"I make *you* sick?" he asked his papa.

Papa Markum's eyes finally left the television screen to meet his son's. "That's right. You fucking *disgust* me."

On "disgust," spittle sprayed from Papa's mouth and rocketed through the meager light pouring in from the kitchen. The spit resembled a shooting star amid the stationary balls of gas that were actually floating dust motes.

When he'd first arrived, Frank had thought there seemed to be an acre between them. Now Papa Markum seemed too close—close enough to smell. Papa Markum stunk of pit sweat and aged corn chips. Of filth and failure. Papa Markum made Frank sick. Had suddenly become so vile that Frank thought he'd vomit in his father's lap. But instead of throwing up all over his papa, he crashed down atop him. Frank could not recall having crossed that acre of carpet, nor did he remember straddling the old man. Rage drove and blinded Frank. Fists came in flurries. Punches were returned, but more were given than received. Papa Markum shoved himself out of the chair, spilling Frank onto the infested, crawling carpet. Papa kicked him full force in the ribs, but Frank managed to wrap his arms around his father's leg before it could be retracted.

Frank yanked and rolled.

Papa Markum spun three-sixty, like a mafia enforcer trying out for the Bolshoi Ballet Company, and came down face first on the edge of his antiquated television set. The stiff cartilage of his nose was stabbed into his brain. The impact also snapped his neck. He died instantly.

Frank sat up, unaware that his papa lay dead not an inch in front of him, and rubbed his busted, bloodied knuckles. He nudged Papa Markum's corpse with the tip of one shoe. Papa didn't stir. Frank crawled to his father, felt for a pulse, and—when he found nothing to assure him that the elder Markum had survived his tumble— began to laugh boisterously. A bright relief washed over Frank, and he'd continued to laugh. Oh, how he had guffawed.

Then he had cried. Oh, how he'd wept.

Now, Papa Markum—decade-and-a-half-in-the-grave patriarch of the Texan Markums—stood beside an unmarked state vehicle under a midafternoon sun, stabbing Frank with steely eyes.

"Huh, faggot? You fucking hear me? *Answer me*, cream puff!"

What was the question? Frank couldn't remember. He rubbed at his forehead, massaging away this strange hallucination before someone snatched him up and slipped him into a pair of leather bracelets and accompanying vest. Frank had never been a fashion queen, but he thought the apparel of a crazy person might cramp his style.

"You want me to forgive you, you pussy douchebag? Does the assclown want Papa to say all's forgiven?"

In a voice no louder than a whisper, Frank said, "No. I don't want your forgiveness. I never wanted that. I liked it when you died. I liked it *so much* that I used all the training the state gave me in reverse. I covered my tracks, and you died a drunk old man who'd stumbled over his own feet. I came around a day later—because I hadn't heard from you in a few days—and found you on the floor. I called the authorities. You died, and I *walked* away. I walked away *happy*." Frank took two steps toward the Papa Markum hallucination. "You hear that, Papa? I walked away happy. And every night, I go home to the man that I love, and—"

Markum's pocket vibrated. A split second later his ringtone chirped.

Papa continued to bait him. "You're a fucking disgrace to the Markum name."

"Shut your cocksucker... whatever you are."

Without taking his eyes off Papa's ghost, Frank brought the phone up so he could see the name on the screen in his peripheral vision.

The caller ID read: NATALIE.

Frank slid the bar at the bottom of the display, answering the call. "This better be good."

Natalie's voice came quick: "That thing in the street, that isn't my father."

"No shit. He's mine."

"Huh?" she asked.

"Never mind. You got that woman under control in there?"

"Nell? Yeah, she's fine. In fact she's the one that broke this thing's spell for me. It's… I don't know what the hell it is, but it's ugly."

"That woman have any idea what this thing is? I'm not taking too kindly to it impersonating my dead family members."

A short silence, then: "She says, 'no.' She also says you need to get in the car so we can drive away. Like, *yesterday*. Got me? You got me, Markum?"

"Yeah. Be right with you."

Frank disconnected the call.

He addressed the apparition. "I don't know what you are, but I'm pretty sure you're not my papa. But, if I were you, I'd run. 'Cause if the old man ever finds out some little bitch who likes to hide behind parlor tricks has stolen his identity he'll crawl out his casket and beat the magic out your ass. For now"—he hitched his thumb at the cruiser—"I'm gonna leave, and you're gonna go to hell."

Papa Markum's eyes retreated into his skull, were replaced by two black holes.

A fetid odor scaled Frank's nose hairs. He cringed.

Years of feigning bravado had given Frank the stones to stand his ground. Though Papa Markum's transformation had about emptied Frank's bladder into his tighty-whities, Frank managed, "Nifty trick."

Papa Markum, ogling Frank with those obsidian orbs, cocked his head. "I've already fed on the Nell-lady, so I no longer require sustenance, but like many Americans, I don't eat because I'm hungry. I eat because I like the taste of my food. I've been known to eat until I burst. Then I eat some more. I'm going to devour you,

Frank Markum, and when I shit out your remains, you'll be prettier because of it."

"Sticks and stones, asshole."

Frank rushed for the driver's door and yanked it open.

Papa Markum called in a sing-song voice over the top of the car to Frank. "Do your peers know you murdered your father, Frankie? Huh? Huh, do they, you little fag—"

Frank dropped inside the cruiser and slammed the door. "Hold on," he commanded the ladies in the back, while he ripped the gear shift into DRIVE and, weaving in and out of traffic, tore hell down Main Street.

Next stop: Far-the-fuck-away from whatever-the-hell he'd left back there in the middle of the road.

THE SHOOTOUT

*N*ice *and easy. Smile for the ladies in the nurses' uniforms. Smile big and bright and proud, like you just won a lifetime supply of Lacuna Coil albums. While we're on the subject, that thin one looks like Cristina Scabbia.*

Twon endeavored to stay cool and calm, and thinking about his favorite band's sexy lead singer reminded him of Laurie, and thoughts of Laurie made him happy. Happy enough to smile like a man getting a hand job from a Shake Weight enthusiast.

"You keep grinning like that," Ollie said, from his place to the right of Kirk's wheelchair, "and these nurses are going to call the cops just on principal."

"Shuddup, muddahfuckah," Twon growled through gritted teeth.

He pushed Kirk's wheelchair by the nurses' station, nodded to each of the multi-gendered crew (four women, two men), and slowed down a smidge as he tried not to look like he was rushing for the elevator. He could feel the cold steel of the red-handled butcher's knife where it hid in the crack of his ass, sharp side pressing against the seat of his pants.

Will trudged along to Twon's left, looking as if a grizzly bear had dropped a big sturdy turd in his corn flakes. The deaf boy held his broken arm to his flank as if the appendage were in danger of falling off if he became unmindful of it.

The four of them made it to the elevator without any nonsense. Twon pressed the down button.

What kind of hospital is this, Twon wondered, *where you can just walk in and steal a patient, then stroll right out the way you came in?*

"Excuse me?" came a voice.

Here we go, thought Twon, as he turned to face the fat white lady in the orange scrubs. Her five o'clock shadow was darker than his.

"Has he been discharged?" she asked, with her hands on her hips and attempting her best impersonation of an overweight, crimson-cheeked Nurse Ratched. Then, before Twon or Ollie could answer, she continued. "I don't think he's been discharged. 'Chelle"—she called to a thin woman leaning over the edge of top of the nurses' station, as if she were a cat and someone had shaken the treat container—"Get me the chart for four-thirty-eight, will ya? I don't think he's supposed to be leavin'."

"A-M-A," Kirk grunted.

In tandem, Twon, Ollie, and Chubby Nurse Ratched all said, "Excuse me?"

"I'm leaving A-M-A... *against medical advice*." Kirk said, this time a little louder. "You bitches are slow with the pain meds and quick with the back talk. Ain't never heard bitches so yappity in my life. Y'all need some real niggas in yo life to show you what's up. If you were my bitches, I'd—"

The elevator slid open and Twon shoved Kirk inside with a mule kick.

"Ya heard da man. A-um-A. Again' medic services... or some shit." Twon stepped aboard the lift, and Ollie followed. Will had already pressed himself into a corner of the elevator, his damaged arm cradled like a newborn across his chest.

"Well, I..." Chubby Nurse Ratched's voice trailed away as the doors closed.

Twon slapped Kirk hard across the cheek. "Next time, you don' talk unless we tell you what ya need to be sayin', seen? Muddahfuckah tryin' to get his ass killed, Ollie! I's tryin' not to murder every muddahfuckah in this bombaclot hospice, but I'm mad impatient, seen? Mad fuckin' impatient."

"He saved your ass," Ollie said. "Calm down."

Twon slid the heavy knife from the crack of his ass. "You keep tellin' me to calm down, Ollie, and I'll calm down ya throat with dis 'ere blade!"

"Yo! Get that out my face, dog!" Kirk, mindful of the sharp edge, waved the slimy blade away. "You nasty fucker."

Twon whapped Kirk across the forehead with the side of the knife. Kirk erupted from his seat. Ollie shoved the wheelchair back under Kirk, forcing the body builder to crash back down.

"Watch yourself, swole boy, or I'll let him stab your ass again," Ollie warned.

"Fuck you, man. That's fucking disgusting! You saw where he had that knife!" Kirk raged, as he wiped at his forehead.

Twon didn't see anything smeared across the knife, or Kirk's brow for that matter, but there was now an underlying odor of warm-man-ass permeating the elevator. He tried to recall the last time he'd bathed and came up with zero results. It's a wonder Laurie ever wanted to be around him. He glanced up at Ollie and found his brother bone-white. Ollie pointed to the ceiling, in the corner directly above Twon.

The cook, following the path of his brother's index finger, craned his neck. At first, Twon couldn't figure out what had blanched Ollie's face. The ceiling was mostly acoustical tiles. Nothing odd...

Then he saw the black dome, wherein a pale red light blinked like some insidious one-eyed demon, suckling the breath from the cook's body. Inhaling wasn't the problem. Twon couldn't push out the pent up breath that he hadn't realized he'd been holding. In a great explosion of carbon monoxide, he released fire for his lungs. He only wished it were true fire, the kind hot enough to melt that black carapace and the camera hidden inside its shell.

Norman Chambers—gun enthusiast, father of three, grandfather of six, and former police chief of Endeavor Springs, Colorado—sat in front of a bank of monitors within his security office, which was located off the lobby of Kerr County Medical Complex. He'd been working for Omni Security (the group that the hospital outsourced for security personnel) for the past nine years. After retiring from his role as head of Endeavor Springs' police force, Norm had relocated with his wife Veronica to Kerrville in an attempt to live a boring, downhome kind of life. His cholesterol had skyrocketed soon after, and a heart attack seemed to be on the horizon for the once-fit police chief, so Norm had applied for a position as head of security with Omni, but had only been given an entry-level position. Still, it was work—work that would see him healthy if for no other reason that he'd be mobile for twenty minutes out of every hour during his eight-hour shifts while he made his rounds of the hospital.

He was one of the lucky ones. Most cops died within five years of leaving the force, but after taking the security job, Norm's blood pressure and bad cholesterol had dropped like the booty of a video vixen.

Norm filled out his rounds report, noting everything as clear and undisturbed, while he rolled a toothpick back and forth across his lips with his tongue. His stomach grumbled, and he wondered briefly where Tony was with the subs they'd ordered from Pompeii Café over an hour ago.

As if Norm had spoken of the devil, he heard the latch click on the door to the office and witnessed all five-foot-nothing of his coworker enter the small confines of the room.

Tony was a Hebrew pervo, or at least that's what Norm called him. Tony always eagle-eyed the monitors during the nurses' change of shift so he could ogle the swaying, swiveling asses of the scrub-adorned ladies as they ambled out to the parking deck and their respective rides. Once, Norm had even caught his middle-aged partner rubbing crotch. When Norm suggested that Tony quit tugging his tube steak at work, Tony had shrugged off the comment, saying he'd had an itch. An "itch" was a good thing to call it, but Norm would have gone with "compulsion".

Tony's hooked nose seemed to bob independently of his body's movement, an anomaly Norm couldn't quite wrap his mind around. The nose didn't seem to move until Tony was stationary, and likewise was inanimate while the man was in motion. Norm had seen many a Jew schnoz in his days, but Tony's stood out further than all the rest. The man looked like an eagle's head had been attached to some squat fellow's torso. Norm figured Tony looked down his nose at him, but then again, Norm didn't think the kike could see that far. And to think, this was the kind of person that had killed Christ.

"Buncha bullshit cloggin' the road out there, Normy." Tony dropped a greasy bag down atop the desk and wiped his nasty hands on his wrinkled uniform slacks, leaving dark trails in the khaki. "Some bitch tried to off herself in the Guadalupe. I swear, I thought I was back in New York, what with all the people fuckin' about. Hope you're hungry. Those sammiches ain't gonna be hot much longer."

Tony talked. A lot. That was Tony, though, all words and nose hair.

"Thanks," Norm grunted.

"Didja hear 'bout that serial killer's momma? What's his name? Been all over the fuckin' news today. That Rest Stop Dentist motherfucker Arkansas executed a year back? His mom killed herself. Blew her brains out.

Killed some lady and her kid 'fore she done it, too. Guess she couldn't live with the fact she raised—"

Norm was elbow deep inside the greasy paper sack which held his sandwich when Tony broke off. He glanced up at his partner. Tony's brow furrowed, nose crinkled, and the man seemed as if he'd seen a ghost.

"The fuck that guy doin'?" Tony asked.

Norm followed Tony's line of sight to the monitors. His gaze floated over each screen, looking for whatever oddity Tony was talking about.

On camera eight, the one located inside elevator two, a black man was waggling a butcher's knife in the face of a chubby white man. Another black man was seated between the two, but this one was in a wheelchair.

"Goddamn it," Norm said, as he rose from his chair. He popped the leather strap from over his .357 and strode toward the door. "And I was fuckin' hungry, too."

He spat his toothpick into the trash can beside the desk and opened the door.

Ollie could have killed his brother if it wasn't for the fact that Momma would hunt him down and shove an ample amount of voodoo up his ass until he vomited juju all over the carpet of their unfurnished home if he so much as thought about laying a finger on Twon with violent intent.

"You're fucking retarded, you know that? Huh? You're a fucking moron with an anger problem, Twon, and you're going to get yourself, or me, killed."

Twon looked down from the black dome in the corner of the elevator's ceiling. His face suddenly ashen, Twon looked like a specter who'd just realized he was no longer among the living.

"You t'ink they watchin' those things this time o' day?" he asked Ollie.

"Don't know, but you better hope and pray they ain't. If I gotta fight my way out of this goddamn hospital on account of you being a goddamned idjit, I'll have your balls for breakfast."

The body builder in the wheelchair chuckled softly.

"What's so funny, asshole?" Ollie growled.

"You guys are like motherfuckin' Keystone Cops without badges."

"What you say, muddahfuckah?"

"Shut up," Ollie ordered his brother. "We ain't got time for this shit."

The elevator's floor display signaled with a shrill ping that they'd arrived in the lobby. The doors rolled open, and if Ollie had eaten this day, he quite possibly might have shat himself.

Lumbering across the lobby, his hand on a rather nasty looking revolver, was a man in a khaki rent-a-cop uniform. Ollie wondered when the hell hospital security had started carrying firearms and decided that information could be gleaned another day. First, they had to get out of Kerr County Medical Complex without getting arrested... or filled full of lead.

"Exit the elevator... slowly," the gray-haired rent-a-cop commanded, his hand still hovering over that cannon on his hip. Behind the older man was a short-shit guy with a sharply-pointed nose that hung down over his cupid's bow and almost touched his upper lip.

"Gitcher hands up!" called the Nose.

Ollie kept his eyes trained on the cavalry coming to the rescue of the body builder and his deaf companion, but he could see Twon pushing himself back against the wall. Ollie smiled, knowing that the two men couldn't see Twon hiding behind the door controls.

"Where's the guy with the knife?" the old man asked.

"Yeah, where is he?" echoed the Nose.

With his peripheral vision, Ollie saw Twon press the CLOSE DOOR button. Finally, his brother had done something with that brain of his.

"He fuckin' vanished, guys. Poof! Damnedest thing I ever saw." Ollie clapped his hands. The old man glared at him with squinted eyes.

"All you get out here, now. I'mma count to—"

The elevator doors began to slide closed.

"Uh-uh, no you don't!" the Nose hollered as he rushed forward, arm outstretched, and shoved his hand in, causing the motion sensors to reopen the doors.

Twon slashed at the man's wrist. The knife entered flesh, sliced upward, and peeled back a layer of the man's forearm. The Nose squealed in pain and fell against the open frame. Twon stepped forward and shoved the knife into the side of the Nose's neck. The blade slid through easily and caught in the rubber gasket of the elevator door.

"Jesus Christ," the old man barked, as he drew his revolver from its holster.

Ollie shoved Kirk out, ducking low behind the body builder in the wheelchair so as not to be an easy target. Rolling backward, Kirk braced himself on the armrests of the chair. Ollie almost laughed when he saw the big guy screw his eyes closed, as if waiting to be shot in the ass.

Ollie slammed the chair into something that he hoped was the old man with the hand cannon. It was not, for when he glanced around the chair Ollie found a potted palm frond gaily waving its branches at him.

Ollie glanced right, directly into the barrel of the old man's gun. The old man thumbed the hammer, drew it back, and then the side of his face exploded, showering Ollie with meaty chunks and warm blood.

Twon stood in the open elevator, his feet wide, double-fisting the .45 he'd stolen off the Nose, whom he'd pinned to the elevator door with the red-handled butcher's knife.

"Giddup, Ollie. Shum on!" Twon reached back inside the lift and snatched the deaf boy's hand, and then yanked the teen out into the lobby.

Ollie's ears were whining from the blast of the gunfire, but he could hear people screaming and calling for someone—*anyone!*—to call the police. Ollie, steeled by the fact that the cops would have to first be called, and then have to travel to the hospital, stood, feeling slightly unsteady on his feet.

Ollie spun Kirk—who was swatting bits of brain from his face—around and shoved him toward the sliding glass doors and the safety of the turnabout.

"Gotta do everyt'ing myself," Twon growled, as he yanked the deaf guy forward and pushed him toward the hospital's entrance, where Ollie was gliding the body builder through the turnabout and toward the parking deck.

All in one fluid motion, Twon shoved the .45 into the waistband of his pants, bent, scooped up the .357 from the dead man he'd shot, and jogged up behind Will.

"The parking deck, muddahfuckah! *GO!*" He jammed the gun in between the teenager's shoulder blades and ground in. The kid made a high-pitched sound, like a mouse sneezing, and shuffled forward faster, still holding his broken arm to his chest.

Twon and Will followed Ollie and Kirk into the darkness of the parking deck, leaving behind the gawking faces of a few bystanders and looky-loos on the street. Twon was highly aware of the state in which he lived, and Texas was known for its high population of individuals with concealed-carry permits, so he continued to glance over his shoulder for would-be heroes, of which he found none.

Ollie had the parking deck's elevator wide open and waiting for Twon and Will, when they finally joined them. Inside, Kirk was still wiping the contents of the old man's skull out of his eyes.

Everyone onboard, Ollie pressed the button for the third floor, and upward they rode.

All the while, as they piled into the car and raced away from the deck, Twon wondered when their luck would run out. They had their prize and an extra soul for Momma, and now all they needed was their money, which the deaf fucker would help with.

"That was like some wild west shit, bro," Ollie said, as Twon navigated through traffic.

After a moment's silence, Ollie added: "No sirens yet?"

"Don't look a gif' ho'se in the mout'," Twon said. "They had cameras e'erywhere in that place. They know my face now. They be comin'. Best belie'e they be comin'."

INNIS

"Won't'cha be my neighbor," the boy with the eye patch had said. And then he was gone.

Innis, shivering from a chill set deep in her bones, lingered in the roiling fog of this strange world. She snapped her head back and forth, looking for the obtuse child. It seemed that the more anxious she became, the thicker the mist grew, as if the fog were an extension of her own clouded psyche. Strangely, she'd have given anything for another horror to step from the white. She didn't care, as long as she had a companion in this alien realm.

The houses that had lined the street where her brother had been murdered were now hidden behind a veil of fog. Innis could only see two to three feet in front of her. She wanted to press forward, or perhaps in reverse, but her feet were planted firmly on the asphalt. Only… it was no longer asphalt under her, but sod. She pushed down with her toes, shoving her shoes into the moist earth, and was welcomed by a spring back.

"Now where the hell am I?" she asked aloud.

"Hello?" a man's voice beckoned.

Innis started to answer, then stopped herself before the first word was birthed. She had no idea who this stranger was, but deep down she was terrified he would only prove to be another monstrosity hell-bent on driving her mad.

"Hello?" the voice repeated, a tremor adding a bit of vibrato to his tone this time. He sounded as scared as Innis felt.

Don't answer, her mind pleaded.

He might know the way out of here. He might even know where here *is.*

That last voice sounded very much like Bruce the Nefarious Cocksucker, and she didn't like that one bit. Odd how, even though she was currently trapped in this unrelenting dreamscape, her ex-boyfriend continued to lurk in the shadows of her mind.

Rage burned brightly at her core, and she stoked that fire with the memory of Bruce's infidelity. How he'd been on his knees servicing another man when she'd come home from work. How she'd yelled and protested, called him a butt pirate and shit pusher. How she'd grabbed the leash, hooked it to Merlo's collar, and dragged the poor dog into a nightmare.

Talking to Merlo. Him falling asleep in the passenger seat. *BAM!* She hit something. Running it over. Bouncing and shaking as she rolled into the scrub. The car on the side of the road. The phone to her ear. The form rising from the road... rolling toward her... dragging... *something...*

Innis vomited into the grass at her feet. Even though violent tremors wracked her body, she still wondered how she could be upchucking in a dream. She recalled the way her face had hurt, the searing pain at her hairline and down her temples, across her cheeks and under her chin, until finally the pain ended and she was left... empty. Completely—

(They'll make you regret)

—hollow and uncaring. Then, all at once, every emotion had flooded back, and the boy with the eye patch had vanished. Now she was alone, her heart and mind heavy with questions and memories, but mostly fear—a crushing terror so heavy that it had rooted her in place.

"*HELLO?*" the stranger wailed. Innis, who'd been lost in thought, started and took a step backward. Her foot landed on soft, dewy grass, and slid, twisting her ankle.

A bolt of lightning arced up her calf and into her thigh, collided with her tailbone and exploded in brilliant bursts of agony. For the umpteenth time, Innis Blake ruminated on how unfortunate it was that she could feel so much pain in this nightmare masquerading as reality.

"Who... are you?" she stammered.

"My God, are you real? Please, tell me you're real!" begged the stranger.

"I don't know what's real anymore." Her voice was meek. It made her sick to think of how weak she sounded.

"Where are you?" Was the stranger crying? Innis thought the stranger was indeed bawling like a child who'd just found their puppy turned into a pancake on the road outside their house. "Can you follow my voice? Can you find me that way?"

Innis didn't think it possible. The man's words seemed to come from all directions: from the sky; from the earth; from the inky darkness above; from inside her very skull.

"No," she whispered. "I can't follow your voice."

"Goddamn it!" he roared.

"God's not here right now," she murmured. "He's abandoned us."

"Mah-Mah," cooed the fog.

Innis shuddered as the mist parted and the baby doll shuffled into view. Even at no more than a foot tall, the plaything unsettled her. The white dress with fringe around the collar and arm holes, the skirt billowing in an unfelt breeze that didn't disturb the fog, the doll's cherry-red cheeks and haunting yellow eyes, the mechanical way it lumbered toward her, heavily, as if it weighed a ton; all this melded together to make the harmless toy seem utterly sinister in nature. For Innis Blake didn't think this doll was quite what it seemed; instead she believed it a precursor to the real threat.

"What was that?" cried the stranger.

Innis assumed the man was talking about the doll.

"Mah-Mah," it repeated.

"Shut that thing up!"

She remembered how, earlier, she'd punted the doll into the mist. She sighed heavily. "I can't. It'll just come back."

"Mah-Mah."

"*SHUT THE FUCK UP!*" the man's voice screamed.

The stranger continued to rage, unseen, as the fog churned and enveloped the foot-tall baby doll once more.

Then, silence.

"Hello?" Innis called, not fully expecting an answer. Unsurprisingly, she received none.

The mineral-heavy aroma of dry dirt overwhelmed Innis's nasal passageways. She sneezed twice, violently, and when she recuperated, was shocked to find herself no longer standing on green ground but brown sand. Ahead, dust swirled into the fog, darkening the ethereal substance and weighing it down, until the mist disappeared altogether and she was left in the middle of a sandstorm.

Coughing and spitting, Innis stumbled forward, covering her face with her forearm to protect her eyes from the abrasive maelstrom. Fighting for air, she pushed through the churning dust. She attempted to reassure herself that this was nothing more than an unreality, that if she choked to death on the sand she would simply wake up. The thought did little to calm her, for she knew what awaited her in the waking world—the life-sized devil in the doll mask.

Her foot collided with something stiff and she went sprawling. The wind howled around her as she struggled to push herself back to standing. Wood under her now, Innis realized she was currently on someone's porch. A rickety rocker lazily swayed back and forth on her right. A tin can, the size and kind coffee had come in once upon a time, sat beside the chair. Behind the rocker was a four-pane window, which had a crack in the bottom left panel. The crack bisected the curious face of a platinum-haired little boy who seemed awestruck by her presence.

The groaning storm calmed to a shushing whisper as Innis stood. She dusted off her front and when she glanced back to the window, the boy was gone. She was growing tired of all the parlor tricks, the comings and goings of strangers and the souls that haunted this odd world.

A door sat ajar directly in front of her. Without thinking, Innis pushed through into the shack, for a shack it was: run down, smelling of mold and dust and sweat. An aged bench and table sat dead center of the foreroom. A fireplace lay cold and bereft of flame on the far wall. On the mantle, a single picture of the boy she'd seen gawking at her from behind the window. The kid stood next to an angry looking cowboy with a shock of platinum hair and a shiny blond beard. The older man's piercing blue eyes chilled her. The boy resembled his father, sans beard and wrinkled brow. In fact, they looked so much alike that the kid could have been the man as a boy, or the man as the boy grown up and weathered by a hard life. In the background, purple mountains lay like slumbering gods of jagged stone. Innis made note that there was no woman in the picture, and figured that was why the older man scowled so deeply.

"Who is you?" asked the boy.

Innis started, spun, and found the kid behind her, gazing up with soft, almost feminine eyes.

"Where am I?" she asked.

"I asked you the question first. Who is you?"

"Inn—Innis Blake."

"You injun?"

"No."

"Why you so dark then? Ain't seen nobody brown as you that weren't injun, and my daddy kills injuns, so's I s'pose you better git, 'fore he kills ya."

"This isn't happening." Of all the crazy she'd found herself swimming in, this little boy and his thick country drawl seemed craziest of all.

"What ain't happenin'?"

"You're not real," Innis said plainly.

"What makes you so real if'n I ain't?" The boy put his hands on his hip, and all of a sudden he was a Podunk Peter Pan devoid of tights and pointed green hat. His faded blue jeans and flannel shirt of some thick material hung loose on his frame, as if someone had let the air out of a hillbilly.

Innis shook her head, trying to dispel the nonsensical child standing before her. He couldn't be real. He was simply another apparition that would vanish once he'd served his purpose, whatever that turned out to be.

Strong hands grabbed her biceps and squeezed hard. Innis shrieked, bucked, but was not entirely surprised to see the boy begin to laugh. Hot breath played across the back of her neck, coming in raspy expulsions, as if a dog panted over her right shoulder.

"Who're you, squaw?" growled the rough voice of a man.

"Let me go," she commanded, yet knew she sounded weak.

Wet sandpaper lapped at her neck, but it didn't take long for Innis to realize that what she was feeling wasn't truly moist sandpaper at all. No, someone was licking the nape of her neck. She grimaced and tried to pull away, but her assailant only squeezed her arms tighter.

"Nuh-uh, missy. You taste too good to be lettin' go right this minute. Lody, fetch my iron from under the bed. Go'n! Git!"

The boy disappeared to the left. Innis heard a door creak open and slam shut.

The man pressed himself against her back and dug his jutting crotch into her ass. She stiffened, sensing further violation on the horizon.

The man slid his sandpaper tongue up her neck, across her ear, and over her cheek. She squirmed, praying for another shift in reality, begging to be anywhere but here. When would this acid trip end? What was the purpose, if there was one at all?

"I'm go'n bed your pretty brown ass. How you feel about that? Ever been bedded by a white man, squaw? Huh? Ever had a white dick in ya? Have ya? No difference, 'cause I'mma slide"—he pulled away and slammed back, crotch first, into her rear end—"this here white dick so far in you, you'll be spittin' seed 'til Jesus comes back."

"Please—"

He yelled into her ear: "Shuddup!"

Then: "Hurry up, Lody, or ya ain't go'n watch when I take this squaw to bed!"

"Yes, Pa!" Lody called, and a second later the boy was standing in front of her, an old-timey gun held aloft in his left hand.

"Good," the man said. "Point that at her, and if she fights, shoot her in the belly. Ya wanna shoot her in the gut so's that we can still play with her, ya understand? Takes a long time to die of a gut shot, but if you hit her heart she'll rot on us, quick like. Her squaw poon ain't no good to either of us if she's dead."

Innis bucked with everything she had and managed to wrench an arm out of his grasp. As quick as she got loose, she was captured again. He slammed his forehead into the back of her skull, and stars exploded in her vision.

"You try that again, you squaw bitch, and I'll make sure to gut you after I done drained my balls."

His rough tongue found her ear and burrowed deep.

CRUELTY

RANDY

Sheriff Randy Miser navigated his cruiser through the winding, one-way road of Eternity's Gate Cemetery. In the passenger seat, Merlo whined softly, gazing at the sheriff with rheumy eyes.

"Just gotta make sure, pup. Once I make sure, I can try and wrap my mind around what happened back at the station. I just hope that thing's gone 'fore Nick comes on."

Merlo chuffed in agreement.

Randy glanced down at his silent radio, to the dial he'd switched off. It wasn't like him to weigh personal conflict over the job, but seeing one's dead wife turn into some black-eyed demon tends to hold priority over the old nine-to-five.

(I AM FUCKING HUNGRY.)

Randy shivered. How God could allow such a thing to walk His earth was beyond him, but he knew the abomination had been no hallucination. He'd seen it with his own two eyes, smelled its breath, felt the wind of its words on his face. Whatever had come to visit him at the office had been real. There was no doubt in his mind about that.

Pastor Wally had spoken of possession during one sermon or another, and Randy wondered if Flo's appearance was something akin to that. Had some nether-beast inhabited the love of his life, then crawled from her grave for a reunion with her still-living hubby? As asinine as that sounded, Randy could come to no other conclusion. So here he was, Flo's final resting place, to find out whether or not his wife's eternal rest had been disturbed.

He parked the cruiser toward the back and left the door open so Merlo could follow if the dog saw fit. It did, and padded alongside the sheriff, panting, its drippy tongue lolling from its mouth.

"I don't wanna be alone either, big fella." Randy bent down and scratched the dog behind the ear without slowing his pace.

He stepped over the curb and into the field of the dead. Eternity's Gate was a newer cemetery and was mostly devoid of the tombstones and crosses of old. Nowadays, burial sites were marked by a small stone plaque set into the ground at the head of the grave. Randy even knew a handful of the people whose graves he passed on the way to Flo's. There was Carmen Venezuela, the woman who'd cleaned house for Randy's mother. Here was Ginger Birde, the barber who'd cut Randy's hair every Saturday afternoon while the sheriff was growing up. There was Booth and Gina—laid to rest side by side—the married couple whom Randy hadn't been acquainted with until he supervised the removal of their smoldering corpses from Booth's pickup; the drunk who'd killed them, Henry Walsh, was buried elsewhere in the world, as he had only been passing through when he'd crossed over the double line and crushed Booth's truck between his own Chevy van and a hundred-foot oak. It had been Walsh's gas line that caught fire, but that made no difference to the drunk. He'd been thrown through the window, over the hood of Booth's truck and impaled on one of the oak's branches. Randy recalled thinking Henry Walsh had looked like a bill someone had pinned with a wooden stake to a telephone pole.

Yes, Randy knew many of the dead who resided within Eternity's Gate, for one reason or another. But only Flo mattered today. He found her in her usual spot (not that she could have moved if the need had arisen), under a palm tree in the rear of the lot. His own plot lay undisturbed beside her, nothing but shiny blades of grass that would one day be ripped up so that he might once again sleep next to his beloved. Flo's own grass was just now starting to cover the dirt that'd been used to bury her. Six months wasn't any great length of time, and it seemed for a while there that her plot would be forever marred by dark brown earth instead of capped with bright green. Now, Randy could see patches coming in here and there, and he wondered if Flo herself were the food nourishing the new growth. She'd always been a giving soul.

Above him, the palm's leaves clicked together like fingertips tapping glass.

"Everything looks all right," Randy told Merlo. "So what the heck came after us, buddy?"

Merlo didn't answer.

Though the breeze was cool out here at the cemetery, Randy felt sweat on his brow. He wiped it away with the sleeve of his uniform shirt. In his pocket, his cell phone's ringtone played "That Old Rugged Cross." He dug out the device and answered: "Miser."

An excited female voice barked, "Randy? Thank God! It's Sherry, you know, with dispatch... why aren't you answering your radio? Never mind, we have a situation at the hospital. You there? Randy, are you—?"

"Yeah, sorry. What's going on at the complex?" He truly didn't want to know, but had to remind himself he was still on duty.

"A group of men killed two security guards before leaving in a car, headed west. Nick's already on scene. George and Stanley, too, but I kinda think you want to be there. DEA's on site, as well. They're thinking that lab rat had something to do with this. You know—God, what's his name—Chatham! Twon Chatham. You got me, Randy? Damn it, will ya say something?"

"I got you, Sherry. I'll... I'll be out there ASAP. I'll call in by radio when I'm on my way."

"Randy, you all—"

He hung up on her. Running a shaky hand down his face, Randy wondered what had happened to his uneventful life as a small town sheriff. Last night, some insane killer in a doll mask had killed and injured several people, leaving only a deaf kid as a witness. This afternoon had seen Randy set upon by some crazed entity capable of mimicking his deceased wife. Now someone had killed two of the hospital's security staff. If he were a cussing man, he might have asked, "What the *fuck* is going on around here?"

"They mean to drive me into retirement by way of psych eval, pup," Randy told the dog lingering at his calf. Merlo gazed up with those wet eyes, as if to offer his condolences.

"Come on, I guess. We'll figure this out after we figure out this new nonsense. Lord Jesus, gimme the strength. Sure as fire gonna need Your help."

Randy held the door open for Merlo, and the dog leaped into the car, once again taking his spot on the passenger seat. Randy plopped in, started her up, and followed the winding road back toward the exit. He stopped at the egress, checked right, then left, and found a black car speeding in his direction. Instead of chancing pulling out in front of this reckless driver—who was lucky the sheriff had more pressing business than pulling someone over for ignoring the posted limit—Randy waited for them to pass.

As the car shot by him, all four tires locked up and a gray cloud of spent rubber rose from where the tires met the road. The vehicle slid a good twenty feet before it finally came to a stop, and then the reverse lights came on. Randy recognized the car, but couldn't place from where. The driver hooked the car onto the roadside and began slamming the horn. The passenger-side door popped open and a woman with long black hair tied up in a ponytail exited the unmarked sedan. She wore a yellow tee and blue jeans. A handgun rested in a holster on her hip.

Randy slammed the gearshift up into park and got out. He met the woman halfway.

"Sheriff," she nodded at him, and Randy finally recognized her.

"Natalie? Natalie Holden, that you?"

"Yes, sir. You got a minute?" She kept glancing around, as if she were a drug dealer about to make a deal with a client.

"There's been a situation at the hospital I need to get to. Can you make it quick?"

"Hang on," she said, before rushing back to the sedan. She bent into the open door, stayed there a minute, like she was telling the driver something, then threw the door closed and jogged back to Randy.

"I'll ride with you. This might take a minute to explain. Is that okay?"

"Yeah, might could use some back up on this, anyhow. Get in."

Randy let Merlo out of the front and coaxed the dog into the back. The beagle stretched out on the bench seat and began licking himself.

Randy had met Natalie several times during her time as a state trooper, mostly when she brought in drunk drivers or those involved in fights she broke up at bars on the edge of town, out of his jurisdiction. She'd always been a pleasant lady, but as they drove back toward town, she seemed upset and frazzled, as if today had been equally as upsetting as his own.

"I... *we*... we saw something, today," she informed Randy as he drove.

Randy thought about his run-in with Undead Flo and took his eyes off the road for a second to gauge Natalie's expression.

"What did you see?" he asked.

"Not quite sure." She shook her head, as if she were attempting to disagree with herself. "I mean, it kinda looked like my dad, but Nell—Tom Morgan's wife—says it looked like Tom, and Frank Markum—"

"Wait, whoa, how'd you all get together? Why isn't Nell at the hospital?"

"Long story. Look, some freaky shit is happening and I don't know how to explain it. All I know is… something's not right."

Randy laughed mirthlessly. "You can say that again. Say you saw some weird crap, eh? I had an experience, too. Thought I was crazy."

Natalie said nothing, only stared slack-jawed at the sheriff.

"By the look on your face, I'm guessing you thought I wouldn't believe you. Heck, Nat, I don't know what I saw, but I know I saw something."

Natalie nodded.

After a short pause she asked. "Your dog?" and hitched her thumb at the rear compartment.

"Merlo's a stray some guy dropped off this afternoon. The dog's nice enough, if a little talkative. Doesn't know it's not polite to discuss religion and politics in mixed company. You know how mutts can be."

"Do what?" she asked, confused.

"Sorry, you gotta ignore me sometimes. I tend to fall back on humor when I'm nervous. My deputy says I ain't a bit funny, but what does he know? He ain't older than a tadpole himself."

She smiled, as if to say she agreed but didn't want to hurt his feelings by vocalizing such.

"It's okay, Nat. I know I'm a strange old man. Now, what brought you and the statie together?"

Natalie went into great detail about the case she and Frank were currently working on, how the DEA was involved in the Twon case, and that's when Randy stopped her.

"The DEA is already at the hospital. They're thinking Twon Chatham is responsible for the chaos at the complex. What do you guys know about him?"

"He's been cooking out at a place on Ranchero Road for a while now, and Frank says he has friends in drug enforcement who're working a stakeout of the cook's place. But it gets even deeper. That guy they found in the cooler of Bob's Bait and Fuel, well, he was one of Twon's suppliers of methylamine. Frank thinks Twon's competition—whoever that might be—took out this Landover guy to disturb Twon's production. Sick fuck was dressed like a baby doll."

Randy slammed on the brakes. Natalie braced herself on the glove box as he maneuvered the cruiser into the scrub.

He threw the car into park and twisted in his seat. "Say that again."

"Jesus Christ, you could've warned me you were going to sling us into the weeds!" she hollered.

"What about a baby doll? Or do I need to talk to him?" Randy gestured to the sedan that was following, which was now pulling to a stop behind him on the side of the road.

"Frank said the DEA has cameras out at Twon's place—that the feed caught the guy who killed John Landover, and the nutjob was wearing a baby doll mask. What? What is it?"

"One of the witnesses to the crap that went down at Bob's last night said the guy responsible was dressed in body armor... and a some kind of doll mask. Kid's name was Longmire, and I let him go. He"—Randy hitched his thumb to the black sedan and the statie inside—"told me to let him go. Sweet baby Jesus, girl, what have we stepped into? This is like some damned teledrama!"

"Can we get in touch with this Longmire guy? Maybe he can give us some more info? I don't know—give us a better idea of what we're dealing with?"

"Maybe, but we gotta sort through this mess out at the hospital first." Randy shifted into drive, signaled, and pulled back onto the road. Behind him, Frank Markum followed.

WILL

Will couldn't stop crying. He kept seeing that guard pinned to the elevator door, and the other one's head exploding. These two—the black guy and his chubby partner—had proved their respect for life to be nonexistent, so what future lay ahead of Will? Nothing good, he suspected.

Kirk sat hunched over next to Will in the backseat. Every now and then, his roommate would shake his lowered head, as if he couldn't believe the shit he'd gotten himself into. The chubby one, on his knees in the passenger seat facing Will and Kirk, kept a gun trained on both of them. Will couldn't help but think of John Travolta in *Pulp Fiction*, the way he'd accidentally shot the dude in the backseat, painting the inside of Samuel L. Jackson's car with brains and blood; Quentin Tarantino's character repeating "Dead Nigger Storage" over and over again, and Will wondering how he'd gotten away with spouting that line on set, in front of Jackson. Will hoped the chubby guy didn't have a twitchy finger, that him and his partner wouldn't need "Dead Cracker Storage" before the end of the day.

They pulled off the main road onto a secluded street. Trees stood sentinel on both sides of the road, bearing witness to the car's passing. The car passed a cabin on the left that obviously was home to an artist of some kind—various statues resided on the front lawn and side of the small home; a gargoyle perched upon the roof above the porch looked forever menacing. It had something wedged inside its mouth, something twisty and long, like a snake, but Will didn't get a good look at it as the headlights swept away and the car rounded a curve. Two minutes later, the black guy parked the car in the driveway of a two-story house. Will could see very little of the home before the headlights were switched off, but he thought that what he'd been able to view seemed rather ordinary. He didn't know what he'd expected, but a double-level Victorian wasn't what he imagined a pair of psychos would call home sweet home.

Both Chubby and his partner exited the vehicle at the same time. Chubby yanked open Kirk's door and tugged the muscular man out. Will waited for the black guy to do the same to him, but he didn't. Instead, the man pointed a gun at Will and made a come-hither gesture with his free hand. Will got out on unsteady knees and closed the door behind him with his good arm. Chubby was already at the front door, his gun shoved into Kirk's back. Kirk opened the door and was made to step inside. Will glanced at the black man once again, who was mouthing "Go" repeatedly. Will did as he was told. He expected to feel a gun in his own back, but his captor only followed close behind. Will could feel his presence, though, and that was enough to make his heart race.

The living room was aglow with soft light, which poured down from a motionless ceiling fan. The entire room was barren, absent of furniture and unwelcoming. Directly under the fan sat a woman on the floor, her legs crossed and eyes closed. She resembled the old black lady from *The Stand*, the miniseries based on Stephen King's novel of the same name. Only this old woman seemed unwell, too skinny, and Will marveled at the jutting angles of her collarbones and the skeletal features of her jawline and cheeks. She looked as if someone had vacuum-sealed her bones in aged leather. Her lips moved almost imperceptibly, and if it was English that she spoke, Will couldn't decipher the words.

Kirk was made to sit against the far wall, and Chubby motioned with his handgun that Will should do the same. Will approached, turned, and slid his back down the wall beside his roommate.

Now I wait to die, he thought.

You don't die here, *William Longmire,* a voice hissed in his head.

He grimaced, suddenly feeling as if he were not alone in his own skull. A pressure built as the alien presence stumbled through his mind like a toddler learning to walk. He felt violated by the invasion, and attempted to throw up mental walls to keep his secrets safe.

The old woman chuckled inside Will's mind.

The deaf man and the prostitute moseyed on down the road... How cute. Is this where your story starts, William Longmire? On a dark road? It is, isn't it? And what's this... what's this thing *that you met? A doll? How very, very interesting...*

"Get out of my head!" Will screamed, and it was only after he noticed Chubby, Kirk, and the unnamed third man staring at him that Will realized he'd yelled it aloud.

In front of him, the old woman placed her palms on the carpet, lifted her entire body off the floor, and turned herself around to face Will. Her eyes remained closed, but she offered him a smile.

How long's it been since you heard another person's voice, William Longmire? Twelve years? My, my, child, you've been in silence so long. No wonder you drew the doll. You do know you drew him, don't you? That no one crosses paths with it unless their fate decides such. But it wasn't you it sought, oh no—

The old woman opened her eyes and bore into Will's own.

—it was the woman who came along after you that it wanted. You were but a bridge... a means to an end.

"How can I hear you?" Will asked of the woman.

She clasped her hands over her bony chest, just above where her purple sundress showed the wrinkled lines of her sagging breasts.

Now her lips moved, but he continued hearing her with his mind and not his ears. "I speak in all worlds, William Longmire, and where I come from, you need not ears to hear."

"Who are you?" Will asked, though he'd wanted to say: "*What* are you?"

"I am but a pawn on the chessboard, *bon ti fi*. I have my masters, as do you. My boys, as violent as they can be, are good men. They only wants what is best for Momma. You understand that, don't you, William Longmire?"

Will nodded, although he hadn't a clue what she was talking about.

"Twon," the old woman said, and looked toward the black man. "This young man doesn't know where your money is, but he does have a role yet to play. The other one is... not important. Ollie, would you be so kind?"

The one named Ollie spoke, but Will only caught the last word his lips formed: "Momma." It was not lost on Will that the woman was the only one he could hear. This both excited and terrified him.

Ollie approached Kirk, said something else Will didn't catch, raised his gun, and shot Kirk in the forehead.

Will screamed so loudly that he thought he heard it. He shoved off the wall, crawled speedily with one arm past the old woman, and scrambled awkwardly to his feet. He was inches from the foyer when something collided with his back, crushing him against the front door. Fingers grabbed his hair, yanked his head back, and shoved his face into the wood. Blood came, flowing from his broken nose and filling the back of his throat. He choked and spat, leaving a crimson splatter painting the door. He was dragged back by his roots. His feet tangled and he dropped to his ass. Fresh pain soared from his tailbone to the nape of his neck. The fingers released him, and Ollie, still brandishing the gun he'd used to execute Kirk, stepped into Will's field of vision.

"Get up!" Ollie mouthed quite clearly, possibly for the benefit of Will's lipreading abilities.

Will did what was commanded of him.

"Turn around," Ollie ordered.

Again, trembling uncontrollably, Will acquiesced to his captor's demands.

The man named Twon was already dragging Kirk's body by the feet into the kitchen area, a wake of blood staining the beige carpet. Will averted his gaze, not wanting to get a good look at what had become of his roommate's head. Instead, the security guard's exploding skull flittered past his mind's eye, and Will was sick. He retched onto the carpet—nothing but bile and foam—and was instantly dizzy. The world canted, righted, swayed starboard.

"He gone to hell, that one," the old woman mused, chuckling. "He wasn't a good man, William Longmire. Remember? He the one got you into this mess in the first place. At least you blamed him for it, didn't you? You the one wanted to get your dick wet, but he the one took the blame for trying to he'p a friend. Look at where *that* got him. What a sad, sad, *sad* bidness it is knowing you. Sad bidness, indeed."

The old woman cackled while William Longmire bled and wept.

CRUELTY

MARKUM

Frank watched the tape one more time. He, Natalie, and the sheriff couldn't believe their eyes. There was no doubt in Frank's mind that Twon was the man in the elevator, but no one knew who the chubby white guy was.

"The kid holding his arm is William Longmire. You remember him, don't'cha, Markum?" Randy asked, looking obstinate. "He's the one you told me to let go. Said he wouldn't be needed after all. Recall that? Now here he is, tied up with your billy goat and his buddy. What I want to know is, who's the Hercules in the wheelchair?"

Frank ignored the sheriff's jibes. "I haven't a clue. Natalie, you know him?"

She shook her head, and her ebony ponytail wagged back and forth like the tail of an excited colt.

"His name's Kirk Babbitt," Deputy Nick Wuncell said, from the corner of the small room. "They took him out of 438, up on med-surg, fourth floor. He'd been brought in with a stab wound, but wouldn't say who did it. Nurses up there said Twon and the unknown perp were taking him home against medical advice."

"Looks like your boyfriend hurt his arm," Frank said to Randy.

Randy stabbed Frank with a gaze sharper than an ice pick. "Had I kept the kid in custody, maybe we wouldn't have another two dead bodies on our hands," Randy barked.

"On what grounds were you going to keep him detained? Being young in public? Oh, I forgot, that's not fucking illegal, is it, Sheriff?"

"Boys, please." Natalie sighed. "This crap isn't getting us anywhere. Frank, what are your DEA cohorts saying about this?"

"That we should mind our own fucking business," Frank said.

"Do you have to cuss like that?" Randy asked. "Some of us can get through the day just fine without all the language, I assure you."

"Fuck off, old man," Frank said, feigning a smile as he said it.

"How do you put up with this guy? I'm just getting to know him, but the way he's acting isn't good for my view of his character."

Natalie shrugged. "He's harsh, but smart."

"Which is more than I can say for you." Frank directed the statement toward Randy. The old man's cheeks blushed with anger, and Frank felt like he might have won this round.

"So, the DEA isn't going to do anything? They're still sitting on Twon until they have the drug wrap thing locked down? Is that it?" Natalie asked.

"Oh, no, they're on their way out to Twon's now. If nothing else, they'll get him for capital murder, and tack on whatever drug-related business they've collected on him thus far. He's going away for a long time, as will the fat bastard he's chumming around with."

"Oh, thank God," Natalie said. "Wait... what if they don't find him?"

"Stupid shit went back home after he left here. My connection said they pulled in about thirty minutes ago. They have eyes on several rooms of Twon's house. They'll lock down that street, every ingress and egress, then come down on him with extreme prejudice. After what he did to Tom Morgan, or what they think he did, I doubt he'll ever walk again... or be allowed to continue breathing, for that matter."

Natalie eyed the live view of the turnabout outside on the monitors, and Frank caught what she was looking at in his peripheral vision: Nell Morgan, pacing back and forth between a DEA van and Frank's cruiser.

"She's gonna get her closure," Natalie said, with a weak smile.

Randy chimed in. "Now we just need to figure out what it is we all saw this afternoon."

"Does it matter?" Frank asked. He, for one, didn't want to ever think about that thing again, much less try to explain its existence. One Papa Markum was enough for this lifetime.

Let bygones be bygones, Frank thought, and smiled inwardly.

"Yeah, it kinda does matter," said Natalie. "What if someone else runs into this... this thing? Protect and serve, remember that? It's rather our motto, us law enforcement types, but you want to ignore that and say the hell with it? What's wrong with you?"

"Calm down. We have bigger fish to fry. What about this doll-faced fellow? He's still out there and no one's looking for him. Aside from us, no one knows he exists. I say we track *him* down, and make the bust ourselves."

"What do we have to go on other than this kid's"— Natalie tapped the still image of the elevator scene with the knuckle of her index finger—"testimony to the sheriff? Other than that, we don't have any leads, right, Randy?"

Randy seemed to think for a moment. "You say that whoever killed John Landover and left him in Bob's freezer was some kind of competition to Twon, Frank?"

"Yeah," Frank said, with a nod.

"Well, one of the bodies recovered from the scene had a history of selling meth. Jennifer something. I have her address back at the office. Maybe we check out her acquaintances, see if they'll spit up anything about how she came to know this doll-faced fella. Worth a shot, ya reckon?"

"Sounds good to me." Frank grinned. "How long will it take you to get the info?"

"Should still be up on my computer back at the station. It was the last thing I looked up before I ran into... whatever that was."

"Okay," Natalie said, "I need to see if Nell wants to go home or stay here to see what they've done with Tom, then I can head out with you two."

"That's a plan," said Frank. "You do that. I need to make a phone call. Sheriff, you wrap up whatever you need to here, and we can run you by the station."

Randy nodded.

"What about me?" Nick Wuncell asked from his corner. Frank started, having forgotten the young deputy was still in their midst.

"Can you handle the aftermath here?" Randy asked him.

"I don't see why not. DEA's pulling all the rank, so there's not much we can do. You go ahead with your buddies. I got this."

"You sure?" Frank asked the young man.

Nick shrugged. "I don't have any other pressing business."

"Good kid, this one." Randy patted the deputy on the shoulder.

"I have to be to put up with your sense of humor." Nick smiled.

"It could be worse," Randy said, "I could completely lack one, like you."

Frank had no idea what the sheriff and his deputy were on about, but he was glad he wouldn't have to wait around for Miser to finish up at the hospital before they left the scene.

"I'll make that phone call, and we can get out of here," Frank told them, and left the group to stare at the monitors in the security office.

Out in the lobby, he pulled his cell from his jacket pocket and dialed Dennis at home. His boyfriend's shift would have ended around an hour ago, and Dennis would have had plenty of time to get home, but the phone only rang until their voicemail picked up.

"You've reached Dennis Lariat and Frank Markum's humble commode. (*It's abode, dingle fritz.*) We're not at home right now, but you can leave a message after our dulcet tones die away into the ether and we'll get back to you before the end of days. Toodles and stuff. (*We're not using that.*) Oh, yes we—"

Beeeeeeeeeeeep!

"Hey, hon, you home?" Frank waited a count of ten then disconnected. Thinking that Dennis might have been asked to stay over because of the recent development in the Twon case, he called Dennis's cell phone. That too went to voicemail. Frank didn't bother leaving a message. As much as he disliked the man, Paul Johnson was Frank's last hope to connect with Dennis. He dialed Dennis's partner, but the balding bigot didn't answer his phone either.

"Shit," Frank growled, as he put his phone away.

"Sorry?" Moxie, the county medical examiner, asked as he strolled by pushing a covered gurney.

"Nothing, corpse monger. Mind your own business."

"Xanax, pal. Works fucking wonders. Maybe look into it sometime?" Moxie continued out, toward the coroner's van, and, before the hospital's front doors slid shut, Frank heard the man say, "Prick."

"I got a prick for you, breeder. Maybe you suck it for me?" Frank grumbled as he headed back to the security office. He shoved his cell back into his coat pocket. "Damn it, Dennis, where are you?"

He knocked on the door to the office.

Natalie let him in. "Everything all right?"

"Yeah, fine. Why?"

"You look like you could eat lead and piss bullets right about now, is all."

"The coroner pissed me off. Called me a faggot," Frank lied, and had no idea why.

Natalie's jaw dropped. "Moxie? Moxie called you that word? He seems like such a nice guy, too."

"He is," Randy said. "He's a damn good judge of character, too."

"What's that supposed to mean?" Frank asked, scowling.

"Oh, nothing," Randy smiled. "You ready?"

"Yeah. Come on before I reenact Clapton's 'I Shot the Sheriff.'"

"I prefer Marley's version, myself," Randy said, as he slid past Frank.

"You would, you old bastard."

Randy stopped in the middle of the lobby and turned slowly around. "I was in Vietnam. Did you know that, Markum? That I fought in a war, and then came home to get spit on by my fellow Americans?"

"What do you want from me, a medal?" asked Frank.

"No, I have plenty of those. What I was getting at is, I'm used to being looked down upon by people who think they're better than me for one reason or another. In other words, you don't bother me, so keep flappin' your jaws if'n you want to. Ain't no skin off my teeth. But at least I ain't hidin'."

"And what is it that I'm hiding, Sheriff?"

"That, I don't know. But when I figure it out, you'll be the first to know." Randy squinted his eyes at Frank. "What I do know is, ain't nobody as angry and downright rude as you without having a few skeletons in their—oh, what's the word?—closet? Yeah, *closet*. That's a good solid word. Fits, don't'cha think?"

Randy, whistling, turned and ambled out the doors.

"I'd like to stuff you in a closet," Frank growled. When he looked away from Randy, who was now crossing through the vehicles in the hospital's turnabout, he noticed Natalie eyeing him. "What?" he asked.

"Do you practice pissing everybody off, or does it just come naturally to you?"

"Not you, too." He sighed.

Nick Wuncell exited the office, weaved through Natalie and Frank, and approached two crime scene analysts in navy blue uniforms. Natalie waited until the deputy was out of earshot before she spoke up again.

"I don't know what your deal is, but I've been through seven levels of hell today, and the day isn't even over yet. How about we all get along until we find out who this baby doll asshole is, and perhaps lay hands on the weird fucker we met earlier today? Can you help me with that, or would that be too much to ask of State Investigator Frank Markum?"

"As you wish, m'lady." Frank curtsied.

Natalie squinted one eye at him. "You think you're funny?"

Frank shook his head. "I'd never think such a thing. One must be of a certain intelligence to crack wise, and I find that my IQ drops more and more when I'm in the proximity of people as retarded as Kerr County's beloved Sheriff Miser."

"There's no dealing with you, so I'll stop trying."

"Just go talk to Nell so we can get out of here, okay?"

Natalie crossed her arms and glared at him. "Apologize."

"Thought you weren't going to—"

"Apologize, or I go to your superiors right now and tell them you've withheld information on the murder of John Landover in an attempt to better your position on the force."

Frank ran a steady hand through his charcoal hair. "Seriously? You want to do this? Here?"

"Good a place as any."

"Fine." He exhaled sharply. "What do you want me to apologize for? And to who?"

"For starters? Yourself."

"Me? Why should I apologize to myself?"

"Because you're making yourself look bad, for one. For two, you're not this asshole you keep parading around pretending to be. I recall you being very kind to me earlier today after I got off the phone with my grandmother. Now, all of a sudden, you're this abominable asshole who can't stand being in the company of other humans. So, yeah, apologize to yourself, because you're the only one you're hurting."

"I'm sorry, *me*, how can I ever make it up to you? By shutting the fuck up. Oh, really? Yeah, you sound like an idiot when you talk to yourself aloud. Sorry about making us look bad in front of Trooper Holden. Apology accepted. Is that better, Natalie?"

"Eat a dick, Investigator."

He laughed at her, perhaps to loudly.

Natalie growled unintelligibly and rushed, stiff-legged, past him, headed for the exit. She stopped hard before storming through the open doors. She spun on him and waggled a finger in his direction.

"On second thought," she said, "eat an entire bag of dicks. A barrel of penises. A *buffet* of cock, is what I wish for you to devour. Please and thank you."

She marched outside, her apple-shaped ass swinging back and forth in a forced, mechanical sway. He found himself jealous of her ass for some odd reason. Laughing and shaking his head, Frank left the hospital.

CRUELTY

INNIS

Innis Blake slammed the balls of her fists against the inside of the closet door, screaming to be let free. How long had she been in here? Days? Weeks? Months? She couldn't tell. Time seemed to come and go at random intervals, speeding past then creeping by, her only way to judge time the crack in the roof through which she could see either sun or starry night. What had they done to her? She remembered threats of the most disturbing variety, but had the platinum-haired man and his son actually gone through with any of those threats? Damn it, she couldn't remember.

She couldn't recall the last time she'd slept, either. The last time she'd eaten wasn't even a memory anymore but a vague idea that she must have, at some point in her life, consumed food for nourishment. Ages had passed since the platinum-haired sicko and his equally disturbing son locked her in this three-by-three room. Wire clothes hangers continuously worried her hair. Untangling the knots had proved impossible. Even now they dug into her scalp or tugged at her roots, depending on how close or far she was from the cross bar.

"We're not letting you out until you've become," the man had said, an eon ago. "Once you're ripe, the Midnight Man will come for you, and you'll love every minute of the attention he plans on showerin' over you."

She reassured herself that this was only a dream. Time and time again, no matter how real everything seemed, she continually promised herself that she would wake up. There would come a period when she would open her eyes and cry out in joy because a new day had dawned. Her old bed would be under her, and she'd be wrapped in warm sheets. Bruce the Nefarious Cocksucker would be there, too, but he wouldn't be the stranger he'd become, because that had been a dream, as well. She hadn't walked in on him blowing another man. He hadn't cheated on her. How foolish was she to believe that her sweet man could betray her so? She hadn't run from the house with Merlo in tow. No, no, no, that had all been a hallucination brought on by a spot of mustard or a bit of gravy. She was Scrooge on Christmas Eve, and all she had to do to wake up was believe in the true meaning of the holiday.

Madness. All madness. And the further she slipped into the icy waters of insanity, the more sane the situation became to her. Now, time was a pretzel. It didn't pass. It overlapped. And in the interim, her mind would decay while her body remained whole and unmarred. The closet was provisional. The closet was life. If she stepped out of this alcove, if she so much as dared to restart time, her body might catch up to her soul, and her mind would implode, collapse under the ruin of decay.

God, what the fuck am I going on about?

The sun rose, lancing through the crack in the ceiling like a blade through a flimsy tent, and stabbed at her eyes. There was no subtle strengthening glow, only immediate daylight. Utter darkness, then blinding light. Midnight to afternoon in a heartbeat.

Timidly, she stared at her bruised hands, at her bloodied fingers, to the long claw marks where crimson pooled in the scratched wood of the door. Her hands were numb, unable to relay pain to her sleep-deprived brain. She'd done so much damage to herself, more damage than even the man and his creepy little boy had done.

What had they done? Had they done anything? When had they stuffed her in this closet? When had she begun her spiral into the hell that is lunacy?

Mind your matters or matters won't mind.

What the hell did that mean?

Why was she talking to herself? Did she honestly expect answers? Hadn't she answered herself plenty over the millennia she'd spent trapped in this glorified box, wherein she was anchored to hangers and babbling gibberish?

I suggest you crawl—

What?

He wuz a firmer—

For the love of God, what're you talking about?

I'm the tooth fairy, Momma, but I don't leave no—

Please, stop...

Pardon my French —

STOP IT!

His lies how they hide in the shadows he wears—

"You there?" squeaked a small voice, from the other side of the door.

"Yes! Yes, please, *help me*," Innis whimpered.

"He's coming... for *you*," whispered the boy.

"Is the bitch ready?" asked the platinum-haired man, his voice muffled through the wood.

"Oh, Papa, she ain't talkin' to nobody but herself."

"LET ME OUT OF HERE!"

"Give her more time, and she be ready, I swears it!" the boy pleaded.

"I reckon we have time. Ain't nothing but time now. Nothin' but sweet, sweet time. When the Midnight Man comes, give him my regards, you squaw cunt!" Barking laughter faded as the platinum-haired man walked away.

Innis's legs betrayed her and she collapsed. The clothes hangers tore clumps of hair from her scalp, and warm blood ran down her face in torrents. Agony washed over her, as if lava had been poured from a great height.

I am the fallen blessed—
The teeth'll lead—
Suffer the little—
Whataya lookin' at—
Canned Sir—

"What do you want from me?" she asked, in a voice so low she barely heard it herself.

"From you?" whispered the boy. "Nothing."

"Why am I here?"

"You're awaiting forgiveness."

"Forgiveness?" she sobbed. "For what? What have I done?"

"All will be known. For now, regret. Regret will welcome forgiveness."

"Fuck your riddles, you little shit! *LET ME OUT OF HERE!*"

The light through the crack in the roof vanished, simply winked out, and Innis could once again see stars through the gap. Shaking, she stood. She reached toward heaven, but her fingers could no more grasp the edges of the crack than she could remove herself from this prison. She relaxed back on her heels, leaned against the rear of the closet, and wept into her bloody palms.

"Innie?" said her brother, from somewhere inside the cramped space.

"Gerry?" she cried. "Where are you?"

"I'm home. With Mom. You coming?"

"I… I can't. I'm trapped."

"Oh," was all he said in response.

"Can you get me out of here?"

"Nuh-uh."

"Then why are you here? Are you another game they're playing with me? Huh? Using my dead brother against me… for what? What the fuck did I do to deserve any of this? *ANSWER ME!*"

"Another time, Innie, I promise. Right now, I'm late for dinner. Bye!"

Madness. Loads of it. A flood of aberrations. Neurosis personified. Her becoming. Her wasting away. Mind numb. Body slack. Giving in. Overcome with wariness. Drunk with fatigue. Collapsing. Falling.

Innis Blake raised her head from the floor. Cinderblock walls welcomed her. The chair in the middle of the room was occupied, but not by her. No, not this time. Caitlyn Blake gazed upon her daughter with morose eyes. Mother made to reach for daughter but stopped, shaking her head.

"Nine days I cried. Nine whole days after that man shot Gerald. You counted. Made tally marks on the headboard of your bed with a dry erase marker. You remember, Innis? Do you remember how many days I cried for him? And now that you need me, I can't manage a single tear. Isn't that funny, honey? Doesn't that make you want to laugh and cry at the same time? It does me, but I can't do either. Why is it that I can cry for my dead child but not for the one with a pulse? Do you know? Tell me if you know. I need to know. I need to—"

"I'm sorry, Mommy," Innis cried, her entire body hitching with emotion. "I'm sorry I let him walk home alone. I'm sorry I went off with that guy from work. I can't even remember his name, but I chose him over Gerry, and then Gerry died, and I can't remember that fucking guy's name. Gerry died because I wanted to fuck some stranger, some temp at the office, and you cried for nine days and I counted because I wanted it to end. I wanted to know how badly I hurt you because I'm the one who killed Gerry. I killed him by not being there for him! I'm sorry," Innis said, as she crawled toward her silent mother. "Please, Mommy, please forgive me?"

Everything came back in a tidal wave of memories. The cute temp with the braces smiling at her in the break room. Him asking for her number. Her saying, "What if we just, you know, went somewhere after work, huh? Do you have somewhere we could, you know, be alone?" And the guy with braces nodding, nodding because he had somewhere. Even though he had a gold band on his ring finger, he had somewhere they could go. His wife worked evenings and wouldn't be home until after midnight. Oh, how the metal in his mouth gleamed. Shone. Sparkled like stars. She wanted to kiss that mouth. Feel those braces on her neck... her breasts... between her legs... Gerry didn't want to walk home, but fuck him, she wanted this boy with the braces so badly her guts ached with yearning.

She'd called Gerry's school and had him paged to the office. He'd answered fifteen minutes later. She tried to hide her excitement, played off her true intentions as a need to work late.

"Come on, Innie, I don't wanna walk home! Band doesn't get out until after dark, and that road's scary as balls!" he'd whined.

"Speaking of balls," she'd said, "you need to grow some hair on your own. Man up, chump! Hell, wait for me if you want. I won't be long. Wait for me in the bus lane, and I'll pick you up after I get done with this new business the boss is shoving at me."

Because she was conducting business, or at the very least, she was going to show the guy with the metal in his mouth what The Business actually pertained to.

After a moment's silence, Gerry had said, "Fine. I'll wait for you."

"There you go, being a man. I'm all proud of you and stuff." She'd faked a sniffle. "Wish you could see me through the phone, kiddo, I got tears in my eyes because my baby bro's finally becoming a man. See you later, all right? Love ya!"

"Whatever." And Gerry had hung up. The next time she saw her brother, he was on a slab. Mom hadn't been able to bring herself to verify that the body was Gerry's, so Innis had gone in Mom's stead. A quiet man in green scrubs led Innis to a television set in the wall. He pressed a button, and an image flickered to life. Gerry's face, calm, serene, most assuredly dead. That hole in his neck seemingly forever wide, gaping, silently beckoning her come hither. Innis had backed away from the monitor, both nodding and shaking her head at the same time, her skull making odd oblong patterns toward the man in the green scrubs.

"Is that your brother, miss?" the attendant, or whoever he was, had asked of her.

"Yea—yes," she'd managed, trembling.

"All right. You can go back to your mother now."

Nine days...

Nine days of tears...

All because Innis had wanted to fuck the guy with braces. And what was his name? Even now, in this place of nightmares and revelation, she didn't know, if she'd ever known to begin with.

"I'm sorry, Mommy. I'm sorry I killed Gerry."

A smile slowly stretched across Caitlyn Blake's mouth. Her head tilted back, and a great darkness rose from her, like a shadow thrown against a wall. The Midnight Man stood tall above Innis's mother, roiling and mercurial, seamless and wicked. He began to chuckle, deeply, as he gazed over his new child with lustful pride.

The Midnight Man said: "Hello, Regret, and welcome to the Withered. I'm Forgiveness. How pleased I am to make your acquaintance."

CRUELTY

Dusk turned to night, and Cruelty paced across the floorboards in the main room of the cabin. It fretted over the whereabouts of its master. Never had Forgiveness been gone this long, nor had Cruelty ever been concerned about its Creator's safety before. But something was wrong. It could feel as much in the depths of its ticking heart.

It shouldn't have left the dark woman alone with Regret, but Cruelty saw no reason to bear witness to her becoming. The process had begun, and there was no stopping it now. Regret only needed time, and Cruelty could not help with matters such as these.

Ninety long years Cruelty had played its game, and memories of its many playthings were still fresh in its mind, but Cruelty lusted after new toys. Perhaps when Forgiveness returned, he would allow it to find another with which to have fun. Cruelty would bend and twist and break, and feed off their agony, whoever they might be. But first, it needed the master's permission.

Engine sounds from outside drew Cruelty to the window that faced the street. It shifted the curtain, only slightly, so that it might gaze out into the dark unseen. Yet darkness is not what it found. The road outside was ablaze with bluish-white light, and the sight caused Cruelty's eyes to burn. It had no eyelids—squinting and blinking were impossible. The light dimmed as a car crept past. Then another. And another, followed by a boxy van. Without adequate illumination inside the vehicles, Cruelty could not judge how many persons rode inside the conveyances. Many, would have been its guess, but there was no way to be certain.

Unless it went outside.

Yes... *outside.*

No, Forgiveness would be angry. He would punish Cruelty. It had been many ages since Cruelty had felt its creator's wrath, but it remembered the event well. An entire month without playthings, and Cruelty had felt as if it were going mad. Forgiveness had teased it by bringing home playthings only to suckle them himself, leaving Cruelty mere empty shells that could feel no pain. No fun, they were. No fun at all. How long ago had that been? A decade? Two? Half a century? Cruelty could not remember, but did not want a recurrence of that horrible period in its life.

But what if something had happened to Forgiveness? What if its master had been harmed or captured in some way. Cruelty wasn't sure if such a thing was possible, but nothing was out of the realm of possibility. Even the Bastard in his chasm had been beaten once, so why not Forgiveness? Wasn't the Creator always telling Cruelty that some things end so that others might begin? What if Forgiveness must die so that Regret could achieve her full presence?

So many questions, so few answers.

Cruelty watched as the boxy van rolled past, followed by no other vehicles. What if every conveyance was filled to capacity? How many souls might Cruelty rend and feed upon? Its heart ticked quicker in wanton anticipation. Its porcelain fingers tapped at the glass and matched the workings of its tinker toy heart.

So many playthings, so little time.

Forgiveness had said to be ready, that they'd be moving along soon, so why not a final harvest? Why not step out for one last night on the town, to play with the men and woman who were all but within Cruelty's grasp already? Oh, it could taste their suffering. Sweet and filling. Tart and sustaining. *Nourishing...*

CRUELTY

Below, Regret or the dark woman—it knew not which—made a noise akin to a grunting hog. There were snorts and whines, guttural, bestial sounds, and then silence. Cruelty wondered what kind of birth Regret was having? One of pain? Of agony? Of joy or hatred? It attempted to recall its own becoming, but aside from the fog, Cruelty remembered nothing. Had there been a boy? Perhaps a boy in the fog...

No matter. As Forgiveness was wont to say, "The mind only matters to the matters of the mind." Whatever that meant. What Cruelty gleaned from the saying was that, if you didn't mind things, things didn't matter. To the winged beast, the wind matters not. To the crawling creatures of the world, the earth is only a thing to be traversed. And, to Cruelty, playthings meant a reprieve from its mind. And if there was a boy in the fog of his past, it mattered not a bit to Cruelty. Where it played, destruction was conceived, and chaos was a blessed child. Cruelty needed its namesake like man needed air, fish need water, and devils need fire.

"Mah-Mah," it cooed at the window. It was the closest thing to what Cruelty truly wanted to say, which—had it the capability of actual speech—would have been, "What's the worst that could happen?"

Mind set, it rolled toward the door and, once outside, lumbered down the porch steps, journeying into the night. Toward its playthings. Toward satiation. Destruction. Chaos.

Tonight, this evening of Regret's birth, blood would flow, as if from a mother's womb.

THE TEAM

Captain Leonard Baumgartner navigated his black Crown Victoria onto the scrub, past the cabin on the left. He radioed for the team members in the cars ahead to block off the road, then called in to the special operations van to pull in behind him.

The team had been waiting for this call for two months now. Agency funds were running low, and all they had on Twon Chatham were possible drug producing activities, and not a shred of evidence that would stand up in court. The techies in the trailer at the KOA campground were good (Dennis being the more professional of the two agents), but this Chatham guy was smart, or had been smart up until today. What had changed? Baumgartner didn't know, nor did he care. What he did know was they now had video of Chatham murdering two hospital security guards. That was enough to appease the director, and now they could move in. Possible hostages could complicate the situation, but Baumgartner had a taste for blood, and anyone who stood in his way of busting this area's meth supplier could take a flying fuck on a rolling doughnut for all the shits he gave.

Twon Chatham's residence was still half a mile away, around a curve and down a ways, but wholly out of sight. Baumgartner could set up operations here and not be noticed. That was, of course, unless Chatham and posse decided to make a break for it. The road on which Baumgartner was currently parked hit a dead end two miles down. There was no place for the cook to go, aside from deeper into the woods. If that were to happen, Baumgartner's team would hunt him down like the dog that he was.

"Forward to Lion, you read?" called Hank in car one.

"Copy. Hold position. We're waiting on go ahead from KOA." They'd yet to hear from Dennis and Paul about the situation inside the house. If it took much longer, Baumgartner would have to go in blind to save face with the public. No doubt media leaks would bring news crews, and the last thing he wanted was to explain why they'd blown the shit out of a residential house with the knowledge that civvies were inside. If only he knew whether or not the two unknowns were part of Chatham's crew. He hated not knowing above all else. He wasn't one to play dollar scratch-offs, much less risk the PR nightmare that was dead hostages.

"Holding," called Hank.

In his rearview mirror, Baumgartner saw Gregory Hyatt (Hotel to his friends and coworkers) step out of the cab of the Spec Van. Hotel waved with one hand while the other fished in the pocket of his flak vest. A second or two later, Hotel lit a smoke and blew a cloud of red smoke—tinted that color by the brake lights from Baumgartner's car—into the night air.

A ciggy sounded good. Baumgartner got out to join him, making sure the window on the Crown Vic was down so he could hear the radio when Dennis or Paul checked in.

Four heavily armed grunts, with whom Baumgartner had only a passing acquaintance, resided in the back of the Spec Van. Technically, Hotel was in charge of the squad, but Baumgartner was in charge of Hotel. Trickle Down Rank, was what Baumgartner called it. Still, he respected Hotel enough not to step on his toes in front of his men.

"Got an extra one, Hotel?" he asked, as he approached the clean-shaven, square-faced white man.

Hotel nodded, causing the night vision goggles perched atop his head to shake, and took the cigarettes from his pocket again. He shook a smoke from the soft pack. Baumgartner took it with a smile. "Got a light, too?"

"All ya brought was the habit, huh? Thought they paid you fuckers the big bucks, but I gotta support your habit, too?"

"What good is all this money if I'm burning it up?"

"You could give some to us little folks. Shit, least you could do is put in a good on my a getting promotion."

"Duly noted," Baumgartner said, nodding. "I should do this more often. Shoot the shit with you guys. Get to know my team during these excursions."

"Naw, boss, ya shouldn't."

Baumgartner eyed the grunt with suspicion. "How you mean?"

"Feels like you're the ugly girl offerin' blowjobs to the football team, if you buy what I'm sellin'. We're gonna do our job whether we like you or not, ya see? You playin' nice with the front lines don't do nothin' but make you look like a brown-nosin' pussy. Better to share a smoke and a story once in a while and call your public relations done for the month."

"Duly noted."

"And stop sayin' that. You sound like a paper-pushin' fuckwad."

"Right."

"How long this gonna take, anyway?"

"Just waiting on our tech guys to ring us back. They have eyes on the inside, but we haven't been able to call them up. I might have to send a car out there if—"

Over Hotel's left shoulder, something moved at the tree line. Something big. There and gone, like a bear crossing from one tree to another in the darkness. The glare from the headlights didn't reach far enough into the woods, but were bright enough to make Baumgartner squint.

"What?" Hotel said, cutting his eyes to the side but not turning to face the trees.

"Shhh," Baumgartner hissed.

Hotel grinned, whispered: "You think this guy's smart enough to have lookouts?"

The thought hadn't even crossed Baumgartner's mind, and he chided himself inwardly, because this noodle-brained lackey had figured it out before him.

"Take two men," Baumgartner told Hotel in a low voice, "and flush whoever this is out. Nonlethal and quiet, you got me? I want to question this person."

"Yup, boss, I got you. I love a good hunt." The way Hotel grinned caused a shiver to run down Baumgartner's spine.

Hotel was kind of glad to be away from his limp-dick captain. The man was all right for short periods of time, but his getting-to-know-you act rubbed Hotel the wrong way. At the back of the van, he tossed his smoke into the street and yanked opened the doors, and then gave hand commands for Felix and Jules to follow him. When both men climbed down, Hotel patted them on their utility belts, directly over their stun guns. Felix nodded, and Jules held up his AR-15. Hotel shook his head, and they slung their rifles over their shoulders. Hotel tapped their NV goggles, and both men brought them down over their eyes. Hotel did the same.

He pointed to his eyes then held up one finger. They were searching for one man. Then he shrugged. Maybe more. He laid a finger over his lips, signaling the need for silence. Hotel hitched a thumb toward the woods, and his crew advanced into green-tinted darkness.

Though fear was not an emotion with which Hotel bothered himself, his heart rate accelerated all the same. Memories of hunting moose with his uncle Kerry during winter trips to Maine came flooding in, and Hotel smiled.

He passed glowing green tree after glowing green tree, noting not much difference between any of them. He could hear the barely audible footfalls of Jules and Felix as the two men moved away from him, on the diagonal, as they'd been trained, to cover as much of an area as possible.

Hotel hadn't a clue what or who he was looking for, but he kept his stun gun out in front of him all the same. Any hint of movement would prove a shitty day for the party at the other end of his stun gun's barbs. Whoever was out here knew how to be quiet. As silent as the woods were, there was no doubt in Hotel's mind that Jules, Felix, or himself would hear, if not outright see, someone fleeing, should their prey decide to bolt for it.

He progressed.

Baumgartner had watched the team of three enter the woods, and now stood at the back of the van, smoking his cigarette down to the filter. When the end burnedhis lips, he flicked it into the scrub. He could hear nothing coming from the two men who remained in the back of the van, but was oddly certain that they spoke of him. He always thought that these grunts didn't have an opinion of him, but the way Hotel had acted made Baumgartner think that, perhaps, he was the butt of some joke, as if he were some superior to be laughed at.

The need to know what the remaining two men were talking about caused him to turn.

Fingers grasped his neck, crushed his throat, and lifted him high above the ground. His feet slammed into something solid, over and over again, and he was vaguely aware of a soft tick-tick-ticking, like that of a clock at half speed.

The way the hand held him, Baumgartner could not look down, for the fist dug into the bottom of his chin, forcing his head up at a sharp angle. He couldn't even see his attacker's face, and that scared him even more than the fact that he could no longer breathe. His head slowly twisted left then whipped hard right, and the last thing Baumgartner heard was the sound of his own neck snapping like a twig.

Henson and Clark were not talking about their superior, Captain Leonard Baumgartner. In fact neither man spoke one word because each man hated the other. Rumor had it that Henson was an informant for Internal Affairs, and Clark had a cocaine problem he didn't want anyone at the DEA to find out about, so the last person he wanted to chitchat with was a possible snitch. Henson was not working for IA, but he did know about Clark's obsession with nose candy. Everyone did. It was a running joke about how Clark couldn't be trusted on site of any major busts because he might snort up all the evidence. The only reason no one turned Clark in was because, like the criminals they fought in the war on drugs, all problems were to be dealt with in-house. They tended to their own, and rats were no better than the enemy.

So both men stared at different points on the wall across from them, until there came a knock on the door. Clark didn't move. Neither did Henson.

The knock came again.

Clark sighed, stood, and went to the rear of the van, his footsteps ringing out on the steel floor and resounding off the wall, making Henson grimace.

Clark opened the doors, and took a step back. "What the fuck?"

Henson saw nothing of what Clark saw, for the other man was in the way. In a blink of an eye, Clark was on his back, being dragged from the van by one leg. The man rolled, dug his fingers into the corrugated steel of the floor, and tried to hold firm. His fingertips left eight neat, bloody trails as he was ripped from the van.

Henson, who'd temporarily been shocked into immobility, shot to his feet. He aimed his rifle at the darkness outside. The glare of the overhead lamp made it hard to see, so he dropped his NV visor and clicked off the overhead.

For a split second all Henson could see was bright white, then his goggles adjusted and he was left staring into the mouth of the open van. His breath was ungodly loud in his ears as his lungs raced to keep up with his now-speeding heart. He swung his rifle left and right, sighting every flaw in his vision. He almost shot a pothole behind the van because it looked vaguely human shaped. The team all wore vocal cord communication devices, but Henson refused to take either hand off his gun to activate his radio. Surely Hotel, Jules, and Felix had heard Clark screaming. They'd be headed back. No doubt about it. All he had to do was wait.

What about the suits in the other cars? Where were they? Fuckers probably had their windows up and their radios blaring Miley Cyrus.

Or maybe they were dead. Jesus jumped-up Christ, they could be dead, couldn't they? Henson's heartbeat and respiration quickened further, and he felt suddenly dizzy. Remember your training, he tried to tell himself. Training said—

Something round and heavy was flung into the back of the van from the edge of the doors, as if someone had tossed a ball in without looking at their goal. Henson almost shot it, would have had his finger been on the trigger instead of alongside the trigger guard. The black orb whizzed by him, and against his better judgment, he turned to look at what had been thrown.

Clark gawked up at Henson in horror. But not all of Clark. Just his head.

Henson was screaming, and he couldn't stop himself. Shriek after shriek shot from his mouth, for he had never seen anything so horrible. Hell, he didn't even watch horror movies, was too squeamish. All of a sudden, Henson wasn't so sure he'd picked the right profession.

The back of the van dipped, so much so that Henson stumbled backward. He feared he would stagger right out the back of the van, ass first, so he twisted and smashed face-first into a barrier of some kind. He was scooped up under the arms and shoved upward, like a battering ram, into the ceiling of the van once, twice, a third time. Henson was unconscious well before his skull gave way.

Hotel had heard Clark's scream, as had Jules and Felix, and now all three were regrouping. Hotel reached the side of the road first, actually saw the big fucker climbing into the back of the Spec Van. He raised his stun gun, but the guy disappeared beyond the edge of the doors before he could get a shot off. Hotel sidestepped, slow and steady, until the perp's back was in view. He pulled his Taser's trigger, and the barbs found homes in the man's back.

Nothing happened. The man didn't so much as flinch. Several great thuds came from the back of the van, and in the dim glow of his night vision goggles, Hotel could vaguely make out a shape being shoved repeatedly into the ceiling of the vehicle.

Where were Henson and Clark?

Was *that* Henson or Clark?

"Man down! Sweet fuck, somebody took his head!" Jules called from the tree line. Hotel glanced away for only a moment, to see what Jules was talking about, and saw that he must've stepped right past his dead team member when he'd exited the woods. Whether it was Clark or Henson, Hotel didn't know, but the human shape was definitely missing its head.

When Hotel faced forward he had a brief moment of hesitation before dropping the Taser and unslinging his rifle. This didn't make any sense. Not one fucking shred of explanation was to be had.

Was that—?

Couldn't be—

A statue of the Mother Mary stared down at him with hollow eyes. A dark, fleshy mask clung to an otherwise stone face. The being stepped down from the van, and the shocks, having been released of their heavy cargo, rose a good foot.

"I will make you"—the thing said in a tremulous female voice—"*regret.*"

CRUELTY

TWON & OLLIE

Twon crouched in a catcher's stance in front of the deaf kid, who was sitting with his back to the fridge, next to his dead friend.

Twon stuck the gun under the kid's chin. "I'mma ask you this one more time, seen? Then I'mma blow the top of your head into my icebox. Where at my money?"

"I don't know," Will sobbed. "I don't fucking know."

Twon thumbed back the hammer on the .357 he'd taken from the dead security guard. "Goodnight, muddahfuckah."

"Quit that shit. Momma wants him alive." Ollie had been pacing back and forth from the living room to the kitchen, but now he stood next to the dining room table and leaned on a wooden chair with latticework and angels carved into the back support.

"Twon!" Momma called from the living room, and her voice echoed throughout the house. "Leave that boy be, now. I told you he don' know where your money is!"

"You gonna talk, blood. Belie'e that." Twon ground the barrel into the underside of the kid's chin again before standing. He kicked the kid's leg, and Will squeaked in fear.

From somewhere outside, a sound akin to someone cooking popcorn resounded through the night.

"What that?" he asked his confused-looking brother.

"Is that gunfire?" Ollie asked.

"Sure hell sound like it."

"Ah, the time, it has come, boys. Come 'ere. Come 'ere and see for your own eyes!" Momma cackled, as Twon and Ollie raced to where she stood at the window.

The curtains were drawn, and diffuse light from the ceiling fan reached out across the front lawn like seeking hands.

Standing at the edge of their property, where the grass met the road, was a hulking shape. Twon rubbed at his eyes until they burned, and then took another look.

No doubt about it, the person was wearing an old baby doll mask. And he was huge. Fuck-all big, with curly black hair framing that silly-ass face.

"Who this muddahfuckah?"

"He's dead, whoever he is," Ollie growled.

"No! You don' go out there! Ollie!" Momma staggered and grabbed after Ollie as he made for the door.

"We're sittin' on a basement fulla cash, and a shed fulla dope. I ain't letting some weird fucker draw any unwanted attention to us before we can collect everything and leave. Get off me, Momma!" Ollie ripped his arm from Momma's frail grip, threw open the front door, and headed down the stone path that bisected their front lawn. Twon didn't follow. The kitchen, even though silent, called to him. He crept back into the dining area.

"Muddahfuckah!" he roared.

The back door stood wide open.

And the deaf kid was gone.

Ollie aimed the gun at the bigger-than-life baby doll, holding it sideways, like a true gangster, and spewed his threats, "I'm gonna give you until the count of three to get your fat, Halloween-giddup-wearing ass off my property before I blow what little brains you got out the back of your head. One!"

"Mah-Mah" it cooed.

"Two!"

The baby doll rolled forward, tossing its shoulder out first, as if it needed the momentum before it could even begin moving forward.

"Three!"

Ollie pulled the trigger three times, and three times he heard the bullets ricochet off whatever body armor this bastard had on. He fired two more rounds with the same result. The baby doll, unaffected by his bullets, continued forward, building steam. Its lurch became a hobble. Its hobble turned into a limping jog. It bore down on Ollie like a runaway locomotive.

He emptied the .45's magazine into the doll's face. A round plinked off its cheek, rebounded, and struck Ollie in the neck. Red arced from his carotid across the doll's cracked and peeling countenance as it collided with Ollie, driving him backward onto the porch.

As he slammed down onto his back, what little wind he had inside his lungs kicked from him. Blood spurted from the jagged wound in his neck to splash back down on his face, as if his artery were nothing more than a fountain in front of some grand casino. He grabbed at his neck with slick hands. Shoved a thumb into the wound. Tried to catch his air.

The doll loomed above him. It raised one boot-clad foot and brought it down on his chest. His ribs and sternum shattered like movie glass. Ollie's mouth erupted in a great expulsion of blood and spit. Ollie realized he was drowning. Drowning in his own blood.

The doll did not attack again, only lingered, cooing above the broken man.

"Dah-Dah," it said, and visibly shuddered.

Ollie wanted to tell the thing to fuck off. Wanted to tell it where it could shove its "Dah-Dah," but without air, words were an impossibility. Not to mention the river of blood clogging his passageways, or his collapsed lungs.

How long could one survive without oxygen?

The answer was: not long.

While his blood brother lay dying on the front porch, Twon chased the boy toward the tree line. When he saw that we would not catch Will in time, he hollered, "There's landmines! You go'n kill yo'self!"

Then a thought so crystal clear and utterly alarming slammed into Twon so hard that he almost dropped to his knees.

He don' hear me, Twon thought. *He fuckin' deaf.*

Twon hit the dirt.

MOMMA

Momma stood stoic, unflappable, in the center of her home as the doll strode through the front door. It paused when their eyes met, and she saw its confused soul, the soul of a lost child. Its mind whirred and its heart ticked; mechanisms made it work, but somewhere within the machine hid the true source of its power. And that power rooted Momma to the carpet.

"I see you, *bon ti fi*, you poor little one. I see you in the fog. You come for me, been searching for me, been so close to me this entire time, and you don't even know it."

"Mah-Mah," it cooed.

"What that thing done to you, child? What horrors have you seen to bring you to this state? Oh, Lody, your father... your father was an *evil* man."

She saw it all, every moment of torment and anguish the young Lody had been through, the cruelty he'd suffered at the hands of his platinum-haired father. The things the child was made to witness. The rape, the murder, the dismemberment...

"It don't gotta be this way, Lody. You can revert. I can he'p you. I can make you *whole* again."

Cruelty cocked its head to the side and judged her with those jaundiced eyes. Yes, that's what it called itself: *Cruelty*, for that is all it had ever known.

"Mah—" Cruelty stopped, shaking, unable to finish even such a simple sentence.

"Oh, *bon ti fi*, you poor child. Momma will make it all better." She raised her arms, as if to welcome Cruelty unto her bosom. It stumbled forward, still favoring an injured leg. So long had it been a tool that its only compulsion was to seek retribution for the crimes of a past hidden by shadow and fog. It only knew the commands of its master.

Maim.

Torture.

Harvest.

Feed.

"Come to, Momma, Lody. Come on."

The doll stiffened, and its eyes came alive with a fiery hatred that she recognized at once. The Master was not absent. He never was. Inside Cruelty lay the greatest power known to man.

"Forgiveness," Momma managed, trembling all over.

"Dah-Dah!" it raged.

Cruelty pivoted and headed for the back door.

Momma dropped, sobbing, to her knees. She hitched and bucked, her body wracked by emotions so overwhelming she knew not the words for them.

This wasn't the end. Nowhere near it. Forgiveness had a goal. And then she would suffer for it.

A second later, Twon rushed in from the back door, and helped her to her feet.

"What the fuck was that thing? That thing in the doll mask? It... it walk right past me. Momma? Momma!"

"We have to leave," Momma moaned. "We have to leave now."

"You damn skippy we leavin'. Lemme get the mon—"

"Forget the money, and your poison. It don' matter no more, boy. Nothing matters but the distance we can put between us and that monster's master. Here, he'p me up."

CRUELTY

WILL

Will sprinted into the dark wood, unmindful of where he was going. He only wanted to be away. Away from the crazy men with the guns. Away from the skeletal woman and her magic. Away from Kirk's hollowed-out skull.

His feet pounded grass and snapped fallen branches as he clutched his broken arm to his chest. His lungs burned. Eyes welled with tears. He thought of the woman he'd abandoned in the ambulance last night, and how he'd had a hand in her murder as he'd had a hand in Kirk's. So much death, and it had all been his fault. Even the security guards' blood marred his hands. And Jennifer, the country pro; he couldn't forget about her. Yes, she was sick and under the control of a substance that brought the user a little closer to death every time they snorted a line or shot a vein or smoked a pipe, but she hadn't deserved to die. Even after waggling that gun in his face on that deserted back road, she still didn't deserve the fate she'd received: run over in the road like a stray dog.

The deaf man and the prostitute moseyed on down the road...

He'd thought that line funny last night, in a gallows-humor sort of way, but he no longer found the humor in it. Now, dashing through a dark wood with no safety in sight, William Longmire found nothing humorous.

He blasted past a tree on his right, and his foot caught on something. There was a concussive explosion of fiery light, and Will was stopped dead in his tracks as something slammed into his middle. He groped for his stomach, and his hands came away sticky and moist. He was on his face in an instant. Unable to feel his legs, he'd collapsed.

He loosed a soul-shattering wail that echoed through the trees. Indignation poured over him, the sheer unfairness of it all. He'd come this far, had escaped the madman in the doll mask and the armed killers, and now this? This is how he died?

He found he could move everything from his chest up. Whatever had hit him had only paralyzed his lower body. Adrenaline roaring through him now, he pushed himself up a little with his good arm, glanced around, and saw the smoking barrel of a shotgun that had been anchored to a tree trunk. He recalled the thing that had caught his feet, obviously a tripwire, and chuckled morosely until blood choked him.

Not like this. Goddamn it, not like this...

Will shoved himself over so that he could look at the stars through the trees. Something cold and hard pressed into his back. Something round. A piece of it gave under the pressure of his body, and he couldn't for the life of him imagine what it could be.

He whined, like the sorry coward that he was, as his body grew colder... and colder... and colder...

"Mah-Mah," the doll said.

Will opened eyes that he hadn't known he'd closed, and saw the behemoth in the baby doll mask standing above him, leering.

"You... again..." Will coughed.

The doll bent down, grabbed Will by the hands, and lifted him from the landmine.

William Longmire felt the cold chill of coming death. He felt the fiery heat of hell on his back. Then, he felt nothing at all.

CRUELTY

LODY

Pointvilla County Institute for the Insane: Children's Care Ward.

    Bay's End, Ohio, 1908...

The boy with the eyepatch doodled in the day room, the light from the floor-to-ceiling windows shining down on his busy, hunched form. The boy twitched almost imperceptibly.

Lody had seen him on several occasions, but didn't see him here every day. The boy had hair the color of mud, and his one blue eye sparkled—a sapphire floating in cotton. His drawings were creepy things, mostly stick figures with wispy threads of shadow coming off them, or swirling chasms of darkness that seemed to bore into the page. He gave Lody the chills.

Lody scratched at his bandaged crotch, the cotton wrappings itchy between his thighs. The tube of a catheter exited the right leg of his shorts and traveled to the bag dangling from the side of his wheelchair. He watched amber urine trickle down the line and into the bag, disgusted by what he'd been reduced to.

It was all his father's fault. Lody knew this, but some responsibility did reside on his side of the fence. He'd helped Dad hold the women down. He'd enjoyed watching his old man rape and murder those unlucky souls. Even though Lody was only ten years old, his father's actions had aroused some base part of him, and now he would pay for that fact for the rest of his life.

"Mornin'," Sean Murphy said, his Australian accent as strong as ever. The orderly carried a hardcover book in one hand, the spine nestled in his palm, as he always did while traipsing around the floor of the children's ward. He ran his free hand over the bristles of his shaved head as he cut his eyes to the boy at the table. "He's a strange one, eh?"

"Fuck off," Lody said.

Sean smiled down at him, as unflappable as ever. "Might want to say hello. From what I hear, his father's a shit. Ya both got that in common, right?"

"I wouldn't know." Lody reverted his gaze to the doodling boy. Something about the kid seemed to beckon him. Though the kid kept his eye trained on his artwork, Lody felt as if he were watching him. As if something behind the boy studied Lody. Assessed him.

"Go on. Say hi. What's it gonna hurt? You two can share horror stories about your fathers."

"I ain't got nothin' to say about him."

"Don't ya? That's a cracker, if I ever heard one. How's the bag? Need emptying yet?"

"I said, fuck off," Lody growled.

"Listen," Sean said as he squatted beside Lody's wheelchair and placed a thickly callused hand atop the boy's forearm. "My pa was no champ either. You'll get past this, mate. Things won't always be this bad. I assure—"

Lody had his father's temper, was quick to anger. He'd seen his father change from a fun-loving man to a feral beast in the flicker of an eye. For this reason, Lody wasn't all that surprised when he shot forward and took hold of the orderly's nose with his teeth.

Sean first screamed then screeched as Lody tore into the soft skin of his nose. His incisors crunched cartilage. Lody had given the man plenty of warning. Sean had not heeded this warning, so now he would be scarred for the duration of his days upon this earth.

Lody cocked his head in one sharp moment, clamping down harder with his teeth as he did so, and three centimeters of Sean's nose found its way across Lody's tongue, down his throat, and into the boy's stomach.

Lody burped.

Sean backpedaled, wheeling his arms like an unbalanced tightrope performer, before crashing into one of the dayroom's benches. He came to rest, prostrate, atop the table to which the bench had been welded. He slid his hands across his bloodied face, and squalled. Curse words flooded from the orderly, and all Lody could do was smile.

His shit of a father would have been so proud.

Lody glanced to the doodling boy to find the kid staring back at him. They shared a grin before the other child went back to his drawings.

Shortly after, chaos ensued, and Lody was returned to his room. A nurse came into his padded cell less than an hour later to take his blood pressure and administer a shot of some clear fluid.

Lody drifted off into dreamland, where he tore numerous noses from various snide, intrusive faces.

The next week, Lody made a new friend.

After breakfast one cloudy fall day, Lody was taken to the dayroom, where he presided over a puzzle that did not interest him in the slightest. All birds and flowers and blue skies. *Sissy shit*, his father would have called it. Such things were for babies. Absently, he stared at the nurse in the corner, and wondered what her pussy smelled like. Dad used to say, "The stinkier a squaw's cunt, the better. Means she'll be slipp'ry when you fuck her." But Lody wouldn't be fucking anybody, no matter how old he grew to be. The man with the knife had made sure of that.

He scratched at his bandages, inwardly cussing his loathsome, albeit loving, father. Dad had not been the best role model, but he had taught Lody the basics of survival. Kill or be killed. Rape or be raped. After all, violence was simply man's survival instinct being proactive. It was only a matter of time before someone came to hurt you. If you hurt them first, they were less apt to come calling.

And hadn't Dad been right? Hadn't the men come? The men from town? Hadn't they taught his father the ultimate lesson, a lesson that father had tried to instill in Lody since the boy was old enough to understand English? Cruelty is the way of the world.

Lody glanced up from the disaster that was his untouched puzzle and noticed the doodling boy once again looking in his direction. Not exactly looking at Lody but just over Lody's shoulder, as if someone lurked behind him. Lody craned his neck and found no one there. Facing forward once more, he saw the kid had gone back to his sketches.

Again, even though the boy no longer looked his way, Lody felt watched, studied.

At the end of the day, he still wouldn't know why he backed his wheelchair out from under the table where his puzzle lay in perpetual ruin. He couldn't have told a prying soul why he navigated his chair toward the doodling boy with the eyepatch. And he most certainly hadn't the foggiest idea why he'd introduced himself to the strange kid. Lody had never been the social type. Having a murdering rapist as a father tended to do that to a child.

"My name's Lody."

The boy continued to sketch.

"What's your name?"

"Scott," the strange boy said without looking up from his project.

"Scott what?"

"Fairchild."

"As in *the* Fairchilds? As in Waverly Fairchild?"

Scott nodded, adjusted his eyepatch, and went back to drawing. A black hole was forming in the center of the paper, and Lody felt pulled in, it was so seductive.

"What are you—?"

"What did his nose taste like?" Scott said.

Without hesitation, Lody answered: "Pennies. Like copper."

"Did you swallow it?" Scott asked, his charcoal pencil swirling faster and faster with every revolution.

"Yeah."

"Did it make you sick?"

"No."

"Why'd you do it?"

"Because he wouldn't leave me alone. I don't like being bothered."

Scott's head snapped up. "I'm always bothered. You don't see me biting off their noses."

"You're going to break your penc—" Lody began, but it was too late. The instrument snapped, and its jagged edge pierced the webbing between Scott's thumb and index finger. The boy didn't seem to notice. He flicked the broken half off the edge of the table and into Lody's lap, and then returned to his swirling darkness. Blood mixed with charcoal making the drawing look like a hypnotist's tool.

"I don't like drawing," Lody said, not sure why he hadn't left this boy alone yet.

"What do you like?" Scott asked.

"Dolls."

Scott, hunched and suddenly trembling, glared across the table at him. His eye gleamed. "You're throwing shadows, Lody. The Bastard likes you."

Lody wanted to respond, felt compelled to say something, anything, but only sat there in a kind of stunned silence. He couldn't fathom why Scott's statement had unnerved him. Something familiar, maybe? Something important that lay just outside of his understanding...

"You'll do great things, child," Scott hissed, only it wasn't the boy's voice that said the words.

His trance broken, Lody wheeled backward and returned to his jumbled puzzle. He picked up two pieces, tried to fit a corner and a middle piece together. He did this for some time, until lunchtime came, and someone whisked him away for his afternoon meal.

Food tasted of cardboard, and his apple juice reminded him of the urine inside the bag at his side. Every so often, he'd twitch, as if a goose had strolled over his grave. He kept seeing Scott's sapphire eye, glaring at him, and hearing that new voice—that dark, sibilant voice—issuing out from his boyish mouth. Lody attributed an immense sense of age to that kissing tone, and felt crushed by its timelessness.

You'll do great things, child...

A ripping feeling between his legs brought him back to the real world. At some point, he'd tugged down his sweats to reveal the bandages covering his groin. One working hand dug around inside the now blood-soaked rags. He shrieked as he yanked his hand from his wound. His trembling fist dripped gore onto his lap. He slowly opened his fingers to reveal the small oval ball resting in his palm.

"Oh, my sweet mother of God," a portly orderly said, and gasped. A nurse standing across the table from Lody covered her mouth and her eyes went wide.

"What is that?" the ginger-haired boy next to him asked. "Ewww... is that your—?"

Lody fainted before the boy could make real the horror in Lody's hand.

Lody awoke on his back, in a familiar place. Posters hung from the beige walls. Health sheets displaying hand-drawn, see-through, anatomically correct humans. Sterile instruments sat on a tray beside him, and on another tray lay bloodied tools floating in glass jars. He smelled alcohol and oysters.

He was inside the nurse's office.

Soft voices chatted somewhere off to his right.

A man's voice: "He reopened his wounds. Ghastly sight. I've sutured him, but he's lost the one. The other is... intact."

A woman's whisper: "Who removed his—?"

"He's awake."

Two forms, nothing but shadows at first, loomed over him. Their features bled into existence, and Lody recognized Dr. Struthers and Nurse Fleming at once.

"You've done a number on yourself, Lody, but I've managed to fix you up again. How are you feeling?"

Lody had not considered how he felt until that moment. His stomach was upset, and he told the doctor as much.

"That will be the morphine. It's for the pain. Not too strong. Same stuff that's in toothache medicine. You should be fine after a short respite. Nurse." Dr. Struthers nodded to Nurse Fleming and disappeared from view.

Nurse Fleming looked sadly down on the boy. "You shouldn't have done that. Why would you do such a thing to yourself?"

"Sca... Scott," Lody said. His throat seemed full of cotton batting.

"Scott... Scott Fairchild? The boy who draws in the day room?"

Lody nodded drunkenly.

"What does he have to do with you trying to mutilate yourself?"

"I'm going... going to do great... things," Lody managed.

"Not if you keep hurting yourself. Here, let's have another shot, shall we? You need the rest. To think, what you've been through. What those horrible men did to you..."

A prick, then dreams.

The men came at night, to the cabin, and Lody's life was forever changed. They carried torches, these men, and most brandished guns and knives along with their firelight.

Dad was in bed with one of his squaws when the first of the mob burst through the door. Lody had been standing beside the bed, touching himself, trying to make his penis stand up like Dad's, but it didn't work the same. Dad had said it would come, but Lody would never know such pleasures of the flesh.

The men of the mob were savage in their brutality, almost as savage as Lody's father was with the women he stole from town. While Lody hid in the closet, the men dragged his father outside, castrated him, and hung him from the tree beside the porch. Lody heard every grunt and scream as the men of the mob tortured and mutilated his platinum-haired father.

It was a man named Johnson who found Lody in the closet. Johnson had returned to the house to check on his daughter, the squaw Lody's father had been raping when the mob arrived, when Johnson heard Lody crying in the closet. Johnson tore open the door, his face red and furious. He locked eyes with the cowering boy.

"Who're you?" Johnson growled. Lody was surprised Johnson didn't recognize him. Lody had been inside Johnson's General Store on several occasions with his father. "Speak up!" Johnson demanded.

"He... he were a part o' it!" the squaw on the bed wailed, as she clutched a stained flannel blanket to her trembling form. "He did me like his pa!" she lied.

"You little monster," was all Johnson said before filling the closet with his presence.

Johnson's knife worked.

Lody squealed and wailed and kicked and bucked, but they were fruitless ventures.

It took four men to pull Johnson from the bloodied, mutilated child, yet even though they'd saved Lody's life, Johnson had claimed his prize.

The squaw's father had left Lody's balls, but little use they would do the boy, for clutched tightly in Johnson's bloody fist, Lody's penis dangled lifelessly, forever removed from its owner.

CRUELTY

Present day...

Cruelty sat up, heart ticking in triple time. It raised its hands to its porcelain face and checked for damage. Cracks. New ones. A chunk was missing from the left corner of its jaw, and another empty space gaped at its hairline.

The woods surrounding it were covered in a layer of acrid smoke. Two fires, no more than candlelight and already dwindling, lit the scene. Body parts lay smoldering all around Cruelty. It could not remember what had happened, how it had come to be in this forest. But it recalled the mob. It remembered, for the first time in over a century, the boy it had once been. And the man it had become...

Lody...

Anger coalesced into rage, and Cruelty rolled over. It pushed itself to its feet and stumbled into a nearby tree. A boot squished down in a pile of steaming guts, but Cruelty did not notice. Blinded by fiery hatred, it lumbered off into the woods, intent on finding answers to unknown questions.

Inside, its black heart ticked away, powered by shadows.

TWON

The night crackled with automatic weapons fire, far off and muffled, like fireworks heard from underwater. Momma, standing beside the car, called for Twon to hurry, a shrieking urgency to her beckoning. Twon ignored it all.

He knelt beside Ollie on the porch, swept his brother up, and cradled his bloody corpse like a lover. Twon rocked, repeating one word over and over again: "Muddahfuckah."

An explosion caused the porch to quake under Twon's knees. Possible outcomes flitted across his mind's eye.

The landmines.

The deaf kid.

The doll.

The doll had followed the boy off into the woods. For some reason, it hadn't been interested in Twon, who had hit the dirt in expectation of the kid setting off the landmines. He remembered the thing (because it felt better to think of it as a *thing* instead of a man or a woman; seemed apt, though he knew not why) sailing over him, not paying him an ounce of attention. Twon had shoved himself from the ground, run inside, and found Momma quivering in the living room.

He'd never seen her scared. Not once in his life. Not even when the Christian men and their dogs had come. She'd remained stoic in light of their obvious deaths. And if it hadn't been for Ollie...

Ollie.

You muddahfuckah.

A hand alighted on Twon's shoulder. In one fluid movement, he pushed up, spun, and pinned a thin figure to the wall beside the open front door.

Momma.

"Twon," Momma whispered. Her face was slack, emotionless, but her eyes were filled with a frenetic energy. "Twon... lemme go, son. We need to go."

"Who done this?" he asked, jabbing a finger at the body on the porch. He didn't sound like himself. His throat seemed full of gravel, his words nothing but spittle and wrath. "Who killed Ollie?"

"You have no power over that thing. Leave it be, or we all be dead." Momma's eyes, sunken and wet inside her emaciated face, pleaded with Twon.

"I'mma kill it, seen? And that be that." He backed away from her, turned, and dashed into the house. Up the stairs and toward the room he'd once shared with Ollie, Twon barreled through the door, splintering the hinges. He frantically glanced about the room until he laid eyes on Ollie's trusted Remington over-and-under, the one his brother had used to disintegrate one unlucky pixie's kneecaps once upon a time.

He strode across the empty room and snatched up the shotgun. He snapped the breach open. A shell rested in each barrel. He slammed the gun closed, grabbed a box of shells from the closet, and left the room.

Huffing and puffing, a bull fit to charge, Twon descended the stairs two at a time. He twisted at the bottom, leaned into the turn, and headed for the kitchen, all but running now. Behind him, Momma still protested, but her words meant nothing to him.

He had a man-sized doll to kill, seen?

In the kitchen, Twon tore open one of the utility drawers next to the sink. He ripped a flashlight from its contents. He flicked the device on and off once to check that it worked. All good. He dumped the box of shells into the sink, grabbed a fistful, rammed them into his front pocket, and repeated the process with the other pocket. Done, he bolted from the rear of the house.

Outside, he raised the over-and-under and held it out in front of him, like a marksman preparing to shoot skeet. He crossed the expanse of his smoky backyard and entered the tree line. Cautiously, he navigated the booby traps until he came to the wreckage of the deaf kid.

The landmine had not been gentle on the boy's corpse. Pieces of the kid hung from branches while others littered the forest floor. One tree, felled due to the blast, leaned across the kid's hollowed-out torso.

Serves him right, Twon thought. *He shouldn't have ran away like that.*

"Come out, muddahfuckah!" Twon raged, spittle as much as hatred flying from his lips. "*SHOW ME THAT CUTESY FACE, SEEN! I'MMA BLOW IT OFF, MUDDAHFUCKAH!*"

Through the smoke and gore, Twon hunted his prey.

CRUELTY

HOTEL

Hotel bounded through the woods. Was he actually crying? Were those tears rolling down his cheeks? And what the fuck happened to his gun?

The thing that had stepped from the back of the spec ops van had torn everyone to pieces. Each of his men. They now lay in the scrub in so many glistening piles. One image in particular haunted him as he fled: Felix's AR-15, still gripped in a white-knuckled embrace. Only, the arm whose hand held the rifle was no longer attached to its body. And neither was Felix's head. That had rolled under the operations van. Hotel had seen Felix's dead eyes glaring at him from somewhere behind the rear tire. Then, he'd run.

That statue... What was it? Nothing about it made sense. It seemed carved of stone, yet it moved. Fluidly. Stealthily. Knowingly.

A root caught Hotel's foot and he went flailing, down to the forest floor like some sad horror movie cliché. His face skidded across a patch of damp detritus, and his face became smeared in offal. He choked, though nothing had found its way into his mouth. He tried to push to his feet. Failed. Shouldered a tree. Slid up.

A voice seemed to come from all around him. Softly, femininely, it whispered: "I will make you regret."

"No," Hotel huffed. "God, no."

Shoving off the tree, Hotel barreled into the unknown. His heart skittered behind his rib cage. The blood in his veins seemed intent on bubbling from every orifice in his body. Pressure built behind his leaking eyes, and he thought he might go down again. Not tripped this time, but simply out of sheer fright. He was a stranger in his own body, and it was intent on ejecting him from his skin.

Hotel slammed full force into another tree. He'd been looking over his shoulder. Why? Because he felt chased. Surely this statue thing couldn't move as fast as he could. He was flesh and bone, limber, not carved of stone. Perhaps it could travel quickly over short distances, but chase a man through the woods? Fuck no.

Still...

Hotel felt like a fox set upon by hounds. Oddly, he could even sense hunters atop steeds pushing toward him.

The statue (had it really been created in the likeness of the Mother Mary, and had that really been *skin* covering it's face?) had taken a full magazine to the chest without so much as staggering. Hotel's finger had clicked and clicked and clicked a trigger that worked a hammer that had nothing left to fire. Stoned with fear, Hotel had watched the figure turn away from him and toward Felix and Jules. Jules fired. The gun was ripped from Jules's hand even as Felix began pounding slugs into their unholy adversary. Jules had been torn in two. Just like that. Bisected. Shit like that didn't happen. It wasn't possible, that Hotel knew. The human body couldn't be torn down the middle like a sheet of fucking paper. Could it? But he'd seen it. Had watched, rooted in place, as Jules became two.

Done with Jules, the thing's attentions had diverted to Felix. Hotel had watched in stunned stupidity as Felix was pulled apart. Like a Mr. Potato Head in a bored child's hands, Felix had been repurposed into the equivalent of a cow upon a butcher's block.

Christ on a pogo stick in a hurricane, had he really witnessed all that? Had he really stood around and watched helplessly as his men were murdered before his eyes? Had he really run away? Was he still, truly, fleeing like a son from a parent's belt?

No. He was fleeing like a man hell-bent on living. Fuck the dumb shit; Hotel planned to live another day. He'd made it out of Iraq in one piece, at least physically. Never mind the mental bullshit—the hiding in the closet during storms because the thunder sounded like being shelled, or having to pull over on the side of the road because a car's backfiring tailpipe had sent him sobbingly into a maddened state. Forget lifelessly fucking his wife like she was some Saudi Arabian whore because something had gone very, very wrong with his ability to show compassion. All that was an aside. Because Hotel wanted to live. Even if that meant continuing to live with post-traumatic stress disorder.

Something struck his face, and, for a moment, Hotel was horizontal, like a boxer having just received a haymaker to the jaw. Pain lanced across his brow. Blood came even before he crashed to the ground. His wind exploded from him. He came up to a sitting position almost instantly. He snorted in his attempts to fill his lungs. Lungs fighting him, he sucked and sucked, but no oxygen was to be found. Torrents of syrupy blood flooded his eyes, cascaded down his nose and cheeks, and dripped from his chin. He inhaled some of it.

Inhaled!

He gagged and spat. The next breath was meager but enough. Shallowly, rapidly, he drew his breaths until his vision spun. Whether his dizziness stemmed from his head wound or lack of oxygen, Hotel didn't know. He simply focused on his respirations.

The more air he was able to take in, the calmer he became. Even knowing that death might be close on his heels, he remained seated, breathing in and out, until finally he could muster the strength to stand.

When he got to his feet, something was standing in front of him, mere inches away.

Cold, rough hands gripped the sides of his head. One even gouged into the flesh behind his left ear. Instinctively, Hotel snatched himself away.

His ear did not come with him.

He staggered in reverse, one hand out in front of him fending off his attacker, and the other at the side of his face. His fingers slid around on a smooth, blood-soaked surface. Distantly, Hotel knew what he was feeling was the side of his skull.

In the darkness, Hotel could see little. He could just make out a hulking shape, almost feminine in nature, but for whatever reason his mind couldn't put two and two together. A part of him remained certain that the Mother Mary statue couldn't have kept up with him. After all, it was stone. He was a living thing. He continued to tell himself that, even as his eyes adjusted further and the figure before him took shape.

He shrieked. The sound was high-pitched and full of an animalistic terror.

"You're not real!" he wailed, still staggering backward, still hunting safety.

The figure stopped. Studied him. Its voice was most definitely female. "Do you regret leaving that place? Do you wish you'd died there?"

"Wha-what?" he stammered. He swiped blood from his leaking forehead even as a sheet of it ran from his ravaged ear down the side of his neck.

"I have my own regrets. Tell me yours?" It was a question. Hotel, even in his current state, could hear the inflection at the end of the sentence. "Tell me your regrets. I'm only just learning how to"—it quaked—"use them."

"Go the fuck away!"

"Tell me, Gregory Hyatt, do you regret coming out here tonight? This night of my birth?"

"I regret you, you fucking monster. How's that for some motherfucking regret?" Hotel barked laughter. He'd lost too much blood. He was going mad. A thought came to him: do the mad feel pain? Is it going to hurt when this fucking thing tears me apart like it did Felix and Jules?

That thought drove a spike of sanity through his brain. Here he was, talking to a fucking statue when he should be running. He wasn't down and out yet. He was still on his feet. Still alive.

His old mantra came rushing back.

Fuck the dumb shit. Hoo-rah!

Hotel stumbled to the left, threw his right leg out in front of him, and bolted for anywhere that wasn't his current location.

Behind him, the statue loosed an exasperated sigh.

Hotel sprinted from the tree line. Before him, a squat structure. A square of illumination. Lights in a window. A cellar's entrance. Unlocked and seemingly waiting for someone to descend. He threw open the doors and thudded down the steps.

It smelled of an abattoir. Back in Iraq, his company had come across am Iraqi death pit. The corpses inside had bloated and burst in the sun. At the bottom of the stairs, Hotel entered a room that smelled exactly like that pit.

The walls were bare, nothing but support studs and cinderblocks. A bulb dangled from the ceiling by the length of an orange extension cord. Directly below this bulb lay a body. No. Not a body. A woman. And she was breathing.

Her face was gone.

He clapped a hand over his mouth and nose, as much to stifle the stench as to suppress any shocked sound that might issue forth, and rounded the stout table, locked in his own static curiosity.

One of this woman's hands was bent awkwardly back, the wrist obviously broken. The other hand was short its middle finger. A pool of dark, coagulated blood lay under the palm and had dripped over the edge of the tabletop. Other than the injuries to her wrist and hands, and her AWOL face, she seemed intact. The fact that she was breathing saddened Hotel more than it terrified him. What atrocities had befallen her, yet she remained among the living.

The mouth worked itself open and shut, forming a single word: "Regret."

That part of Hotel's brain that couldn't put two and two together earlier fired a cannonball of correlation through his synapses.

The face on the statue. The dark skin.

This woman. Her face missing.

Footsteps sounded on the stairs. Not the stairs leading out of the basement, but the ones leading up into the cabin. Hotel froze, overcome with an abstract horror of the unknown. For he knew, most certainly, that he should never have come down here.

"There is a place inside us all, a place where we go when the savagery of the world becomes too much for even our lizard's brain to process," said a soft male voice. "It hides like pornography on a preacher's computer. Like bodies under a murderer's home. It is known as the Withered. It is where we collapse when hope fails us, and it is where you, Gregory 'Hotel' Hyatt, find yourself on this night of regret."

A young man, no more than four feet tall and rail thin, appeared at the bottom of the stairs. He wore a gray cardigan over neatly pressed gray slacks. One shiny black shoe tapped an impatient rhythm on the floorboards while the other remained stationary, balancing him. He looked like a child. No more than ten or eleven. But his eyes were so very old. Their age alone caused a shiver to scroll down Hotel's back. The eyes were why Hotel first thought "young man" and not "little boy."

"Who the fuck are you?" Hotel managed.

"Oh, goodie," the boy said. "This one sees me. You know," the kid said as he turned and began to pace with his hands locked behind his back, "not everyone can. See me, that is." The boy flashed Hotel a bright, beatific smile. Hotel realized he was trembling. "You don't seem to harbor any... issues. Fascinating, Hotel, because you've seen and been through so much. I rather think you enjoyed it."

"Fuck you, pip-squeak," Hotel spat.

"Marines on the ground in Iraq, killing and trying not to be killed, would have tendencies toward instability. At least one would think, anyway. You're a real odd duck, you know that?"

Hotel did not answer. The tremors coursing through him gained speed until he was agitating like a washing machine.

"You don't want forgiveness for... *anything*?" The child looked flummoxed, yet continued to pace, eyes locked on Hotel.

"I didn't do anything wrong," Hotel said, even though he hadn't meant to speak.

"Oh, didn't you? I would fancy a guess that you did plenty wrong. The thing is"—the boy stopped in front of the stairs and faced Hotel—"whether or not the evils of man are done knowingly doesn't matter. They're still evil deeds. Just because you don't think so doesn't mean a squirt of piss down your quaking thigh. For, Hotel, my dearest man, you're a coward. You always have been. See?"

The boy snapped his fingers, but Hotel did not hear the snapping of fingers. He heard a gunshot, heard the bullet whistle past his ear, and dropped to his knees.

The boy approached him. "They fired at you so you fired back. You killed them out of self-defense, right?"

"No." Hotel was barely aware that he was now blubbering. "No, not all of them."

"Right," the boy said, his tone silken. "There were a few that didn't have the chance to shoot at you first."

Sobbing, Hotel nodded.

"There was... a girl, wasn't there?"

The boy's face shimmered like heat waves on scorched asphalt. Features swirled. The cheek bones became higher, the eyebrows darker. Baby blue eyes washed away to reveal ones the color of coffee. The skin tanned, and the body grew taller. A veil appeared over the lower half of the woman's face. She gazed at Hotel in starstruck horror.

"You killed her," the woman said. The accent was thick and Arab in nature. Yet... had there been an accent? Had she even spoken to him in English?

"You were crossing the street. In my line of fire. I didn't see you... or her."

Because the "her" in question hadn't been the woman who now stood in front of Hotel. The "her" was the baby she now cradled in her arms. The one with the hole in her chest.

"I didn't see her!" Hotel bawled.

"You owe me something," the woman said.

"What? God, what?" he whimpered.

"An apology," she rather plainly said. "An apology for murdering my baby girl."

"I'm sorry," Hotel said. A snot bubble burst in his nose. "I'm so fucking sorry, okay?"

"Oh, Hotel," the woman smiled, "I forgive you."

MOMMA

"T WON!" Momma cried, but her son paid her no heed. From the back door, she watched him flash into the tree line and out of sight.

Ollie's loss could be managed. But Twon? She didn't think her failing body and mind could handle the shock of losing her own flesh and blood. When Twon's father Huxley had died, she had mourned as one mourns the loss of a familiar, a pet. When her own mother died, she was equally ambivalent. But Twon was of her. He'd been ripped bloody and naked and screaming from her womanhood, and his death would cripple what few faculties she still harbored.

"Ya damn fool child! It'll be your end!" she hollered, only this time with less fervor. The black was closing in on her, threatening to lay her flat, and she could not have it. She hadn't the strength to chase after her son, but she could do other things. She could empower him, if only she could recall the proper words...

Limping with exertion, Momma made her way back into the living room and up the stairs. She entered her room, then went to her closet. The woman standing in the full-body mirror, which hung from the inside of the closet's door, looked haggard and drained in the soft light of the room. Her wispy gray hair curled about her head. Most of it had found it's way out from the bun atop her skull, and she resembled a windblown wraith. Her lips were as gray as her elbows and knees, and the pink silk gown she wore did little to hide her jutting bones. Oh, how she'd wasted away since they'd escaped Union

Island. The place where Ollie and Twon had become blood brothers, and Ollie had murdered a dozen men while trying to save the three of them.

"I nevah shoulda ate that preacher," she told her reflection. "Gave my heart the burns, he did."

Why was she here, standing before her open closet and talking to herself? Oh, yes, the claw. That's right.

She pulled a bit of sackcloth from the tippy top of the closet, where it had hung from a rusty nail since they'd moved in to Ollie's father's old abode. She took a few steps back until she felt the mattress on the rear of her thighs, and sat down. The springs squeaked under her meager weight.

Heavy twine encircled the sackcloth's middle. She unwrapped the package, set the rope beside her on the comforter, and unfolded the cloth. In the center of the package was the withered, mummified right hand of a preacher named Samuel Lessing. Father Lessing had once threatened to damn Momma to the fiery lakes of hell (*as if such a place existed*, she mused) if she would not repent (what had he called them?)... her voodoo ways. As if her dark magic had anything to do with French Creole nonsense. No. There were other planes of existence, yes, but they had nothing to do with deities and religions. There was, of course, the Withered, where the Bastard and this new one had come from, but there was also the Roaming. One plane in constant flux, the other in a state of perpetual limbo. Both places of the mind. And with the advent of the power that ran this doll-thing (*his name is Lody... or it was*, she thought) Momma feared certain lines had been crossed. A meeting of the planes had finally happened. The Withered and the Roaming as one.

Oh, the horror. She shivered violently.

What had she been concerning herself over? The doll? No. Father Lessing; that was it. The auburn-haired fool had tried his white magic on her, brandishing that cross as if it were more than just a wooden trinket, and she'd laughed in his Christian face.

"I'm gonna eat you, Godly Man. Momma's gonna eat you all up!"

"Back away, spawn of Satan!" Father Lessing bellowed, holding the cruciform high over his head.

They stood less than ten feet apart, in the vestibule of a church located on the outer rim of Union Island. Momma had heard tell that the father plotted against her and her boys, that he sought big, brave, strong men to hunt them like dogs, and Momma could have no such thing. She'd cut the cancer before it could spread, she would. Cut it out and devour it.

"No matter the strength of your faith, Godly Man, because it be in vain. Ain' no gods here. Ain' no gods anywhere. Only death. And the After."

"My father, which art in—"

"*Bladoch!*" She spat the archaic word, and the preacher dropped immediately to his knees. The cross seemed to grow heavy in his hand, as if it had been suddenly filled with lead, and his wrist snapped under the pressure. Bone protruded from the father's forearm as he wailed at the wound.

Momma giggled. "*Bladoch sha romday,*" she whispered.

Invisible fingers hooked themselves inside the father's cheeks and stretched his mouth into an absurd rictus. Farther and farther, the corners of his mouth drew upward and away, until they all but touched his dangling ear lobes. His cupid's bow split, and a curtain of blood veiled his bottom lip and chin. The tearing continued, bisecting his face completely. His skin came away like the coat of some perverted flasher. His muscly, bloody countenance pulsed.

Faceless and panting, the father slumped forward. His face smeared the vestibule's floorboards a thick purple.

"Oh, bon ti fi, how will you ever face your creator now?" Momma chuckled.

She approached the dying man. "You gonna taste *so good.*"

Her reverie over, Momma glared down at the portion of gray wrist and palm and digits lying in her lap. Two fingers were missing. She grabbed hold of the thumb, wrenched it away, against the joint, and it snapped off in her hand.

She closed her eyes.

"Protect my child," she begged. "Protect the idiot, for he know not what he face."

"Yoo-hoo?" a voice called from downstairs. "Anybody home?"

Momma's eyes shot open. Her visitor's presence seemed to follow his voice. Cold. She felt so suddenly cold that she expected to see her breath frost in front of her face. She exhaled, as if to test this theory, but no fog formed.

And she could smell him. The death and wrongness he exuded almost choked her.

Could he sense her as she sensed him? She couldn't be sure. She reached out with her mind, knocked on his door, and was denied entrance. Was she simply too weak after her ordeal, or was this man (*this thing*) blocking her?

"Your parlor tricks don't work on me, witchery woman. Why don't you come on down here so we can talk? I have no time to chase after you, but we both know I will." She heard an impatient tapping, and assumed it was his foot upon the hardwood floor of her foyer. "I'm waiting, but I won't be for long."

"Time to face your maker, Laurette," she told herself, and rose.

"Oh," the man-thing called, "and do leave that monkey's paw on the bed. Thanks."

Momma glanced behind her and saw that the father's withered hand was indeed lying upon the sheets. She didn't remember placing it there.

The dried up thumb she'd torn from the hand lay at her feet like a fat worm.

She exited her room and went to the stairs. Descended the stairs. She found no one in the foyer, only Ollie's corpse resting on the porch just outside the door.

"In here," the man-thing beckoned.

She faced the kitchen.

Her breath caught in her chest at the sight of him. No, not him. It. It, in all its terrible glory.

The boy (for sometimes it was a boy, nothing but a child, while others it was darkness itself) was perched upon the lip of her kitchen skin, kicking its legs as if it didn't have a care in the universe.

"Here," it said, smiling with its black maw, "let me do something about your trepidations."

The image of the boy solidified, and Momma found his gray cardigan and slacks so utterly banal that she might have laughed if she wasn't in the presence of a true-to-life monster.

"What you want, demon?" she managed to eke out.

"Demon?" The boy laughed. "That's so... unimaginative of you, Laurette. So uninteresting. You know who I am. You can call me by my name, if you wish." The boy's grin was inviting and warm, yet she shivered when faced with it.

"I will not name you in my home."

"Sad. It's been so long since I was on a first name basis with a flesh sack such as yourself. Oh, I almost forgot..." The boy leaped down from the sink, jabbed his thumb and forefinger between his lips, and whistled.

A vacant-eyed man in black clothing stumbled in through the back door. He wore boxes on his belt, as well as a can of some unknown material and a pair of handcuffs. His hair was cut in a military fashion, and his face and cheeks were scarred from previous battles with acne.

He shouldered the fridge, and for a moment, Momma thought he might topple it. Ice rattled in the freezer, but the refrigerator remained upright.

"Are you hungry?" The boy burped. "You look like you could use something to eat."

The zombie-like individual shoved past the boy and shuffled toward the knife block beside the sink, where it withdrew a long, serrated bread knife. The walking dead man lifted the front of his shirt and began sawing at his flank.

"You don't scare me, demon. I been seen worse things than this puppetry. What would you have of me? Take it and be done!"

"Have from you? I'd—You can stop that," he told the zombie. The man left the knife jutting from his side, backed up against the pantry, and slid down to lie beside the deaf kid's friend, the one with the hole in his head. The boy returned his attention to Momma. "Where was I? Right. What would I have of you? Now that you mention it—and you're so very kind for thinking of my needs—I could use some information. It seems I've lost one of my wards. I can't... reach him, and he's so very dependent on me. Tell me, have you seen a big-as-shit baby doll running around, perchance?"

CRUELTY

NATALIE

After dropping Nell Morgan at home, Natalie followed Markum and Sheriff Miser to the addict's home.

She would never get used to seeing dead bodies, and Simon Allison's bloodless corpse was no different. The naked man's arms had been duct taped to his flanks, and his throat had been slit. His head rested on the back of a worn leather sofa. His penis looked like a purple tennis ball.

"Why?" Natalie asked, pointing at the man's engorged member.

Frank shrugged. "Blood has to go somewhere."

"Eye's on the prize, troop," Miser said, adjusting his belt. The sheriff stood opposite the emaciated druggie, looking down on the dead man. "Who you reckon, statie?"

"Sorry, are you talking to me?" Frank Markum asked. "Because, you know, Sheriff, I have a name. Investigator Markum will do."

Miser snorted laughter. "Whatever, fancy-pants. Just answer the question. You think Twon had something to do with this?"

"More than likely," Frank said.

"I actually know this guy," Miser informed them. "He doesn't go by his real name. Goes by Turtle. Funny, I never had any run-ins with his old lady, though. Shame."

"Why's it a shame you never ran into her?" Natalie asked.

"Oh, no, sorry. I was just saying that this—him—is a shame. Waste of life. Drugs do funny things to people. Makes 'em crazy. I mean, you'd have to be nutso, batcrap crazy, to deal with someone the likes of Twon."

"Ah," Natalie said. "And, why are we here again?"

It was Miser's turn to shrug. "Best place as any. Following up leads, and whatnot. At least we found him. Might not have come across him had his lady friend not ended up in the morgue. Besides, maybe it weren't Twon at all. Maybe your doll has something to do with this."

"Could be," Markum said, nodding. "Doll Face kills this guy to send a warning to Twon, only Twon never finds the guy because he's busy causing chaos at the hospital."

"You want me to call in crime scene?"

Miser nodded.

Natalie pulled her cell phone from her jeans and was about to call in the body when Markum raised a hand.

"Hold up. Phone."

At first, she had no idea what he was talking about, but then she leaned around him to see where he pointed. In the corner of the room, atop a rickety table, lay a telephone with a message system. A red light throbbed dully.

Miser went to the phone and pressed play.

A computerized voice relayed the date and time followed by the announcement of fourteen messages.

Markum sighed and combed his fingers through his hair. "We might be here for a while. Go on. Play it."

All but two of the messages were from Twon. The Caribbean cook didn't sound pleased. As the space between messages decreased, Twon became more vehement, until the final message, which was mostly expletives mixed with adverbs.

The penultimate message caught them all off guard.

"Hey, dickhead. I know you're hiding from Twon, but that don't mean you can't call me back. For Pete's sake, he ain't gonna kill you! Lemme talk to him, and all this will be swept under the rug. He can wait for his money, trust me. He's fuck-uck-uck-ing load-ded! He's just all paranoid and shit because some guys are after his sweet ol' mommy. You should see this bitch, bro. Wicked Witch of the West ain't got shee-it on her. Anyway, call me back, you dickless wonder. Laurie, out!"

Natalie said, "Do you think she's really his sister or—?"

Markum cut in: "Shhh!"

The next message began.

"Turtle, man, where are you? Jennifer's dead, and they're pressing in on Twon. I would have called you earlier but I've been tied up since that bullshit out at Bob's Bait and Fuel last night. Now I'm getting called into some shit at the hospital. Anyway, none of this looks good. Call me back."

The message beeped, and Natalie watched Sheriff Miser deflate.

"What? Who was that?" she asked.

Miser slowly shook his head. He chuckled, but it wasn't a jovial sound. "That? That's Nick Wuncell. My damn deputy."

CRUELTY

ANNE-MARIE

Anne-Marie Monlezun studied the rental agreement for lot F with a fretful eye. Loopholes. She hated loopholes. If this douchebag thought he was going to live in her park for free he had another think coming. Still...

Loopholes. If they existed, she was going to find them.

She should be online, surfing the web and conversing with friends and chatting about her favorite novels on BookLikes. Instead, she was hunched over this piece of paper, brooding over loopholes.

"God!" she growled, flinging the page across her kitchen table, where it fluttered off the side and out of sight. She got up to fix herself another pot of coffee. She discarded the thick dregs of the previous carafe into the sink, rinsed it, and sat the pot back inside the maker.

She was reaching for the cabinet that contained her Folgers Dark Roast when Pau, her Shih-Tzu, started yipping at the front door. Gertie, the alpha Shih-Tzu, soon joined in.

"What? What is it?" she asked, not upset, only exasperated. She was not the type of person to become vicious with her best friends.

The dogs ignored her, continued to bark and yap at the closed entrance of her double-wide. From her open kitchen, she could see clearly through the blinds of the front window to the right of the door. Sickly light from her bulb lamp made her porch glow an ugly citron. No one stood on her deck. Just to make sure, Anne-Marie went to the window, parted the slats of the venetians, and gazed outside.

Somebody clomped up her porch steps. They were huge, whoever they were. Their face was covered by curly black hair, and their head was down, but the style of the hairdo suggested a woman. A big woman at that. She (because she didn't know what else to call this person) was clothed in all black, and Anne-Marie could see glistening spots here and there, as if puddles of ink clung to the apparel.

The woman stood motionless and silent in front of Anne-Marie's front door. A feeling of unease drew icy fingers down her back. She noticed the fingers that held the blinds apart were now shaking slightly.

Why isn't she moving? Anne-Marie asked herself. *Why doesn't she knock or something?*

The woman cocked her head to the side, and the curly black hair slid off the face.

Anne-Marie backpedaled, stepped on Gertie's front paw, and fell down hard. The terrier skittered away, yelping. She spider walked backward on her palms and heels until she hit the coffee table. The corner stabbed her between the shoulder blades and she cried out.

A soft, muffled voice came floating through her front door: "Mah-mah…"

"I'm calling the police!" she screamed, but did not move. Her body betrayed her. All circuits were busy. Please try again later.

"Mah-mah…" The thing outside cooed.

Now it was a thing, not a woman, for she had seen its face. More importantly, Anne-Marie Monlezun had seen what hadn't been there and wound poured from the emptiness.

Darkness.

Cold and utterly complete darkness.

It fled the missing places in the face like smoke from the windows of a burning building. Black tendrils reaching out for—

"Mah-mah…"

"Go away!" she wailed.

All was silent aside from her heart's attempt to vacate her ribs. She clutched her chest, between her breasts, and willed her pulse to calm. How long had it been since the thing had spoken last? A minute? Two? God only knew.

Wait?

Silence?

Where were Gertie and Pau?

As if in response to her thoughts, a wet nose nudged her hand. She craned her neck to see Pau's white face peeking out at her from under the coffee table. The unadulterated terror in her little one's eyes kindled a response in her not unlike a mother who fears for her child. Hell, Gertie and Pau were her children, and she would protect them.

Cops.

She had to call the cops.

Where was her cell phone?

On the kitchen table.

Good.

Go!

She shoved herself to her knees and rolled forward, throwing a leg out in front of her before she did a header into the floor. Up, she rushed into her kitchen, where she found her Nokia sitting atop a pile of paperwork.

What was she going to tell the police? That some horror movie villain was currently standing on her porch, threatening her babies? Forget that. They'd never believe her. Tell them—

Just dial the fucking number! a voice of reason shouted within her head.

She pressed the nine… the one… the—

Something hit her front door hard enough to bend the aluminum frame at the hinge. The attack so startled Anne-Marie that she jumped. Her finger pressed down not on the final one that she needed to dial to reach emergency service but on the nine.

Gertie and Pau rocked past her and into the hallway, where they took shelter in her master bedroom. Following their lead, Anne-Marie began backing in that direction, never taking her eyes off the entrance to her trailer. Her grip on the phone was now sweaty, slippery, the device all but forgotten.

Another crash, and the upper section of the door gave way. The door folded inward, the top hinge a shattered memory of its former self.

The horror movie villain peeked inside.

"Mah-mah."

Anne-Marie Monlezun screamed her loudest scream yet.

And then the baby doll with the shattered face was gone.

She stood trembling in her hallway, her damp thumb playing over the keys of her forgotten phone. Her breath came in quick shallow gulps. She terribly needed something to drink; her throat was so dry, and her tongue seemed to have swollen to double its size.

She glanced timidly down at her phone, saw the 9-1-9, and pressed end, clearing the screen. She looked up, quickly, to check the door, and then back down to her phone. She dialed the proper combination of numbers this time, shoved her thumb into the send key, and slapped the phone to the side of her face.

A grinding metallic sound cleaved through the silence of the hallway a mere second before the phone began ringing.

Something was moving around under her trailer.

The phone rang a second time.

She took another step in reverse, her eyes locked on the floor.

The trailer shuddered. The entire thing, as if earthquakes had come to middle Texas.

"Nine, one, one, how may I direct your call?"

CRUELTY

"Please," she whispered into the phone, "help me."

"Ma'am, what is your emergency? Can you say?"

"Something's under my—"

The floors of modular homes are thin, made mostly of plywood and metal and sheets of insulation. This evening of her death, Anne-Marie wished she had chosen a more substantial place to call home.

The baby doll came ripping and grinding and tearing through the floor of the hallway. Pieces of ravaged wood and metal bent and twisted around it, and pink cotton candy exploded into existence. At least, that's what it looked like to Anne-Marie. In reality, it was only insulation.

Instinct drove her to throw whatever she had in her hand at the monster emerging from beneath her home. Her cell phone shattered against the doll's cracked and peeling mask, and she knew her foolishness had killed her.

"*GET OUT OF MY HOUSE*!" she bellowed.

The baby doll refused. "Mah-mah."

Anne-Marie turned to flee, to kick her leg out, to make for one of the windows in her bedroom, but a hand around her calf stopped her cold. The viselike grip bore down until her femur exploded in her leg, as if it had been packed full of plastic explosives. The pain sent her wailing to the floor. The pressure on her leg increased. Her calf was snapped to one side. And then the grip was gone. She dug her fingers into the eggshell carpet under her and tugged, tugged, tugged herself forward. Her uninjured leg slid through something wet. The shattered one caught on nothing, as if it weren't even there. Funny thing, that. Of course her leg was there. It was just broken, right?

Anne-Marie chanced a glance down her flank. At the same time, she brought what was left of her left leg out to the side.

Did I get bit by a shark? was her crazed thought as she glared at her halved appendage. Gore spouted and dripped from the end of the enormous wound. *It's not even Shark Week.*

The doll loomed behind her, big enough to blot out the meager light emanating from the living room. The darkness pouring from its cracked face got her going again. Adrenaline fueled her. She clawed and dragged her way toward the safety of her bedroom, moving faster and faster. Actually impressed with her progress.

Who needs two legs? she thought maddeningly.

She pulled herself into the bedroom, and without a thought about her mutilated leg, tried to push to standing. When she tried to shove off with her missing leg, she went head first into her nightstand. Bright flashes of light pulsed in her vision. She rolled and writhed, clutching her head, and for the briefest of instances, she forgot about her leg.

Something fierce latched onto her right ankle, and it was like a startlingly intense feeling of déjà vu.

Didn't we just go through this? her pain-addled brain mused.

A feeling of sudden weightlessness, as if someone had flipped the switch to gravity into the off position. Then she was flying. Flying away. Flying...

CRUELTY

Cruelty slung the woman across the room by the ankle. She slammed into the mirror above the dresser with a satisfying *crunch*! It loosed her, and she landed atop a pile of knickknacks and forgotten clothing.

Cruelty studied the woman's inert form. Glass from the mirror was embedded in her face and jutted from her tan blouse, circled in sticky pools of ever-spreading redness. She had the cutest chocolate brown hair styled in a pixie cut. Cruelty ran its fingers through the short strands.

The agony coming off her was ecstasy itself. Cruelty shivered as it suckled up every ounce of the woman's pain.

She moaned. Her eyes fluttered. They locked drunkenly on Cruelty, and Cruelty cooed.

"Mah-mah," it said.

And then a flash of pain so intense that it buckled Cruelty's legs lanced through its ticking heart. It shambled backward, fighting to maintain its balance. Hands groped at its chest. It tried to breathe for the first time in a century, but it had no lungs with which to gasp.

You will do great things, child...

"Dah-dah!" Cruelty cried. It blundered to the far wall, and braced itself there, its ticking heart click, click, clicking away inside its chest.

What was happening?

Was it dying?

It slammed a palm into the wall, and its chest bucked. Once... twice... three times.

Cruelty took in a great rush of wind, and it actually tasted the air. A cloying aroma. Perfume mixed with dirty laundry.

Breathing! It was breathing!

The ticking of its heart accelerated as the old woman from earlier that night flashed before its mind's eye, and Cruelty remembered. It remembered lumbering out into the woods after the boy. It remembered the explosion. It remembered the memories.

The institute.

The doodling boy.

Throwing shadows...

And then that too was gone.

The mind only matters to the matters of the mind, Lody...

Forgiveness?

Come home, dear one. That's a good Cruelty...

Its master's voice was unmistakable. Forgiveness was beckoning, and Cruelty should—

No. It needed to feed. The woman on the dresser should be harvested. Forgiveness could wait. He had to wait. Cruelty was hurting.

Cruelty needed sustenance.

It needed power.

Needed...

Freedom.

That last word echoed quite largely in Cruelty's thoughts.

Still unsteady on its feet, it ambled toward the dresser. The woman gazed wide-eyed at Cruelty. She was fully awake, but had yet to move. It wondered if it had done something to her back. Perhaps it had snapped the spine. Maybe she couldn't move even if she wanted to. Then again, Cruelty knew how fear could root someone in place. Make them immobile. Easy prey. Yes, Cruelty knew this all too well.

"Mah... m-m-m-m... moh... mother," it cooed.

CRUELTY

"Puh... puh-lease... puh-LEEEEEZE!" the crippled woman squeaked.

Cruelty laid a single hand on her elbow, squeezed, and grasped the woman's arm at the wrist. It jerked the forearm up, shattering the elbow joint. Cruelty twisted and pried as the woman squealed and blubbered. It ripped the arm off at the joint and showed it to her. She gawped at it, mouth working like a fish out of water. Her stump pinwheeled, spurting blood all over Cruelty's scorched clothing.

"Mah... mah-mother," Cruelty vocalized. "Dah-dah... dah-dadd-ees... Daddy's coming. Shhhh..."

Cruelty nursed from the woman. It watched the damage to its face mend in the unbroken shards of mirror that still clung to the frame. It was unaware that it had spoken. Did not know the meaning of the words it had uttered. For all Cruelty knew, it had been the woman who had warned Cruelty of "Daddy's" imminent arrival.

When it was finally satiated, Cruelty relieved the woman of her head. Her skull would make a nice plaything.

INNIS

Innis Blake continued to exist, but just barely. She simply *was*.

She lingered in a dusty theater seat, her gaze drifting lazily, while Regret moved silently on the floor-to-ceiling screen. Innis didn't breathe, for breath was not required here, in the Withered. She did not hunger, for Regret had found nourishment this night.

Innis and Regret were duality personified. Two within one. Master and puppet as a single entity. Yet Regret had a mind of her own, and Innis was not privy to the entity's thoughts. Had she been, Innis Blake might have found solace in unbeing.

The flesh of her predicament was this: her body was technically still alive, as Gregory "Hotel" Hyatt had recently discovered, but like Hotel in the clutch of Forgiveness's psychic embrace, she was not entirely aware of her body. She knew that her physical self rested somewhere other than here, that she was, somehow, strangely outside of herself.

The bones of the matter was such: she would not be among the living for long. That is, unless someone came to her rescue.

An odd word hung in her subconscious like the proverbial carrot before the horse. The single word repeated ad infinitum. It seemed to be missing something, the equation incomplete—a fraternal twin without its sibling.

Nefarious...

On the screen, Regret exited the woods. The cabin lay directly ahead, its basement door flung wide. Had Regret moved down those steps Innis might have been able to look down on herself, in turn having a true-to-life out-of-body experience. But Regret found nothing of interest regarding the cabin. The visage of the Mother Mary diverted her course and headed for the road.

The stone of her body moved fluidly, a living thing. Down to the molecular level, Regret was indeed a carved thing. But man had split the atom, and the likelihood of her existence was not so farfetched. Within, she ticked, not unlike her brother, but there was far more flesh to Regret than there was mineral. Innis could feel Regret's lungs working, though the entity's respirations were few and far between.

The oddest thing for Innis was that she sensed the possible presence of a womb within the statue's abdomen. Innis could feel a tightening in Regret's guts that was not unlike menstrual cramps. Had she been fully conscious and capable of rational thought, Innis might have considered the horrible idea that this thing could become pregnant.

Once again that half-statement flitted through Innis's brain—

Nefarious...

—and she shivered.

Something interesting was happening on the screen, but Innis Blake was only vaguely aware of it. Regret began to move faster. Not so much running as gliding.

And then Regret began to come apart.

Perhaps this event held no uniqueness in Innis's mind because she had seen it before, back when Regret had hunted the DEA agent, the man named Hotel. Regret had finished her business with the men in the spec van, and then focused her attention on the three armed men outside. Innis had watched in a narcotized state as Regret ripped the men asunder. Then, Regret had pursued the final agent. Yet "pursue" wasn't the right word, because that word inspired thoughts of a chase. This was more of a stalking, a languid passing from one section of the woods to the other. Hotel dashed and rushed and bounded through the woods, but Regret simply moved. She shifted, as it were, from one location to the other, coming apart and reforming again, as if teasing her prey. Only when the man injured himself on the tree branch and the game grew boring did Regret finally confront him.

Then Regret had spoken in riddles. Something about having only now gotten used to her... powers. Only that wasn't the right word, either. A more apt description would have been "abilities." Because one did not possess the power to feed oneself. One has the ability. Because feeding was exactly what Regret planned to do. Not to sustain *her* power, though. She needed to sustain another, for Regret was nothing more than a proxy.

"Hello?" a man's voice called loudly. The word echoed throughout the empty theater, a tired entreaty.

"Yes?" Innis asked languorously.

"Hello? Is someone there?" More insistent now. A frantic sense of hope clung to the man's every word.

"Yes..." Innis moaned.

"Where are you?" he called.

"Here..."

And there he was, coming, quite literally, into her vision from stage right. He sidestepped across the front of the riser, caught sight of Innis in the front row, and hopped down the stairs. He seemed almost jubilant, jovial, but Innis assumed this was only masked relief.

The man was in his forties, and had brown hair, or at least from what she could tell given his wide, flat-brimmed hat. He was dressed in an oddly familiar uniform that Innis could not at first categorize. An officer of a kind... Perhaps a policeman... Or—

"Thank God, I finally found someone. I been banging around this place for hours. Probably a full day by now. Ain't nobody around, sister. It's damn eerie out there."

Innis nodded, not really paying attention to this strange man. After all, he wasn't real. Like the boy with the eyepatch, this man was just another specter, a shadow that roamed the withered halls of this unlife. This officer was no more substantial than the kid in the cabin, or the platinum-haired loony who'd threatened to rape her.

"Say, lady, what's wrong with you? Are you drunk?"

Innis shook her head.

"Listen, we need to get out of here. I'm not sure how the hell I got here, myself, but I'm sure as shit getting gone in a hurry. You can help me. We can help each other. I'm Tom, by the way. Tom Morgan. I'm a Texas state trooper. What's your name?"

"Regret..." she murmured.

"What? Regret what? Lady? Hey, lady?"

"Nef..."

"Huh? Yoo-hoo?" He snapped his fingers in front of her eyes. She didn't so much as flinch.

Then it came to her, and quite suddenly, too. Her head snapped up and Innis Blake remembered. The pain of betrayal coursed hotly through her veins. The crushing agony of her own regrets: loving a man who had not returned her love.

Nefarious...

Bruce.

Bruce... the Nefarious Cocksucker.

While this Tom Morgan fellow continued dumbly on, Innis focused on the screen as Regret hunted. For Regret had known Innis's true heart all along. Innis would proudly watch Regret gift Bruce with her namesake.

But first, Bruce's plaything would suffer.

We're coming for you, fancy-pants, and when we find you, we will make you...

CRUELTY

MARKUM

Regret was not something Special Investigator Frank Markum bothered himself with. He knew that everyone had a conscience, but some were better than others at not listening. And some were plain old fucking deaf. Frank was the latter.

He still had not heard from Dennis, and like most people guilty of infidelity, Frank worried that Dennis might have another guy on the side. Or worse, Dennis had found out about Bruce.

After the crime scene team arrived, Frank bid farewell to his knew companions: the ever-pleasant and bright Natalie Holden, and Sheriff Randy Miser, who had proven a shitty jokester incapable of serious investigation. After all, he'd had a viper in the form of a deputy lingering right under his nose the entire time, and Miser had been completely oblivious. The man was laughable, at best, and Frank assumed the old fart's time as sheriff was coming to an end.

Frank had not said goodbye to the dog in the back seat of Miser's patrol car. Saw no reason to, even though the pooch did look awfully familiar.

Where had the sheriff said he'd gotten the beagle? From some fat guy in coveralls? Frank thought he had that right, but couldn't be sure. Miser had a horrible habit of rambling on to the point where his words turned into warm Jell-O and drained through the strainer of Frank's brain, leaving a sticky, unpalatable residue behind.

CRUELTY

Frank strode across the gravel turnabout in front of Turtle's trailer and to his cruiser. Natalie would be riding back with Miser. Frank was now, by his own standards, off duty. The outcome of the Twon sting could be garnered tomorrow. He was tired. But, more importantly, he was horny.

Long days at work tended to rile something deep within the state investigator. Like action movies with sex scenes, they belonged together. There was, to Frank Markum, nothing better than fucking after a long day at work.

So he decided to kill two birds with one stone.

He started his cruiser, backed out, and hit the highway, speeding along at well above the posted speed limit. He withdrew his cell phone from his coat pocket and speed-dialed Bruce.

Bruce was what Frank referred to as an undercover brother. A dude on the down-low. Bruce had a girlfriend (a rather pretty woman that Frank had found himself being jealous of on more than one occasion), but the man also loved the cock. Loved sucking it, to be exact. Bruce was no bottom, power or otherwise. He simply enjoyed pleasuring other men.

They'd met in a gay bar called, quite aptly, Flamingos, which was located on the outskirts of Fredericksburg. Frank had been on the prowl all night, looking to tap a little strange while Dennis was hung up at work, when he came across Bruce in the bathroom.

Now, gay bars are not as seedy as the straight community would have one believe. Sure, men fucked in stalls from time to time, but breeders did the same thing in their breeder-friendly clubs under breeder-friendly lights. Coke was sometimes snorted from the tops of toilet tanks, commodes could back up due to discarded condoms clogging the pipes, and one might find themselves skating briefly across the linoleum on a spot of blood, but that also could be found in any other entertainment venue across the world. And don't get him started on breeder-friendly strip clubs. If the girls' teeth outnumbered their tits, it was considered a great night in the Topless Texas scene.

Bruce answered on the third ring.

"You feel like swallowing something long and stiff tonight, Brucey?"

"Frank? That you?"

"Jesus, man, how many other guys are you currently blowing on a regular basis? Of course it's—"

"She ain't answering my calls, Frank?"

"What? Who?"

"Innis? My fiancé? She's not returning my calls. And the dog's gone. I noticed this morning. I think... I think she left me. Why else would Merlo be gone?"

Gooseflesh rolled like an ocean wave over Markum. He pulled the cruiser over to the side of the road, killed the engine, and staring at the scrub brush at the tree line.

The dog. That fucking dog. The one in the back seat of Miser's patrol car.

Merlo.

"Hello? Frank, are you there?" Bruce's trembling voice said.

"Yuh... yeah. Sorry. When was the last time you heard from her?"

"Last night. Well, I didn't actually hear from her. She called while we were... you know, and left a message saying she was on her way—Oh God, Frank... Do you think she saw us?"

Frank's mind flashed to the scene from the night before. He thought he would have remembered seeing someone watching him, so he didn't focus on obvious possibilities such as those. Instead, he honed in on the subtle changes. If someone had come in while Bruce had had his mouth full and working then something must have changed. His memory panned, like a camera with a wide-angle lens, and zoomed out.

No one in the window. He was sure of that. He'd been watching Bruce do his magic in the reflection on the pane. Just beyond that he could see the neighbor lady cooking dinner in her kitchen. Boy, if she would only look up and out she'd get an eyeful! His vision drifted left, across the closed bedroom door, to the closet, where no one lurked among the clothes and hangers and shoeboxes. He scanned the ceiling, looking for cameras. Nothing. His vision descended. Down over the cracked bedroom door. Down to Bruce's bobbing head. To his own heaving chest. Climax. Swallow. "You taste better every time, Frankie." Smile. "What can I say, Brucey, you bring out the best in—"

His memory flashed back to the bedroom door. Even in his passion, Bruce had remembered to close the door. It was a safety precaution. If his fiancé came in, surely she'd make some kind of noise (at least that was the assumption) and with the door closed, Frank might have time to hide in a closet or flee out a window like some fifties adultery cliché. But... But when Frank had gotten up and dressed and left, he hadn't needed to open the bedroom door. Because it was already open. Because someone had been watching.

And what if that someone was Innis—

(*of course it was, you fucking idiot!*)

—and what if Innis had some way of finding out who Frank was? Could she have solved the crime in a single day? Could she have called Dennis and told him of Frank's cheating ways? Is that why Dennis, oh lovely and sweet Dennis, *his* Dennis, wasn't answering his calls?

Frank huffed and puffed, his breathing suddenly car exhaust in his throat. He swallowed and his throat clicked. The hand on the steering wheel shone with glaringly white knuckles. He tried to pry them off the shiny leather but was unsuccessful.

"If your bitch called my boyfriend I'm going to kill her, him, and you."

"What the fuck are you talking about," Bruce asked angrily.

"I'm warning you, Bruce, if I find out she... she did something to fuck up my relationship, I'll drop that cunt down a well."

"What's wrong with you? Listen to yourself. This hasn't got shit to do with you, fucker!"

"Doesn't it? The bedroom door was open when I left, Bruce. It. Was. Open. Let that shit sink in for a minute, faggot."

"Oh, I'm the—"

"You better find her before I do, asshole. You just better."

Frank disconnected, feeling wholly depressed that he didn't have an old school telephone to slam down on its base. Pressing an end button was just so goddamn anticlimactic.

CRUELTY

TWON

Twon Chatham was lost.

With his flashlight and shotgun leading the way, the cook frantically skirted trees and kicked through fallen leaves. The woods' various scents assailed him: moss, bark, moldy dead things. But there was another stench lingering on the air. His own body odor. He could not recall the last time he'd bathed, and likened the waves of funk rolling off of him to that of pulped roadkill.

But he could shower later. After he killed the doll. The doll was the only thing that mattered now. Ollie would be avenged, and that big fucker would beg for death by the time Twon was through with him.

A woman's scream cleaved the air. Twon stopped, listened. Another peel of terror clenched his jaws. The screams seemed to be coming from off to his right, but he couldn't be sure, not in the woods, where everything sounded as if it were an intimate neighbor. Not knowing where else to go or what to do, he strafed in the direction of the woman's shrieking protestations.

Moments later, Twon exited the tree line and found himself at the rear of a trailer park. Monlezun Estates. He'd been here several times to drop off product with a dude who used to sell for him, until said dude went up the river, that is. Now that salesman (what was the guy's name? Hermes? Herbert? Heathcliff?) was some Aryan's bitch. My, how things could go south on a person in a hurry.

Directly in front of him sat a double-wide. He was facing the rear of it, but could see lights on within. For the moment, all was silent. Bracing the shotgun on his shoulder, Twon swung around the trailer in quick steps.

Skirting lay in disarray all about what constituted the place's front lawn. It seemed someone had ripped the plastic sheets off in a fuck-all big hurry in an attempt to get under the trailer itself. Through the gaping hole that had been left at the bottom of the trailer, Twon found nothing but darkness and quietude.

Another scream. This one most definitely to his right. Twon swung around, hunting the sound.

In between a pale blue trailer (Twon saw all this by the glow of a single arc sodium lamp, which was perched atop a telephone pole in the middle of the park) and one with maroon trim around the roof, was a short, fat woman in a housecoat and curlers. She was pointing and squealing at a dark shape that was just now moving out of sight and into the road.

"Hey!" Twon barked.

The woman spun, wide-eyed, and gawped at Twon in a state of utter shock.

"It... it had a head!" she yelled.

"Get the fuck inside, bitch. Now!" His command had nothing to do with the woman's safety, only his need for no witnesses. He planned on laying waste to the sack of shit in the doll mask, and didn't want some fat bitch with her hair in rollers taking the witness stand against him in the future.

She jiggled her way up the steps of the trailer with the maroon trim. She disappeared inside.

This was it. This was the end. He was actually going to kill the fucker who had murdered his brother. In his excitement, Twon didn't realize his dick was hard. It throbbed, unnoticed, against his zipper.

"COME BACK HERE, YOU MUDDAHFUCKAH! GET WHAT COMIN' TO YOU, SEEN!" Twon roared.

He rushed forward, shotgun at the ready, flashlight swaying madly. At the exit of the trailer park, he swung his flash side to side, searching the direction in which his prey had fled. Down the street, maybe fifty yards from where Twon stood, the doll lumbered along under the glow of a streetlamp.

He's headed for town, Twon thought, before bolting after the immense shape.

Something swung from the doll's hand. It looked like a bowling ball on a leash. Only it wasn't a leash in its grasp. It was hair. And that bowling ball had a fucking face.

The shock of what he was seeing caused Twon to come to a skittering stop. He hopped on one foot in an attempt to keep his balance.

"The fuck that is?" he breathed. "The fuck that was?"

The doll rolled on, tossing its shoulder out before sweeping its leg along. Twon thought it looked injured, what with the odd motion of its gait. Didn't really matter, though, as it would be dead a few heartbeats from now.

Twon leveled the shotgun on the lurching doll, took a bead on it down the sights, lined up nice and neat as you please, and squeezed the trigger.

The dual hammers of the over and under clacked on dead shells.

"Goddamn it!" Twon raged.

As random memory often does, images flitted into his mind. Ollie standing in the basement, cussing, soaked to the bone. Billy Yearling was on his knees in the corner. The skinny kid had shorted them over a hundred bucks on the tweak they'd fronted him. He was sobbing. Snot ran down his face, as if invisible snails were racing for the finish line of his chin. The over and under was cocked open, resting in the crook of Ollie's arm. He'd been about to scare Billy by blasting a hole in the wall next to the kid's head, but the shotty hadn't fired. Ollie fumed. "Fucking shells are worthless, man. Remind me to kill that motherfucker Charlie, will ya? Dickbag sold me bullshit buckshot!"

Now, Twon was the one who dropped a string of expletive-laden sentences as he snapped the breach, removed the shells, and replaced them with two from the pocket of his jeans. Ahead of him, the baby doll lumbered on, seemingly unaware of Twon's presence.

He flipped the shotgun closed, aimed, pulled the triggers.

Snap.

No boom.

"*MUDDAHFUCKAH!*"

He reloaded twice more, but each time the gun misfired. Every shell he'd brought with him was a fucking dud. Goddamned useless!

Headlights approaching. High beams at that. Twon bolted for cover, finding it behind the big rectangle of the trailer park's signage. Behind the words MONLEZUN ESTATES, he hid, and very carefully plotted his next course of action.

CRUELTY

PAUL

An hour earlier...

Paul Nelson closed his H. R. Chatman paperback and glanced around the truck stop's dining area. He felt watched, and his instincts rarely betrayed him.

There was a tubby white man seated by his lonesome at the diner's bar, three rows over from where Paul sat at a table in the epicenter of the restaurant. The man's ass cheeks resembled bulldog jowls. Paul assumed that, given enough time and gravity, the man's rump would eventually come to puddle like candle wax on the floor around the stool. Still, this man was facing the kitchen area and could not be blamed for Paul's nagging sense of being stalked.

The heavy-breasted black lady at the booth next to the entrance was equally innocent, though Paul wouldn't mind her attentions. A proper shag with him would knock the kink out of her hair.

Two ankle-nibblers jounced by—a young boy and an even younger girl, neither over ten years—and he wondered where the bloody hell their parents had gotten off to. It was almost one in the fucking morning, and here these two were rabblerousing like a couple of nitwits.

Fucking children. He was glad his own daughter was of age and out of the nest. Charmaine had hit eighteen and the road at roughly the same time. Seeing his daughter leave home had been such a bittersweet occasion that he'd caught the diabetes. All jokes aside, his doctor had said he'd had the sugar disease for years, but they were just now finding it because Paul hated everything having to do with hospitals. Doctors and their diagnoses were like a bunch of poofter psychics dooming everyone to a life of medication and finger-up-the-arse examinations. He was still considering allowing them to put an insulin pump inside him. He was so very tired of needles.

His eyes continued to roam the mostly empty restaurant, until finally they alighted on their prize.

The woman was all of twenty (he hoped, anyway) and, on a scale of one to ten, a perfect fifty. Long, ash-blonde hair, the kind you could tug and wouldn't have to worry about it falling out in your hand. Breasts shoved up to her chin (they'd probably sag outside of that Wonder-doodad she had elevating them at the moment, but a sandbag was better than a silicone doughnut any day of the week), the cleavage long and inviting. Her knit top was a putrid shade of shit brown, but Paul was more interested in what the shirt contained than the fashion statement it made. The rest of her was concealed under the booth, yet he imagined a tight ass, one he could bounce a quid off to make a hundred pence. But the best part about her were her eyes, and the fact that she couldn't keep them off him.

Paul glanced back at his copy of *Timber*, riffled the pages, and thought long and hard about his wife. He generally didn't play away from the marriage bed, but he was roughly a fucking world away from Debra. And, besides, how would she find out?

The woman's stare burned a hole the diameter of his boss's ass in the back of his shaved head, which was to say, a big bastard of a cavern. His meat and two veg pressed warm and heavy against the inside of his thigh, and for the first time in his life, he was upset he hadn't worn any underwear.

"Get ahold of yourself, mate. She'd fuck you into the ground and leave you for the gophers."

Would that be such a bad thing…?

CRUELTY

The waitress—a chunky gal with a face like a pushed-in fender—brought Paul his plate of eggs and toast, asked if he needed anything else, and when he said no, shambled off like an extra on *The Walking Dead*.

Paul ate with fervor, soaking up the runny yellow of the yoke with slices of crusty bread, and washed it all down with a cup of coffee. America didn't do much right, but their roadside coffee was better than English tea any day of the week.

The curious woman in the shit-brown blouse took a seat across from him. Paul still had his mug to his lips when she flopped down, her hair bouncing, and he almost choked on the final swig. She beamed at him, the smile on her face rimmed with such a dark shade of red that her lips looked almost purple.

"Hey," she blurted.

"Can I help you?" Paul asked over the rim of his coffee cup.

"Sure. Help me all you want." She smiled wider, and Paul could do nothing but blink at her.

Debra, mate. Your wife's name is Debra. She's the mother of your child, and not at all bad in the bed. Keep the safety on your cock before you shoot the wrong lady.

When he didn't answer, his new breakfast companion (could you call it breakfast at one in the morning?) slapped a palm down atop the novel he'd been reading and slid it over in front of herself. She picked it up, opened it to its bookmark (which was currently an email he'd printed out about his new training assignment here in the States), and began reading a passage.

"*She watched the creature made of wood devour her friend. The impossibility of this monster, the insanity of it, locked her in place, as if she, herself, had roots.*" Her eyes flitted up. "Who writes this shit, huh?"

"H. R. Chatman. He's a midget. Real name is Donald Adams. Chatman's a pen name. Been reading him for years." All this came out in a steady tone, and Paul thanked whatever deity had kept his voice steady. Women didn't, as a rule, flummox him, but he was currently so worried that he might traipse willy-nilly into the realm of adultery that a tremor in his voice wouldn't be such an unlikely exception to the rule.

He was a handsome bloke, he knew that; someone women pined over and men hated. He'd had to deal with overzealous females since he had completed his apprenticeship as an electrical engineer, which was a fancy way of saying that he fixed shit other people had mucked up.

"Midget?" she frowned. "I think they prefer 'little people.'"

"Never been one for using safe words, sorry. I've offended you, then. My apologies, but you've seemed to come over here and not the other way around." Paul realized he still hadn't lowered his cup, then did so.

"Meaning?" she asked.

"Meaning, I guess, that you're the one who was interested in me. Awkward, innit? You come over here expecting James Bond and find yourself chatting up John Cleese. Fuckin' tragedy, that."

She laughed, and it was musical. He enjoyed the sound of it very much, and had to think about Debra to keep from ripping this woman's clothes off right here and now. Jesus, but her tits were amazing.

Settle, mate...

"So," she said after a moment's silence, "you're... British?"

"Staffordshire. United Kingdom. Born and raised, and God save the bloody Queen, if it pleases ya." He was laying it on thick, but Americans were quite stupid. Especially those that frequented truck stops.

"I'm not one of those girls that swoon over Englishmen just because they're from across the pond. Your accent is nice, but you're kind of a jerk."

Paul took another sip of his coffee, then laid the mug back on the Formica tabletop. "What's your deal then?

Why're you still sitting here? I'm forty, got a spot of gray in my goatee, and"—he held up his left hand, twirled the gold band on his ring finger—"I got someone waiting—how did you say it?—across the pond."

She nodded at his raised hand. "That's exactly why I came over. I like married men. They're safe. No worries about you wanting some lovey-dovey romance with me. I like fucking 'em and sending them home to their women." She leaned across the table, her breasts smashing and expanding against the Formica. "Spent. Drained. Dripping."

"Jesus, you're a brash one."

"I'm offering, is all. Is she still in... where was it? Staffordshire?"

Paul nodded, not because he had been rendered speechless, which he hadn't, but because he was coldly calculating stuffing this woman like a turkey.

"There's quite a few miles between the two of you. What would it hurt? Really, who'd know?"

Paul sighed. "Unfortunately, I would. So, unless you're paying for my breakfast, I suggest you find another sausage for your morning meal. Go on now, my coffee needs refilling. That's a good lass."

The hungry, seductive quality of her face vanished like a tube up a chute at a drive-up teller. She was suddenly, ferociously ugly. He wondered if this is what she would have looked like after sex, once she'd gotten what she'd come for.

"Fuck you, asshole."

"That's mighty U. S. of A of you. Carry on now."

"Eat my ass," she said as she rose.

"Thought I already took a pass on that?" He forced a smile.

"Cocksucker."

He laughed. "You're one to talk."

She left. Paul went back to his coffee. It was cold. He blamed it on the needy twat with the ash-blonde hair.

He paid his ticket and walked outside to his car, a Toyota Corolla he'd rented from a Hertz inside Houston International. The night was ungodly cold, or perhaps his internal temperature was up due to the coffee. Or the girl. One of the two, anyway.

His tool kit and luggage lay in the passenger seat. Force of habit, really. Anytime he travelled he kept his belongings beside him to mimic a passenger. Made traversing the highways and byways of foreign lands a little more bearable if he maintained the illusion that he wasn't all alone.

As he backed out and got back on the road, he considered his reasoning for not taking the ash-blonde girl up on her offer of a one-night stand. Could it be he was actually a decent guy? He laughed aloud at the thought. He was having a go at himself.

Truth was, he loved Debra, and couldn't see himself diddling some college sophomore while his wife waited at home. Alone. Like him.

Get a grip, you poof. Leave the mushy shit out with the bins.

He took the highway into Kerrville, intent on bypassing the interstate on his way to Fort Hood, where he'd be training a group of greenhorns in the various intricacies of installing wires and other boring equipment. Four years at university and twenty years on the job. Nowadays he trained younger blokes with his knowledge and experience, and collected a mighty wage for his time and effort. When Newfoundland Prime opened a warehouse in Fort Hood, Texas, USA, Paul had jumped at the chance of travelling abroad. Sure, it was the farthest he'd ever been from Debra, but the duration wouldn't be half as long as some of his other jobs. He'd be home again, home again, jiggedy jig, in two shakes of a whippoorwill.

These thoughts occupied his mind as he drove through downtown Kerrville, on a course that would forever alter him. He passed the strip of stores that housed Pompeii Café's dark storefront, as well as the medical complex a little way farther down the road, before crossing the Guadalupe and heading out of town by way of Highway 16.

Twenty-four hours earlier, a deaf kid looking for his first sexual encounter had stopped at the gas station Paul was just now tooling by. His rental car rolled over a handgun in the middle of the road, one that had gone surprisingly unnoticed over the course of the day, that had once belonged to a meth addict named Jennifer, who currently resided in Moxie Macleod's cold storage room inside the Kerr County Medical Examiner's office. A few miles down, Paul passed a broken down Pontiac Bonneville, which sat in the scrub, dark and squat like a lurking beast. No one would ever come to claim that car. Paul made no note of it.

On this dark highway, Paul Nelson approached his fate unknowingly, oblivious to the horrors awaiting him.

He came across the doll's path at a quarter to two in the morning. He was considering calling Debra—there was six hours difference between them and she would be just now getting out of bed to start her morning routine before heading off to work—when he saw the hulking figure step out into the road. He had time to note the object dangling from the figure's right hand before he swerved and slammed on his brakes, in that exact order. Anyone who has driven more than a handful of times will tell you that this is not the recommended way of avoiding something in the path of your speeding automobile. The brakes caught, the traction on the tires became inconsequential, and Paul went careening into a telephone pole at a little over forty miles per hour. The impact slung him face first into the steering wheel, where his nose was ruined in an explosion of cartilage and blood.

Even after all this, Paul remained conscious. He was quite with it when the driver's side door opened and night flooded in. His mind tabulated these events with an eerie calm: he was dragged, moaning and bleeding, from the car; his chin was then propped up on the frame at the bottom of the car door, and he could see the gas and brake pedals in the glow of the interior light; an immense force crashed down on the back of his head and the nape of his neck, and suddenly he couldn't feel his legs; the force returned, abated... returned, abated.

He was rolling. When he came to rest he was looking over at himself. His headless, twitching body lay perpendicular to the car. The driver's side door was closed, and a thick liquid dripped from the bottom of the frame onto his back.

Dreaming. He was dreaming. He was dreaming that a huge baby doll was watching him from where it stood motionless under a streetlamp, beside his beheaded corpse. He was dreaming that the doll had a woman's head dangling from one hand by its hair. He was dreaming about the girl who had wanted to fuck him. He was dreaming of Debra. He was dreaming of not being alone. Of not dying alone. Of... of... of...

CRUELTY

Cruelty regarded the man's head thoughtfully. Should it take the head with it? Probably not. It already had the woman's head. That was enough.

It turned its attention to the Toyota. The front left headlight was smashed in and it was a wonder the air bag hadn't deployed. Faulty, maybe? Cruelty imagined the car would drive all right, as it was currently still running. It bent down and dug its fingers into the flesh and gore of the body's draining neck. It hefted the corpse up and tossed it into the woods. It left the head on the side of the road—a meal for crows.

Cruelty was saddened that it hadn't the chance to suckle the pain from the driver, but oh well. It was still full from feeding on the woman. Gluttony didn't serve its purposes. Besides, there would be more. So much more. An entire town. A town full up with delicious suffering. And if he came across those that did not suffer, it would make them suffer. And Cruelty would be satiated to the point of bursting.

Cruelty adjusted the seat and stuffed itself behind the wheel of the Corolla. It threw the car into reverse and backed into the road. It had been a full day since it had driven, and it already missed the feel of the road: the way the tire rumbled over the pavement, the cool night air pouring in from the open window, the feeling of freedom. The feeling that it could go anywhere it pleased.

Five miles from town, Cruelty was wracked with another wave of hot agony. Its chest burned. Its eyes

341

watered. Pulling into the dark parking lot of Bob's Bait and Fuel, Cruelty found it was weeping uncontrollably. It hunted the reasoning, barreling through its own thoughts, trying to make sense of this pain, this fiery, soul-scorching pain.

Its breath came in hot bursts, and Cruelty was only vaguely aware that it shouldn't be breathing. After all, it didn't have lungs, and its heart was nothing more than a device powered by dark magic. It blinked, and was stunned motionless.

I have eyelids...

The thought came like a brakeless semi down a mountain pass, and caromed recklessly through its mind. When had it grown eyelids? What was happening to it?

But you've had them, child. You've had them all along. Remember? Remember winking at that boy? It was here, inside this very gas station. You winked at the deaf boy.

An icy fear the likes Cruelty had never known—

(*but maybe it had known such a fear, yes, maybe, once upon a time*)

—coursed through its veins.

No! I don't have veins!

It was nothing but a toy, a tool, a possession. It had no lungs to breathe, no eyelids to blink, no veins to pump blood... and yet... and yet it did. It could now feel the thudding of a muscle in its chest. Not a ticking, but a beating. A heart... beating.

Cruelty wailed. It thrashed about the inside of the sedan, pounded the steering wheel into a shapeless mass, smashed in the radio's face, cracked the dash, shattered the driver's side window.

"*H-h-h... HELP ME!*" This wasn't a coo, nor was it some prerecorded baby doll voice. This was a voice. A real human voice. And that scared Cruelty. This monster who had never known true fear—

(*yet maybe it had*)

—was now in the grip of a crippling terror.

CRUELTY

The old black woman flashed in Cruelty's vision, and suddenly, it (*HE!*) was back in her home, standing in her living room, listening to her talk, taking in her words, processing them... understanding...

I see you, bon ti fi, you poor little one. I see you in the fog. You come for me, been searching for me, been so close to me this entire time, and you don't even know it.

Now, Cruelty loosed a tormented wail into the ceiling of the car.

What that thing done to you, child? What horrors have you seen to bring you to this state? Oh, Lody, your father... your father was an evil man.

"STOP C-C-C-CALLING MUH-ME TH-TH-THAT!"

Cruelty descended into madness.

You are Lody.

I am Cruelty.

You were only a child.

I am a monster.

You weren't always like this.

There's never been anything else.

He made you this.

My father's dead... No... No, I have no father.

Not your father. Him. The Midnight Man.

No.

Yes.

Lody is dead. DEAD!

Now, the old woman spoke in his head (*its head*), and her words were new, not of the house, not of that time before he awoke in the woods surrounded by the pieces of a deaf man:

Lody, his grip on you is faltering. You can be free, bon ti fi. Seek it. Seek freedom.

Then another voice, this one ancient and wise:

You will do great things, child...

Cruelty exploded from the car. The driver's side door went careening across the empty parking lot and came to rest beside one of Bob's gas pumps. Cruelty, sobbing, stumbled from the wreckage. It twisted, set its sight on the vehicle, and rushed it. It hit the side of the Toyota like a bull moose smelling a female's scent on a tree. Cruelty dug its fingers into the roof, attempted to rip it off, but the entire car came with it.

Such power, such dark, horrible power, coursed through Lody (*CRUELTY!*). It slung the car—as if the Toyota weighed no more than a baseball—into the woods surrounding Bob's Bait and Fuel. The car mangled three trees and ripped a fourth from the ground.

"*I AM CRUELTY! I AM—*"

—*a scared child*—

"*—CRUELTY! I AM CRUELTY!*"

Its voice was not unlike a young boy in the fit of a temper tantrum. High and screeching were its wails. Cracking and indecipherable were its words.

In the dark of early morning, Cruelty lamented.

And Lody, if only briefly, was mourned.

RANDY

Sheriff Randy Miser tried Nick Wuncell's cell phone number eight times before dropping Natalie off at her car. She said her goodbyes, yawned, and wished Merlo, who was in the back seat licking himself, a pleasant night.

"Good luck with your deputy, Sheriff," Natalie said as she began to close the door.

"Hey," Randy called after her.

"Yeah?" she said, sticking her head back into the car.

"Do you work this mornin'? I might need you to fill out a statement. You know, about what we heard on that message machine of Turtle's?"

"No, I'm off for the next two days. Call me if you need me. Do you have my number?"

Randy shook his head. She ticked off the numbers while he punched them into his phone.

"It's going to be all right, Sheriff. Everything passes. This will too."

"Right. You're not the one that's gotta interrogate your own deputy. Get some rest, Nat. We'll be seeing you."

"Night." She closed the door and went to her car, where it sat alone in front of Pompeii Café. Randy waited until she got in before pulling away.

"Well, looks like we're all alone, Merl'. Whatcha say we hit the strip club?"

Merlo continued to lick his balls.

"Right. I gotta confront Nick. I'd hate to have to put out an APB on him. Doesn't seem right, you know?"

Merlo met Randy's eyes in the rearview mirror and chuffed, as if to say, "Sounds good to me. Now, back to my regularly scheduled tongue bath. If you'll excuse me..."

"Sheriff?" the radio asked. "Sheriff, you there?"

"God bless it," Randy growled as he reached for the transceiver. "Go ahead, Shirley."

"Finally, I got someone," her voice crackled over the speaker. "I've been trying to get Nick or Robert or anyone to answer my damn—sorry—my dang calls, but no one's so much as telling me to go jump in the river. I have a lady out at Monlezun Estates says some fat guy in a doll mask and—she used a much uglier word than what I'm about to use—some black guy with a shotgun just rolled through there, one chasing the other. Says she heard screaming coming from her landlord's house, so she went outside to check on her, and that's when the— how'd she put it—the nightmare parade come through."

"Oh sweet baby Jesus, Shirley... Ain't nobody answerin'?"

"No, sir, not a one."

"All—" That's when what Shirley had said hit Randy full in the gut. It took his wind away, and he sat there, gaping at himself in the mirror.

"Didja say one of them had on a baby doll mask, Shirley? Please don't tell me that's what you said."

"If I changed my story I'd be lying, Sheriff. She most certainly said baby doll mask. Them exact words."

"God willin' and the creek don't rise, I'm going to wake up at some point and all this hootenanny horse crap's gonna be just some terrible dream, I swear it. Listen, Shirley, you call this number I'm about to give you, and you raise the guy that answers the phone. You be real nice to him, you hear. You get him to put on his gun, and meet me out at the Monlezun's trailer park. He's going to be mad you woke him, but you remind him he owes me a favor. Will you do that? He goes by the name of Matthew. You tell him he owes me for the birds, all right?"

"What's all this about, Sheriff?"

"Well, if none of my deputies want to answer the call, I'll just have to deputize someone else, won't I. Keep trying to raise the rest of the men, but hold off on Nick. I'll phone him myself, you got that?"

"Yessir."

Randy rattled off Matthew's number, then hung the receiver back on its cradle. He dialed Natalie, and she answered on the fourth ring. She already sounded groggy, but Randy doubted she'd already made it home.

"Need you again, little lady. I got a bead on your guy in the doll mask."

"Goddamn it," she groaned. The sounds of pop music emanating from Natalie's end of the line waned then disappeared altogether. He figured she'd been listening to the offal to keep her awake. No grown person with half a head on their shoulders listened to that teenybopper crap.

"Might not want to blaspheme, Nat, we're gonna need all the help we can get tonight. God's included."

"Yeah, yeah, where should I meet you?"

"Go back to Pompeii Café. We'll take my car."

"If it's all the same to you—"

"It's not all the same to me, Nat. You're technically off duty. If something happens to you while you're driving your car, I'm responsible... er, well the town is, at any rate, and I think we have enough trouble on our hands as it is. Pompeii, okay?"

"Yeah. Be right there."

Randy disconnected. He made a U-turn and asked the Lord for the strength to get through this night. The sheriff had no idea what was going on in his town, but he intended to find out. Sleep deprived or not, he had a job to do. He yawned wide and blew a cloud of foul breath into the car. The smell could have killed cancer.

He parked in front of the café's glass frontage and killed the engine. Two minutes later, Natalie came rolling up. She got out and the lights on her vehicle flashed on and off twice. She'd obviously set her alarm system. She jogged up to the passenger side of Randy's cruiser, popped the door open, and slid in.

"I tried reaching Frank, but he's got his phone turned off. Looks like we're on our own."

"Yeah, none of my graveyard boys are answering the horn, either. I got someone else coming in. Guy owes me a solid," Randy said as he pulled away from the curb. "He's the son of an old friend of mine. Both him and his pa used to be cops, once upon a time."

"What happened?" she asked.

"What? You mean, why ain't they cops no more?"

"Yeah."

"Well, his pa's retired, and Matthew... well, let's just say Matthew left the force for personal reasons. He wasn't a cop around here, though. Kid's a Yankee, born in Ohio. Here I am callin' him a kid, and he's your age." Randy loosed a spatter of nervous laughter. "Anyway, he moved down here after his pa took ill, so's that he could see after him. He'll do in a pinch, believe you me."

"What happened to your night shift?" Natalie asked.

"That, my dear, is the question, ain't it?"

NELL

Nell Morgan sat on her living room sofa, staring at her television screen. The TV was off and the house quiet. She'd forgotten something, something important, and she could feel other things slipping away as well.

For instance, there was a strange man in all the photos scattered around her house. He was a handsome looking sort, but she had no idea why he should be in so many of her pictures. There was even a photograph of him kissing her. She wore a wedding gown in this picture, and the handsome man wore a tuxedo. The only explanation she could find for this was that she'd done a bit of playacting after a night of drinking and someone had captured the odd snapshot. She wasn't married. Surely she would have remembered something like that.

"Oh, Tom," she whispered.

Her mind cycled from forgotten things to remembrance in the flutter of an eyelid. This had happened four times in the hour since Natalie and the sheriff had dropped her off at home. She'd told them she hadn't wanted to go to the hospital to check on Tom because she could recall no reason to do so. Who was this Tom person and why should she want to check on him? So Nell Morgan had simply answered Natalie's question of "Do you want to see about Tom?" with "No. I'm too tired."

Now, Tom was all she could think about. Well, he was all she could think about when she remembered to think about him. My, but she was terribly confused.

She ambled to the front door, pulled it open, and stepped out into the cool air that lingered about her porch. It was quarter past two in the morning. The streetlight down the road looked like an orange sun burning in the darkness at the edge of her vision, and her lawn shone a sickly yellow. The scene made her uneasy: plain, autumn-stricken front yard, its grass brown and crispy, like overcooked bacon; dead leaves scattered about, dotting her lawn with spatters of red and yellow; the hose coiled snake-like. Everything seemed dead or dying or dangerous, and Nell wanted Tom home more than ever. But he wouldn't be coming home, would he? No, not ever again.

Though she did not remember the previous times, she checked her driveway for her Ford station wagon. The LTD was, of course, not there. She'd left it up at the hospital when—

What was she doing out in the cold? She tried to rub away the goose bumps, which rose from her forearms like headless pimples, but they remained. She couldn't recall stepping outside. Couldn't think of a single reason for her to be shivering on her front porch.

—she'd checked on Tom earlier that day, when they told her they were going to pull the plug on her husband. That they were going to kill her Tom. Then she'd run. Out of the hospital. Through the turnabout. Into the street. Someone had tried to console her, and Nell had run screamingly from them. She'd fled to the bridge that crossed the Guadalupe, had mounted the low wall and dangled her feet over the river. She'd planned to jump, until—

Why was she so damned cold? Her shivering intensified, and her teeth began to chatter. She gazed out over her dull orange lawn, and smelled a hint of woodsmoke on the air. Before too long it would be winter, and it would be even colder. She really needed to get back inside.

CRUELTY

—Tom had appeared next to her. No, not Tom; some *thing* that was most definitely not Tom. It had the yellow mustard stain on the lapel of its uniform, yes, but that thing was most assuredly not her Tom. Her Tom was dead, or soon would be. If that heartless hospital staff had anything to do with it, Tom Morgan would be a flesh Popsicle by morning. My, but that was—

A child stood in the middle of her yard. Nell Morgan gave off a short squeak and took a step in reverse. Why this lonesome looking boy should have such a frightening effect on her was beyond her. He was small, almost wraithlike, and clothed in a blue button-down top and black slacks. One sapphire blue eye sparkled with knowing life, while the other was covered in a leather eyepatch. The boy smiled a withered smile and approached the steps of the porch. No, he did not approach. He glided, as a ghost will glide down the corridors of its haunt. This boy came on the wind, and it whispered his welcome.

—a morbid thing to think. *Flesh Popsicle*? How cruel and unlike her. This was her husband of whom she thought, her poor, broken, lifeless Tom. The man she'd shared thousands of meals with, the gentle man who'd made love to her, who'd cuddle with her when she felt the weight of existence crushing her very soul. Tom Morgan, her heart, her love, her—

"Who... who are you?" she asked.

"A second chance," the boy said.

—companion while traversing the dark waters of this world. But, if the thing on the bridge had not been Tom, what had it been? And what had it done—*what was it doing*—to her? Black threads of wispy ink had come off her, and she had felt lighter, almost drunk, as the thing suckled those threads from her person. It had been eating. Feeding off her. And it had taken something of import. Something—

"What do you mean," Nell Morgan asked the boy with the eyepatch.

"I can help you remember, just as he's made you forget." The boy took a gentle step up onto the first of her four steps. The boards did not creak under his weight, and Nell thought this was because he wasn't touching. Not in the least.

—dire and needed and blissful. It had taken a piece of her. She suddenly could not recall Tom's face, and it was only after a tremendous inner struggle that she had been able to remember that it was Tom whose face she couldn't recall. Someone had stuffed her inside a police vehicle (she'd assumed as much anyway, for there was a Plexiglas partition between the front and rear seats), and then she was looking at Natalie Holden, the woman who'd come to see her when Tom was first admitted. But what lay over Natalie's shoulder had been far more pressing. It had been—

"It dwells in shadows and feeds off memories. I was once like him, but I've since been released," the boy said from the second step now.

—darkness. A full and unyielding darkness where light goes to die and hell itself quakes in its presence. A cold, dank pit of despair, where tragedy and suffering lingers, breathing… Sustained… Nourished. A place of death that is unending. A withered, gnarled plain. Nell had seen all this in the thing's twisting shade. She had—

"Go away. You're not welcome here."

From the third step, the boy said, "You need me, Nell."

"I only need you to go away!"

—come to then. Poor Natalie had been locked in its gaze while Nell was away, and with some effort, Nell was able to draw Natalie back. And who was it Natalie had said she'd seen? Her father? Nell had wondered absently what forgiveness Natalie sought from that particular man. What had the trooper done to her father? What shadows—

"I'm the only one who can help you. All of you," the boy said as he stepped up onto the final riser.

CRUELTY

"What are you?" Nell quivered.

The boy smiled his haunted smile. "A friend."

FORGIVENESS

F orgiveness roared. His bellow shook the woodwork of the witchery woman's home. She cowered away from him, fear shining brightly in her aged eyes.

It couldn't be. It wasn't possible. Not him. Not... *Him*!

Yet Forgiveness had known *He* was here. Forgiveness had foretold that he wasn't alone. Back in that hospital room, back with that comatose state trooper in that bed surrounded by machines that were meant to keep Tom Morgan alive.

If Forgiveness had believed in a one and true god, this is where he would have begun to pray.

"Oh, the demon looks scared," the witchery woman said. Her terror had vanished, and now she seemed utterly pleased with the course the night had taken.

"Shut up, bitch!" Forgiveness growled.

He was losing control, had to reign himself in. He would not let this affect his plans. *First thing's first*, he thought. *Find Cruelty, find Regret, and then tear this town asunder*. Kerrville would be stricken from the map by daylight. Every soul writhing in the Withered by sunrise. Forgiveness had had quite enough. It was time to harvest the crops.

He glared at the empty shell that had once housed Hotel and released the man from his bonds. The agent crumpled beside the body of... *Who the hell is that*? Forgiveness asked himself. The thick-bodied black man (the guy obviously made a habit of the gym) didn't look familiar, but there was something about him, something... residual. Forgiveness had touched so many souls during his travels that he supposed he'd come across this one at some point. Still, if he had come across this one, this body-builder with the gunshot wound in his thinker, it had been when the man was just a boy. Perhaps that was the shadow that clung to this corpse: a memory of youth.

"Your boy is either dead or dying by now," Forgiveness said, averting his gaze from the corpse and pointing a thin finger at the witchery woman. "My Cruelty will tear him limb from limb, but that will only be the beginning of his suffering."

"Twon might not defeat your puppet, demon, but he know the lay o' the land, he does. What he don' got for brains he make up for with anger... *seen*?" She chuckled, and Forgiveness could find no reason for her joviality.

He snapped his fingers. The witchery woman shot to the roof. He stuffed her into one corner, her neck twisted at an unnatural angle.

"Call him back, woman. Call that boy of yours back. Cruelty will follow, I have no doubt."

The witchery woman cackled breathlessly. The angle of her neck made her words come at ragged intervals. "You think... you think the doll is the hunter here, demon? You... you... you should think twice ah... about that!"

"*WHERE IS HE*?" Forgiveness thundered.

The witchery woman continued to cackle.

He eased himself into his next words. "Answer me, witch."

"Oh, so you know... know me after all?" The top of her head had reached her shoulder, and one of her ears was now plastered to her chest. Another inch or so and her neck would snap like a pretzel stick.

In the calmest tone Forgiveness could muster, he said, "When I'm through with you, you're going to wish Cruelty had killed you."

"I got bigger t'ings... than you and your puppet to worry about, demon. *He comes*. You sense him. I sense him. My boys... my boys been tryin'... to save me. But e'ery circle 'ventually... 'ventually come back around, it does."

"Help me find Cruelty and we'll destroy Him together."

The witchery woman barked mirthless laughter. Her breath came harder now. "He been... been hunting me longer than I can 'member. This ending... seems best, it does. I won' live in a world with you in it. If that means we all perish, so be it."

"So be it," Forgiveness repeated somberly.

"Come, demon," the witchery woman said. "Come to Momma."

Forgiveness fed, and the witchery woman's life unfolded like a pop-up book in Forgiveness's mind.

CRUELTY

RANDY

So much death and destruction in such a small amount of time. Kerrville had once been a peaceful place. A town were you could let your kids play outside long after the streetlights came on. A place where a murder might pop up maybe once every couple of years, and only then because Jim couldn't hold his liquor, or Susie caught Bobby with his sword in a different sheath. Murder around these parts was never for sport, but someone had had their fun with Anne-Marie Monlezun.

He stood in the sullen light of Monlezun's bedroom, minding his steps, skirting the blood, neither of which was an easy task. There were pieces of the woman everywhere, and more blood than a bucketful. Her torso lay on the dresser. Shards of silvery glass jutted from her face and chest like shiny tombstones. She'd obviously been thrown into the mirror at some point.

An idiot with brain damage could have recreated the scene. The blood trail began at the gaping hole in the floor of the hallway and led to the splatter painting that was Monlezun's bedroom. Before entering the landlady's home, Randy had noted the torn away sheet metal that had once served as trailer skirting. Randy surmised that whoever her attacker had been (this killer in the baby doll mask, if Beatrice next door was right. He'd find out once Natalie got done talking to the woman), the Halloween reject had come through the god-blessed floor like some kind of hellish jack-in-the-box. Cue dismembered Anne-Marie Monlezun and one thoroughly confused sheriff.

"Sheriff Miser! Randy?" Natalie called from outside.

Randy sidestepped over the pit in Monlezun's hallway and went into the living room. The front door had been open when he got here, but he hadn't realized the state it was in. The dang thing was bent to almost an L shape. The sheriff wondered what kind of drugs this character was on to be able to do something like that to Monlezun's door. Not to mention Monlezun herself.

When they'd first arrived, he'd sent her to question Beatrice O'Neil, the woman who'd called in the disturbance in the first place, while he scoped out Monlezun's trailer. Now, Natalie stood at the bottom of the landlady's steps, looking stricken and more than a little green.

"She's dead," Natalie said, and swallowed hard.

"Yeah, she is. In a whole bunch of pieces, too." Randy shook his head sorrowfully.

"Who?"

Randy perked up. "Monlezun." He hitched a thumb to the open front door behind him. "The landlord. Who're you talking about?"

"Beatrice, I think is what you called her. The woman who phoned? Yeah, her. She's dead, too."

"But..." For the first time in nigh on a decade, Sheriff Randy Miser was speechless.

"Her door was ajar, so I pushed it in. She's lying in the middle of her living room with her face caved in. There's a shotgun on the floor next to the body. It's one of those old over and unders, and the butt is covered in blood. Not hard to tell that that's the murder weapon. Funny thing, though, 'cause she ain't shot, and the gun's got shells in it."

"You didn't fool with it, did you?" he asked, concerned.

"No. The breach is open. I imagine whoever beat her to death snapped the latch while... well, you get the picture."

"I don't get it. I just don't see none of this adding up to anything, Nat." He ran trembling fingers through his thinning hair. "I mean, I got a woman in here that could moonlight as one of those thousand-piece puzzles them old folks do up at the retirement home, and now you got someone with their face bashed in. There's no rhyme or reason to it. No modus opera—"

"Operandi," she corrected.

"I don't care if it's Oprah dang-blasted Winfrey! What I'm saying is, crazy is usually methodical, right? What I mean to say is, Jeffrey Dahmer ate people. Gacy killed kids. Bundy strangled women. Get me?"

"Yeah, I catch your drift. I'd fancy a guess and say that nobody's ever seen anything like this. Which raises the question, what do *we* do about it? Should we call it in to... I don't know... the fed or something?"

"Heck if I know, Nat. All I do know is that I'm tired and my brain is mush. And, if I don't have a heart attack by morning, I'm going to retire by sunset. Come on. I need to hit the office for some numbers to call."

"What about these folks?"

"I don't think they're going anywhere, Nat, do you?"

"But what if your neighbors—?"

"For cripes' sake, woman, I. Don't. Know! Do you get that? I ain't ever seen anything like this, and there ain't no book on the subject, so I'm doing the best I can. Do you wanna stay here? Would that please you?" Randy leered at Natalie, saw the fright in her eyes, and softened almost instantly. He let out a long breath and tried to compose himself.

"I'm only trying to help, Sheriff," she said after a moment's silence.

"I know, Nat. I know. I just... I just got a lot on my plate, and... and I don't like feeling stupid. Like someone is running circles around me, playing keep away with my favorite ball. It's... well, it's damn annoying and not a bit pleasant. I'm supposed to be protecting these people, and they just continue to pop up dead. And not peaceful dead, either. That at least would be comforting. But no, these folks are getting ripped to shreds and I don't have the first suspect aside from a description of some sicko in a mask. I just... I... I..."

Natalie only nodded. He could see his own sorrow reflected in her eyes, and he hated it. No, hate wasn't a strong enough word. He despised that look. Loathed the knowledge that he was something to be sad over.

"If you want to stay here, stay. I don't want to be here. I want to find someone who can actually help this god-blessed town, because I'm doing a piss-poor job of it."

Speaking of piss-poor, Sheriff Randy Miser thought, *I think I need to change my Pampers.*

"I understand," Natalie said at last. "And I don't want to be out here by myself either. Let's go."

They strode across the gravel toward his cruiser, passing Beatrice O'Neil's open front door and empty driveway.

"Wait a second," Randy said. He walked over to the dual worn sections of grass that sat beside Beatrice's trailer. He bent down and studied the strip of green between the two ruts. Something thick and dark glistened on the grass. He pinched an inch-long section and ripped it off, sniffed it. It was most definitely oil, which meant only one thing.

He stood and returned to Natalie's side. "You reckon Beatrice O'Neil lived alone?"

Natalie nodded. "I made myself known before entering and no one answered. Doesn't mean a husband or kids aren't out working a graveyard shift somewhere, though."

"Right. But I'm thinking it's far more likely that someone stole her car."

"This could be true."

"I'll have Shirley run her name and see if anything comes back registered in her name. Until then, we'll run down my contacts back at the office. See if we can get some aid from somewheres."

"And if we can't?"

"Why wouldn't we? This is central Texas. It's not like we're cut off from the world out here."

Back in the cruiser, Randy radioed Shirley. She ran the plates and came back with an affirmative. Beatrice O'Neil had registered a 1981 Grand Marquis back in the summer of last year, and though the car's tags were expired, there was no record of anyone else registering a vehicle with the same VIN number. When she was done relaying this information, Randy told her to call Matt back at the number he'd given her, and that Matt should meet him back at the station in town. She agreed and signed off.

"Should have asked her if she heard from your men," Natalie said as she reached back to scratch Merlo under the chin.

"I think if she'd heard from them she might have told me, right?"

"Whatever you say, Sheriff. I'm just along for the ride."

The drive into town was heavy with their silence.

CRUELTY

MARKUM

Dennis wasn't at home, but his stuff was still there. Frank tallied his boyfriend's underwear, socks, shirts, and pants, along with Dennis's various toiletries. The other man's extra supply of Speed Stick and Cool Water cologne remained in their usual place under the sink. The half-empty tube of Crest sat under Dennis's purple electric toothbrush, where it dangled from its charger. The extra tube resided in the drawer to the left of the sink. Dennis hadn't taken his towels—the ones he'd brought into the relationship—with him either. All these clues combined told Frank a very clear story.

Dennis hadn't left him. This was good. But, if his live-in lover hadn't hit the road, where the hell was he?

Frank had dialed his boyfriend's cell phone four more times as he walked from room to room, counting items and looking for anything that might be out of place, but reached Dennis's voice mail every single time. The fear that Dennis had simply left without taking anything with him lingered somewhere in the back of Frank's mind, but he tried not to focus on that. That possibility was dangerous, insidious. That thought brought on images of a man so angry that Frank pictured the Incredible Hulk swelling and bursting from his clothes, then escaping, unmindful of the important items he was leaving behind.

All signs pointed to the fact that Dennis had never come home from work. Everything remained where Frank had left it after being called to Bob's Bait and Fuel last night... or the night before... or whenever. His days were beginning to blur together. His rage toward Bruce wasn't helping either. It clouded his thoughts, coated everything cycling through his gray matter with a patina of guilt and horror. Dennis couldn't be gone, but if he was, it was all Bruce's fault.

Exhausted and distraught, Frank left his apartment with the intention of checking the last place he might find Dennis: the KOA campgrounds and the trailer inside which Paul and Dennis were tasked with watching the Twon household.

On his way, he considered stopping by the location of the sting operation to see how things were moving along. Since he hadn't heard from Dennis, Frank had no idea whether or not Twon was in custody. He didn't know anyone else in the DEA, not as well as he knew Dennis, anyway, so he had no one else to call.

Tom Waits sang "Come on Up to the House" over the cruiser's stereo, and Frank found himself singing along. He didn't know the tune, but the ditty was so repetitive that didn't matter. "Words and words and words and stuff... Come on up to the house..." And so it goes...

Frank arrived at the KOA campground shortly after two-thirty that morning. He drifted through the open front gate while eyeing the sleeping fat man who had replaced the acne-ridden teenager from earlier that day. The chunky bastard didn't stir, and Frank continued unimpeded. He pulled the cruiser up in front of Dennis and Paul's trailer and killed the engine.

The first thing that hit Special Investigator Frank Markum when he exited the car was the overwhelming scent of dead things. The sickly-sweet aroma of rot hung on the air like heavy drapes, and Frank felt as if he might need to physically part the odor before he would be able to press on. The closer he came to the trailer the stronger the smell, and the greater his sense of dread.

Don't be stupid. What you're smelling is week-dead animal, and you just saw Dennis earlier today... yesterday... whatever.

Paul was absent from his lawn chair, the one beside the front door of the camper unit. This struck Frank as quite odd indeed. Standard operating procedure stated that, during a stakeout, one man must stay on the outside while the other watched the cameras inside. Dennis had told Frank as much on numerous occasions. Going against SOP was unlike both men, and Frank's dread became a charcoal briquette inside his stomach. He wouldn't have been a bit surprised if he'd managed to belch smoke.

His guts burning and his mind reeling, Frank Markum tugged the door to the camper open an inch at a time.

"Hello?" he said, and his voice sounded full to the brim with abject terror.

Once the door was open a foot there was no doubt in his mind where the cloying stench originated. The scent of super-sweet Juicy Fruit chewing gum wafted out of the opening, and Frank snatched himself away to dry heave onto the gravel. He knuckled tears from his eyes as he backed slowly away from the camper unit.

"Dennis!" Frank hollered, unmindful of the other campers asleep in their trailers. He didn't care anymore. He only wanted Dennis to be okay, for Dennis to answer him. The smells pouring from the unit shouldn't be so strong. Even after a day in the summer sun, roadkill didn't smell *that* bad, because Frank wasn't simply smelling death and rot. There was an underlying scent of sickness... of infection. The aroma of a hospital's isolation ward. "Dennis! You fucking answer me!"

There was a thump. Something began to move unsteadily through the trailer. Another thump as that someone hit the ground.

A light came on in Frank's peripheral vision. He'd woken someone, but didn't give a shit.

"Dennis?" he called again.

"Ffffff... ffffrrrrr..." came a voice from the grave.

Instinctively, he took a step backward. He could hear someone moving again. A slap, then a shushing sound.

Slap!

Shhhhh...

Slap!

Shhhhh...

"Dennis? That you?" Frank's voice cracked, as if he were a prepubescent boy confessing his love to his crush.

Slap!

Shhhhh...

Slap!

Shhhhh...

Crrrrrrrreak...

The screen door floated open on unoiled hinges, and something monstrous spilled out from the camper. The humanoid shape dripped and drooled onto the gravel. A piece of glistening flesh slid off the right side of its face to splatter down onto the rocks below. The exposed jawline twisted up in a hideous mockery of a half-smile. The hands were nothing more than bones and exposed muscle. The spine canted at an extreme angle, and the legs curved outward to the left, giving the body the shape of a question mark. It pulled itself along like a snake with arms.

"Frrrraaaaaaaaank..." the creature bubbled.

And then Frank knew the truth of the slimy thing that beckoned him. After all, weren't the clothes familiar? Hadn't Frank purchased those shoes, and told the owner how sexy he looked in those jeans? Hadn't he watched this creature change into these clothes today after he'd made love to it? Because then it hadn't been an *it*. Yesterday, this thing had been Dennis, his beloved Dennis...

"My God," Frank gasped.

"Shhhheeee... cur-cur-curse... sssssss..." hissed the creature that had once been Dennis. All life (or whatever had been powering Dennis thus far) fled from the living corpse. Its head struck the gravel with a sickening *crunch!* and Frank took a quick step back. He might have yelped, but he couldn't be sure. He was trapped in the moment, watching Dennis's skull liquefy before his eyes. The body boiled beneath the clothing like the surface of a witch's cauldron. Pink and red goo oozed from the sleeves and the space where pant legs met shoes.

The smell was a tangible entity in Frank's nose. He retched, but nothing came of it.

And then he was running. He blew past his cruiser, ignoring it. He was only vaguely aware he was even moving. His feet were in control, and they seemed hell-bent on getting him as far away as they could from the bubbling thing that had once been his lover. As he fled, horrible, detestable thoughts flitted through his mind.

Good old narcissistic Frank Markum was suddenly quite concerned that maybe Dennis had been ill, and that his lover might have passed along whatever ailed him. Frank could feel his guts churning with sickness, and even sensed that his skin was looser... drippier... sloughing off...

"What the fuck is that?" someone hollered as Frank fled, carless, out into the road. He'd already sweated out his dress shirt by the time his feet traveled from gravel to asphalt, and his breath came like locomotive steam from his trembling lips. He spun, tottered, and dropped to his ass so hard his teeth clacked painfully together. He sat in the middle of the road, panting, looking back the way he'd come.

At first, Frank Markum thought that the someone who had hollered had found Dennis's oozing corpse. But that was not the case. If that had been the case, this night might have ended on a better note. Had the most terrifying thing this night had to offer been the putrefying body of his dead lover, Frank Markum would have shouted hallelujah and amen to a god he didn't necessarily believe in. Alas, what stalked Frank this night was far more menacing, and far less dead than his former lover.

The man (for Frank now saw that it was a man who had yelled, "What the fuck is that?") was smote against the windshield of a recreational vehicle. The figure that had shoved the man mostly through the glass of the RV studied its work for a moment before focusing its attentions on Frank Markum. While the man's feet twitched and spasmed, the figure drifted away. Under and out of the lights shining down from the power poles KOA had set up throughout the park, it came, floating, as if on a gentle breeze.

It's what it can't be, Frank's mind thought confusedly. *That's not possible. Just not fucking in the realm of possibility...*

And still, the figure came. Under the lights. Out of the lights. Illuminated. Darkened.

"First you," it hissed through stony lips, "then him. I'll make you both regret what you did to me. Do you understand me, sissy man? I will make you... *REGRET*!"

And regret he did.

CRUELTY

TWON

Twon Chatham pulled Beatrice O'Neil's busted-up Grand Marquis into the parking lot of Bob's Bait and Fuel. The car in the trees piqued his interest.

Before bashing the fat bitch's face in and stealing her car, Twon had witnessed the big-ass baby doll acquire this very vehicle. He'd not seen the fate of Paul Nelson, though, because as soon as Twon realized what the doll intended to do with the Toyota, he'd scurried off to Beatrice's trailer. He'd kicked her door in, and set upon the woman in a fit of rage. Five licks to the face with a shotgun put Beatrice among this evening's body count, and Twon was on his way. Poor old Beatrice; nothing but a speed bump on Twon's road to destiny.

He didn't tarry too long at Bob's Bait and Fuel. The car in the trees was empty; its driver had escaped once again into the night. Cursing his shitty luck, the cook returned to the Grand Marquis. His prey couldn't have gotten far. It was big and fat, and walked with a ginormous limp. In fact, if Twon closed his eyes and ruminated on the doll-faced fuck, he could see it tossing its shoulder out and moseying on down the road.

"Roll right along, seen? I'mma getchoo 'fore sunrise, belie'e that, muddahfuckah." Twon snarled at himself in the rearview mirror as he backed out of the gas station. His face was a death's head mask of insanity, but the crazy do not know that they've tipped the scales into the land of the unstable, and thus Twon continued his hunt unabated, pleasant in his madness.

Moments later:

He can see you now... I can no longer protect—

The voice whispering through his thoughts cut off, and Twon was left wondering if he'd heard anything at all. The tone and inflection had been familiar, almost intimate, but intimate wasn't quite the word, either. He shoved the thought to the back of his mind and focused on the task ahead.

The highway unspooled before him, the broken yellow line coming at him like citron lasers fired in the deepest reaches of a starless void. Trees sucked by, and their fallen children spun out behind the stolen car like dervishes.

At his best guess, he was less than a mile from town, but he couldn't be sure. Kerrville wasn't a huge city, and the streetlights down its main drag cast only a subtle illumination and nothing like the halo glow some major residential areas gave off.

When he reached the Guadalupe, Twon's heart sank. He'd come all this way just so he could lose the baby doll in town. The road ahead was devoid of traffic; even the curbsides were empty, all aside from a small sedan parked in front of Pompeii Café. It was at this vehicle that Twon's gaze lingered. He allowed the car to roll forward until he could see more clearly into the car at the curbside.

Someone was most definitely inside. He could see the massive shape shifting and stirring, and the car rocking on its suspension.

Broken glass twinkled below the driver's side door. Whoever was currently behind the wheel didn't own the vehicle.

Twon killed his headlights.

A 1981 Grand Marquis is a wide-bodied tank of a car with a 5.0 liter engine. It's a monster of a battering ram when you get it up to speed.

Twon slammed the gear shifter up to the ceiling, then eased it back down into reverse. He backed to the beginning of the bridge, giving himself roughly a quarter of a mile between him and the car at the curb. He jerked the shifter down past drive and second and left it in first. He rammed his foot into the accelerator, and the car rocked forward, its body heavy enough to keep the tires from smoking and, in turn, losing traction.

He swung wide, careening into the oncoming lanes. He barreled through the flashing red light at the intersection, spun the wheel hard right, and slammed into the side of the parked car at forty-five miles per hour. The smaller car took the brunt of the impact on its driver's side door, and the vehicle went tumbling into the glass storefront of Pompeii Café.

The Grand Marquis flopped lifelessly down the road. Its front right tire was now cocked at a forty-five degree angle, and the car didn't roll as much as hobble along. Tongues of smoke licked from the crushed radiator and drifted up into nothingness. The car, which had been reduced to nothing more than a junkyard's poster child, hit the curb at the Walgreens on the corner and came to a stop.

The driver's side door screeched open and Twon spilled out into the road. He could taste the metallic perfume of antifreeze on hot engine. As he stumbled in the direction of Pompeii Café, he heard the dying clicks and whines of the Marquis's life-support system. They were the only sounds other than his shuffling footsteps.

Then: "Mah-Mah!"

The voice was high-pitched, childlike and frantic.

"H-h-h-*HELP ME!*"

"I'm... I'm gonna help you... muddahfuckah," Twon grumbled as he limped toward the now smoking store front of Pompeii Café.

The smell coming out of the store wasn't entirely unpleasant. It reminded Twon of jerk-style chicken on a hot grill. Or perhaps barbeque of another kind.

With a tremendous flash of blue light, the night exploded. The resulting concussive wave blew Twon cartwheeling through the air. He landed in a heap next to the ticking Grand Marquis. Something inside of him had let go, had broken open. He could feel heavy liquid sloshing around in his gut. He seemed to be bleeding from every orifice as well. Everywhere he touched his hand, his fingers came away soaked in gore. He was only vaguely aware that something was moving in the background. The figure looked as if it were walking up the side of a building, but Twon soon realized that was only because he was on his side, observing the world at a ninety degree cant.

The figure was round and smoky. It seemed to roll itself toward Twon. Its flesh shone brightly through the scorched holes in the fabric of its clothing. The thing's body glistened, but not wetly. More like a piece of china will shimmer under the light. Twon had the smallest inkling that this baby doll was more than just some guy in a mask. This thing was actually porcelain. It was actually some overgrown toy. And it was coming... coming... coming for him.

"*You... you muddahfuckah... Come on!*" Twon spat. "*COME 'N AND GET ME, YOU FUCK!*"

"Wuh-wuh-why?" the doll asked.

Twon ignored the thing. He managed to extend his arm. His fingers bit into the asphalt, and he tugged himself an inch or two farther down the road.

"Why?" the child's voice asked again.

"Why what?" Twon choked and spat a lump of blood (and something else?) onto the street.

"Why... why are we so... so bad?"

Twon stopped all attempts toward escape. He rolled onto his back, and the baby doll filled his vision as it loomed over him. The cutesy mask stared down at him, haloed by the streetlamp above. All of its curly black hair had been singed down to nothing. Wisps of black smoke reached for Twon. Jaundiced eyes gazed into him. Not *at*, but *into* him.

"I'm not a bad man, seen? I do what I do... for Momma. I only... I only did what any good son would... would do."

"We're all evil," the baby doll with the little boy's voice said.

Twon bubbled up a bit of laughter. "Evil? Ain't no evil, seen? Not even you. You're just some toy, seen? *Seen*? You're just a walking tink-tinker toy. When *He* finds you... oh, oh, you gonna wish nobody created you. Now... get the fuck out my sight, muddahfucker. I wan'... I wan' die in piece."

He was gurgling now, rumbling and wheezing like a flooded engine. He rolled onto his side so he could breathe better. His lungs were water balloons. But he was still alive. Twon Chatham clung to life like a cruise disaster survivor clings to a bit of driftwood. Because of this, he was quite aware that he was now being dragged across the rough asphalt. His fingers tried to impede his progress and claw him away from his fate, but his nails failed him—snapped off like dry bark from a dead tree.

He was sobbing and choking when they reached their destination. He was lifted into the air, held aloft by the doll.

"We're all evil," the doll's childlike voice said. "And we'll all... burn."

He was thrown screaming into the flaming wreckage of Pompeii Café. He landed with a thump and sizzle atop the car. Fire massaged him, and he felt its heat for only the briefest of instances before everything went cold. Every hitching breath he took in was a torrent of lava poured down his throat. He tore his arm from the hood of the car, and left a substantial amount of flesh behind. It mixed into the bubbling paint, where it was devoured.

Twon Chatham screamed until his vocal cords split in the intense heat. Then he was still. His eyes burst and flash-boiled upon his cheeks.

CRUELTY

Outside, the doll paid witness to Twon's passing. When Twon's body began to curl up into a fetal position, it turned and lumbered away.

MERLO

Merlo could smell the Lady. Mostly he could smell the Lady through the slats on the dash, the place where air flooded in and felt amazing on his damp nose. Though the Lady wasn't famous for bacon, Merlo did miss her. He wondered where she was, and if she was going to come looking for him.

Merlo had recently been allowed to sit in between Big Gut and New Woman. New Woman was nice. She liked scratching Merlo under the chin, and he could not complain. In fact, he thought he liked it far more than she ever could.

A new scent tickled his nose, and Merlo stood up on the seat and stretched. He leaned forward, out over the dark void of the place where Big Gut and New Woman had put their legs, and sniffed the slats.

Yup. No doubt about it.

Dead tree rat.

Merlo growled low in his throat. His hackles rose, and he was suddenly very afraid. Shaking even. Wherever the thing that smelled of dead tree rat was, it had better not show itself. Merlo had grown quite fond of Big Gut, and New Woman wasn't half bad herself, but Merlo wouldn't hesitate to run away again. No amount of bacon and lovins could fix Merlo if the thing made of shadows found him.

"What's wrong, boy?" Big Gut asked. A hand touched behind Merlo's ear, and he snapped at it. Got a piece of it too. That would teach it.

Big Gut squealed. "Shee-zus, he bit me!"

"Then don't touch him. You see he's aggravated by something," New Woman said. "Haven't you ever owned a dog?"

"I'm bleeding, Nat!"

"You'll live."

Merlo let them drone on. He had other problems to consider. He'd been able to escape the shadow monster back at Big Gut's place, but would he be so lucky a second time?

Merlo hopped back and then sideways. He bounced over New Woman's legs and stuck his nose on the cool glass of the passenger side window. He drooled down the glass as his breath created a canvas for his lolling tongue to paint.

"What is it, boy?" New Woman asked.

Merlo barked. Once. Twice. A third time.

"Think he has to pee?" Big Gut asked.

"I don't know. It's your dog."

"Only for a couple days. Say, boy, you gotta pee?"

Even though Merlo didn't know what Big Gut's words meant, he barked anyway. Barked several times, each instance more insistent than the last.

"Pull over," New Woman said as she scratched Merlo under the chin. "Let the good boy relieve himself."

"We're almost there. Just around this curve. He's held it this—"

Merlo smelled bacon. Or something like bacon. The dead tree rat was gone from his nose, and now he smelled cooking meat. Oh, but it smelled delicious. Smelled like a pile of Good Boys and a house full of lovins.

Merlo bounded off New Woman and jabbed his forepaws into the dash. He hovered over the darkness at the bottom of the car, his tender bits open to any kind of assault imaginable, but Merlo didn't care. He wanted at whatever smelled so good. He wanted it bad. Wanted it more than bacon, and that was saying something.

An orange glow spread out over the street. Merlo saw scary fire spitting from the front of a building, and the black smoke that churned up into the heavens. Some of that smoke attacked the car as Big Gut pulled the car to a stop several yards away from the blaze.

Merlo thought that the smell that was better than bacon was hidden somewhere in that black smoke. In fact, it might *be* the black smoke itself.

oh boy oh boy oh boy ohboyohboyohboy

"When is this night going to end?" Big Gut groaned. He sounded very sad. Merlo thought he might share this new deliciousness with Big Gut if he found out where exactly it was coming from.

"Is that *my* car?" New Woman asked. "Inside the store?"

"I'm thinking it is."

"Goddamn it!"

"And there's our Grand Marquis. I guess our guy in the doll mask didn't appreciate you parking in front of his favorite coffee shop."

"Real funny, Sheriff. Just hilarious."

Merlo waited for a door to come open, prayed to his doggie god for one of these idiots to open their door, please! open the door, open the door and let me at that new smell.

Neither Big Gut nor New Woman opened their doors. Merlo wondered what would happen if he bit Big Gut right on the nuts.

FORGIVENESS & MIA

Oh, but the witchery woman was powerful. Forgiveness had never known such sweet anger, such unharnessed rage. He dove deeply into the hag, uncovering lost secrets, tales she had hidden even from herself. In the Withered, everything was visible, and Forgiveness saw—

—Laurette Fabiano standing beside the baby's crib. Laurette, now only fifteen years upon this earth, gazed upon the mewling infant, which lay in its crib, swaddled in pink fabric. The cloth had been quite expensive, and Laurette had spent the last of her allowance buying the blanket as a gift for her new sister. Momma had balked, but Laurette remained firm. Her baby sister Penance would have the best things in life; of that, Laurette would make sure.

The new child's gifts lay all about the room. A spinning top and a rag doll with orange hair clothed in a red-and-white polka-dotted dress sat upon the small room's only dresser. The top drawer held all the new baby clothes, while the next two drawers contained Laurette's hand-me-down garments. Atop the single bed, a golden-brown teddy peered at her with button eyes. A chain of wooden links hung from the bedpost nearest to her—a toy made by one of the village elders.

This part of Union Island was sparse as far as community was concerned, but those who lived here remained here. All knew all, and one cared for the other. The oak rocking horse tucked in the corner next to Penance's crib had been made by Agwe Laba, the local carpenter. Agwe was an amiable gentleman, and quick with gifts. He'd crafted Laurette's bed, as well as Momma's, and had made both women, young and old, ornamented bracelets, one of which Laurette now hiked up her arm to the elbow as she thought of the woodsmith. One day, she hoped to meet a man like Agwe whom she could marry. One day, indeed.

A prayer shawl hung from a rafter above, directly over the cooing babe. Mia Labaj—"the Witch" to some—had knitted the shawl as a present for Penance. Momma's pregnancy had been a rough one, and Mia had helped Laurette's mother through a terrible time. And if magic had been a part of Penance's survival, so be it.

Laurette sang: "God's pretty thing, may life be given to you! Devil, you naughty one, let no light cleave the dark ahead of you!"

Penance cooed in her crib.

"Laurette!" Momma hollered from the front of their meager shack. "Mind me, girl!"

"Yes'm!" Laurette called, as she hiked up her worn blue dress and bolted for the foreroom.

Momma stood in the exact center of the living room, studying a spot on the round rug that covered two-thirds of the shack's aged wooden floors. For the briefest instant, Laurette thought she might've spilled something, that Momma was about to lay into her for messing up the rug, but when Momma faced her with a smile upon her dark face, Laurette's heart calmed.

Momma was a fat but short woman. Laurette would outgrow her in height in a year or so, but she would never match her mother's egg-plant-shaped girth. Zidane Fabiano—Momma—had hard hands covered in gray calluses and chubby cheeks two shades darker than her otherwise chocolate features. Black patches of skin roughened Momma's elbows and knees. She was the village's washerwoman, and spent most of her time in the sun, on her knees by the spring in Tidal, the next village over. Here in the village of Perchance, Zidane was known as Zed, but Laurette knew not why. Today, Momma was dressed in a flowing white gown that fit tightly over her amble bosom and loosely at her grand hips. She had a rose tucked in her hair above her left ear.

Laurette gawked at Momma's dress. No wonder she'd called her to the foreroom. That was Momma's Sunday dress, and by the arc of the shadows across her feet, they were late for church.

"Oh, Momma, I sorry, I am. Don' be but a minute, right?" Laurette pleaded.

"Aye, go'n git dressed, girl. Pastor won' be waitin'?" And without another word said between them, Momma went back to studying the spot on the rug.

Laurette rushed back into the room she shared with baby Penance, reached into the crib, softly pinched the infant's cheek, and spun around. She dashed to her closet, snatched her Sunday fines, and tossed the silk dress onto the bed.

In the crib, Penance cooed.

"Aye, it be a fine day, Pen! Momma's in a fine mood!"

Penance snorted in agreement.

Laurette drew her old blue dress over her head and threw it on top of the rocking horse in the corner, where it hung from the long face like a funeral veil. She slipped inside her pink silk dress, flattened it to her stomach, and spun again, watching the skirt spread out like an umbrella.

"I look pert fine, right, Pen? Pert fine, indeed!"

"Hurr' up, ya silly girl!" Momma called. Her tone was jovial, but Laurette knew that could change at any moment. Momma wasn't a happy woman these days, not since Papa had run off, so Laurette minded as her mother bid.

Laurette turned to grab Penance from her crib.

Bored, Forgiveness drew back into his own mind, collected himself, and struck out again. He cycled through the witchery woman's memories as a businessman might a Rolodex. He was looking for the Source. If he could find the source of her powers he could make them his own. And then nothing would be able to stop him. Not the Bastard. Not even the Creator himself.

Soon enough, Forgiveness realized he had skipped too far ahead. Here he was at Twon's birth, and that was much too far, for Laurette had already become a "Momma" herself. He rotated back, back to the day Laurette, her mother, and baby Penance had visited church together for the final time. Forgiveness heard—

—Christian hymns. Mostly melodic voices praising and worshipping. Laurette sang, but only slightly. She didn't like her voice, thought it sounded like a loon in a bear trap. Momma didn't mind the sound of her own voice, although Laurette thought she should have, and so she bellowed, unmindful of the angered glances from random church parishioners.

When the music finally stopped, and the praying began. Laurette prayed for money, as she normally did, and was in the middle of asking God for a great vein of oil or gold to be found on their property when she heard something strange coming from her mother.

Momma, seated beside her and clutching baby Penance to her chest, was saying: "Lord, forgive me for what I haf'ta do."

Her mother's voice drifted into a mumble, and Laurette stopped listening. What could Momma have to do that worried her so? Did it have to do with her? Did it have to do with the baby? Laurette tried to shove the questions away that she might enjoy her Sunday, her Lord's day, but Momma's prayer echoed in her mind, rolling around in her skull like a ball in a cauldron.

Church over, Laurette and her mother left their seats and headed for the church entrance. Father Lessing, the church's young preacher, lingered at the front doors, shaking hands and bidding parishioners farewell.

As Laurette approached the man, he said, "The Fabianos! How good it is to see you? Did the Lord speak to you today? Did you feel the Holy Spirit in your hearts?"

"Yes. Thank you, Father." Momma's voice was clipped. She seemed upset.

Laurette only nodded at the preacher, fearing words would only anger her mother.

They went down the three long steps of the church's porch and stepped out under a high, hot sun. Sweat burst instantly upon Laurette's brow, and she wiped it away with the back of her hand. Church attendees had gathered in sporadic groups about the front yard of the church, and Laurette could feel as much as hear the happy buzz God had given the throng. She was rather jealous. No such amiable feeling coated her heart in joy. God, for the most part, was quiet in her head.

Momma handed Penance across to Laurette, and Laurette took the sleeping babe unto her bosom. At the white picket fence, Momma turned left instead of right, the way they normally took home, and headed down the tree-bracketed length of the old dirt road.

Father Lessing's unnamed church fell away farther and farther as Laurette continually glanced back over her shoulder. Still, she asked no question, once again because she was worried any inquires would send Momma into a fury. So she walked. And she walked. And she walked some more.

At some point, Momma quickened her pace, kicking up clouds of red dust behind her, and Laurette, although far smaller than her mother, began to tire. She wasn't sure if her exhaustion came on quickly because she was carrying the extra twenty pounds of her baby sister, or if they really had been moving along for a long passage of time. Either way, there was no denying burning calves and scorched feet.

Up ahead, the dirt road curved slightly, where it dead-ended at a tree line. Upon a stump sat a gleaming white skull with a raven's feather jutting from a crack in the top.

Suddenly, Laurette knew exactly where they were. The realization raised both feelings of happiness and of confusion. Why should they be visiting Mia on a Sunday? The Witch (*Mia*, Laurette chided herself) kept no gods but her own, and was rumored to play with white as well as dark magic. Her door was not one to be seeking on the Lord's day.

"Mind me, girl," Momma said as she faced Laurette. "If you value your head, you'll mind me this day over all others. Where we go, we go 'cause we haf'ta. Inside these woods, you mind me."

Why this day shouldn't be like any other bothered Laurette deep inside. Her guts swirled in her stomach, and she felt a sudden urge to void her bowels, then and there.

As the two women and the slumbering babe pressed into the wood, a faux darkness enveloped them. The sun did not shine here, and whether because of magic or the tightly knit tree branches overhead, Laurette did not know. She could smell the ocean on the wind, but below that was the musty forest odor of wild animals and their droppings. She squeezed Penance harshly to her breasts and followed her mother into blackness.

Rumor told that no matter which way you entered the Witch's Wood, one would find their way. No matter the direction one went, no matter which way one should choose to flee if fright bettered one's judgment, one would find the old woman who lived here. Because one couldn't leave until one's business was done.

Two months before, Laurette had accompanied her pregnancy-swollen mother to this dark place, but had been told to wait outside the house's gates. Today, Laurette didn't think she would be so lucky. The way had been long, hard, and Momma had collapsed twice in her exhaustion. Laurette thought the second time would finish it, and she would be left out there in the pitch black all alone, with her mother decomposing beside her and the corpse of her unborn sister putrefying in Momma's womb.

Then, it had seemed like days passed before they came across the old woman's plantation-style mansion.

Now, they reached Mia's home within minutes.

"Mind me," Momma repeated as the wrought iron gate came into view. Metal ravens were perched upon the tips of the gate, and each one seemed to eye Laurette morosely.

Beyond the gate, the mansion dashed up toward the sky, its white columns stretching on into infinity. At the top, a widow's walk. At the bottom, a wide-mouthed front door waited to gobble her up. The home had been white once upon a time, and now that paint peeked through the black coat that had been more recently applied. The walls gave off the impression of lightning striking in a black sky. Weathered shutters were closed over the eight massive windows, and no light peered through them. Glowing torches on five-foot lengths of wood illuminated all that she saw, but gave no warmth to the crypt-like presence the house exuded.

Laurette gazed up at the sky hoping she might find sunlight and blue eternity, but only darkness awaited her. Though there were no trees blocking her view of the heavens, all was night.

"Momma... I'm scared," Laurette mumbled helplessly.

"Shhh. Mind *me*," Momma said again, and this time there was much more venom in her tone.

CRUELTY

The sound of a rickety door opening and closing rose on the wind. *Creak, shush... creak, shush...* A glacier formed in her chest as she sidestepped, following her mother through the open gate. The noise persisted, and the night was suddenly redolent with smoldering things. Smoke came from the enormous front yard in wispy tendrils as the sound—*creak, shush... creak, shush*—grew louder and louder still. She imagined corpses under the earth, fanning their casket doors as they wallowed in flame.

She shivered violently.

"Who go there!" a shrill voice beckoned, the "there" sounding much like "dare." "Who visits Mia in 'er home place?"

"Zed and her children, Mia!" Momma called. "I bring the one I promised you!"

Laurette's head snapped to look at her mother. "Momma," she cried, "no! Not Penance. You can't—"

"Mind me!" Momma hollered. No, she'd roared. Roared like a lioness protecting its pride.

"Send her up then," the old woman said, her voice not much more than a whisper now.

"Laurette," Momma said, "hand me the baby."

Tears came in hot torrents as Laurette backed away from her mother. "No, Momma! Why? Why her?"

"Laurette, you mind me, girl!" Momma thundered toward her, and the smoke she inhaled came from her nostrils in big steaming plumes as she exhaled. "You mind me 'fore you git us bot' killed!"

"No, you can't have—"

And then Laurette was falling. She crashed down onto her back. Something scorched her shoulder. She trundled to the side, unmindful of the baby at her chest, and came down on top of Penance. Realization flooded in, and she rolled once more. She came down in a patch of grass that stabbed her through her dress, lancing into her flesh like porcupine quills.

Then Momma was upon her, tearing the baby from her. "You stupid little bitch!"

"Why?" Laurette sobbed as she shoved herself forward and crawled toward her backpedaling mother. "You went through so much to have her, and now you give her to... to... to this witch."

"You stupid little bitch," Momma repeated. "I'm not giving my baby away. I'm giving *you* away."

"Wha-what... ?"

"It was planned, Laurette. Once your blood came, you were to be given to Mia. Don't'cha see? She let Penance be born if I gave her you. Why lose one chil' to death when both may live? You won't be wit' me, but you'll be *alive!*"

"Momma... Momma, no..."

"It's for the best, girl. You'll see."

Were those tears in Momma's eyes? Laurette thought so. Funny thing, that. She couldn't remember having ever seen this old washerwoman weep. That's when something irreplaceable broke inside Laurette.

One for the other, she thought. *One for the other.*

Coldly, Laurette said, "I wish Papa would have taken me with him when he left."

"This is for the best," Momma said, before turning for the gate. She never looked back. Not once. But forever on, Laurette would see those tears in her mother's eyes and feel an icy jealousy, for Laurette herself would never cry again.

The front gate clanged shut.

Laurette sat back on her haunches and screamed at the darkness above. "Damn you, Momma! Damn you! I curse you! You gonna lose that baby, and then you'll die alone! Alone! *ALONE!*"

From the porch of the grand house came soft laughter. "No use there be screamin' at the top o' your lungs, little girl. Come on up. Let Mia show you a trick or two. That's right, lemme show you what a real curse sounds like."

385

The laughter returned, and Laurette went to the sound like a widow to her lover's grave.

Forgiveness pulled back into the Withered. He was smiling from ear to ear.

"Mia," Forgiveness mused. "How very nice to meet you. Now to see where this is going..."

Mia sat in a rocking chair—*creak, shush... creak, shush*—to the right of the plantation home's double doors. She was so tiny, seemingly a toy two sizes too small for its dollhouse furniture. She wore a pilgrim's dress, adorned with white apron and bonnet, and her dark eyes glinted from the shadows cast over her brown face. She was kneading a gelatinous mass. Red dripped from the flesh-colored ball. The smell coming off the pale globe reminded Laurette of a pit barbeque. Soft squelching sounds could be heard under the *creak, shush* of Mia's rocking chair.

"I wan' go home," Laurette said, and steeled herself for the worst.

"Aye, I know you do. We go 'ventually... Aye, 'ventually." Laurette didn't believe one word the woman said and refused to raise her own hopes to expectations laid out by this old witch. "You want food, girl?" Mia asked, holding out the throbbing ball of skin.

Laurette shook her head. She didn't have the emotional capacity to be disgusted.

"This all there is to eat, girl. The Roaming only provide one meal, and it's nothing but man. You'll get used to man. He taste like chicken, he do!" Mia softly cackled.

"Where am I?"

"I jus' told you. You in the Roaming. The Roaming is where you is. Some place between heaven and hell, if you believe that sort of nonsense. Kin to the Withered it is, but we don' harbor no evil here."

"I don't understand." Laurette's voice wasn't much more than a monotonous whisper; she couldn't manage any greater volume or inflection. It was as if everything inside, all her hope and love and joy, had been sucked from her. She felt drained, both physically and mentally. Now, she only existed.

"You ain' got to understand for things to be true. They jus' be. I live here, but I don' be here. Only my soul's what you see. My body died long ago, and now... now Mia is jus' this. Come 'ere. Lemme feel you."

Laurette did as she was asked. When she was within snatching distance, the witch's hand struck out and grasped Laurette's forearm. Laurette didn't flinch or cry out. Again, she didn't have the energy for it. But she could feel every wrinkle, every moist fold of flesh, on that old woman's palm. If her hands were any clue to how old Mia was, Laurette guessed the old woman no younger than a century.

"Aye, you do nicely, you do. Come inside, girl, and we'll get you ready."

"Ready for what?"

"For what you gonna become. We gonna see some things, me and you. We gonna see the world." Mia cackled as she rose, back popping, from her rocking chair and led Laurette into the house.

Forgiveness pulled back into the Withered. He was smiling from ear to ear.

"Mia," Forgiveness mused. "How very nice to meet you."

The Roaming interested Forgiveness very much. He'd known of its existence for some time now, nigh on a hundred years, but had never had the pleasure of visiting. The Bastard didn't offer vacations. Once you were damned to the Withered, in the Withered you stayed. Forgiveness continued—

—Watching. Laurette spent a great deal of time participating, but mostly she watched. Mia didn't explain much, but when the old woman did, Laurette listened intently. Days became weeks... became months... became years. Time was inconsequential. The girl forgot what daylight was, and allowed the hope of sunset to fade away completely. For all intents and purposes, Mia was keeping her promise. Laurette was learning the intricacies of curse and cure, the subtleties of shade and fog.

"Among all t'ings, there must be balance, girl," Mia had said. "For every wrong there be a greater evil, because good is only an illusion. Do you see? Man be judged by his most dastardly deeds, and those that offer forgiveness, oh, them be the strongest. They hold all the power. Do you see? But before there can be forgiveness there must be regret. And before there can be regret—"

"There must be cruelty?" Laurette had asked.

"Oh, but she's a bright one, she is!" Mia had tittered loudly before going back to her teachings. "There is this place, this *plane*, known as the Withered. It lives right next door to us, always, but it be inescapable, girl. Do you see? It is where our hearts, our very souls, go to die. It is the absence of humanity, a hell of a kind, if you can see that more clearly, and it feeds on our humanity until we're nothing by shells. The creatures that live there, the lords of that keep, they feed on our hope. They find our suffering delicious. And me, I plan to find 'em, I do. I plan to find 'em and I plan to kill 'em. And you, you girl, you gonna he'p me. Aye, so you is."

CRUELTY

Every forty-second day, villagers from the surrounding towns would come. Men and women, but never children. They came bearing gifts of fruit and idols and gems and precious metals. For some time, Mia would tell them to leave their offerings at the gate, but at one point she started allowing Laurette to retrieve the items. Meat was never a gift, and one thundery night, with the fire blazing in the hearth and Laurette sitting beside Mia's rocker (the one she kept indoors), Mia told her why:

"Animals aren't welcome here, girl. Neither are they welcome in the Withered. Animals *see*. Do you see? They see the world in a way we can't, in a way the Creator never intended, because they come from a time 'fore us, 'fore humanity, and it shows. Egypt, they worshipped cats. Buddhists be worshipping cows. Even as backward as it seem, some God-lovers worship snakes. Shamans—goats. Witch doctors—the wolf. The list, it be going on, but do you see? For that reason, they don't come, and when they do come, they throw everythin' into turmoil. We don' like being seen, girl. None of us. None." Mia had spat something black onto the hardwood, and set to rocking, once more lost in her own thoughts.

Over a time, Laurette was shown how to enter someone's thoughts, how to bend their minds to her own ways. Mia had described it as nothing more than reaching, and Laurette had found this an unequivocal truth. With the arms of her mind, Laurette could pull and massage and bend and hide the thoughts and emotions of the men and women that came from time to time from the village. She would meet them at the gate roughly every month and a half, and she would make them do things. She liked to watch the women hit themselves because she imagined they were her momma, and she liked the idea of Zidane Fabiano slapping herself silly. The men were made to pleasure themselves before her. They would grasp their members and tug and moan and twitch until they gave up their seed to the earth. The sight of them in orgasm made Laurette shiver, yet she never touched them. Somehow that, above all things, felt wrong.

Until Huxley. Huxley was a completely different story. He was tall and handsome and strong. His dark eyes seemed to look into her very core and were the only things in this cold place that provided her any warmth. Even the fires that Mia kept roaring in the hearth paled in comparison to the heat of Huxley's gaze.

He first started coming around as a preteen, and then more frequently as he grew into adulthood, then less when the gray became obvious at his temples and in his moustache. My, how quickly everybody aged now, while Laurette remained the same dull-eyed teenager.

And then one day, she took him. Fearing that Huxley would soon be too old to enjoy their coupling, Laurette bore into his mind and planted a seed of seduction. He became a slavering, numb-minded extension of his penis, and he took her. Took her upon the trees and the grass and the bushes off to the side of the gate, where his basket of offerings lay forgotten until they were done.

When he spilled his seed inside her, Laurette knew something had changed. The shift was dramatic and instantaneous. She shoved him off, and he went rolling, pants around his ankles and twigs clinging to his kinky hair.

"What did you do!" she screamed as she pushed her up. She dug at herself, into herself, and flicked goo from between her thighs like coffee from a filter. "What did you do, you stupid man!"

Huxley, flummoxed and doe-eyed, gazed up at her from where he lay on his back on the forest carpet. He dumbly grinned, and she realized that she'd broken him. She couldn't be sure when it had happened. Maybe when she forced her will into his mind to pique his sexual interest, but there was no way of telling.

A line of drool ran down the front of Huxley's mouth and pooled on his chest. He slobbered, and she was sickened. She thought about killing him, about delving back into his head and stopping everything, all activity, but she didn't. If his seed would grow in her belly, then she would allow the baby's father to live. In that way, she and Huxley shared a connection, and she was a bit sad when she had to let him go.

As Huxley meandered back the way he'd come, Laurette returned to the house, but never gave birth. Not nine months later. Not nine years later. The baby would not come until her life began for the second time.

The man's rape had disturbed Forgiveness and he couldn't have said why. Something about the inner violation. The physical part hadn't bothered him, but the way Laurette had burrowed into Huxley's mind closely mirrored what he was currently doing to Momma, and that, above all else, caused him to pause. He shook off the unclean feeling that had beset him and—

—Escaped. Laurette had escaped. She didn't remember anything about the time at Mia's mansion, nor did she remember Mia. All these things she would hide from herself until she met a demon in the kitchen of her home half a century later.

She stumbled drunkenly down the dirt road, past the gutted façade of Father Lessing's church, and back home.

The house she had once shared with her mother and baby sister was gone. In its place, a building of concrete and metal. The sign above the door had a red cross on it, and a blackboard next to the front door gave meal times for hurricane survivors, those made homeless by the recent storm. She stood there in the driveway of this new building for some time before finally shambling off, seeking someone who would remember, or a someone she might herself remember.

As she went, her stomach began to swell.

Union Island had been modernized, and there seemed to be industry everywhere. White smoke backlit by city lights drifted like bored ghosts into the heavens. The boiled-cabbage stink of the town's new paper mill clung to Laurette's passageways. She didn't think she'd ever get the funk off her. The dirt road had turned to asphalt back where the Red Cross Shelter had been. The surface was too hard, and took far too much out of her. Laurette found her body sore and winded before she was halfway into town.

By the time she reached a shop she recognized—Agwe's furniture store—her stomach resembled a rolling hill. She collapsed to her knees out front, and wept softly, until John Laba came to open the store the next morning.

John was Agwe Laba's grandson, and had taken over operations of the woodsmith shop sixty-three years after his grandfather opened it. Now, Agwe was dead, and his son was retired, but his grandson made a fine dining room set—that is, if you listened to the old women around town. The apple sure hadn't fallen far from the tree.

An indescribable amount of time had passed. Laurette recalled how she'd once thought Agwe would make fine husband material, and now the man was decades in his grave. The grandson was just as sweet as his grandfather, and drove Laurette—who had been in labor for four hours by the time he'd found her—screaming to the hospital in Tidal, where she gave birth to a perfectly healthy nine-pound boy. The boy, who was as dark—if not darker—than Huxley, would be named Twon, and would share Huxley's last name. The Fabiano name would die with its women, or at least Laurette hoped it would.

Laurette was diagnosed with a severe case of amnesia, and released fourteen days after having been admitted. The Red Cross provided her with aid until she got on her feet, and for a while, Laurette forgot the talents Mia had given her.

"Oh, no you don't," Forgiveness growled. "You get back here, witchery woman. Even if that girl doesn't know how she escaped, I do. Sneaky bitch. You sneaky, *sneaky* bitch..."

Forgiveness parted the folds of Momma's mind and found what was hidden at her depths... he found—

—Mia. Laurette hadn't escaped. Oh no. Like a stowaway, the witch had hidden herself inside the girl, and Laurette was never the wiser. Even now, as the demon toiled inside her, the woman who had once been the girl, didn't feel any different. Their minds had melted together perfectly, and Laurette had simply become Mia—she had become *Momma*.

Momma found it all too easy to get the residents of Perchance and Tidal and, well, all of Union Island, to do her bidding. She took up living at a two-story home located between Perchance and Tidal, and had paid for it with nothing more than the suggestion of money. She purchased her food and baby clothes and diapers all the same way. She even bought a wonderful invention called a television. A new invention to her, anyway. The rest of the world had been watching television so long that they now enjoyed reruns of *I Love Lucy*, which Momma had also fallen in love with. The eighties were good to Momma, and Twon grew big and strong like his father because of it.

When the boy hit puberty, he was next to unmanageable. Momma never suggested things to Twon like she suggested others. He would grow into his own man, and if his mother blinded the world to his doings once or twice, why should he be privy to such information? Plenty of days rolled by when Momma would cloak the teenager and Twon would come home, bragging about skirting one authority figure on Union Island or another, and Momma would listen and smile.

He started cooking after dropping out of high school. The educational system in Tidal and Perchance wasn't exemplary anyway, and the only reason Momma had sent Twon to school in the first place was because she wanted a bit of normality for the boy, a bit of normality Laurette had never experienced. Twon had learned to read and write, and that was also more than Laurette had accomplished in her youth. (That she had never wondered how she'd been able to read that Red Cross blackboard caused Forgiveness to chuckle inwardly.)

Twon learned the meth trade quick, and he learned it well. His mentor Charles had a boy Twon's age, a pasty pale fat kid named Oliver, who Twon turned to calling Ollie. Twon had said he liked that name better, and it had stuck. Even the boy's father came to call his own son by the nickname.

Charles and Ollie had been run out of America by the Drug Enforcement Agency, or so told the father. He'd left a house in Texas, which he still owned, but couldn't go back to, lest the government caught on to him owning it. Charles's wife had died in 1981, and Charles blamed her death on a man named Ronald Reagan, someone Momma had no acquaintance with.

"Once George Bush's war on drugs dies down, Ollie and I will come back. Until then, the law's more lenient around here, so I guess the boy and I will stay a few more years. Besides, they say Bush is only good for one term. I think those fellow Americans are going to go for some guy who plays saxophone during his campaign appearances. Imagine that? A jazz musician running the most powerful nation in the world. Shit, Reagan was an actor, so I guess it's not that far-fetched," Charles had said all this one morning over tea. The decade had changed over to the nineties, and both Twon and Ollie were in their twenties. He'd grown accustomed to visiting Momma on the weekends, while the boys were cooking, and she didn't mind the company.

"You don' t'ink you'll ever get caught? I mean," she smiled "if you go back, that is?"

"If I went back now? Sure. In ten years or so? Who knows? Twenty years would probably be best. Yeah, I wouldn't mind living here for that long. Already been here ten. You got some more of this tea? It's damn good."

"Oh, I got all the tea you'd ever want, *bon ti fi*." Her smile widened.

There was no tea in the man's cup.

Charles didn't make a scene of dying. His eyes went wide and his cheeks flashed red before his head slammed down on the table. Ollie would miss his father, sure, but all this was for Twon's benefit. After all, what mother didn't want the best for her child?

Momma buried the man in the backyard while Twon and Ollie cooked their poison in Charles's garage. As far as Ollie knew, his father had simply disappeared. Product of the game, he assumed. It was suggested to him that masked men had captured and killed his father, and he took to the thought easily because he'd always figured something like that might happen. Ollie came to live with Momma, and the boys became kin of a kind. In Ollie's mind, Twon was his brother, and vice versa. This coupling pleased Momma. Now, not only did she have one protector, but two.

She could feel a presence coming, something barking on her heels. Something in America, hidden in a chasm. She knew her time was running short, only she didn't know from what direction she would be attacked.

CRUELTY

Two decades later, Father Lessing's great-grandson came to Union Island to finish a job started a century ago, to convert the voodoo-believing locals into Christians. The converts would prove overzealous, and Momma would be threatened. And although this new preacher was an amiable, passive man, his flock was a murderous breed. The sins of the father's congregation would have the father dead and digesting in Momma's belly before long, and then that same congregation would descend upon Momma and her boys like the Wrath of God.

Forgiveness skipped past Father Lessing's murder because he'd seen it before, just hours ago when he first came to the witchery woman's home. She'd been ruminating on the scene inside Lessing's church when Forgiveness strode in. Lessing's death had been an awful thing, something the likes of which Cruelty would have enjoyed. Forgiveness breezed ahead to the final bit of the story, wherein Momma's story closely resembled his own, wherein—

—The men came at night, their faces covered in pillowcases and potato sacks with the eyeholes cut out. A modern day lynching is what it looked like, but the faces under these masks were black, not white, and somehow that angered Momma more than anything else.

Ollie was at the window, picking off whom he could with that old over and under shotgun he'd inherited from his father, and Twon was in the back room, gathering supplies. They would need food for the trip, not to mention clothes in case they became wet during their trek through the woods and to the dock.

Momma sent a slight suggestion to Ollie. He would die for them. No matter the danger, he would die before he would let any harm befall her or Twon. It would take another three years for that suggestion to get him killed.

Somehow, Ollie managed to keep Father Lessing's congregation at bay until Twon was ready.

Twon, a duffel bag over each shoulder and a pack on his back, appeared in the hallway. He jerked his chin toward the back door, and Momma followed. Ollie soon came after. The three of them journeyed as quietly as was possible through the dark wood. Shouts from men accompanied their escape, and after a while smoke from their burning house filled the night with a sickening odor of hot metal, scorched insulation, and blackened wood.

They reached the docks on the eastern end of Tidal just before sunrise. At some point, the men had discontinued their chase, or they had simply lost Momma and her boys.

Charles's Bayrunner was where Ollie had left it. The luxury boat had been taken out of storage months before. Momma had had a feeling they would need it, and as per usual, she hadn't been wrong. While Twon unloaded his baggage in the sleeper units below, Ollie got the boat going.

As they pulled away from the dock, Momma stood at the bow watching the smoke from their burning house rising from the trees to obscure the hunter's moon overhead. Soon hunter would turn to harvest and all this would be over.

(On this day in America, the Bastard had been beaten, but the boy with the eyepatch had survived. Forgiveness was just finding this out, as was Nell Morgan, though both parties were miles away from each other.)

Back in her kitchen, Momma was dying.

"I would ask why you didn't just toss a suggestion or two to Father Lessing's congregation, but I know what it's like to try and talk to Christians." Forgiveness said, smiling. "I've about eaten my fill, and you look like you're about empty, so what say we call it a night?"

Momma, crumpled into an indistinguishable lump in the corner by the back door, grumbled weakly.

"What? What was that? Couldn't quite hear you." The image of the boy in the cardigan was a toothy thing. The demon was still hiding, though, and that was good.

"Did... did you..." Momma stopped, choked on her own blood, and, once the coughing fit abated, continued. "Did you stop... stop to ask yourself... why she let you see all that?"

"Who?" Forgiveness asked, his brow suddenly creased in confusion.

"Did you ever consider that she... that she wasn't hiding from me?" Momma bubbled. The bubbling became a chuckle, and soon the dying mess of flesh and bone in the corner was cackling.

"Who the fuck are you—?"

And that's when Forgiveness knew. It was quite funny, really, when he thought about it. Damn near hilarious. "Oh, you sneaky little bitch."

"I'm here, demon," Mia said from inside Forgiveness. He could almost see her smiling that aged grin. "Remember what I said to the girl? Remember?"

"Yeah," Forgiveness muttered. He no longer found any of this funny.

—*I plan to find 'em, I do. I plan to find 'em and I plan to kill 'em. And you, you girl, you gonna he'p me*—

The witch said: "Story time's over, demon. Come to *Mia*."

CRUELTY

NELL

Nell Morgan sat beside her husband on the couch, enjoying his warmth. She didn't recall sitting down, nor did she remember the events that had occurred on the bridge yesterday afternoon. All she was certain of was this: she was with her Tom and that was the only thing that mattered.

"I don't wish to startle you, Nell," Tom said without looking at her, "but I needed to bring you somewhere that seemed safe. A memory that seemed safe. Something has been taken from you, and I intend to return it."

"All right," she said dazedly.

"I need to step inside your head for a bit, but Tom will stay right here. He won't talk to you, so don't ask him any questions. You two just watch that box on the wall, and I'll only be a moment."

Nell had the oddest sensation that something was crawling up the back of her neck. Fingers danced across the back of her skull. Those fingers pressed hard, and broke through. There was no pain, only pressure, and suddenly she wasn't on the couch in front of the TV, nor was she in her own home. She was at the altar. Tom had his hands interlaced with hers, and he was speaking his vows. Then they were sitting in his car, at the drive-thru in Lubbock, and *Pet Sematary* was playing on the screen. Stephen King was the preacher because Stephen King acted in all his movies, except for the ones he didn't write. Nell had read that somewhere, and she was telling Tom this until they were no longer in the car, but at school, high school, and she was walking down the hall and Tom was walking her way and he had a smoke behind his ear because he was supposed to be some big hotshot jock and all the girls wanted him but Nell Chandler didn't want to have anything to do with some big dumb—

"Say, your name's Nell, right?"

She nodded, was rendered speechless by those hazel eyes. That cigarette tucked behind this jock's ear became a faraway concern.

"Yeah, I know you. Thanks for helping my sister with her math homework. You done good on that. Say, you don't... maybe... wanna help me with my stuff some time, wouldja? See, I wanna go into the air force, and they don't take dummies, and... Say, are you all right?"

She was running. Running down the hall to the girls' room. Shoving into a stall. Lurching toward the porcelain. There was a bloody tampon peeking out of the drain but she didn't even care. She threw up violently. Epically. The water turned pink then green and finally yellow. The restroom smelled like musky vagina and vomit. She was sick twice more before she left the girls' room. The jock with the smoke behind his ear hadn't waited around for her. And that was a good thing because her breath reeked and her hair was a mess.

She went about the rest of her day without bumping into the jock who had made her so suddenly ill.

The following day, though, her problem arose again. She was back in the hallway, breath fresh after a morning cleaning, and waiting for the bell to ring for first period. Donna was complaining about her parents burning her Tesla tickets, and Julie was lifting Nell up on high for all the wonderful work Nell had done tutoring her in math, when someone tapped Nell on the shoulder.

It was the jock. Julie's brother Tom. He was as gorgeous as ever.

"You never answered me yesterday. In fact, you kinda just ran off." He smiled quite goofily. He had a small space between his front teeth, but it added something to the image of Tom. Made his smile unique. It would be that smile she would fall in love with.

"Yeah, sorry 'bout that, but I don't think I can help you." She pointed to the cigarette (hopefully this was a new one) that currently resided behind his ear. "I don't like the smell of those things."

"Mouthwash is a thing. And I promise not to smoke around you." He continued shining that ridiculous smile at her.

The knees, Cap'n, we're losing them!

"Your clothes will still stink, though. I don't know, I just... I just don't see it happening, sorry."

And she was running again, running away before her knees gave up the ghost. Running away before he kissed her, as if that had been his one and only intention this morning.

She burst through the doors to the girls' room and rushed the first stall. Locked. The second. The same. The third. *Are they all fucking locked?* And then the fourth swung open effortlessly. By the time she'd stepped inside, spun, locked the door, and then faced the toilet bowl she felt loads better. Her stomach was in the eye of the storm and everything was going to be fine. She'd finally beaten off the jock with the smoke behind his ear and now things would go back to normal. All she had to do was move on with her life. Sure, Julie was her friend and she might bump into Tom again, but she wouldn't have any reason to talk to him, and—

"Nell! Nell Chandler, you come out here right now!" Julie. Fucking Julie. Goddamn, fucking *Julie*!

Nell slid the bar, unlocking the stall door. She gazed out at her friend, she of the long peroxide-blonde hair and perfect eyeliner. She of the heavy breasts, small waist, and tight rear end. Julie wouldn't understand being scared of boys. Julie was perfect. She'd already had sex, and now Drake, the football team's quarterback and captain, was in her pocket forever more. Sex made everything forever. What would Julie know about being a virgin and having absolutely nothing to offer a guy like Tom?

"Why won't you help my brother with his homework?" Julie asked. She had her hands on her hips and her head cocked. Her hair-sprayed bangs danced atop her brow like a cobra under the influence of a charmer.

"Because I'm a virgin!" Nell squalled, and heard a sudden burst of snickers from the three closed stalls to her left.

"What the hell does that have to do with anything? He wants help with his algebra not his zipper." Julie smacked gum to punctuate her statement.

"What I meant to say is, I'm worried that he's going to want more than just tutoring."

"Why would he—?" Julie's eyes flashed wide. "You *want* to screw my brother, don't you? You think he's hot!" The latter was not a question. "That's kinda *ewwwww, grody*, but I can kinda see how—never mind. You should totally help him though. Totally. He's an idiot. Been hit in the head too many times. Just kidding. He's totally smart for a dweeb."

How is this airhead my friend? Nell asked herself, and could find no logical explanation.

And so it was that Nell Chandler allowed Tom Morgan to harness his mathematical powers under her close tutelage. He also unharnessed her bra. But that was later, after he aced his algebra test.

As the months went on, the two kept in contact even though they had never technically dated. High school ended, and graduation saw Tom at the A&M on a college scholarship and Nell down in Florida, where she rooted for the Gators. It wasn't until Nell returned home to Kerrville to live with her parents until she could find a job that she ran into Tom once again.

College had been a wonderful thing for Tom, and had almost completely destroyed the stupid jock he had been in high school. Though he had been amazing in high school, he was only a subpar lineman when it came to college level, and that had had quite the sobering effect on him. He'd moved back home, where he was sometimes substituted for Paul Cooley, the junior high's gym instructor and first period history teacher.

Nell and Tom ran into each other at the gas station one summer day and were dating a week later.

That night at the movies, while the movie about pets and family returning to life after being buried in an Indian graveyard played across the screen, Nell asked, "What ever happened to the air force?"

"You did."

"Huh?" she asked, honestly taken aback. "What do you mean?"

"I been through this class and that class and all the classes in between. I played high school ball and college ball. I been all over Texas, and I ain't found a woman yet that makes me feel the way you used to make me feel. I ain't even talking about making out after studyin', or the fun we had when you finally let me—you know. I'm talking about how happy I was just to be next to you. Just to spend time with you. I coulda went off and been an airman. I mighta even flown one of these days. But I wouldn't've been happy. Not as happy as I was with you, anyways."

She swallowed. Hard.

"We didn't just bump into each other at that gas station, Nell. I didn't stalk you or nothing, don't get me wrong. But I was drivin' by, and you was filling up, so I swooped in. I made it sound like—"

"Shut up," she said, and grabbed his cheeks.

Then they were kissing. And she didn't care about the slight hint of smoke on his breath. She didn't mind the yellow stains on his fingers as they combed through her hair. She melted into him, and that pack of Camels in the car's drink holder disappeared.

She wouldn't think about his smoking again until they were married. As the years rolled by and the drive-thru vanished, she had never forgotten about that night in his car. That was part of the reason she rallied for him to stop smoking. She couldn't lose him, and if she did, it damn sure wouldn't be because of some nasty habit.

Now, in her living room, Tom Morgan vanished, as did her living room. She was once more on her porch, with cold autumnal air circling her like wagons.

The boy with the eyepatch gazed up at her, smiling.

"I have what I need." He turned to go.

"What are you?"

"Like I said, I'm a friend. Goodbye, Nell. I'll send him back to you, if I can."

"Wait!" she cried, as she ran down the steps. "Do it again! Please, do it again! I want to live that again!"

The boy did not answer. He came apart in the breeze like so many fall leaves, and drifted away on the air.

Nell Morgan dropped, sobbing, to her knees in her front yard.

CRUELTY

NICK

Deputy Nick Wuncell parked in front of Kerr County Dispatch, killed the engine of his cruiser, and got out.

KCD was a small cube of a building, which was the soft wooden color of brown eggshells. The location had been built on the outskirts of Kerrville, on the opposite side of town to Bob's Bait and Fuel, and was surrounded on three sides by trees. The door was a shocking red, and a small white sign in the center read: NO ADMITTANCE. A cement walkway bisected the grass, and Nick took this path toward the door. He knocked three times and waited, with only the hum of the power lines to keep him company.

Shirley answered less than a minute later. She looked like hell, haggard and drained. Her normally high color had gone sallow. She twitched almost imperceptibly. Acne had won the war and her face was a bombed-out battlefield of pits and scars. When was the last time Nick had seen her? One day? Two? A week? He couldn't remember. The state Shirley was in now reminded him of Jennifer on her last days. Turtle's girlfriend had become a zombie, and Shirley wasn't far away from such a state.

"Where have you been?" she asked. There was a hollowness in her voice, as if certain tones were missing and had been replaced by flat notes.

"I had to finish up that bullshit at the hospital. How bad is it?"

405

Shirley shook her head until it seemed her neck would snap from the force she exerted. "Don't really know. I been good. I told Miser you haven't been answering, but that's only going to hold over for so long. He wants me to call in some guy named Matthew. You know some guy named Matthew? Huh?"

"Calm down. He's been blowing up my cell for the past hour but you don't see me shaking. Where's George and Hank? Danny? Any of them? Your car is the only one I saw in the lot."

"Nobody's here. Not one of them. Far as I know the DEA knows about them too. Maybe they took in all of Twon's boys, I don't know. The radio has been quiet. Quiet other than Miser, that is. You really should call him, Nick. He's going to wind up calling one of the other deputies himself and they're going to tell him that I ain't really called and then what am I going to do? I can't afford my shit if I ain't got no job, Nick!"

"Jesus, you fucking junkies, I swear." Nick said this more to himself than to Shirley. "I got half a pound in the trunk. Keep up the good work and you'll have a quarter for your trouble. Okay?"

"A quarter of your half, or a quarter of a pound?" Tweaker bitch or not, she wasn't stupid.

"A legitimate quarter, okay? Maintain radio and cell silence with anyone other than Miser. I don't want our discussions recorded without our knowledge. If something comes over the radio about Twon finally giving up, call me. But"—he stuck his finger in her face—"you don't mention shit about us leaving once this is all over, you hear me, Shirley? Nothing about us. You only call me and say something like, 'Thought you'd want to know they finally caught Twon.' Okay? That's all you say, Shirley, or so help me God, you aren't getting a pinky nail's worth of the product I got in my cruiser. You got me?"

"Yeah." She trembled under his gaze. "Yeah, I got it."

"Where is he, anyway? Has he said what's got him on shift so late?"

"No. He's been out to Monlezun Estates, but other than that he's just been around town. He went to the hospital—but you know that—and then he... then he went to Turtle's house and—"

Nick grabbed Shirley about her twig-thin arms. "What the fuck did you just say? He went where?"

"To Turtle's... I... I thought I told—"

"No, Shirley, you didn't tell me anything about him going out there. What the fuck is wrong with you? He could get anything out of that sorry fucker. Hell, I can't even get him on the phone. What if he rolled on Twon? Fuck, what if he rolled on me? Jesus Christ, is that why he wants to talk to me so bad?" He was shrieking now, losing his shit, and that wasn't like Nick Wuncell. No, not at all. Nick Wuncell had survived that cave in Pakistan and Nick Wuncell would survive some pot-bellied sheriff with a shitty sense of humor.

"Don't worry about Turtle," Shirley said with a shaky smile. "He's dead."

"He's dead? He's... what the fuck do you mean he's dead? Turtle? Simon Allison? Simon is dead?"

"That's what Miser said. He called in the coroner and everything. Someone slit Turt's neck. So we're good."

"No, we're not good."

"Why not? How's Miser going to find out—?"

"Because I left a message on Turtle's answering machine, that's why we're not all right. Shit, here I thought he just wanted me in to help with the Twon sting, and now I can't be sure. I can't be sure of any-fucking-thing right now."

"I don't know, man. He said he wanted to talk to you. Maybe you should call him, you know? Maybe he don't know shit, and you're fine, right? I mean, you're kinda starting to sound paranoid."

He slapped her hard across the face, and was more than a little surprised when she crumpled to the floor.

"Shirley?" Nick said timidly. "Shirl', you all right?"

He knelt beside the woman's immobile form. He put a hand on her back to check for respirations but felt none. He checked the side of her neck for a pulse. There was something thumping in there but it was so ungodly shallow and weak that Nick felt his own heart rate double.

Had he murdered the dumb bitch? If so, how? He raised his right hand, the one he'd used to strike Shirley, and looked at the blushed palm. It was crimson and hot from the slap, but was otherwise just his palm, the same old palm he'd been born with, except for his class ring.

"Oh, goddammit it… " Nick muttered, as he stared at the treacherous silver ring. If he'd somehow managed to connect Shirley's temple to the underside of his ring… "Goddamnit!" he growled again.

He checked her neck for a pulse once more and found that the weak beat was now entirely gone. He even fancied that her skin had dropped a few degrees.

"Why'd you make me do it, Shirley?" Maybe if he made this her fault he would be able to live with killing her, would be able to sleep again. "You shouldn't have called me a pussy, Shirley."

Had she called him a "pussy"? Probably not, but that was better than nothing.

He laughed. He suddenly couldn't remember. What had she said to set him off? What damning word had she used to ignite that secret fire inside him?

Paranoid…

Oh, yeah, that was it. That was most definitely it.

Most people would skip right over such a word, but not Nick Wuncell. Because, once upon a time, someone else had called him paranoid. And that someone was every bit as dead as poor Shirley. Still, he couldn't think about such things right now. He had to do something with Shirley's body before he could figure out what he was going to do about the sheriff.

He stood once more, glanced down the short hallway that led to Shirley's small office, then back to his car. Should he hide her inside the building or in his own cruiser? Good question. He scratched his chin and tapped his foot, unaware that he was currently the clichéd vision of a man lost in deep thought.

Finally, Nick stepped inside and eased the door shut behind him. The lock caught with a snick that echoed down the short corridor. He took one long, leaning stride over Shirley's corpse. He planted his foot on the carpet just past her and swung his other leg over. He felt more than a little foolish for being so cautious. Here he was, out in the middle of nowhere, trying to be stealthy in a building whose only two occupants were him and a dead woman. He loosed a mighty sigh and continued on into the building.

At the end of the corridor was a branching hallway, and directly across the hall, Shirley's office, where she routed and connected calls from Kerr County's four major burgs. He ignored the rest of the hallway and entered Shirley's office.

He'd been inside the county's switchboard more than once, and it was no different from the past two or three times. A single flat screen sat upon an L-shaped desk. A keyboard had been set up directly in front of the monitor. Beside the keyboard was Shirley's headset. He picked the headset up and placed the muffs to his ear. Nothing. All was quite in Kerrville and its surrounding areas for the moment.

Nick stepped back out into the hall and returned to Shirley. He stood looking down at her for some time before finally bending over and grabbing her about the ankles. He dragged her body down to her office, where he stopped just outside her door. He glanced up one hall and down another until his eyes alighted upon a perfect possibility.

He tugged Shirley down the left corridor, watching her shirt ride up to expose her pimply back, and then backed into the building's sole restroom. He dropped her in the open door as to keep it ajar and went about his impromptu plan.

If someone called in and received no answer from Shirley, surely (pun most definitely intended) they'd swing on by to find out if the dispatcher was okay. If they then found the office empty and no signs of struggle, they'd automatically begin searching around the station. Soon enough they would find Shirley, dead upon the floor of the restroom, victim of poor luck.

Nick ran the tap and splashed some water on the linoleum. He then arranged Shirley's body so that it looked as if she'd walked inside, slipped, and struck her head on the lip of the commode. It was then and only then that Nick realized how lucky he'd been that she hadn't bled anywhere.

Before leaving Shirley's corpse, Nick said a silent prayer. More for himself than for her. He prayed that God would see that what he had done was a complete accident, and that this one murder be overlooked on the grounds of criminal insanity. He added a bit at the end about how he didn't want to be caught, and then tacked on a quick "Amen" before heading back out to the hallway.

He was halfway to the front door when some kind of alarm began going off. No, not an alarm. A phone was ringing, that was all. That was enough.

"Fuck!" Nick growled as he spun back around to face the office at the end of the hall. There was little doubt in Nick's mind where the ringing was coming from. Even less of a doubt about who was on the mainline, and it sure as hell wasn't Jesus.

RANDY & NATALIE

"God bless it, Shirley, answer your dang phone."

The sheriff felt fit to cuss, but somehow managed to keep it under check. The smoke roiling from Pompeii Café was giving him one elephant of a headache. The phone line ringing in his ear wasn't helping matters any. He'd stopped counting the rings somewhere around fifty, and only hoped nothing had happened to the dispatcher. Maybe she was in the bathroom. Yeah, sure, that was it. Because if she'd fallen asleep on the job, she'd be in a heap of trouble, especially on this night in particular.

"Come on! Answer!"

After another few rings, Randy hung up. He called up his contacts and highlighted Matthew Pontiff's name. He pressed send.

Three chirps later: "Whataya want?" a sleepy voice asked.

"Where are you?" Randy asked.

"Huh? I'm in bed. It's"—a brief pause—"almost two thirty in the morning, Randy. What's this about?"

"You're still in bed!" Randy nearly screamed into the phone. "Why are you—?"

And just like that, Randy knew. Though he didn't fancy himself a Columbo or Miss Marple type, he wasn't a stupid man by any means. Shirley hadn't been able to contact Nick, and now she wasn't answering the phones. On top of all this, Matthew was still in bed. The why of the matter was still lost on Randy, but he didn't like where this was pointing.

"You didn't get any other phone calls this evening before now, huh?" Randy asked.

"My sister called after dinner last night—Randy, what the hell do you want? What's going on?"

Randy sighed. "I'll fill you in later. I need to call in a favor. How quick can you get to Pompeii Café?"

"I was sleeping."

"Do I have to remind you?"

"About?"

"The birds?"

"That's low, old man."

"I don't have time for this shit, Matt! Get your lazy ass out of bed and get the hell down here!"

"Whoa, all right. Calm down. Since when do you cuss?"

"Pompeii Café. Now."

"Fine, fine. Let me grab a shower—"

"No one's going to care how pretty you smell, trust me." Then a thought occurred to Randy and he said, "Never mind Pompeii. Head on over to dispatch. You know where that is?"

"Yeah, sure. Who's on tonight? Sarah?"

"No. Shirley. Check on her, will you? Check on her before heading out here. Call me the minute you find out why she's not answering the phone, okay?"

"What's going on, Randy?"

"Remember that mess you and your old man got into back in Ohio? Well, this is worse. Much worse. This old man has never needed your help so much in all his life, youngster. Be on point. Oh, and bring your side arm. It's like the Wild West in Kerrville tonight. And if you see anyone in a baby doll mask, shoot them. Don't ask any questions, just plug the bastard."

"Randy, you're starting to worry me."

"Good. Because you need to be worried. Just remember what I said. Baby doll mask. Shoot and ask questions later. In that order."

Natalie stood across the street from the flaming frontage of Pompeii Café, and thought, *Kinda went up like its namesake, didn't it?*

A cool breeze could be felt at her back, and was juxtaposed by the intense heat pouring from the smoking coffee shop. On that smoke lingered the ungodly stench of hot metal and melting rubber, as well as an underlying meaty aroma akin to summer barbecue. She could understand why Miser's new doggy companion was panting at the rear window of the sheriff's cruiser. Merlo (at least that was what Miser had called the dog) had almost escaped the cruiser when the sheriff got out, but Miser had been quick enough with the door to bar the dog's exit.

Now Miser paced back and forth in the middle of the street, his cell phone plastered to the side of his face, mouth working and free hand waving as he spoke feverishly to an unknown someone. Over the crackle and pop of the blaze, Natalie couldn't hear what was being said.

She'd been out there for more than five minutes before she realized her car was gone. She blinked several times as realization dawned.

Where's... ?

No...

Is that my *car in there?*

State Farm isn't going to like this.

The first thought to follow her inner dialogue was, oddly enough, about her kaku. How was she going to visit her grandmother today without a vehicle? Hell, how was she going to get home? Would she be allowed to go home at all given the case she was currently working with the sheriff? All these questions and more assailed her as she tried desperately to think of anything other than her current predicament.

She glanced down the street toward the Grand Marquis that had been left at the curb in front of Walgreens. While the sheriff continued his tirade, Natalie approached the lonesome car. Hadn't the dispatcher said Beatrice O'Neil had owned a 1981 Grand Marquis? Wasn't that what her and Miser were after when they'd come across the burning storefront?

Yeah...

She tried to add everything together. Someone had killed Anne-Marie Monlezun, the owner of Monlezun Estates, and then (presumably) that same someone had killed Beatrice O'Neil and stolen the old woman's car. The perpetrator of these crimes had then crashed into a parked car—Natalie's parked car—before abandoning O'Neil's stolen Grand Marquis at one corner of the intersection. Logic dictated that this someone was now on foot, unless of course they had stolen yet another car.

But look around you. Kerrville is a ghost town. They all but roll up the sidewalk after dark. Even the traffic lights switch to flashing yellow after ten of the clock.

So which way would you head if you were a criminal suddenly without a set of wheels? Which way—?

And then she heard it.

Randy disconnected with Matthew and did a one-eighty trying to locate Natalie. He found her standing by the wide-bodied vehicle that was resting at the curb in front of Walgreens. As he began moving her way, she started walking down Peterson Avenue, which crossed at the southern end of Guadalupe Street. She seemed almost in a daze, hypnotized, and Randy felt a bit of trepidation. He wanted to call out to her, but didn't want to break her concentration. He knew that look. Trooper Natalie Holden was *in the zone.*

"Whatcha got, girl?" he whispered as he followed her into the middle of Peterson Avenue. She stopped with

Walgreens on her left and a seamstress shop on their right. Randy stepped up beside Natalie. He gazed down the empty street with her.

Fifty yards ahead, the shops stopped and the houses that lined the majority of Peterson Avenue began. The housing tract wasn't that old, maybe four years at the most, and Randy had almost bought one of the squat three-bed, two-bath homes for a steal. But when Flo had gotten sick and lost her foot, all hopes of moving flew out the window.

The first house on the right was a white one-story number with an L-shaped porch, which wrapped around the right side of the house and ended halfway down, where the gate to the privacy fence stood open.

The gate creaked softly as it swayed back and forth in a calm breeze. *Someone definitely needs to squirt a little WD-40 on the hinges,* Randy thought. That's when it hit him, and he focused a little harder on the swaying gate.

Natalie began walking toward the house with the wraparound porch. She had her hand on the butt of the gun she carried on her hip, the one she wore while she was off-duty. Her thumb snapped the leather strap off the top of piece, and Randy felt the sudden urge to do the same with his own police-issue revolver. He did as much, but whereas Natalie left her gun in its holster, Randy drew his. He held the old .38 out in front of him, using the palm of one hand to steady his gun arm. He laid his finger over the trigger guard, not the trigger, and continued forward.

What are you doing out here, old man? Randy thought. *You should be back at Pompeii Café calling in the fire department. You should be back at Monlezun Estates waiting with a couple of dead bodies for Moxie to come around with his ice truck. You should be at home, praying. In other words, you should be* not here!

His mind drifted to Flo. But not really Flo. A mimicry of Flo. That thing's impersonation of Flo. Randy recalled how real his dead wife had seemed yesterday afternoon… that is, until her eyes rolled back in her head and her breath turned into a rancid fog. She'd seemed so real that Randy had traveled out to Eternity's Gate Cemetery just to make sure she was still under six feet of solid earth.

And he hadn't thought about her since. He could hazard a guess and say that was because he'd had bigger fish to fry, but he didn't think that was the case. It was as if the thought of that entity, that shapeshifter, had been removed from his memory banks until now. He hadn't thought about it because it hadn't been there to think about. Senility might be the culprit. He was getting up there in years. Still…

He laid a hand on Natalie's forearm and she jumped a little at his touch. They both stopped in the middle of the road and faced each other.

"What did you see today?" he asked.

"Huh?" The confusion on her face, which was lit a drab orange by the arc sodium, looked almost comically confused.

"When you first met up with me outside the cemetery yesterday, you told me you saw your father. That you *thought* you saw your father. Is your father dead?"

"Yeah."

"But you saw him like I saw my dead wife. My Flo. Why haven't you mentioned what happened since then? And why haven't I thought about what I saw?"

"We've been busy. That's all," she said, but he could see in her eyes that she didn't fully believe her own words.

"Is that it? Is it really? Yeah, we been through some hell the past eight hours or so, but does that really account for our memory loss? I'd think seeing our dead loved ones would rank pretty dang high on a list of stuff to remember."

"What about that?" She hitched her chin at the open gate, which was now directly across the street from them. Randy turned and saw that he could see all the way into the backyard, as well as the broken clasp and the shattered wood around which a lock might have hung, once upon a when. "We can't just hang back and reminisce. We have to catch this guy, whoever he is."

"Fine. Let's go, but don't let it slip your mind again. Whatever you have to do, you remember what happened yesterday, okay? You focus on that. Focus on your father, and I'll focus on Flo." Randy punctuated his final statement with a nod of his head before turning toward whatever unknown trouble lay in wait for them in that backyard.

"Go up and see if anyone's home. I'll take the back," Natalie said.

"I'm not letting you go back there by yourself," Randy said, and forced a laugh.

"Listen, I do this shit all day every day. I drive a big fancy state trooper car and handle bad guys all the time. You don't have to protect—"

"All right. Fine. I'm sorry. But be careful."

"No, I was going to shoot myself in the foot."

"Nobody likes a smart-ass, young lady."

"You're one to talk."

Natalie stepped through the open gate and into the backyard. Directly inside the fence, a bin bursting with black garbage bags welcomed her, the plastic fluttering in the wind like waving hands. The stench coming off the can was redolent of stale beer and coffee grounds. A forced heat and air machine hummed quietly under one of the house's side windows. No light emanated from inside, not even the soft glow of an alarm clock or the standby light of a television. But as Natalie strode farther into the main yard she could see the diffuse light of a bug lamp, which reached halfway across the low-cut lawn.

A child's play place sat toward the back of the property—a slide connected to a swing set, which had three seats in all: two regular sized, and one for toddlers. A large round shape sat on one of the bigger seats. The figure's weight bowed the crossbar at the top of the swing. Whoever they were, they didn't seem to be moving. No rise and fall of the shoulders as they breathed. Nothing. The way the light from the bug lamp died halfway across the yard, Natalie couldn't define the features of the figure's face. This, above all else, unsettled her.

Her cheeks seemed packed full of ice, yet her brow felt aflame, as if she were running a fever.

The figure said, "Mah-mah."

Natalie drew her sidearm in one fluent motion. "Put your hands up! Now!"

MATTHEW

"Birds. Old bastard throws the fucking birds in my face."

Matthew Pontiff glared at himself in the mirror. His round cheeks were especially red this morning, and his sandy-brown hair resembled something in which ferrets had mated. He cranked the cold water, washed his face, and wet his hair. After he dried his eyes, he was a bit more presentable. Not that he was headed for a party or something, so who the fuck cared?

Down the hallway, his father snored. The elder Pontiff had had a rough go of the last few months, and Matthew worried that the old man wasn't long for this world. He would hate to see him go, but at least the pain would be gone. This was one of the few evenings Dad had slept through the night... well, most of the night, anyway, as he could still wake up before the sun peeked over the trees. Most nights, Dad would be in a ball, crying and begging for someone to put him out of his misery. Matthew was always quick with the Dilaudid on those nights, but the high-powered narcotic did little to stem the fire in the old man's guts. Stomach cancer was a motherfucker.

"The fucking birds," Matthew said again, blowing out a great gust of wind. His breath smelled as if he'd tossed a bear's salad.

Miser had sounded quite anxious on the phone. Because of this, Matthew skirted the toothbrush and toothpaste. He grabbed the bottle of Scope next to his shaving stuff and headed for the front door.

419

He slid behind the wheel of his Kia Sephia and stuck his key in the ignition. The engine turned over without a problem. He backed out and got on his way.

Kerr County Dispatch was four miles from Matthew's house as the crow flies. By road, however, it was more like six miles. Highway 238 wound around the outskirts of Kerrville like a knotted-up snake, but Matthew knew it like the back of his hand. He slowed at the beginning of every curve and accelerated just before the road cut in the opposite direction. He loved driving. That is, he loved driving when his car wasn't in the shop. The Kia was a 1999 model and spent more time with mechanics than it did under the operation of its owner. Praying that he wouldn't break down was a daily mantra for the former police officer. When Matthew had quit the Bay's End police force and left Ohio to take care of his ailing father, the car had served its purpose during his cross-country jog, but he knew the vehicle was on its last legs. So when the old girl started to cough and shimmy around the halfway point between his house and KCD, he simply pulled over to the side of the road, put the car in park, killed the engine before it killed itself, and, sighing, dropped his head backward onto the rest.

"The *fucking* birds," he told the ceiling. "Why'd he have to bring up the fucking birds?"

Headlights cast an eerie glow inside the car. Matthew drew his chin down and shaded his eyes with his palm. He popped open his door and stepped out, began waving his hands. He could call triple A if he had to, but somehow he doubted Sheriff Miser would appreciate any delays.

The car rolled to a stop beside him. Matthew was shocked to see that it was a Kerr County Sheriff's cruiser.

Nick Wuncell rolled down his window and smiled. "Hey, guy. Car trouble?"

FORGIVENESS

As Mia burrowed deeper into him, Forgiveness fled into the Withered. He planned to hide. To wait. And as he did, he reined in his tethers, pulled to him the powers he had gifted his wards.

Through memory and shadow, the witchery woman followed.

CRUELTY

LODY

Bay's End, Ohio, 1908...

The dayroom twinkled. Tinsel around the floor-to-ceiling windows sparkled, and the Christmas tree in the corner flashed brightly red, green, blue, yellow. The silver star atop the tree caught the sunlight coming in from the windows and speared Lody like accusing fingers. George M. Cohan's voice issued from the phonograph, which was located in the corner opposite the tree. Cohan sang about a small-town gal, but Lody was more focused on the boy with the eyepatch—Nurse Fleming had said his name was Fairchild, Scott Fairchild—than he was the music.

Scott doodled, as he did every day, and Lody considered gliding over in his wheelchair to speak to him. Two weeks had passed since the unfortunate incident—his left testicle fourteen days removed—and approaching the odd kid didn't seem like the best course of action just now. Whether or not Scott had somehow caused Lody to mutilate himself, Lody didn't know, but the interaction had changed him.

The dreams were the biggest change. Before his first conversation with Scott, Lody hadn't dreamed of his father. Now Lody dreamed of him every night. Mostly he dreamed of being dragged out the front door of his home and his father dangling from the tree in their dooryard. Only in this version of that horrific night, his father, eyes bulging and swollen tongue lolling, spoke.

"You will do great things, child."

His father had not said those words, because dead men told no tales, but Scott had. And even though Lody

422

suspected that Scott had somehow forced him to harm himself, he still felt drawn to the boy.

After much back and forth, Lody backed away from his table and went to the one-eyed boy. Lody's wheelchair squeaked and hummed as he crossed the twenty feet of space between Scott's table and his own. Aside from Lody and Scott, there was one other kid in the children's ward; a little girl, who looked no older than seven or eight, resided in a chair by one of the windows. A snail trail of glistening saliva dribbled from her chin, and one eye rolled independently of the other. One of the new orderlies—the man who had replaced Newly-Noseless Sean—lurked by the door to the dayroom, his hands in his pockets as he watched Lody trundle toward Scott.

Lody pulled up to the table and engaged the brakes on his wheelchair. Scott did not look up from his drawing.

"Hello," Lody said.

"Hello," Scott returned, scribbling faster.

"Whatcha drawing?"

"You don't want to know."

Lody gazed down at Scott's revolving fist—wherein a piece of charcoal pencil was tightly gripped—and the swirling black void the boy was creating on the surface of the paper. The longer Lody stared, the more mercurial the black hole became, as if watching the void gifted it life. There soon came a time when he couldn't pull his eyes away. Lody drifted into the void, and a warmth filled him. He felt welcome, at home, and...

"What are you two doing?" came a voice that snapped Lody from the wonderful place within the drawing. He jerked his head in the direction of the voice and faced the new orderly, the guy who had been manning the dayroom door only seconds before.

"Huh?" Lody groaned. He was lightheaded and suddenly weary. The orderly swam in his vision.

"They told me to keep all you kids separate, so come on. Back to your own table." The orderly disappeared behind Lody. Lody was pushed back to his table, where he sat dazed and forlorn, like a toddler deprived his binky.

"We can talk here," a voice whispered inside his head.

"What?" Lody asked aloud.

"No. In your mind. I can hear you just fine."

Lody glanced over at Scott and met the boy's eye; it glimmered blue, a sapphire floating in a sea of cream. A redness in the center of Scott's forehead drew Lody's gaze. At first the crimson glow was dull, like a flushed cheek, but the longer Lody looked the brighter it became, until finally a red eye glared, burning fiercely above Scott's brow.

A shadow emerged from the boy as smoothly as a man pushes himself from bed. The shifting darkness floated wispily over the table, across the space between the two boys, and came to rest in the empty seat on the other side of the table. The entity was a Cyclops, its one eye a ruby in the middle of ever-shifting shade. Darkness steamed from the mass. Lody thought he smelled smoke, but soon realized it was only his mind attributing the odor to the smoke-like snakes coming off the shadow's form. He couldn't parse this creature, so his mind grasped at any similarities to real-world things it could.

With his thoughts, Lody asked, "What are you?"

"I've been called many things throughout time. The boy calls me the Bastard, for I have no father and can be quite... dastardly."

In spite of his fear, Lody chuckled. "That's silly."

"Is it? Aren't you, yourself, a bastard of a kind? Tell me, where is *your* father?"

Lody didn't answer. Instead he glanced at the orderly. The man had returned to the dayroom's only exit. He stared in Lody's direction, but didn't seem to notice the ruby-eyed entity.

"He can't see you, can he?" Lody asked.

"Not unless I want him too. Even if he did see me, he wouldn't see *me*. He'd see a fond memory. I have that effect on people. Well... the boy has that effect, at any rate." It was the shadow's turn to chuckle.

"Who? Scott?" Lody asked. His thoughts sounded far away to his own ears, as if he spoke from the bottom of some grand chasm.

"I prefer to think of him as... as the Creator. He makes all this"—the shadow made a sweeping gesture with one inky appendage—"all this possible. Nifty, huh?"

"I don't understand."

The shadow's chuckling became guffaws. "There's nothing for you to understand, child. You must only see, and that is already accomplished."

"Whaddya mean?"

"You can see me. That is all that matters."

"I'm not scared of you." This was not a challenge but a simple truth. Lody knew that this... this shadow... this Bastard should frighten him. The reality of its existence should have terrified him to his core, but instead of being fearful, Lody felt as if he were in the company of a longtime acquaintance; or more aptly, a friend.

"I didn't suspect you would be. We're kin of a fashion, you see. Our shadows are twins, if you will."

"Our shadows?"

"Our pasts. That which lingers behind us. That which withers. They can be your fuel, or your great destroyer. It all depends on how you use your... your talents."

"So... are you Scott?" Lody hitched his chin at the boy with the eyepatch.

"You could say that. He created me. I am of him. In a way, I protect him."

"Protect him from what?"

"Himself. His memories. If it wasn't for me, Scott would have torn himself apart long ago. But there is a greater power in the Creator's core. More of a place, really. A plane. It is called the Withered, and it is where happiness goes to die. He has learned how to harness its power, though, and thusly, created me from that power."

"Are you talking about magic?" Lody asked.

"Oh, nothing so simple or as boring as magic, no. This is *power*, child. This is the essence of what separates man from animal." At "animal" the being, this thing made of nighttime, shivered. "You see, man is the only species that dwells, that lingers, in the past. Their memories are allowed to control them, to shape them into the men and women they become. A lion doesn't feel bad for killing its prey. To the wild beast, prey is simply nourishment. It's not murder. It's mealtime. A dog doesn't fret over past punishments. It piddles on the floor, has its nose rubbed in it, and moves on. The dog might become conditioned by these things, to associate piddling in a certain area with punishment, but they do not regret previously pissing indoors. Only man knows regret."

Lody studied the Bastard's ruby eye, that cold gem in the middle of its mercurial face, and shook his head in incomprehension. "What's any of this got to do with me?"

The shade sighed at length. "You're a dense one, child. I mean to tell you of the power you carry within yourself. I mean to show you how to use it." The shadow smiled. That smile was a horrible thing. A fraction of a second later, the shadow vanished.

"Dad!" Scott hollered from his table at the other end of the room. Lody's gaze shot up from the empty space that had only a second ago contained the shifting form of a creature who called itself the Bastard to see a tall, thin man in a charcoal suit stride past the orderly and into the room.

Scott ejected from his seat like a wound up jack-in-the-box. He dashed toward the man, and crashed into him. Scott wrapped his arms around his father's waist, buried his face in the man's stomach, and openly wept. The stoic man, this man Scott had called *Dad*, simply patted the boy on the back as he shot furtive looks around the room. He seemed to be concerned with how he'd be perceived, as if comforting his child was an embarrassing act.

"I missed you," Scott said, sobbing against his father.

"Stop it, Scooter. Please."

Scott pulled away from his father's stomach and gazed up at the wraith-like man. "Have you come to take me home?"

"How would you like to visit for a bit, and perhaps discuss the future?" the boy's father asked, as if he hadn't heard Scott's question.

"Yeah. Yeah, sure!" Scott cried excitedly and wiped tears from his eyes.

"That's just fine. Good, even." The man finally managed a smile for his son, and Lody was suddenly very confused. The creature that had emerged from Scott had said something about Scott being a bastard, about not having a father. If the entity and the boy were truly one, then who was this man? Unless the man really was the boy's father, and the creature was a liar.

Or you're imagining the whole thing.

That was a very real possibility, and sadly, Lody knew it. The pain medication the nursing staff gave him to combat the agony of his self mutilation could be to blame, or perhaps the pills the doctor had prescribed to keep him calm were the culprits. Any way he looked at it, his mind was not to be trusted. His blood was tainted, and his brain would be affected. Yes, that was it. He simply wasn't in his right mind. Loopy. Nuts.

This comforted Lody throughout the rest of the day. There had been no creature made of shadow. There was no Bastard, and no place called the Withered. Scott was nothing more than a disturbed child, much like Lody was himself. Where most would grow concerned by the possibility of their own madness, Lody found solace. Because, if a creature like the Bastard existed, the world was a scary place indeed.

After dinner, Lody was rolled back to his room, where he was made ready for bed. If the orderly noticed the red lines stretching out from under Lody's bandages, the man made no mention of it. Lody spent that entire night tossing and turning, mind reeling with fever and body trembling with chills.

When dayshift came in the following morning, the boy was half-dead. Staff rushed Lody to the intensive care ward, which was in-house and located on the first floor. He was given an ice bath to drop his temperature. This kept him alive long enough to undergo surgery.

In the early days of the twentieth century, little was known about sepsis, and so Lody's remaining testicle was removed and his blood poisoned by the infection that had taken root after his episode of self-mutilation. His tainted blood infected his brain, and then his nervous system. Lody disappeared for a while. Doctors called this state a coma. Lody would come to think of it as a rebirth. No matter what it was called, this state lasted for two weeks.

To the surprise of everyone employed at Pointvilla County Institute for the Insane, Lody opened his eyes on Christmas morning. A nurse by the name of Tamara Colton was injecting a rather nasty looking bit of goop into Lody's nasogastric tube when his eyes shot wide. She screamed, and in her shock depressed the plunger completely. The pressure blew the syringe from the tubing and Lody's face was showered with nutritious muck.

Lody began to laugh. And continued to do so until the doctor was called and he was put back to sleep.

Lody awoke for good the following evening. The medical floor was empty and quiet, and the boy felt an overwhelming sense of unease. The shadows pulsed, and every cot in the twenty-bed ward seemed occupied by slumbering ghosts. In a way, Lody knew this was his imagination overreacting, but another part of him recalled the Bastard, and he figured that at any moment the red-eyed darkness would erupt from a shadowy corner to race at him with seeking claws.

This did not happen, but Lody remained frightened until a nurse came in to find the boy shivering under stacks of covers. This nurse's name was Kimberly, and her part in this tale is still to come.

After awakening from his two-week coma, Lody was ravenous. The next morning he devoured two trays of food, which his doctor erroneously allowed due to the boy having lost so much weight while asleep. Lody threw up most of what he ate because his stomach was not used to so much intake, something his doctor should have realized was going to happen. But once the boy was done being sick, he requested more. The orderly denied Lody a third tray. At least someone in attendance had a little sense.

Lunch stayed down. Dinner did not. Lody slept. Lody woke. Breakfast digested without incident, as did lunch and supper.

On the twenty-second day of Lody's stay in the intensive care ward, a gift was left for him on the nightstand beside his bed while he slept and dreamed of his father.

In the dream, his father's bloated corpse swayed languidly from its noose. The balloon-like eyes followed Lody wherever he went. The swollen purple tongue licked puffy lips, as if the dead man found Lody simply scrumptious.

"You will do great things, child," the impossible man grumbled. The voice was thick and full of the grave.

"You're not real," Lody said in the most grown-up voice he could muster.

"You will. Oh, Lody, you will make me so proud. You'll kill her, child. You'll murder the cunt and make that squaw wish she were never born. You'll. Be. Just. Like. Me!"

"No!" Lody wailed as the corpse swung and chuckled, chuckled and swung.

When Lody awoke, he was covered in sweat and what was left of his crotch throbbed like a rotten tooth.

The doll on the nightstand was grinning at him.

He eyed the gift suspiciously, wondering where it had come from but mostly who had left it. The face was cherub-like, with a smiling mouth and chubby cheeks, which were slightly blushed. Two happy blue eyes gazed at Lody with what seemed eager anticipation, as if it just couldn't wait to be in his arms, couldn't wait to be hugged and caressed and befriended and cherished. Its long black hair hung around its face in thick curls. In fact, the hair was so very black that its curls shone purple in places. The doll wore a black settler's dress with white fringe. Both of its hands were curled into fists, and its feet were covered in black shoes, which had been polished to a mirror finish.

Lody reached out with a tentative hand and plucked the doll from where it stood. Under its clothing, Lody could feel the cold emanating from its porcelain body. He'd never touched something so unyielding, so frigidly hard. He squeezed its legs, its arms, its torso, expecting it to give somewhere, but there was no give. The entire doll was made of the same solid porcelain. By its weight,

Lody wouldn't have been surprised to find out that the doll didn't have a hollow spot on it.

He flicked his middle finger at one of the doll's eyes and it clinked. The eyes had been painted on. The hair and the dress seemed to be the only parts of the doll that were not molded. He tugged softly on the black locks and they came off in his hand.

A wig! he thought with a smile.

His crotch throbbed but he paid it no mind. He was lost in his gift.

"Do you like her?" asked a voice from behind Lody. With great effort, Lody rolled over. He grunted with exertion as he settled down onto his back, the doll clutched to his chest.

A young woman in a nurse's cap and dress grinned down at him. Her teeth were rows of pearls and her eyes roasted chestnuts. A brunette ponytail jutted from the back of her cap and hung behind her head. It looked clean, and Lody imagined how soft it would be if he ran his hands through it. This wasn't a sexual idea for him, but a comforting one. He didn't realize it at that moment, but soon enough he would think that this nurse reminded him of his dead mother.

"She's lovely," Lody said in a weak voice. He cleared his throat and swallowed a glob of phlegm.

"It was my daughter's." The nurse's smile lengthened, but Lody saw sadness there. Moreover, Lody saw grief. He would not ask about her daughter, for he knew, from that smile alone, that this woman's daughter was dead.

"She's lovely," Lody repeated. "What's yer name?"

"Kimberly. And you're Lody. There," she said with a nod of her head, "we're introduced then. Maybe we could be friends, too, if you didn't mind. I'd like to be your friend, at any rate."

Lody shrugged. "Sure."

"You were asleep a long time. I took care of you while you were... away, so I know you a little better than

431

you know me, I should say. But I'll listen." She seemed overeager. Almost forceful in her compassion. Oddly enough, Lody found nothing strange about this. His life had been so full of such extremities—extreme horror, extreme abuse, and now, with Kimberly, extreme kindness—that he found nothing strange about her overly cheerful demeanor. "I'd listen to anything you have to tell me."

"All right," Lody said. "All right, Kim."

"No. Kimberly, please. *Nobody*"—but Lody saw something in that word, something in "nobody" that made him think she meant "somebody" instead—"calls me Kim. Is that okay? Will you call me Kimberly?"

"Yes. If ya want." Lody absentmindedly caressed the doll's dark hair.

She bent down and patted the edge of Lody's hospital bed. "Can I sit down? Do you mind?"

Lody shook his head. Kimberly spun and dropped down, crossing her legs almost instantly. There was a brief moment when the old Lody peeked through (no, when his father peeked through) that Lody wondered what she was hiding, wondered what hid between those long legs covered in white pantyhose. Would it be soft? Would it be welcoming? Would it—?

"She doesn't have a name. I mean, you can name her if you want." Kimberly motioned toward the doll lying on Lody's torso.

"I'll think about it."

"Now, some of the orderlies around here can be quite... brutish. Do you know what I mean?"

Lody shook his head.

"They might say cruel things. Like... stuff like 'A boy shouldn't play with dolls,' or they might call you names. You ignore them, okay? You just love your doll and you forget it... You know, if it ever happens."

"Okay."

"So, what would you like to talk about?" she asked, twisting a bit so they could face each other fully.

432

"When do I get to leave here?" Lody asked, for that was most present in his mind. He wanted to get out of here, away from the hospital feel of this place, and back into general population. Mostly though, he wanted to see Scott again. He didn't necessarily miss the strange, doodling boy, but the shadow attached to Scott intrigued Lody.

That was all in your head, remember?

But was it? Was it, really?

"Not sure. That's up to the doctors, and one of them I'm not. It won't be too long, though, I wouldn't think. Your infection is passing, which surprised many of us, let me tell you." She forced some laughter, and Lody found that he didn't like it when Kimberly pretended to laugh. It made her ugly. "Needless to say, you worried us. Gave everyone quite a scare. You're fine now, though. Nary a bit of fever. We must make sure your infection does not return, though, so that is why you're still here. Do you understand?"

Lody nodded.

"Good. She looks happy with you," Kimberly said, pointing at the doll once more.

"She makes me happy, too. She makes me think about my mother," Lody lied. He was thinking about his mother, but the doll was not why.

"Your mother?"

"Yeah... she, uh, she... she died. It was bad. She bled a lot."

Kimberly flinched. Her hands had been in her lap, but now one of them reached for her mouth, as if to cover it. She thought better of the action and dropped it back to her lap. "That's... that's horrible."

"She was having a baby. Woulda been my sister. But something ripped open and they died. Both of them. And Pa buried"—this word came out "burr-rayed"—"them under the house. We got this cellar, ya know. Pa says it's a cellar and not a basement cuz it's got a dirt floor and not a wood one. 'Nyway"—he was getting excited, and the faster he spoke, the more broken and country his words became—"Pa buried them down there and said I could go down there whene'er I wanted, long as I didn't try and dig up the old bitch. Something about letting the dead rest, or some such, and that bitch deserved to sleep. Pa said if ever there was a bitch what deserved sleep, it was Ma." Lody nodded to punctuate his final sentence.

Kimberly gawped at him.

She looks mighty scared, Lody thought.

"Lody," she said and swallowed, "that's not a nice word. You shouldn't call a woman that. Especially not your dead mother. It's disrespectful. Do you even know what that word means?"

"What word? Disrespectful?"

"No, no. That B word you said." Kimberly hesitated then pushed forward. "'Bitch' is the word I'm talking about, Lody. It's what some folks call female dogs. You don't think of your mother as a dog, do you, Lody?"

"Naw," he drawled. "She weren't no dog. She were a nice lady. Like you."

"Why, thank you. You aren't so terrible yourself, young man." Her smile was diamonds, finely cut and invaluable. "So, what made your mother such a nice lady?"

"She gave me presents, like you. Pa ne'er gave me no presents."

"He didn't give you *any* presents," she corrected softly.

"What?"

"Saying your Pa never gave you no presents is like saying he did give you presents. It's a double negative. One no cancels out the other. Do you understand?"

Lody did not comprehend, but he wasn't about to let Kimberly know that.

He nodded. "Pa never gave me *any* presents. After Ma died from losin' too much blood, Pa changed. He started stealing squaws and doing things to them. He let me help sometimes."

Kimberly was making that face again, that face that said he'd spoken something terrible. He knew that face because Ma used to make the same face when she stepped into the outhouse after Pa had been in there for a while.

"That's why they killed him, I think," Lody added. "I think the men from town hung him from that tree because he'd done something wrong with one of those injun bit—uh, women he took from town."

"My good heavens, Lody," Kimberly said weakly, as if his story were draining her. "You do realize that your father was a bad man, right? What he did was rape and murder women. I read as much in your chart. You were living in Nevada at the time. You were brought out here because of your... condition. The women your father tortured weren't *squaws*, honey, they were just women. Negro women, but women all the same."

"What's a 'negro woman'?"

"Don't worry about that. Some people think folks with different colored skin should be labeled, but I don't think that's very nice, do you?"

"But... but you called them that name. That label." Lody was so confused.

"I did, didn't I? I'm sorry, Lody, but even I'm not perfect. Things become habit after a while. But you shouldn't call other people names. After all, even if our skin is different colors, we're all the same on the inside."

"No we ain't," Lody said very plainly. "Some of us got brighter blood. Some of us have more fat. Some of us have our playgrounds on the inside and others on the outsides. Naw, we ain't all the same. Pa showed me that much. Some of use are darker... much, *much* darker on the inside."

"Oh, Lody," Kimberly moaned. "Oh, my dear child."

You will do great things, child, that serpent's voice said in Lody's mind, and the boy shivered.

That night, Lody's sleep was dreamless, and when he awoke the next morning, Kimberly had left him a new present.

Under the six-inch-tall statue of the Mother Mary, Kimberly had left a note. This note said:

> Lody,
>
> *This is a symbol of my faith. I'm not sure if you or your family was religious, but I am. I believe that JESUS CHRIST is my lord and savior, and this is his mother. I think she could stand in place of your own mother, if you let her. Not replace your mother, but stand in her place. Do you understand? If not, we can speak about her later. I'll try to bring you a Bible later on this week. I'm working upstairs today, so we will not see each other again until this weekend. I pray that your day is good and pain free.*
>
> Love,
> Kimberly

When he put the letter back under the figurine, Lody was surprised to find tears in his eyes. He couldn't remember the last time he'd cried. He hadn't shed a tear for his father, but maybe he'd cried after his mother and sister had perished? Maybe? With some hope in his heart, Lody imagined he had broken down and sobbed at the place where half of his family, half the people he had ever loved, had been laid to rest. The truth was, Lody hadn't cried. Lody hadn't missed the bitch in the slightest.

So what was different now? Yes, what indeed?

Four days went by before Lody saw Kimberly again, and when she did return to his bedside, she didn't seem herself. A dark cast had fallen over her usual affable features. Dark splotches rested under her roasted-chestnut eyes. Her cheeks weren't as cherry-red as they normally were, and she favored one side. Every time she twisted at the waist or bent to pick something up she'd groan and clutch her flank. Once again, Lody was reminded of his mother.

"You gotta go to sleep, Lody," his mother said, holding her ribs and forcing a smile.

"What's wrong, Ma? What's wrong with your side?" a much younger Lody asked.

"Sometimes I do bad and your Pa has to remind me what's right, is all. Don't worry about it, baby. Your father knows best, he does. Yes, father knows best."

"Do you like your new gift?" Kimberly asked. She sat down on the edge of his bed as she had on her previous visit, but this time the action fetched a grimace from her.

"What's wrong with your side?" Lody asked, ignoring her question.

"I fell coming down my porch steps. Ice, you know. Nasty stuff. It's gotten so cold outside. Hey, maybe we could ask the doctor if we can take you outside. The brisk air might do your lungs some—"

"Who hit you?" Lody asked. He hadn't expected to ask as much, but some part of him, some inner darkling, shoved the question from him. He felt it rise from his gut into his throat then pour like mud from his mouth. No matter his intention, the question sounded ugly. Sounded filthy. He thought less of himself for asking it.

"What makes you think somebody hit me?" Kimberly plastered on a fake smile that was somehow dirtier than the question he'd asked her.

"You ain't gotta lie for him. Some man hit you, and he doesn't deserve you being dishonest for him."

"It isn't a man. I'll leave it at that. I have to get back to my duties now." She rose, turned, stopped, and faced him once more. "If we're going to be friends, Lody, please don't ever ask me questions like that again. Okay?"

"You said you'd listen to me. I was... I was just returning the favor."

"Thank you, Lody. But, please, honor my wishes."

"Yes, ma'am," Lody said, and even as he said it he regretted it.

"I'm not a 'ma'am,' Lody. I'm Kimberly. Your friend Kimberly." She flashed that ugly smile again before turning and walking away.

Lody saw no more of Kimberly that day, and he was very, very sad because of it.

Lody got better, so much better that he was allowed to start therapy again. Before his self-mutilation, Lody had seen Doctor Andy only twice, and both visits had ended in Lody trying to strangle the man. Every time Doc Andy mentioned Lody's father, Lody became enraged and his hands found their way around the bespectacled-man's bearded neck.

Today, much was different, and not only on Lody's side. Doc Andy had the curtains open, something he never did. The view of the institute's inner courtyard was lovely. There was a birdbath in the center of a grassy knoll, which was surrounded by wrought iron benches. A haggard-looking woman roughly the age of Father Time sat on one of the benches, screaming so hard at the sky that bands stood out in her neck from the strain. Lody believed that at any moment this old woman's head must surely explode. The scene was building to such a payoff, at any rate.

Lody was lost in watching this woman rip the heavens apart with her very voice when Doc Andy said,

"I've been informed you've made a friend, Lody. Care to tell me about that?"

"Kimberly. Her name's Kimberly." Lody continued to look out the window. If the geriatric lady's head did indeed explode, he didn't want to miss it.

"Right. Kimberly. She's a nice lady, isn't she?"

Lody glanced away from the straining, screaming face of the old woman on the park bench long enough to judge Doc Andy's eyes, and then he snapped back to the view outside.

"How do you know Kimberly?" Lody asked quietly.

"Well, that's easy enough to figure out, isn't it? I mean, she works here, as do I, so we're bound to run into each other from time to time." Doc Andy smiled. Lody hated Doc Andy's smile. That smile made Lody want to hurt Doc Andy, because Doc Andy had the type of face that welcomed punches. Begged for them, really.

"Okay," Lody said, sounding dazed.

The woman outside still hadn't exploded. In fact, to Lody's disappointment, she was starting to lose steam, like a teakettle after it's taken off a burner. A dark-skinned man in an orderly's uniform came into the picture, as if he were an actor traipsing out onto stage in the middle of a performance. This man (*Is he a* negro, Lody asked himself. *I think he is, 'cause his skin's the color of Pa's squaws...*) sat beside the wailing woman and threw an arm around her shoulders. She quieted instantly. She rested her head on the man's shoulder, and he started to pet her hair. There was something sweet about the scene; even though Lody didn't exactly understand what the word *comfort* meant, he understood at a base level that this was the exact opposite of his father. He wondered, absently, if these brown-skinned people weren't nicer than people with paler flesh. After all, those with pale flesh had—how had Kimberly put it?—labeled those with darker flesh than them. Lody wondered if that made him a bad person by default. Was he a horrible human being simply because of the color of his skin, or did it take actions to make you a bad person?

"They hung the men who killed your father." Those words broke through Lody's thoughts, and he faced forward with a snap.

"What? Why?" Lody stammered.

"Those boys killed a white man, Lody. It didn't matter that they had proof of your father's actions. They still murdered a white man, and if you're of nigger blood, that's a crime. I thought you'd want to know. Maybe knowing will give you some—oh, I don't know—some closure."

Lody realized he was shaking. Or perhaps he was trembling.

Is there a difference?

"Why would that give me closure?" Lody asked, and had no idea just how adult he sounded. "My father was a bad man. He deserved to die. He was... he was cruel."

Doc Andy shrugged. "The world's a cruel place, Lody. I think, deep down, we're all bad, and we must fight daily to be good. But when we are idle, we're the most evil species on the planet. I should write that down."

Lody sat in silence while Doc Andy hunted for a notebook. The doctor found one, pushed his glasses up his bumpy red nose, and began to jot down his thoughts on the matter of human evil. Lody considered leaping across the table and giving the doctor's neck a firm handshake for the third time, but he suddenly felt weary, drained.

If Doc Andy was right about humanity, were people like Kimberly the exception to the rule, or had she simply not given in to her demons? If man was, at basement level, bad, then what did that say about Lody's father? Could a man be blamed for giving into his basic urges? And could his child forgive him. Lody thought he could.

Before the orderlies came to take him away, Lody thought he had come across the truth of the world.

CRUELTY

Cruelty was the way of the world. But true power lay in forgiveness.

CRUELTY

MIA

And that's the difference between Scott and Lody, between the Bastard and Forgiveness, Mia thought from her place in the Withered. *The Bastard was only darkness, the darkest of human suffering, but Forgiveness is so much more. All it takes to vanquish the dark is a fire, a light in the black. But what happens when that light is part of the darkness? How do you destroy the dark without snuffing out the light? What is this creature's weakness if not light? What lies between Cruelty and Forgiveness?*

Mia pulled out of Forgiveness's memories and found herself standing in an arid wasteland.

Well, this is unexpected.

Sand blasted her skin, and she was quite surprised that she could *feel* it, as if her flesh had become her own again, and not Laurette's.

Interesting...

Dunes bracketed her, and she realized she was in some kind of valley.

In the valley of the shadow of death, I shall fear no... well, I shall not fear me.

She cackled softly. The sound would have made a grown man's blood run cold.

She'd spent so long in the Roaming that the Withered seemed alien. Though this plane of existence was only what the mind made of it, she knew that she was not in her own mind. She was in the demon's mind, and this monster obviously fancied sand. Sand was good at hiding things. That was an inarguable truth. But what was the demon hiding? She hadn't had to dig too far to find the demon's childhood. Forgiveness's memories rested on the surface of it all. What on earth could be beneath?

I don't yet know the before of the matter, Mia thought. *I know where he ended up, but I do not know what happened before his father's death.*

A voice rose in her the likes of which Mia thought she'd never hear from again.

Laurette—Momma—asked a simple question, and Mia chided herself for not seeing it.

If Lody grew up to be Forgiveness, then who, if anyone, resides in the doll?

Oh, Laurette, you ain't so stupid after all.

Is they one and the same, ya think? Instead of master and ward, be they one? One scared child what never grew up? How does that strike ya, Mia?

It strikes me as deadly possible, Laurette. Deadly possible, indeed.

Mia giggled as she kicked and trudged through loose sand.

That explains the doll, but what of the other? Laurette asked. *What of the statue?*

That, bon ti fi, is what I hope to find under the sand, at the root of the matter.

Regret?

Yes, Laurette. Remember what I told you?

Before there is forgiveness, there must be regret.

And before regret, Mia answered, *there must be Cruelty.*

FORGIVENESS

The bitch just wouldn't give up.

Forgiveness paced inside his cabin, throwing screaming shadows across the walls. Here, in the Withered, he was his incorporeal form, nothing but shifting darkness, much like the Bastard. He considered how long it would be before she found the Source. If Mia found that, he was done for. The Bastard would no longer be the only one of them to have fallen.

He could feel the presence of the Creator. That little fucker was out there somewhere, screwing everything up, destroying Forgiveness's plans layer by layer.

And what of him—Forgiveness? A prisoner was all he was now. A prisoner hiding in a place where he had once been much like a king. At least after the fall of the Bastard. The Withered was where Forgiveness belonged, but not under these conditions. Not like a rat in a damn trap.

Wait...

He stopped in the middle of the cabin's foreroom. He had another option. If he used the dark woman to harvest, he could regain the strength he'd lost by losing track of Cruelty. If he harnessed Regret's energy instead of allowing her to feed, he would be able to rejuvenate himself while he hid.

And by the time Mia found him...

Oh, yes. Yes, this was very good.

Outside, the winds of this desolate land blew down the eaves. Sand crackled as it kissed the roof and thin walls.

CRUELTY

Let the Creator and the bitch come. Let them come together. And when they found him, death would welcome them. No, not death. Oblivion.

Because they were finite and he was not. Not as long as he could feed.

Still, in the back of his mind, he worried, because one question continued to pester him:

Where is Cruelty?

THE LOCK-IN

Bruce was beginning to regret coming to the mystery party. Innis was still missing, and here he was, hanging out with friends and hiding from his guy on the side. No telling what Frank Markum would do if he dropped by Bruce's apartment, the apartment he shared with Innis Blake. Frank had been extremely unstable on the phone. Feeling unsafe in his own place, Bruce had called up an old friend to see if maybe she wanted to get a drink.

Sarah Frost now stood next to Bruce in front of a crowd of fifteen. Four more people Bruce didn't know lingered in a line to the side of Sarah. The goal of the mystery party was simple. The crowd would leave for thirty minutes, someone in Sarah's group of six would fake-murder someone else, and the crowd would return. It was then the crowd's job to figure out who the murderer was. Weak sauce, but easy enough.

Instead of drinks, Sarah had offered Bruce a spot in the mystery party. The crew of twenty—twenty-one with Bruce included—would be locked in their office building until six o'clock the following morning. Bruce had been a part of several lock-ins when he was just a lad, mostly during his time with his church's youth group. He could recall playing volleyball (shittily) and running track (even more shittily) with the other guys in the gym while the girls did their nails and gossiped about good little church boys they'd fucked without their uppity parents' knowledge. Even in those days, Bruce had wanted to be on the girls' side of things. He

446

wanted to talk about boys and hear all the tricks of the trade from the best cocksucker in the business—the pastor's adopted daughter Cheryl. It was known among the public trust that Cheryl could suck a basketball through a straw. Rumor had it even her father knew, and at times, the pastor would partake of his daughter's talents. It wasn't incest, the kid spreading the rumor would say, because Cheryl was adopted. Who cares if she swallowed his Twinkie filling? No one seemed to care that Cheryl was only fourteen, or that, if the rumors were true, Pastor Thomlin would be serving jail time instead of Christ.

Bruce first realized his oral fixation included penises around the time he hit junior high school. He found women attractive, but there was something about a guy's engorged dick that made him salivate. His buddy Charlie had brought over a porno movie wherein two girls fought over a purple cock as if the thing were a rocket pop. Bruce spent more time imagining his own mouth on that swollen thing than he did picturing those girls slobbing on his knob. About two minutes into the fuck flick, Charlie whipped out his shifter and started shifting gears. Bruce tried to keep his eyes off Charlie's pounding fist and what it clenched, but it was pointless. He offered to blow Charlie, and surprisingly enough Charlie accepted the offer. It never occurred to Bruce that this was what Charlie had in mind the entire time.

Still, he enjoyed women. If he ever traipsed through a headshrinker's door and flopped down upon their sofa, said headshrinker might inform Bruce that he was bisexual, and that there was nothing wrong with this. But Bruce never saw a therapist, and because of this, Bruce thought something was wrong with him. So he remained hidden, hidden from even his fiancée—if Innis could be called his fiancée anymore.

There was a damn good chance she'd caught Bruce going down on Frank. If this was the case, Innis was gone forever. She'd warned him about infidelity, had said there was a lot of shit she could deal with (his obsession with porn, video games, and the BBC's *Sherlock*, just to name a few), but she would never stand being (as she put it) a side-bitch.

This was where Bruce's mind currently resided, so when Sarah started reading the rules of the game to the crowd of fifteen strangers, Bruce had missed every word of it. Now that she had finished and the crowd was moving toward the door of the conference room, Bruce realized he didn't have the slightest clue what the fuck was going on.

"Ready, dead boy?" Sarah asked with a sly grin. Bruce could just hear the slightest Aussie in her accent. He wondered how long ago it had been since she'd left the deepest south there was, but never did get the chance to ask. Sarah was a stout lady—not fat, but "well-built with something to hang on to," as Bruce's father would have put it. She had a gorgeous smile, which consisted of two rows of shimmering white teeth. As far as Bruce could tell, she wore no makeup. He liked that. Hated when Innis wore the stuff. A woman should go throughout her day the way God made her. Everything else was a lie. The same could be said for high heels and pushup bras. Bruce liked his women all natural as much as he loved the feel of a stiff one in the back of his throat.

"Sorry?" Bruce asked, smiling.

"Are you ready to die?" Sarah asked.

For the briefest of moments, Bruce's heart fluttered uncertainly in his chest. He had no idea what was going on, and believed he'd been lured here under a ruse, that these six people (all of them grinning at him manically now) planned to skin and eat him. Before he came to his senses, he had the horrible thought that he was trapped. He'd watched the old man lock up the front of the building (this geezer was hunched over and wore an old-school mechanic's jumper with the name Earl on the patch over his heart, and Bruce thought that death wasn't far from this guy's door, if it hadn't already started knocking), and knew that there was no way out. The double doors of Stannis and Pessl (the law office where Sarah worked as a paralegal) were locked from the outside. There was no turn bolt on the inside, Bruce had seen. The single rear exit was much the same. No turn bolt on the inside. Only a key would open it. On the ride over, Sarah had mentioned that someone else had a key, in case of emergencies, of course, but she wasn't going to tell who it was.

"Where's the fun in giving away that information?" she'd asked, and Bruce had laughed, but only because she'd started laughing herself.

"Danger is fun!" she had cried next, and slapped Bruce's thigh. "Buck up, Bruce, she'll come back eventually." This non sequitur had been brought on by the story Bruce had told Sarah over the phone. As far as Sarah was concerned, Innis had left Bruce and he didn't feel like sitting in an empty house feeling sorry for himself. Sarah was more than happy to help him out. In fact, she planned to keep him out of the house all night. They'd be going to a party, a mystery party, one where someone would die.

Oh yeah...

"Oh... I'm the victim?" Bruce finally managed. The Asian man dressed in a tweed jacket and tweed slacks and, well, tweed everything, who stood at the end of the line, chuckled into his fist. Bruce ignored the man.

"Yes, dear," Sarah said. "You're it, as it were. So, are you ready to die?"

Bruce shrugged. "Sure."

"This is where it gets fun. Jonathan down there"—Sarah pointed to the Asian man—"will be the murderer, but Isabelle and Monica will be the red herrings. Izzy's shoe will be found next to the body. Monica's lipstick will, too. She's the only one wearing makeup, so it should be obvious whose it is. Izzy, of course, will be short a shoe, and—"

Sarah droned on and on, but Bruce thought he got the gist of the game. The items left by the body would serve to throw the crowd off the scent, but there'd also be evidence to lead to the capture of Jonathan on Bruce's person. Whatever. At least he wasn't at home, shaking in his boots, waiting on Special Investigator Frank Markum to show up and put two between his eyes.

"Ready?" Sarah shrieked and clapped her hands together. "This is gonna be fun!"

Bruce lay down in front of the short bookshelf on the far wall while the other placed the evidence around him. The murder weapon was a projector. Jonathan was supposed to have dropped the thing on Bruce's head after they'd struggled. A piece of tweed fabric snatched from Jonathan's jacket was placed in Bruce's open palm, and he was told to close his fist on it.

Well, that's convenient, Bruce thought as he closed his eyes and played dead.

Sarah Frost thought Bruce looked fantastic. Jonathan had smeared some fake blood across Bruce's forehead, and now Monica and Isabelle were lifting the projector from its base and lowering it next to Bruce's head. Izzy eased the projector onto its side and looked up at Sarah. "This good?" Izzy asked.

"Looks fantastic. Okay, everybody, assume your positions!"

The crew dispersed. Sarah's job was to be one of the missing. She'd be hiding in the ladies' room when the crowd was let back in, and George (the oldest of the bunch) would be asleep in Harold Stannis's office, which was a bit of an inside joke around Stannis and Pessl. If you listened to the gossip hounds around the workplace, it was said that George napped in Stannis's office after Stannis went out for lunch every day. The truth of the matter (which only Sarah knew) was George went in there to fuck Izzy. Izzy was a married woman, but neither she nor George seemed to give a flying fig about such details. One afternoon, a month or so back, Sarah had walked in on George's bald head shining in the overhead lights as he thrust his sixty-year-old hips into Izzy's not insubstantial backside. Izzy, who was no zoo prize herself, was bent over Stannis's desk sucking breath like an asthmatic. Though Sarah didn't know if Izzy knew about being caught, Sarah was quite sure George knew, because when he turned his head to see who'd walked in on them, he'd given Sarah a grin and thumbs-up and gone right back to his plumbing duties.

Giggling inwardly, Sarah walked out into the hallway that connected the offices and the conference room. The fifteen people who would be playing detective over the next hour or so, were currently waiting in the lobby and out of view. The door to the lobby lay at one end of the hall, and the back door (the employees' entrance) sat at the opposite end. Sarah slunk quietly down the hall to the ladies' room and pushed the door open. As she stepped into the restroom, the back door banged open.

What came through that door caused Sarah Frost to keep moving. She stumbled into the dark bathroom, rushed for one of the two stalls, and threw herself inside.

"Couldn't be... just couldn't be... couldn't be..." she repeated again and again.

The restroom door swung open, flooding the restroom with light. Sarah wished she were at home, safe at home, with her father's gun cabinet just down the hall. She wished she was there, gun in hand, protected against the horrors of the night, but she wasn't. She was here.

And something was coming for her.

The doors of the restroom glided silently closed, and the restroom was dipped in darkness once more.

"*Pleasepleaseplease*," she muttered, her terror a white-hot coal in her belly, a brick in her throat.

"Bruce?" said a female voice. "Bruce, is that you?"

"Oh God, Izzy?" Sarah asked, feeling quite stupid once she recognized her friend's voice. She pulled the door inward and stepped out, laughing nervously. "You scared the bejesus out of—"

"You're not Bruce," the woman in the dark said, and Sarah could feel this woman's anger, could feel the scorn coming off her in waves. Although Sarah didn't notice, her knees began to quake.

Something grabbed her by the neck, squeezed, and tore out her throat. Sarah dropped to her knees instantly. She didn't cough or choke, such was an impossibility now, but she did manage to buck as she died. That, at least, was something.

The living statue, the thing she'd seen come through the back door, pulled the restroom door open and floated out into the hall.

Just before Sarah died, she wondered why it had been Izzy's voice she had heard, wondered if it had been Izzy's voice at all. Perhaps it had been someone (*something*) that sounded like Izzy. Izzy did sound rather generic. Truth be told, Izzy sounded a bit like every young woman Sarah had ever met.

This was what went through Sarah's dying mind. She didn't fear for her fading life or what she might face in the hereafter. Her life did not flash before her eyes. Sarah Frost died quite plainly, thinking about how unoriginal her friend's voice really was.

The crowd in the lobby had been unconsciously segregated into four groups.

The first of these groups were the minimum-wage staff of Stannis and Pessl: your carriers, gofers, and cleaning crew. These four individuals hung around the front entrance; one of them (a woman named Barbara) actually leaned on the glass. Michael, the Stannis's gofer, was soft on Barbara, but she'd just left her husband, so he simply imagined he was the glass she was smashed against. Johnny, the nineteen-year-old kid who kept the bathrooms clean and the trash emptied between nine a.m. and five p.m., five days a week, was trying to suppress his giggles. He found Michael's boner rather funny. The last of these four people, a Chinese-born woman named Xi (pronounced *Zy*, she would tell people), mostly studied her nails. Her new boyfriend, a body builder named Kirk, had paid to get them done. Xi was the first one to notice the statue enter the lobby by the door that connected to the inner hallway. It came floating in, and Xi was reminded of the balloons in the Macy's Thanksgiving Day parade. Her parents had taken her to see the parade when they first came to America. That would have been around 1983, when she was five. She remembered Snoopy the best. Xi had become so excited by Charlie Brown's dog that she had peed a little. Her mother had been so disappointed in her, and somehow that hurt worse than when mother was upset with her. But this thing coming through the door was no Snoopy. It was made of stone. And its face was dark flesh. Xi didn't so much pee herself a little as much as she pissed her drawers to the point a puddle formed around her twenty-dollar Payless trainers.

The second group of individuals were one step higher up the pay grade, but there were only two. Jessica and Charlene were both administrative assistants. Before the need for political correctness, both women would have simply been secretaries; in fact, this was how Stannis and his partner Joy Pessl referred to Jessica and Charlene. After a dozen or so martinis at Franco's in Fredericksburg, Stannis had even called Charlene a phone jockey to the rip-roaring laughter of his current rum buddies. Both women made the same amount of money, and neither soul wanted to be here. The truth of the matter was, both Jessica and Charlene were lonely ladies and enjoyed one another's company. Jessica had come because Charlene had said she was coming, and it beat staying home to watch her *True Detective* DVDs for the fourth time in as many months. Charlene had attended the mystery party because Jessica had expressed interest in going, and had she not come, she would have simply gone to bed with a bottle of wine, Norman Reedus pictures called up on her tablet, and her favorite vibrating device. Jessica's back was to the door when the statue floated in, but Charlene saw the thing quite clearly. She had one clear thought before she died: "I wish Daryl Dixon was real."

The remaining nine people in attendance were all paralegals, either newly graduated or still in school. These nine souls earned no paycheck, were apprentices. They'd all come this evening for the same reason: each one believed Stannis and Pessl were going to be here, that they could rub elbows with their heroes, their mentors, but neither lawyer had showed. Pessl would drop by later, but that would be after everyone was dead, dying, or badly injured. The only apprentice of import (because they were all much like a collective brain—a hive mind, if you will) was Erika. This young woman would be this evening's only survivor, and only because, much like William Longmire, she was a coward. Erika saw the statue gliding in on what seemed to be a cushion of air and didn't hesitate a single instant. She bolted for the door the thing had just entered through. Three days later, when she finally left the hospital, she'd tell her friends, "Those stupid white motherfuckers didn't know what hit them. They just stood there. Even after I took off running, they just stayed there. This is why so many white folks die in mass shootings. They're stupid. Dumber than they are pale." Erika made it five long strides down the hall before what felt like hot charcoal rained down on her. She would suffer third degree burns all over her back and legs and buttocks, but the doctor would never find the cause of it. Because there had been no fire. There had only been shrapnel, and even that had disappeared.

The statue of the Mother Mary with the dark woman's face hovered in the middle of the lobby, three inches off the carpet. All fourteen people (the remaining "stupid white motherfuckers," Erika would have said) stared at the stone impossibility, many with their mouths agape. The statue tilted its head back, and everyone heard a sound akin to a drill meeting rock.

And then the statue screamed. The wail was eardrum-shattering, but that didn't matter because no one in the room would live to complain about their hearing. Hands clutched ears. The shriek died off.

The statue exploded.

Barbara and Michael were blown through the glass frontage of the office block. Michael landed atop Barbara, his swollen erection pressed against one of her twitching thighs as he died. His organs were liquefied and his bones turned to powder by the concussive force of the explosion. Barbara had been mostly cut in two by the push bar of the door she'd been leaning against. The bar still rested inside her, at an angle, making the woman look like a giant plus sign.

Inside, Jessica and Charlene had been made one with the wall beside which they'd been standing too close. Jessica's arm landed in the hallway, five feet from where Erika had come to rest. Charlene's head was a mass of pulpy flesh and bone and brain and tissue. The first EMT to arrive would say that her corpse reminded him of that one guy in that one movie. His buddy would say, "What, *Scanners*? The movie *Scanners*? When Michael Ironside makes dude's head do like a piñata?" and the first EMT would nod, because that's exactly what Charlene reminded him of.

The apprentices caught the worst of the explosion. Not only did the shrapnel created by the exploding statue turn them all into noodle strainers, but most of them had burst open, their internal organs popping out here and there like glistening jack-in-the-boxes. Each twentysomething's body smoldered and smoked, and gave off an aroma that Merlo the Cowardly Dog would have enjoyed.

When all was dead and done, a muffled voice could be heard, asking, *"What the holy fucking shit was that?"*

The explosion fucked up the motion of George's ocean. Izzy didn't seem to notice.

"What the holy fucking shit was that?" George asked as he pulled out of Izzy's warmth and tucked himself back into his pants. Izzy didn't answer, remained bent over Stannis's desk. After Sarah had sneaked off to hide in the bathroom, George had dragged Izzy to their usual tryst location. Izzy had dropped her drawers without George even asking and bent over the desk, as per usual. George went to pounding, and was about to climax when the bomb (*or whatever the fuck it had been*) went off.

"Hey!" George hollered as he slapped Izzy's pudgy bare ass. She didn't move. Didn't so much as flinch.

"Izzy?" He laid a fat hand on her left butt cheek and nudged her softly at first then a little harder, until he finally shoved her limp body off the edge of the desk. As her body thumped lifelessly down onto the office's carpeting, George made a sound not unlike a mouse squeak.

Something had gone through Izzy's head, from temple to temple, and it had taken her eyes with it. Smoke drifted from her empty eye sockets, and suddenly George knew what had happened. The projectile hadn't stolen Izzy's eyes, it had burst them. Disintegrated them. Annihilated them. However you looked at it (*Looked at it*, George thought madly, *Ha!*), her eyes were no-fucking-more.

George became aware of a faint clicking to his right. He looked over at the wall, where smoke drifted from the center of Stannis's law degree. A smoldering hole lay where the lawyer's first name had once resided. The clicking was coming from in there. In the wall. As if something was trying to claw its way out. Claw its way out to get to George.

He watched in stunned silence (being the stupid white motherfucker that Erika claimed George and his coworkers were) as a fist-sized chunk of what looked like moon rock pushed itself out of the wall. It hovered in front of George, and he simply gawped at it.

There was no acceleration, no build up of speed, as the chunk of rock went from zero to Mach One through George's nose and out through the back of his head. He was dead before his bald head ever hit the carpet.

As Erika lay unconscious in the hallway, the statue re-formed in the lobby. Sadly, as its efforts were quite amazing, no one would see it return to form.

Chunks of stone floated above a center mass—the statue's feet, which were still whole. These chunks drifted lazily, like stars and moons orbiting a black hole. Piece by piece, from feet to head, the statue put itself back together. The flesh covering its face stitched anew, rising from the stone like lily pads breaking a lake's surface. When it was whole once again, the statue smiled.

Monica thumped down beside Bruce as he was opening his eyes and wondered the same thing George was wondering: *"What the holy fucking shit was that?"*

Oh, my god, it's like 9/11! was Bruce's first coherent thought. From where he lay supine on the conference room floor, next to the short bookshelf against the wall, Bruce could see several smoking holes in the thin walls. There were dozens of these holes, ranging from dime-sized to the diameter of cantaloupes. He was lucky he'd been lying down. He was sure that, had he been standing, he'd be dead now.

Speaking of dead...

He glanced to his right, to the headless corpse of Monica, and screamed. He shoved himself away from the body and into the bookshelf, which then toppled and crashed down atop him. He struggled out from under the vaguely heavy particleboard shelving and pushed to his feet. He stood there for a moment, huffing and puffing, trying to collect himself. It was during that time when Bruce realized that Monica was not only headless, but her body had been punctured dozens of times. Truth be told, Monica was nothing but a sweater stuffed with tenderized steak.

Jonathan, the Asian man who'd been so super excited to get started, lay in a crumpled, hole-filled mess in the corner. The man looked as if he'd fallen on a bed of invisible nails.

Bruce found that he was screaming again. Jamie Lee Curtis would have been jealous of his performance.

"Bruce?" a familiar voice called. "Bruce, is that you, dear?"

"Wha—?" was all he could manage, as if pronouncing the T would take far too much effort in his current state.

Something passed in front of one of the bigger, bowling ball-shaped holes, and Bruce thought he saw Innis. Just for a second. Just the briefest glimpse. But it had been Innis. He was sure of it.

"Innis? Wha—?" he stammered again.

The dark face drifted past outside, there and gone through the hole.

"I've come to tell you a secret, Bruce," the voice whispered playfully.

"Innis, there's a woman in here... she's... she's hurt... well, she's dead, but—"

The statue came through the door, and Bruce stopped speaking. He stopped thinking, too. Everything shut down inside Bruce the Nefarious Cocksucker as

Regret, powered by the scorned soul of Innis Blake, went to her betrayer with open arms.

Those cold appendages wrapped around Bruce and squeezed. Squeezed until the man's eyes and tongue bulged from his face. Squeezed until his spine snapped and his ribs shattered like crystal in a vise. Squeezed until Bruce folded in two.

And then, once more, Regret exploded.

Out in the alleyway behind the law offices of Stannis and Pessl, Regret collected Frank Markum's unconscious form from where she'd hidden him inside a dumpster. Together, they drifted off. Regret picked up speed. Began coming apart at the molecular level. Frank did the same. Had he been awake, he might have had a moment of gleeful geekiness. He'd been a *Star Trek* fan most of his life, and had always wished to take a ride on a teleporter. Alas, Special Investigator Frank Markum slept through the trip back to the cabin.

MARKUM

I*'m going to be sick.*

Frank Markum awoke gagging on a mouthful of vomit. His eyes filled with tears as hot sick splashed down between his legs, covering the concrete floor and his pants in pink goop. He spat the remaining nastiness from his mouth and swiped the pooling wetness from his eyes.

The statue with the face of flesh glared down at him.

Startled, he shoved himself back, but could go no farther. He was flush with the cold concrete.

"Don't!" Frank bellowed, covering his face with his hands. He quaked so intensely that every joint in his body clacked together and became sore.

Yet... nothing happened. No violence befell him. And when he gazed between his fingers, he saw that the stone body of the Mother Mary had not moved. Still, she glared at him with hollow eyes. Those vacuous things were far scarier than the idea that a piece of rock could become animated. Because if the eyes were truly the windows to the soul, this entity was bereft of such.

Frank slid himself up the wall, making sure to keep a good six inches between him and the statue. When he was on his feet, he sidestepped away from the thing. It did not move. It did not lash out. It remained static, as one would expect of a statue.

Keeping the statue with the fleshy face in his peripheral vision, Frank scanned the room. Bare cinder block walls with wooden support struts. A staircase directly in front of him, leading to God knew where. He chanced a glance over his shoulder.

He did a double take.

Not believing his own eyes, he reversed, backing away from the statue. He bumped into something at hip height, pushed around it, and continued backward. All this in an attempt to keep a line of sight on the statue. But when the table with the faceless woman came into view, Frank forgot all about the statue.

The woman had been laid out on a rectangular table that resembled a woodworking bench. One hand was cocked at an awkward angle, and the middle finger had been removed from the other. And she was missing her face. Frank looked down at the glistening muscles, the exposed gumline, and rows of bloody teeth, but the eyes disturbed him the most. They were wide and staring, dead.

The woman inhaled violently and Frank staggered away. He stumbled and came down hard on his backside. Something dug painfully into his hip. He glanced back. Here, a different set of stairs led up to a view of treetops and a starry night. Frank could smell bark and moss and dampness. A way out.

There was a part of him that was drawn to the woman on the table, a part of him that felt a need (was *desire* a better word?) to help her, but his survival instinct won out that night.

Frank half-crawled, half-ran up the stairs and into the chilly night. A tree line ahead of him and a road to his right. He went for the road. As he ran, he checked his pockets for his car keys and his phone. Both were missing in action. He wondered where they could be, but he couldn't exactly recall how he'd gotten to this odd location in the first place. He remembered the statue, remembered how it had stalked him at... at... Where?

He stopped when he hit the street, and stood in the middle of the road, breathing heavily.

Damn it, why can't I remember?

Something about Dennis?
Is that right?
Something about Bruce?

Many questions came and went and none of them found an answer.

He had a sudden mental image of a man (a stranger) being swung into the windshield of a recreational vehicle. And then... and then...

Nothing more. That man being slung into the windshield of that RV kept replaying in his mind, but Frank couldn't see the figure responsible for tossing the man through the glass. His memory was blurred, distorted just enough to where he could make out nothing but a seven-foot mass of gray cotton. The harder he tried to focus, the less he saw. The farther he zoomed in, the more the image faded, until even the man lying folded into the front of the RV became nothing more than television static.

Then the figure came for him.

The statue. The statue in the basement of the cabin he'd escaped only seconds before. He turned and gazed over the cabin, over the shadowy figures in the front yard, his breath quickening. He scanned for anything that seemed dangerous, expecting the Mother Mary statue to be hidden among the other still-life waiting in the dooryard. A bull's head without features—nothing but a bust, really—faced blindly forward. The podium it sat on was wooden, but the bust glinted dully in the moonlight, and Frank assumed it had been created from some sort of metal. Above the porch, perched precariously atop the eaves, sat a gargoyle with a snake in its mouth. In the snake's mouth, an apple.

Frank Markum shivered. There was something oddly familiar about the gargoyle, as if he should remember a story... perhaps one of Aesop's fables? A Bible verse? Something...

A loon called out from somewhere unseen. Frank flinched. Under the usual night sounds—crickets and katydids and frogs—Markum could hear as well as feel a subtle hum, as if he stood under a power line. He glanced around and found no telephone poles. He wondered if the cabin here had electricity. And then he remembered the bare bulb that had lighted the basement, the place where he'd awoken this evening... morning... whenever it was.

Thinking of the time, Frank searched his coat and slacks for his cell phone. No use. *Nothing there*, he reminded himself. In either place. At the present moment, he had no connection with the outside world. That was okay, though, wasn't it? People had survived just fine before the invention of smart phones and laptops and tablets, right? Just because he didn't have his cell on him didn't mean he was in any more danger than usual, right?

The loon cried again.

"Fuck off," Frank muttered, addressing his invisible companion.

Frank struck off toward the front lawn of the cabin, toward the dark and lurking figures. If the statue had crept up from the basement to hide herein, he'd find it. Better the devil you know than the devil you don't, right? He wanted to run, to scurry, to flee this odd and, if he was entirely honest with himself, scary situation, but something at his basest level wouldn't allow it. That was the part of him that had confronted Papa Markum, the part of Frank that had slayed the monster in the recliner. Frank would not go running off into the night, because that would leave the possibility of him being followed. Of being chased. Frank refused to be on the run like he refused to hide. In a closet or otherwise.

Fuck that thing in the basement. Fuck that statue. Frank would not be scared of a chunk of rock, whether that hunk of stone moved or not.

He reached for his gun and found his leather shoulder holster empty. He didn't even have his gun. The phone might not have mattered, but his gun, now that was important. He cursed under his breath and trudged on.

The angel of death was the first thing he came across that he could actually name. You couldn't mistake the thing: prerequisite hood, cloak, and grinning skeleton face. The gargantuan scythe clutched in the metal statue's left hand only further cemented Frank's assumption; this was definitely the Grim Reaper.

There were more statues, mostly cast from iron or steel or some other metal, and Frank could find nothing of import about them.

And then he stepped on the baby. Frank dropped down into a batter's stance to study the creation. It was, in fact, not a baby. The body and pose spoke of infancy but, truth be told, it looked more like some kind of demon spawn. Horns curled, ram-like, around its ears, and its eyes were round with square irises. There was something more goatish about the infant than human. Its features had been welded on. Clumps of congealed aluminum had created rather lifelike patches of hair, which covered the lower third of the baby's legs. These legs ended in hooves. The same welding had been used to make the eyebrows and lips, but the eyes seemed to have been chiseled in, if one could chisel metal. Frank sought out the right terminology, but kept coming back to that word: chiseled. Perhaps *scratched in* was the proper verb... but still, it looked chiseled, as if someone had been at it with hammer and spike and force. Frank wouldn't have been a bit surprised to find out that this thing's maker had been rather angry when they'd created it. The work looked violent.

He'd seen enough. It was time to go. He needed to find a phone. But more importantly, he needed to find out what the fuck had happened to him in the past few hours. He studied the cabin's front door, trying to will himself to go inside and find a phone.

No telephone pole, remember? Inner Frank said, sounding an awful lot like Papa Markum. He didn't like that one bit. But the voice was right. No telephone pole meant no telephone. He figured he should check anyway, just to be sure.

But there was that other part of him, the weaker side of Frank Markum, that wanted to turn around and run. Struggling against his better judgment, that part of him that housed his survival instinct, Markum moved toward the front porch.

The wind picked up the closer he came to the door. Gusts tore at his coat and pants. His clothing and hair whipped about him as the wind strengthened. By the time he reached the top step, it had reached gale force, and he had to clutch the banister to maintain his balance. Grit pelted his face, and Frank thought he was being sandblasted. But that was insane. Kerrville was eastern Texas. There was no desert here.

Squinting his eyes and steeling himself against the buffeting winds, Frank rushed forward. His hand touched the wooden doorknob. The door flew open, and Frank Markum stumbled inside.

He shook sand from his hair. But as he gazed around the interior of the cabin, his shaking head slowed. Frank's mouth dropped open, and he stood there in stunned silence.

There was a slatted, wooden floor under his feet, walls on either side of him, but at the end of the hallway directly across from where he stood was a barren wasteland. A world of dunes and blowing sand. He could hear the wind shrieking and the grit assaulting the walls of the cabin, but his mind could not process what exactly was happening. Somewhere in his addled brain, he understood he'd crossed some kind of threshold when he'd walked up the front steps of this cabin, but he also realized that this was an impossibility.

As impossible as seeing your dead father standing in the middle of the road yesterday? As impossible as living statues?

A door slammed shut at the end of the hall, blocking Frank's view of the desert wasteland.

He obviously wasn't welcome here, wasn't meant to be here. Frank wasn't a dumb man. He could take a hint. It was time to make like a barrel and roll out.

Frank spun, and as he did so, everything changed. If someone had asked him at that exact moment what had happened, Frank would have said it felt like he was watching a poorly edited film, two movies that had been haphazardly spliced together. In the first film, he was standing in the middle of the Cabin of Impossibilities, and then he was spinning, turning back toward the door he hoped to escape through. In the second film, he was finishing his revolution inside a movie theater. When he came to rest, he was staring up at the screen. The view on the canvas was of a cinder block wall framed by wooden struts. The view reminded Frank of a shot from a horror movie, one of those scenes shot at the most striking perspective, extremely low camera shooting upward, or elevated and canted downward at a severe angle. Think Alfred Hitchcock. Think Cronenberg. Kubrick.

"You," said a voice. This voice was both feminine and venomous.

Frank twirled, caught sight of the woman in the front row and the cop sitting next to her

(although it wasn't a cop, not really; PD didn't wear blue and gray, only state troopers did, and didn't this guy look vaguely familiar, didn't he look like—?)

and he screamed so loudly that his own ears began to ring. He reeled and stumbled and crashed against the elevated stage behind him. He attempted to press himself into the wall, like he had upon waking and finding the Mother Mary statue staring down at him, but once again he had nowhere to go, nowhere to turn to, and wasn't this bitch in the front row far scarier than the statue? Yes. Yes, she was. This bitch was terrifying, because there wasn't a thing more intimidating than a woman scorned. A woman scorned could burn a hole through you with nothing more than her gaze. And this bitch was trying. Oh good lord have mercy, this bitch was trying to light his nuts on fire with her heat vision.

"You!" she roared, and the entire theater shook with her trembling, rage-filled voice.

"Who's this guy?" the state trooper asked, and he even sounded familiar. Somewhere in the back of Frank's mind, the place where Rational Frank had hidden for the time being, Rational Frank decided he knew this man. This familiar state trooper had been the beginning of this whole mess, hadn't he? Rational Frank recalled approaching State Trooper Natalie Holden at Camp Meeting Creek, where the two of them discussed this very man. Tom, this man's name was (*is*) before he was smashed to bits in the little boys' room at Bob's Bait and Fuel. Thomas Morgan, Texas state trooper, stepped between Frank and the bitch and gave Frank the most confusing look Frank had ever seen. That look said that Frank was an impossibility. But that was crazy, because the bitch and the trooper were the impossibility, not Frank. Frank was solid. Frank was real.

In reality, Frank had begun to crack. Frank had crossed the line between distressed and balls-out bonkers. Batshit. Beautifully and perfectly insane.

"Frank?" Tom asked the broken man.

Frank began to cry.

"Frank Markum? Special Investigator Markum? How... how the heck did you get here?"

Frank continued to sob.

"He's crossed," Innis Blake said from her chair. "He's mine now."

Frank closed his eyes, and tears as warm as blood glided down his cheeks. He realized in that moment that he would never see Dennis again. Memory flooded back in. How could he have forgotten what had happened? Dennis in a puddle in front of a mobile home, wherein Dennis had been working surveillance on the Twon

Chatham case. Dennis bubbling and hissing. Dennis saying something about a curse. Something about how "she cursed" him.

Frank Markum would never know that it had not been Innis Blake who had cursed his lover, and truth be told it didn't matter. Frank was mad now, murderous, and the bitch, scorned or not, would know his wrath.

NATALIE

"Get your fucking hands up! Now!" Natalie screamed at the large figure on the swing set.

It didn't move. A brisk wind blew her ponytail up onto her shoulder. She didn't notice. Suddenly trembling all over, she took two quick steps forward.

"Mah-mah," the figure repeated in its cooing, baby doll voice.

That voice. That goddamn voice. She knew it. But how? From where?

"Put your hands on your head!" she roared. "I will fucking shoot you, man, I swear to God I will shoot you! Put your hands up!"

"Maaaaaaaa..." the voice slowed and stretched out, like a cassette player devouring the final bit of life from its batteries.

"Whatcha got, Nat?" Randy's voice. Finally, a voice that didn't terrify her.

"I... I don't know. But... but... just look."

Randy stepped into her peripheral vision. He seemed bigger than before, wider. Or did she feel smaller? Could that be it? She thought that maybe that was the case. Because something about that dolly voice had rocked her to her core, and Natalie Holden couldn't, for the life of her, think why. It was just a doll's voice. A prerecorded, mechanical child's voice emanating from a speaker somewhere on this fucker. He probably used it to scare his victims. Dude probably got his rocks off by dressing up like a baby doll and wreaking havoc all across town.

"Is that—?"

"Yeah," Natalie stammered. "Yeah. I... I think so."

"Buddy? Hey, buddy?" Randy called as he aimed his service revolver at the shape on the swing. "I need you to stand up, turn around, and put your hands behind your back, okay? Then this nice lady here is going to put some cuffs on you, and we'll all have ourselves a nice little talk, okay? Buddy? You listening?"

Randy snapped a glance at Natalie. She hitched her chin at the huge shape. Both of them moved across the backyard, slowly, with their guns raised, and Natalie's heart trip-hammering in her chest. The baby doll voice kept repeating in her mind, intent on driving her mad.

Mahmahmahmahmahmah... You know who I am. Yes, Natalie, I think you do. You'll remember me, or break. Remember me or break, remember me or break, REMEMBER ME OR BREAK!

She willed her brain to be quiet, to shut up so she could concentrate. The last thing she needed was nonsensical rambling from some idiot section of her brain. She needed to be on her game. In the zone.

"Come on, buddy," Randy continued. "We don't want to shoot you. But if you make us, we will. It's just the way it's gotta be. You come at us, or make any sudden movements, and we'll add some lead to your diet. Okay, partner? Okay?"

Then, in a whispering voice, Randy asked Natalie: "What's up with this guy?"

"How the fuck am I supposed to know?" she snapped. Shit, she even sounded scared. She swallowed, collected herself, and said, "Sorry, Miser. I don't like this. I don't like this at all."

"You think I do, Nat?"

Without another word, they approached the swing set. Randy hefted his Maglite from the hoop on his belt and shone it over the dark shape on the swing.

"Jesus Christ," Randy hissed, sounding more frightened than upset. "What the hell is going on here?"

Randy shone the light into the empty eyeholes of what Natalie at first thought was a baby doll mask. The paint on the face was peeling and chipped. The red circles that had once portrayed blush had faded with age, and she could just barely make out two faint pink spheres. There were no holes in the nostrils, just two indentations at the bottom of the nose. The mouth was grinning, but Natalie could see it wouldn't open. Its lips were, quite literally, sealed. Atop the head, singed black hair stuck up in patches here and there, as if the thing had just crawled out of a fireplace. Thinking back on the current blaze eating through Pompeii Café, Natalie decided that wasn't such a farfetched idea. To further back up her findings, the clothes this gigantic baby doll wore were scorched, and Natalie could see porcelain through some of the really bad holes. Not flesh, but shiny porcelain, like what you'd find in any bathroom.

Randy reached out and knocked on the doll's forehead with his Maglite, startling Natalie.

She jumped back a good foot. "What the fuck, Miser!"

He chuckled nervously. "Sorry. Didn't mean to scare you, hon, but I think this thing's empty. I can see right into its head, Nat, and ain't nobody in there. Looks like our guy ditched his costume."

But something in the back of Natalie's mind spoke up. This new voice sounded amused, giddy even. *That ain't no costume, baby girl,* this new voice said, *and you don't wanna know where its owner ran off to, trust me. You don't wanna know a thing like that* at all.

"Now what do we do?" Natalie asked, more to quiet the eerie voice in her head than anything else.

"I don't rightly know." Randy knocked three more times on the doll's face. Natalie shivered at how hollow and deep those knocks sounded.

Randy sighed and took a step back. He pulled his cell phone out of his uniform's shirt pocket, worked the keypad, and pressed the device to his ear.

"Who you calling?" Natalie asked.

"Matthew. He should've been here by now, I would think."

"Has it been that long since you called him? It's gotta be three in the morning by now. You probably woke him up. He'll have to get ready. Give the guy a few minutes."

Randy waved her off. A second later, he said, "Matt? Hey! Where you at? Car broke down, huh? Damn. Who? You gotta be... No, Matt, you listen to me, and you listen good. Don't let him know who you're talking to. Don't—

MATTHEW

—let him get too far out of your sight, either." Matthew Pontiff cut his eyes at the green face of Deputy Nick Wuncell as the sheriff relayed what kind of mess Matthew had stepped into. Matthew thumbed down the volume on his cell, just to make sure Miser's voice didn't carry. "He's part of the trouble going on, Matt. I ain't got time to explain, but you might be in danger. Stay on point, son."

"No, no, I got you, Rhonda. Right. Wake Dad up to give him the pills at their scheduled time. Don't wait until he wakes up on his own. Thanks. You're a dear."

"Your dad's sick?" Nick Wuncell asked as Matt disconnected.

"Yeah. Stomach cancer." Matthew tried to smile sadly, but was sure that he was failing. Luckily, he doubted Nick would be able to see him in the dark car. The only reason Matthew could see Nick was due to the splash of the dash lights across Nick's face. The deputy looked like Willem Dafoe in his role as the Green Goblin.

"That's horrible. I'm sorry to hear that. Here we are, though. Do whatever you have to do, and I'll run you into town afterward."

Matthew's mind raced as Nick navigated the car into the gravel parking lot of Kerr County Dispatch.

After Nick picked him up, Matthew informed the deputy that the sheriff had asked him to swing by dispatch to check on Shirley. Nick had smiled, nodded, and said he was on his way out there as well, and that Miser must be catching Alzheimer's because he'd told him to do the same thing. Matthew hadn't had a chance to tell Miser this over the phone, of course, so now

Matthew was in a bit of a pickle. He twirled his foot, the one with the .38 inside the holster on his ankle, and took a deep breath.

"I'll only be a minute," Matthew said with a smile.

Fucking birds, Matthew thought as he stepped from the car. *All because of those fucking birds.*

Matthew was not entirely surprised to find the front entrance to Kerr County Dispatch wide open. Nick been coming from this direction when he'd picked Matthew up, so the deputy could have very well been coming *from* dispatch. He sure as shit hadn't been heading *to* dispatch, as he'd told Matthew he'd been doing.

Fearing what he was going to find inside, Matthew stepped through the door.

The first corridor was chilly, as if someone had the air conditioning on. That, in fact, turned out to be the case. The thermometer on the wall at the end of the hall had been set to COOL and turned all the way down to fifty degrees. As if someone were trying to turn the building into a cold storage unit. As if they meant to keep meat from spoiling.

Matthew swallowed hard and called, "Shirley? Shirley, you there?"

When no one answered him, he glanced back the way he'd come, to the open door at the front of the building. He could see the cruiser's headlights, and that was all. The only sounds were the engine clicking and idling, and his own heart thudding in his own ears.

He pushed into the dispatcher's office and wasn't shocked to find it empty. He scanned the floor and the space under the desk. He found nothing but wires and the blinking lights on the fronts of CPU towers. The switchboard glowed a soft orange. Nothing seemed to be out of place.

He turned and walked back out into the hallway. Keeping an eye on the front door, he dipped down and retrieved the .38 from his ankle holster.

"I don't wanna shoot you, Nick," Matthew said as he rose. "Don't make me shoot you."

Matthew looked left. The break room was the only room that way. The door was open, and everything seemed undisturbed. Matthew thought that, if he'd killed someone, the last place he'd hide a body was in a break room.

Then where would you hide it?
In the bathroom.

He moved right, away from the break room and toward the single restroom. He'd never been inside Kerr County Dispatch, but the layout was quite simple. Dispatcher's office, break room, restroom, all connected by a hallway in the shape of a capital T. If Shirley was here at all, Matthew felt in his gut that this was where he'd find her. He pushed the door open, but stopped when it wasn't more than a foot open.

He could feel another presence in here with him. Could feel the weight of this second someone. Before this night, he would have laughed in the face of anyone who said they could feel it when someone was staring at them. He believed it now. Eyes were boring into him. An uncomfortable warmth poured over him and his breath caught in his throat, as if he were drowning in bathwater.

On instinct, Matthew swung around toward the way he'd come, and without a word, brought his .38 up.

I'll be damned, he thought as he laid eyes on Nick coming around the corner, the deputy's own gun up and out, ready to kill.

Nick leaned into his turn and brought his service piece around. Matthew fired three times. Nick fired four. Each man landed two shots.

One bullet hit Matthew in the thigh and tossed his leg out behind him. As he fell, the second slug tore into his forearm. He landed with a thud on the carpet in the hallway outside the restrooms. Somehow his gun remained in his hand. He rolled onto his side, and brought Nick back into his sights.

But it was no use.

Deputy Nick Wuncell was dead. His body just hadn't figured it out yet.

A thin line of blood drooled from a small hole above Nick's left eye. That same eye had rolled up, as if asking, "Where the hell is all that blood coming from?" His other eye stared lifelessly forward, not really looking at Matthew, or anything else, for that matter. The gaze was as dead as the person behind it.

Matthew's second bullet had hit the deputy in center mass. A red balloon seemed to be inflating on the deputy's uniform shirt; it grew bigger and bigger as Matthew watched, and unsurprisingly enough, he expected it would burst at any second.

Nick Wuncell dropped with the quick, unexpected force of a marionette whose strings have been suddenly snipped. The deputy's head bounced off the carpet with a *THUNK!*

The pain came like a brush fire up Matthew's injured arm and leg. Both trails of agony seemed to collide in his abdomen, and he screamed. Bullets were hot things, and while he thought the wound on his arm was a through and through, he was quite sure the ball of fire in his leg had once resided in a .45 caliber police-issue Glock. Something was wrong with his arm, too. It wasn't working, and his brain automatically associated this with nerve damage.

"*Motherfucking goddamn cocksucking birds!*" Matthew raged as he dropped the .38, rolled over onto his back, and rummaged in his pants for his cell.

Wrong pocket. Wrong side.

Using his gunshot arm was an impossibility at the present time, so he tried reaching across himself. No use. His jeans pockets were slanted at such a horrible angle that he couldn't get his other hand inside.

"*FUCKING BIRDS!*" He was in too much pain for this bullshit.

Think of how your dad feels. Something's eating away at the old man's guts and you're bitching about two fucking flesh wounds? Take your fucking pants off already, and quit being such a little bitch!

Matthew wrestled with his belt buckle with his good arm. Once he got it undone, he started sliding out of his jeans. His leg protested at every movement, and his wound flapped and gaped like a chewing mouth. Blood made sticky work of the situation, but after two minutes of bright pain and more than a handful of choice cusswords, Matthew kicked his pants to one wall. He rolled to his pants and dug into the proper pocket. The cell came out covered in blood. He wiped the screen on his shirt, unlocked the device, and phoned Miser.

When the sheriff picked up, Matthew ripped into him: "Fuck you and those fucking birds, you fat fuck! He shot me! Twice! Come and get me before I bleed out!"

CRUELTY

THE HOLDENS

One year ago...

Just outside of Fredericksburg, ten miles north of the Comanche reservation they called home, Donna Holden and her husband Buck had a flat tire. Their 2005 Hopper recreational vehicle had needed new rubber for the past year, but Buck had been far too frugal to buy a set. As they hobbled to the side of the highway, Donna inwardly cussed her husband.

Buck parked half-on, half-off a remote stretch of I-10, and waited on their AAA-designated tow truck to come fix their flat. Buck would've had the tools necessary to install the spare, but when he'd pulled off onto the shoulder, the affected tire had dropped into a rather loose bit of sand. The heavy-duty jack would be useless in such sand. So, they were stranded until Mr. AAA showed his ugly mug. Stranded not unlike a deaf teenager and a strung-out prostitute would be stranded the very next year, just outside Kerrville, on Highway 16, five miles from Bob's Bait and Fuel.

While Buck Holden waited outside so that he might flag down their tow truck driver, Donna chatted with their only child by way of cellular telephone. Natalie had grown up and moved out so quickly that Donna's head was still spinning. Donna could understand Natalie's need to live off the reservation, but she couldn't fathom her daughter's need to take up such a profession as law officer.

"Mom, everything all right?" Natalie asked. Her voice wasn't much more than static over Donna's antiquated cell.

Donna hadn't realized she'd been lost in her own thoughts, wondering where the years and her daughter had run off to. "Yeah, sweetie, I'm here. Sorry. What did you say?"

"I asked if the tow truck is there yet?"

"Nope. Nothing. Not even a spot of headlights. It's pitch black out here. Or at least it is past the headlights. Golly, I can't even see your father!" She'd said the last bit so loudly that she cringed a little and apologized for yelling in Natalie's ear.

"Hope coyotes didn't run off with him." Natalie chuckled.

"Your father's too goddamn skinny to satiate a coyote. Hell, he's barely rabbit food."

Natalie laughed brightly. Donna enjoyed hearing her daughter so happy. Come to think of it, she hadn't heard Natalie laugh so cheerfully in the last two or three years on the reservation. Could being away from your parents make you that content? So content that even your laugh lightened in tone?

"How's Kaku?"

"My mother's a mess, and you know it. I think she has more sex than I do."

"Mom!" Natalie shrieked, cackling.

"Oh come on. We're both grown women. I'm sure you're not a virgin."

"I'm not having this conversation. Nope. Nu-huh. Next topic."

"You thought I was a prude, didn't you. That's a shame. How'd you think *you* got here, young lady?"

"Donna?" Buck called from outside. "Hey, Donna!"

Donna shifted in the passenger seat, covered the phone's mic, and hollered over her shoulder, "What?"

"There's somebody coming. From the rear. You wanna put the hazards on? Thanks!"

"Why didn't you put them on yourself?" she called back as she leaned into the driver's side and pressed the red triangle on the dash.

"Saving battery! Why else?"

"Stupid man leaves the headlights on and the engine off, and he's worried about the battery. Goofball," she whispered.

Outside, the dark flanking the RV pulsed with the orange light of the hazards.

"What?" Natalie asked from somewhere in Kerrville.

"Nothing. Did you say you were at work?"

"Nope. I'm off tonight."

"When's your next vacation?" Donna asked, but she didn't hear her daughter's response. Her eyes had drifted to the adjustable mirror on the driver's door. Donna saw two pinpoints of light in the glass, off in the distance. These glowing dots were growing bigger by the second, and Donna thought that this vehicle couldn't be the tow truck. This vehicle was moving much too fast. In fact, if they didn't slow down, they were liable to have an accident.

"Mom? Fuck... did I lose you..."

"You really shouldn't cuss. It's unladylike," Donna said. The lights were less than a mile away now, at least by her best judgment.

"You were just talking about how Kaku gets laid more—"

"Hang on, Natalie." Donna's heart began to pound dramatically in her chest and her breathing quickened. Had she survived this evening, she wouldn't have been able to tell anyone why she'd become so frightened so quickly.

As the unknown vehicle that was surely not the tow truck blew past the RV, Donna saw that it was, in fact, a tow truck. She also saw the body dangling from the crane on the back of the rescue vehicle. It was most definitely a man. A man with bald head and thick beard. He wore a blood-splattered mechanic's jumper. The legs of this jumper swayed briskly in the wind, and Donna was quite sure there were no legs in the bottom half of that uniform.

She screamed as the brakes on the tow truck locked and the thing went careening sideways down the interstate. Something caught and the truck flipped. It seemed to explode out of the range of their RV's headlights, as if someone had stuck about four-hundred pounds of *plastique* under the left side panel.

"Oh my God!" Donna gasped into the phone.

The side door of the RV slammed open and Buck, breathing hard, rushed in.

"Didja see that? By Christ, Donna, didja fuckin' see that shit?"

"Mom? Hey, what's going on?"

"There's been an accident!" Donna hollered into her phone. "I'll call you back."

Donna did not wait for her daughter's response. She pressed end, dialed 9-1-1, and thumbed SEND.

"I gotta go see about 'em, Donna. You know where we are, right? You know where to tell them?"

"No... no, I don't. Gimme the mile markers."

Buck rambled them off before disappearing out through the side door, leaving it open behind him. A cool desert wind blew in, caressed Donna's neck, and gooseflesh flooded her arm.

Buck ran out in front of the RV and into the glow of the headlights before vanishing beyond their reach. Oddly, Donna expected some extravagant explosion to illuminate the night, like cars in action movies when people do nothing more than fart in their general direction.

Donna spent almost a full minute gazing out the windshield and listening to nothing more than her own thudding heartbeat before realizing the call hadn't went through.

She gazed dumbly down at the Nokia. The phone was silver and phallic shaped, with a keyboard set into the bottom half, and a screen the size of a matchbook. Natalie had been harassing her mother, begging Donna to upgrade before horses dragged her off into the great prairie in the sky, but Donna had parried her daughter's every reason.

"There's nothing wrong with my phone, Natalie. Just needs a new battery is all," Donna had said on more than ten occasions.

"It's not the battery, Mom, it's the clasp that holds the battery in."

"How would you know what it is? It's my phone."

And around and around they would go until Natalie finally gave up and the subject of discussion moved on to other things.

And now, as Donna stared at the slate-gray display on the tiny phone and saw not a single digit or bar displayed, she knew that the battery she'd never gotten around to replacing had finally failed her.

You were just *talking to Natalie. The battery was fine. What did it have, three bars of life? Two?*

She couldn't remember. Instead of fussing inwardly she fingered the power button. When the screen did not light up, she flipped the phone over, slapped the back of the case, and turned it back to her. She pressed the power button again. The phone lit up a second later. The Nokia emblem faded into existence as the device booted.

Something hit the windshield.

Donna jerked backward and thudded her head against the leather headrest. It didn't hurt, not yet anyway. She might have a bit of a concussion in the morning, but...

A dark substance had been splashed across the windshield, obscuring her view. Something about the thick liquid seemed familiar, like it should be instantly recognizable, but currently Donna's brain wasn't processing new information. She had gremlins in her head, and they were scampering.

Donna reached over and flicked on the windshield wipers. They squeaked back and forth across the slippery glass like excited mice. Once a decent amount of the viscous fluid—the *red* viscous fluid—was out of the way, she could see, very clearly, the heels of two Reebok sneakers. Buck had a pair of sneakers just like them. In fact he'd written his name on them—Buck on the back of the left, Holden on the back of the right—after he'd brought them home from Academy Sports in Fort Hood. And either that was her husband laying just out of sight (all but his Reeboks, of course) or someone else named Buck Holden had written his name on a pair of Reebok kicks before venturing out onto a remote section of Interstate Ten this evening.

All at once, the red muck on the windshield, the stone-still legs of the person laying in the middle of the road, and the figure now lumbering into the headlights all made a simple kind of silly sense. All at once, Donna was screaming. All at once she was stabbing her index finger into the SEND button of her phone and shrieking like a tornado rushing through a trailer park.

What Donna Holden did not know was this: She had never dialed 9-1-1. Her phone had already been dead (as dead as Buck) when she started dialing. So now, as she pressed SEND over and over again, and as the huge individual in the baby doll mask stepped around the side of the RV, Donna redialed Natalie's number.

Her daughter answered on the second ring, but Donna didn't hear her. Donna was still shrieking as the improbably large baby doll stepped into the Hopper recreational vehicle and the carriage drooped significantly under its weight. Natalie was screaming by this point, as well, asking what was wrong... wanting to know where they'd broken down... needing to know so she could come help... *Mom, if you don't tell me where you are, I can't help you!*

Donna was fully insane with fear long before the baby doll slid its fingers through her long black hair and tugged Mrs. Holden out of her seat, down the two short steps, and into the desert. Seconds prior to the battery clip failing on Donna's cell phone, one thing was transmitted from that remote section of I-10, across no less than three cell phone towers, and into Natalie's phone as she sat in line at Burger King, waiting for her Whopper combo, with cheese, no onion.

That word was: "Mah-mah."

CRUELTY

NATALIE & RANDY

Present Day...

"I'm not leaving this thing, Miser. Sorry, but you're on your own."

As they stood in some stranger's backyard, regarding a life-sized baby doll with a growing sense of what-the-fuckery, Sheriff Randy Miser began to snap his head back and forth. "Matt's been shot, Nat. I ain't got time to be messing around with you, and I need you. You got me, Natalie, I *need* you."

"I'll explain myself later. You go get your friend. I'll stay here."

Randy must have seen that she meant it, because he sighed and slumped forward drastically. "Don't do this to me, Nat. Not tonight."

"I have my mind set." Natalie took her eyes off the sheriff and faced the doll again. "There's nothing gonna happen. This... this *whatever* it is, is lifeless. But I have a feeling whoever was inside of it—"

"T'weren't no one inside of it! Some sick bastard left it here for us to find and get confused over." He rapped his Maglite against the doll's forehead and Natalie grimaced at the too-loud *clank... clank!... CLANK!* it made.

"Whatever. I know I heard someone. And I think they'll come back. When they do, I plan to be here. Waiting."

"Dammit, girl." Miser snatched off his hat and scratched at his forehead. "Dammit... Fine! I don't wanna, but I can't leave Matt out there to bleed to death."

"Get out of here, Miser. I'll be fine."

Randy jogged away about as fast as his heavy heart could handle. His soggy adult diapers squished and squashed between his soaked thighs as he went. He felt like a toddler fleeing from someone intent on changing him.

He considered himself about the lowest creature on earth for leaving Natalie Holden—state trooper or not—alone on a night like tonight. But he'd also not had time to argue with her. He could still hear Matthew's frantic, enraged voice screaming at him through the phone.

"Fuck you and those fucking birds, you fat fuck! He shot me! Twice! Come and get me before I bleed out!"

If he lost Matthew, it would be all Randy's fault. It didn't matter whether or not Matthew owed him. It wouldn't matter that Matthew had left his home tonight of his own accord. It would all find its way back to Sheriff Randy Miser, and Randy would then be responsible for not only enabling Flo into the ground, but murdering his best friend's son. Wasn't life just a bucket of crap with a bomb in it?

He made it to his cruiser less than two minutes later. The fire inside of Pompeii Café had begun to dwindle, but Andi's Smoke Shoppe on the left and the hair boutique on the right were already catching. Both would be gutted if Kerrville's volunteer fire department didn't get to them soon.

Randy had a sudden epiphany, one that Flo might have asked, once upon a time, if it had hurt him to have it.

What kind of numbskull was he? He didn't need dispatch. The hospital would have numbers on hand for emergency services. Matthew might not make it until an ambulance arrived, but they might be able to contact the firehouse and get someone on this blaze before the entire block went up.

He used his cell phone to call Kerr County Medical Center. While the phone rang in his ear, he jerked open his cruiser's door. He didn't notice Merlo snake stealthily out of the car before he, himself, slid in. The dog bolted off into the night as Randy made a wide U-turn and took off toward his bleeding friend.

In the back of his mind, Randy thought about the birds, and smiled despite the tragedy of the past thirty-six hours.

With her mind on her dead parents, Natalie Holden approached the oddity in front of her. She shined her flashlight into the empty eyeholes.

That voice from yesteryear crept back into her mind: *"Mah-Mah."*

Had she been hearing things? Had her mind conjured the prerequisite baby doll sounds upon seeing the figure on the swing?

No.

She had heard the voice *before* she had seen what was sitting on the swing. She was sure of that.

"What the fuck are you?" she asked in a too-loud voice.

Not *"Who* the fuck are you", but *"What* the fuck are you." She was sure that was right. In her heart of hearts, State Trooper Natalie Holden knew that she'd stumbled upon an *It*, only this *It* wasn't a clown in a horror novel. It was a giant baby doll. And this baby doll was, she felt, only biding its time. Whatever dark engine ran this horror would be back. And when it came back, she'd give its engineer a lead enema. She might not have had the best relationship with her parents, what with her just disappearing and starting a new career without their approval, or even their knowing, but you didn't fuck with family. When you fucked with blood, blood made you bleed.

Her mind flashed back to earlier yesterday afternoon, when she'd seen the broken and bloodied corpse of her father shambling up to Markum's cruiser. Nell Morgan had somehow broken the spell Natalie had fallen prey to, and Natalie had come to feeling... well, feeling quite lost, like a baby without her binky, or a Momma's boy at his mother's funeral.

After Nell had snapped Natalie out of it, Natalie had seen what was underneath the façade, but only for the briefest of instances.

A boy in a gray cardigan.

A boy of about four feet tall.

And then the swirling darkness had overtaken the boy, and the boy in the cardigan was lost in its black depths. Markum had sped away; saved all three of their lives, really. Hadn't he? Well, here she was assuming. She knew this doll-faced thing had murdered at least one person (John Landover, Twon's methylamine supplier), but did she have any proof that the thing in the street yesterday had wanted to kill them? She thought not. But what else could it have wanted if not them dead?

A terrible memory resurfaced, and Natalie shivered.

There had been a moment, not more than two or three seconds, when Natalie had seen *something*. They'd been dragging Nell away from the short concrete wall at the verge of the Guadalupe when Natalie's father (*not your father, you silly girl, only something pretending to be Buck Holden*) had begun sucking something off of Nell. What Natalie had glimpsed had reminded her of squid ink. How it looks like silk in the wind. So pretty...

Now, she considered something else. For the first time since all the weirdness had started, she wondered if all of this was connected: Twon, the four-foot person Burt Waters had seen by his mailbox near Camp Meeting Creek the night Natalie found Tom Morgan's cruiser in a ditch, the ever-shifting shadow-child, the baby doll...

Could this many odd

(be real, Nat, we're talking supernatural shit here, not just odd shit)

things be connected?

Was there really any other explanation? She didn't think so.

But what did it all mean? Where did the trail of breadcrumbs begin and where would it end? Would anyone be able to stop it?

Something nudged the back of Natalie's right thigh and she screamed a horror-movie-victim scream.

She spun around, raising her gun as she did so, and, truth be told, almost blew the top of Merlo's head off. Imagine that: Merlo the Cowardly Dog living through all this hell only to have his thinker painted all over some stranger's backyard by a woman tightrope walking on her last frayed nerve.

"Goddamn it, dog!" she yelled at him, and for the first time, she wondered why no one in the house belonging to this backyard had gotten up yet.

Merlo gave her a truncated bark, dropped to his side, and began lapping at his balls.

Natalie was laughing at this silly doggie when she faced the baby doll once more. Natalie's laughter began to die the moment she saw the bright eyes in what had been previously empty eye sockets. Natalie's laughter turned to night-rending shrieks when the gigantic doll stood up from the swing with unsteady legs.

Merlo started to bark, snapping Natalie out of her terror long enough for her to raise her gun and aim.

The doll cocked its head quizzically and, in an equally quizzical voice, said, "Who are *you*?"

CRUELTY

LAURETTE

Laurette Fabiano was dying. After all this time, finally dying. And she was sated by that thought. Happy.

For the first time in she didn't know how many decades, she was alone inside her own head. The last time she hadn't shared her mind with Mia, Laurette had been a new woman, just becoming acquainted with the trials of womanhood. Momma had abandoned her, left her the ward of a witch in a realm known as the Roaming.

No more haunted mind. No more inner turmoil. She'd be with Twon again, somewhere in the Withered, where their memories would exist together forever. Her and her boy. Surrounded by quietude and nothingness.

Ah, blissful silence.

Now, to die.

"Hello, Laurette."

"Goddamn it," she muttered.

It was him. The Creator.

A boy of about ten strode into the kitchen, wherein Laurette, barely recognizable as human, was crumpled in the corner like a load of dirty laundry. She was vaguely aware that her legs and torso had become one, that her appendages had somehow been folded into and melded with her upper body. This did not truly bother her. She would be nothing but a memory in someone else's head, where she would live on for eternity with her son, unburdened of flesh. Let it be done already.

"Do you know who I am?" the boy with the eyepatch asked. His voice was soft, almost feminine, and his blue eye glimmered in his face—a sapphire in sand.

"Aye, child. You're older than me but younger than this existence." Laurette realized with a kind of intense humor that she still sounded like the witchery woman. Even in death, she couldn't drop the bitch.

"The idea of me is old, yes, but this flesh is far newer. Did she tell you about me?"

"Aye."

"Are you scared?" the boy asked.

Laurette found that she was. She swallowed and nothing happened. She tried to take a breath and could not. Was this death? A pause button on your body's daily operations? Would she move on now? Oh, please…

"Where is she, Laurette?" He sounded so damn innocent, as if all this nonsense, since the beginning of time, hadn't been his fault.

"With the demon, *bon ti fi*," she burbled, not sounding the least bit intelligible. It didn't matter if the boy understood her. He could hear her just fine in his mind.

"How did it come to this, Laurette. How did she get free? How did she get out of the Roaming?"

"Not infallible as you seem, eh?" And Laurette knew that she was no longer speaking. Her synapses continued to fire, throwing speech at this creature, the one who resided in this boy, but her lungs drew no air, and her lips made no sound.

"I see and hear all, but what's not said and done cannot be known. Not even by me. Mia's actions were outside of my vision and my ears. She told you enough about me to suit her plans, but not my trueness. Not *who* I am. Not *what* I am." The boy's eye shimmered beautifully, and Laurette was full to the brim with a love for this creature. In that moment, she could see how it worked, because she wanted him to work. To work on her.

Forgiveness fed on resolution.

This boy fed on memory. On the memory of love.

"Before there can be forgiveness, there must be regret. And before regret, there must be cruelty. But what comes before all of that, *bon ti fi*?"

"In the beginning," the boy said sadly, "there was joy. And I saw that it was good. So I ate it."

"You sound like—"

"It does not matter what or who I sound like, Laurette. Time draws to a close, but yours doesn't have to." He settled that glistening sapphire on her. "I can make this last forever. Pain will be your god, and you will worship at its altar."

An agony so complete and all-encompassing raged through Laurette. Her bones bent and cracked and reset and shattered all over again. Her heart burst in her chest before thudding back to life. Her eyes exploded and returned. She was Prometheus being devoured over and over again by a giant eagle at the base of Olympus.

Even through her agony, Laurette was offered a clear view of the boy—*the Creator*—and what she saw drew frigid fright like a bow across the strings of her soul.

An undulating redness brightened in the middle of the boy's forehead, as if someone had draped the skin of his brow over a flashing stop light. From the center of the child stepped a mass of mercurial shadow in the rough shape of a man. The Bastard stood tall and proud in the kitchen of Ollie's father's old home and began to chuckle.

"No," Laurette burbled.

The throbbing red eye in the center of his face pulsed in time with her fear. "We left something with him, and we want it back. It's not for Mia to have. She would undo all of our hard work."

"Please, just lemme die!" Laurette's mind screamed at the creature.

"Where is he, Laurette," the boy asked most kindly. He stood to the side and behind the swirling darkness of the Bastard, as if he were a timid child hiding from a stranger behind his parent's leg.

"She... she took off after him, through his head, she did. You not gonna catch her before she reaches the Source. The dumb thing let her in." Laurette felt like laughing but her fear crushed such jovialities under its heavy boots.

"But where did *he* go?"

"I... I don't know. He was 'ere, then... then he was gone."

The boy gazed up at the Bastard. There was a sadness in the boy's eye that was nowhere to be found in the presence the entity exuded. The Bastard was nothing but cold indifference. The child, its prisoner. Or, at least, that's how it seemed to Laurette. The truth, she figured, was far more complicated than that.

"He retreated," the boy said. "He's gone home."

"Yes," the Bastard hissed.

"To the Withered?"

"Yes."

The Bastard drifted down, and ice seemed to pour over Laurette. If she were more than a glorified thought, she might have shivered.

"Can I die now?" Her voice was meek and, even though it was spoken only with her mind, trembling.

"Oh, no," the Bastard said. "You don't get to die. She planned to come for me, and, in a way, she did. I know you being tethered to that witch was none of your doing, but I believe you've forgotten Huxley. Rape is rape, my child. You used your powers to steal that man's humanity, and I plan to steal yours."

"No..."

"You've done your share, Laurette, and instead of death, you will know madness. After all, we must have balance."

Her flesh ran like tallow. Her muscles exploded and painted the surrounding walls, the refrigerator, the corpse of Kirk Babbitt and Gregory "Hotel" Hyatt, the cabinetry, and the tile floor of the kitchen in reds and pinks. Freed of her body, Laurette knew an even greater pain than one of the flesh. Her very soul was ripped to shreds, refastened, and destroyed again.

The kitchen was gone. The house Ollie's father once owned disappeared. Kerrville was a distance memory. Texas was an impossibility. Earth was a speck in an ocean of specks. The universe, inconsequential.

Laurette Fabiano was one with the stars.

MIA

"**W***here is it?"*

Mia struggled through sand-heavy winds and shifting dunes. This plane, this world, was nothing more than the imaginings of a creature not unlike her. The only difference being their motivations.

She had to be close. The tempest was increasing in strength. Forgiveness had installed several security measures, many a false floor, but she had beaten them all.

Now, she hunted the Source, the inception of the demon's powers... the Beginning.

Through the swirling sand, Mia could see a structure. She'd seen several buildings like it throughout her time with Laurette—with Momma—and this one was instantly recognizable by its marquee alone.

The theater sat lonely in the middle of this arid wasteland, its signage on and twinkling aside from the fact that it seemed to be perpetually daylight in Forgiveness's version of the Withered.

Sand sprayed and tinkled off the glass of the empty poster cabinets. On the marquee, below a flashing **NOW PLAYING**, were black letters. Although some of the letters were missing, the message was clear:

S rry we r closed

"I jus' bet you is closed, demon," the witchery woman said, tittering with excited anticipation. "Mia go'n get a ticket. See her a show, she will."

The storm—as if wishing to welcome her to this antiquated cinemaplex—died down as she approached the ticket booth. A shriveled skeleton in a faded red usher's uniform with gold piping sat behind the glass. The pile of bones in the red suit glanced up at her, and she saw the pools of darkness inside the sockets of its eyes.

It spoke: "Abandon all hope—"

"Your parlor tricks ain't no good on old Mia, demon."

"I'm warning you," the skeletal usher said. "You've already come too far uninvited."

"Mia's scared, she is. But not of you. He's taken my puppet, the Fabiano girl. We'll be next. Do you see? He knows you're hiding it, and when he finds you—"

"*SHUT UP!*" The right side of the jawbone snapped loose and the mandible swung down to its chest. Still, the thing spoke at her. "You don't know anything, you stupid bitch. I didn't steal anything from him. He *gave* it to me. He *made* me, you stupid cow."

"You can call Mia anyt'ing you want, devil, but she's comin' in there. She's coming in there and she gonna see about your guts, she will. See what make 'em tick. And when Mia's done seeing to your tinker-toy heart, she gonna eat it."

Silence answered her.

"You still there, demon? Huh? You still wit' Mia?"

But she saw those pools of darkness had gone. Now only the skeleton's cobweb-infested sockets glared back at her. The jaw broke loose and fell into the lap of the dead usher's crimson pants. And, with a suddenness that almost shocked her, the skeleton turned to dust before her eyes. Poof. Gone.

"Let's see what's in 'ere, shall we?"

She went to the first set of glass doors on the right, grabbed the handle, and pulled. She half-expected them to be locked by some of the demon's dark magic, but they were not. They opened effortlessly, and she stepped inside.

Everything was alive. Brand new and alive. The red carpet very nearly glowed, like a neon bulb, so much so that Mia found herself squinting in spite of the fact that she was not truly in possession of a body with eyelids which she could squint. She'd been hidden away inside Laurette so long, and old habits died hard.

When her eyes adjusted to the brightness of the carpeting, she tried to focus in on the other details. She had to remember that everything in this world was important, that everything herein had been built from scratch using only the tools of Forgiveness's imagination and memories. So, this—wherever this was—had either been real at one time, or was a complete fantasy. She assumed the former. Nobody would create such a gaudy place. Look at the gold accents on everything. The gleaming silver doorknobs. The glass on the popcorn machine shined to a crystal finish. Each kernel of popped corn the same size. The smell of CO_2 and butter on the air. The taste of chocolate on the tip of your tongue.

"He's trying to seduce me," she said aloud. "Ha! I don't get hungry, demon!"

Or perhaps that wasn't the case.

No.

Now that she had time to consider other possibilities, she remembered Lody. The boy had been split in two, was confused. One side an unstoppable monster. The other side a being who offered its prey forgiveness. Both sides stolen

(He *gave* it to me. He *made* me, you stupid cow!)

from an entity far more powerful than he.

So... what side did this theater represent? The monster, or Lody? Forgiveness, or the doll?

Beyond the popcorn machine and the soda fountain, a flicker of movement caught Mia's eye. White on red. There and gone in a flash.

She eased forward, each footfall landing in a golden diamond in a sea of red carpet. The diamonds were new, she realized. There'd been no harlequin pattern underfoot when she first entered this place. Whether or not that was important, she did not know.

"You!" a female voice growled from somewhere within the building.

"Who's this guy?" came a deep male voice.

The voices were muffled, but Mia garnered their meaning easily enough. The man and the woman had been visited by someone they hadn't been expecting. Which was odd, considering how they were all essentially inside Forgiveness's mind. She supposed even demons could suffer from split personality disorder, and continued on.

She rounded the end of the concession counter and entered a long, shadowy corridor. Three doors on each side, and above each one a sign delivering the films being shown in each theater.

The titles of the movies intrigued her.

First on the right: **Regret**.

First on the left: **Cruelty**.

The voices were most definitely coming from the first door on the right, but the signs farther down the hall piqued Mia considerably.

Second on the right: **The Creator**.

Second on the left: **The Bastard**.

Though she knew she was not in possession of a body, a chill rippled down her spine. She was Mia, the witchery woman, a creature of sorrow and loss, a being of the Roaming, where souls went to wander, but here she was, knee deep in a being's broken mind, and she was ever so confused.

She strained and glared at the final two doors.

Last one on the right: **Joy**.

And, finally, the last one on the left: **Death**.

She ignored the voices coming from the theater showing **Regret** and chose the first door on the left. The sign reading "**Cruelty**" very much interested her. That was the doll, and she felt the doll was the key to this whole mess. Forgiveness had come after Momma—or Laurette, if you prefer—wanting to know where his "ward" had run off to. Logic dictated that, if the doll named Cruelty was important to the demon, it would also prove important to Mia.

The door marked **Death** intrigued her, but she wasn't concerned with Forgiveness's death. Not yet, anyway. First, she needed to find the Source, only then would she best the Bastard.

She crept toward the door to Cruelty's theater, pushed open the door, and stepped inside.

The first thing she noticed was a woman's perfume on the air as she walked down the dark hallway toward the blank screen on the far wall of the auditorium. The next thing she was aware of was a heaviness in her chest. It felt as if someone were squeezing her heart. Had she had a heart to worry about, she might have been concerned, but a memory need not worry about a coronary.

At the end of the hallway, she made a left into the seating area of Cruelty's theater. The screen flickered to life. Mia chose a seat in the middle of the third row, and gazed up at the screen.

Time didn't work the same way in the Withered as it did in the corporeal world, and Mia felt no sense of urgency; only a sense of pique niggled her.

Heavy red tapestries the color of the usher's uniform the skeleton out front had been wearing bracketed the screen, which was slightly wrinkled in the center and stained near the bottom left corner. Such attention to detail struck her odd. Mayhap this place was a true memory after all. Why would Forgiveness have built this thing from the ground up and not make everything fresh and new? There was no excuse. For now, Mia would assume that this place existed—or had existed—once upon a when.

The screen flickered and a film reel stuttered into life. The first image was of a woman tearing at her own teeth and gums with a pair of needle nose pliers. *Cute*, Mia thought. The second image to roll across the screen was of a donkey approaching a woman. This woman was duct taped, stomach down and bare-ass naked, to a wooden saw horse in the middle of a blindingly white room. That image died and the film settled on an overhead view of a dark chasm surrounded by a thin forest. A group of six or seven people were weaving their way toward a chasm. The two in the back—a fat man and his dwarfish companion—had fallen away from the group and seemed to be conversing. She could hear the fat man counting.

1... 2... 3...

What was all this? She had no idea. It nagged at her, whatever it was.

The screen went black. There was a pop, followed by another, and then two more. Another two tiny explosions went off. The screen remained dark.

"Lody?" came a voice so soft and sweet that Mia's stomach roiled in disgust. "Lody, wake up."

The screen flickered, giving Mia split-second views of a tall white woman in a nurses uniform bending over the camera. The gate fluttered three more times before the aperture opened completely. At first, the picture was out of focus, but slowly the image cleared.

"Kimberly?" asked a small voice. Mia thought it sounded like it belonged to a boy-child.

Ah, Mia thought as she leaned back in her chair, *I've been here before...*

LODY

Bay's End, 1908

Lody awoke to find Nurse Kimberly standing over him, smiling.

"Kimberly?" he asked, and rubbed the sleep out of his eyes.

"Hey. Yeah, it's me. I see you and dolly are getting along smashingly." She pointed to the black-haired doll he had clutched to his side.

"She's my friend," Lody said groggily.

"That's good. Say, are you ready to get out of here? Doc said you can return to your room today. That means dayroom visits again. You can visit with your friend Scott. Won't that be nice?"

"Uh huh." He yawned.

"I'll come and see you every now and then if you like. You know, after you return to your room. Would you like that?"

He nodded. Truth be told, though, all he wanted right now was to go back to sleep.

"All right. Good. I'll see you later, after my rounds. Good luck, young man."

"Thanks."

Lody was transported back to his room shortly after nine o'clock that morning. He never saw Nurse Kimberly again.

Lody's first morning back in the dayroom was uneventful. Scott was not in attendance, and Lody didn't feel like asking anyone why. A nurse came in before breakfast and gave him his antibiotics and pain medicine. She disappeared once her chore was finished.

The tubby black guard at the door liked to stare, and Lody wondered more than once what this one's nose would taste like.

He shivered at the thought. He hadn't had one of those inklings in quite some time, not since the Bastard had first shown himself to him. Lody wondered what that meant, if it meant anything at all, as he shoveled cold eggs into his mouth and washed them down with bitter orange juice.

That evening, directly after supper, Lody was returned to his room and helped into bed. His barren crotch had begun to itch something fierce, and before the tubby orderly left, Lody asked if the man would inquire about something to ease the irritation.

"Yeah, sure." The guy smiled big and wide, and Lody realized he knew this man. This was the same orderly that had eased the screaming old woman in the courtyard, the one Lody had eavesdropped on while speaking with Doc Andy.

"You're a good man," Lody told him.

"Thanks, champ. You sit right there, and I'll get someone to look at your... well, I'll get someone to tend to you."

"Thank you..." Lody let his voice trail off, baiting the man for his last name.

"Harold. Name's Harold Babbitt." The orderly's smile widened, and Lody believed he could see every tooth in Harold Babbitt's head.

"Nice to meet you, Harold. I'm Lody."

"I know." Harold winked at the boy and left the room, locking the door behind him.

Lody had no idea how long of a period of time passed before a red-faced woman came to see about his itch. She applied a cool lotion to his healing scars, and the nuisance was instantly relived. She washed her hands in the sink beside Lody's toilet, and excused herself. Lody wondered how awkward it would be to have to rub lotion on a strangers mutilated genitals. Could they even be called genitals anymore? Lody thought, *Probably not*. He reminded himself that they were more than mutilated—they were entirely gone—and drifted off to sleep.

"Wake up, child," a hissing voice beckoned.

Lody opened his eyes, instantly fully awake, and glanced quickly around. A soft red glow hovered in the far corner of the room like a crimson firefly. The glow did not reach beyond the corner, though, and the rest of the room remained cloaked in darkness.

Lody was very cold.

"Are you—" Lody began.

Yes.

The answer was wheezy and chilling, and, Lody believed, entirely in his head.

"What do you want?"

To talk with you, child.

"Why? What do you want from me?" Though he was scared, he was also quite curious.

You will do great things, child.

"What does that mean?"

Don't you speak anything other than questions? I've come to converse with you, not be interviewed. Is that so much to ask?

Lody swallowed hard, bolstered his courage, and asked: "Did you make me hurt myself?"

After a moment's silence, the shadow said, *Yes.*

Lody had not expected such firm honesty.

"Why?"

The shadow chuckled deeply.

Lody found he was sweating and trembling. He swiped a shaking forearm across his leaking brow, and then wiped it dry on his covers.

I see I frighten you. You have no reason to fear me, child. I do not intend to harm you… or make you harm yourself again. I've come to give you something. A… a gift, if you will. I will be going away, and you should have something to remember me by.

"What if I don't want anything from you?"

The red firefly darted at Lody. The boy flinched back against the iron head rail behind him, instantly raising a knot on the rear of his skull in the process. Hot tears of pain dashed down his cheeks, and he stared through the wet clinging to his eyes to see the glowing red dot hanging directly in front of him, no more than an inch away.

You will not deny me, the Bastard hissed. *No one denies me.*

Point proven, the shadow drifted away, stopping in the middle of the room. Its crimson gaze settled on Lody, and the boy could have sworn he could feel the Bastard smiling at him.

You will not be allowed to stay here after tonight. Things will happen, and you will need to find a new home. I suggest you continue to move until I come for what I am to give you. Do you understand?

"No," Lody said earnestly.

Of course you don't. The bastard sighed, and fetid breath stole over Lody. The boy gagged.

No matter, the shadow continued. *With my gift, you will do great things, child. Without my gift, you will be left to rot in this… this den of insanity. Outside, you will need to feed. You will need to harvest and recharge, and as long as you follow the rules, there will be no need for you to ever grow old.*

Lody didn't like the sound of any of what this creature was saying, but he remained silent. Whatever the Bastard gave him, he would destroy. He promised himself this, but said nothing.

I like your doll, the Bastard said. Its crimson gaze drifted toward Lody's small bedside table, where the doll and the Mother Mary statue resided.

"Kimberly gave them to me," Lody told the shadow.

Yes… Kimberly has been good to you, hasn't she?

"Yes. She's my friend."

The bastard chuckled. *After tonight, child, you won't need any friends.*

The shadow vanished, and Lody was left all alone.

For the first time in his short life, Lody prayed, and the silence that answered him seemed the most tragic thing of all.

Lody dreamed he was walking, walking down the hallway outside his room. He couldn't remember having fallen asleep, but surely this had to be a dream. The nurses and orderlies didn't allow the children outside their rooms after dark, and it was most certainly dark.

So Lody walked and dreamed… dreamed and walked…

No. Not exactly. He wasn't walking. He was lumbering, lurching with every stride. His legs felt too big, too cumbersome. Clunky. Somewhere, a clock ticked quickly, as if the minute hand seemed intent on catching the second hand.

At the end of the hall, a lamp shone from atop a desk. This desk was set up behind a bank of bars, the kind one might find in prison. Lody knew this to be the guard's desk.

Seated at the chair, his legs up and heels on the calendar atop the desk, was a man with white hair and more wrinkles than a geriatric bulldog. Lody thought the orderly looked so comfortable, so innocent perched there like that.

And then he wondered, dreamily, what it would feel like to rip the man's leg off at the hip joint. Big fun, he assumed. It would be like biting that Aussie's nose off.

Lody dreamed he tore the bars out of their mooring and tossed the entire thing down the hallway.

In this dream, the guard woke with a start and tipped over backward. He looked up at Lody. Abstract terror filled the man's eyes as he scrambled away.

It was then that Lody realized he was taller in this dream, at least six feet if he was a foot.

The orderly bellowed for help. Lody had heard something like this before. His father had sounded this way as the men dragged him outside the cabin to be hanged.

Thoughts of his father only served to stoke Lody's fire. He tossed his shoulder out and charged forward. He barreled toward the scrabbling orderly, leapt, and came crashing down on top of the man. Blood splattered the walls on both sides of Lody. He pushed himself up and surveyed his work.

The orderly's head had been crushed, and Lody once again thought how odd this dream was. He wasn't heavy enough to crush a man's skull. That was just silly.

A door on Lody's left swung open and two men in white uniforms

(*more orderlies, oh goodie*)

slid into the hall, skating on blood.

One went down hard on his ass, and Lody left him for the moment. The other crashed down face first. Lody stepped on this one's back, and his heavy leg smashed through the man, as if he were no more than a cockroach. The second orderly was screaming,

screaming so loud in this horrible dream that Lody could think of nothing more than stopping his infernal racket.

He tore the man's leg off at the hip and beat the orderly to death with it.

Lody lumbered out through the door the two orderlies had used to enter the hall. He found himself in yet another corridor—black-and-white checkered floor, tan walls, light bulbs shining brightly from steel cages set into the ceiling. He walked jerkily down the hall until he reached another door. He grabbed for the doorknob and stalled.

His hand.

His hand looked so weird.

It shined in the light, as if it were made of glass. He brought his palm to his face, and though he knew it impossible, he felt the cool, smooth surface of his face. He patted his chest. Ran his hands over his thighs.

From head to foot, he was completely solid. Yet he could *feel*.

Sewn into the front of the dress he wore

(*This dream's so weird*)

he found a pocket containing the Mother Mary statue. Good. At least he hadn't left it behind. That would have made him sad.

When he was done checking his new self out, Lody grabbed the knob again and crushed the bronze handle in his massive grip. He shoved the door open and walked into the lobby of Pointvilla Home for the Criminally Insane.

A scream sounded from somewhere behind him—a woman, by the sound of it. He ignored her.

Lody headed for the glass doors at the front of the building. Not bothering to stop, he burst through the frames as easily as a grown man walks through a spider web. Glass exploded outward, and Lody felt as well as heard his feet crunching glass as he strode out into the turnabout.

He walked out from under the overhang and kicked through a row of bushes.

Even if this was a dream, it felt so good to be out.

Behind him, the woman continued to caterwaul. For just a moment, Lody considered going back in to shut her up, but he had no reason to.

He was out.

He was free.

And, having murdered three men, he was… *full*.

He pulled the Mother Mary statue from the pocket of his dress and caressed its sad visage.

"Mah-Mah," he cooed, and disappeared into the tree line at the verge of the hospital.

FORGIVENESS

The cabin existed between the folds of space and time and reality. It existed in a plane known only as the Withered. It was in this place that Forgiveness hid. Because his was a very special hiding place, a secret known only to him, he was rather surprised when he turned from his pacing and found the boy sitting on the bed.

The child was maybe eight, maybe ten, and he had hair so blonde it was almost white. He gazed at Forgiveness with black eyes, and Forgiveness found that he was scared. Why he should be scared of this boy he did not know, but fear nonetheless infused him with icy blood.

"Who are you?"

"You don't recognize me?"

"No?" Forgiveness hadn't expected the word to come out as a question, but his voice raised at the end all the same.

"I don't blame you. I'd forgotten about me too. That happens, you know, when you're locked away for almost a century."

"I—"

"You're confused. I know. So am I. I look at you and I don't recognize you, either. Well, I guess that's not entirely true. I guess I remember you like... like maybe a castaway will remember his face after awhile without a mirror. I know you existed at one point in time. I know I existed right along with you. But I ain't seen't you in so long that I done forgot what I—what you—look like. I aren't makin' no sense, am I?"

Forgiveness shook his head. The boy had gone from a well-spoken child to a Podunk hillbilly in less than the blink of an eye. Still, there was something familiar even about that.

"Who are you and how did you come to be here. Only I—"

And that's where Forgiveness stopped. Realization stole over him in caustic waves, rending the flesh from his memories and exposing their glistening inside.

"Lo... Lody? You're... you're Lody?" Forgiveness stammered, shaken, "You're me?"

"I'm more me than I am you. And you're more Dad than you are me. Damn, this is getting a might confusin' again. Whatcha say, kid? You 'member me, or not?"

"My father didn't have a forgiving bone in his body. He—"

"I think you got your forgivin' nature from me. You got your cruelty from my father. Well, our father. I'm jus' gonna talk like there are two of us, okay? Makes things less strange."

Forgiveness nodded.

"What I think happened is that, at some point, we split up. The Bastard locked up everything good 'bout you inside that doll. You know, when he gave you the gift. You 'member that? Probably not. That old woman's been swimming around inside our mem'ries, but she ain't found that bit. No doubt she will before long, but at this point, what's it matter, right?"

"I don't want to die," Forgiveness said, not truly understanding why those exact words had spilled from him.

"I do. I'm done. We were tricked. Don't you see that? Something happened. The Bastard knew something would happen and he'd be... I dunt know, *lessened* somehow. He gave us a part of himself. That part became you. That midnight part. That goddamn shadow you flaunt around like a purdy cape."

"What?"

"That thing hopping around in the theater? Mia? She showed me something while I was still in the doll. She showed me the truth of the Bastard. She showed me that you ain't Pa and I ain't bad. There was a part of me, the part of me you—it—hid. The good part. We haven't been feeding and harvesting for us. You haven't been running the show. He has. The Creator's first creation. The Bastard."

"I am me. I am forgiveness. I help people forget the painful parts of their lives so they can move on. I feed on misery, and the husks I leave behind are better for it. I do that! Me!" Forgiveness was screaming, although he knew not why he was angry.

"No. You don't. That's him. That's the Midnight Man... the Bastard. All this? The cabin, the Withered, the darkness inside us all—it's him."

Forgiveness reeled. If all of this was true, if he'd been taken over like Laurette had been taken over by Mia, then that made him nothing more than a pawn in someone else's fight. He refused to be a puppet.

He had created Regret. He had used the dark woman to create a separate being. A being that reminded him of... of...

"The dark woman is nothing but a battery," Lody said. "She's powering our memory of Mom."

"No," Forgiveness whimpered. "No."

"Here," Lody said, offering his hand to Forgiveness, "let me show you. It's okay. I was scared, too."

"No!" Forgiveness raged, snatching his hand away from the boy.

"I know how hard it is to misremember, or to not remember at all. I've been stuck in that doll for so long, I forgot what it was like to love. I was powerful. I was untested. I was *Cruelty*."

"If he made us," Forgiveness asked, "who made him?"

"That's the question isn't it?"

(Not "ain't it?" but "isn't it?")

"Do you know?"

"I do not."

("I do not," not "I dunt know")

"Who are you?"

"I told you, I'm you?"

"Well, partner, that's a load of horse droppin' because *we* don't talk like that."

Forgiveness stopped. Had he really spoken in such a way?

"My, don't we sound country," Lody said, grinning.

"This ain't right. I dunt talk like this!"

"Don't you?"

"What the hell you done to me. Stop it! Stop—"

And then there was three.

In this cabin that wasn't really a cabin at all, stood three things that used to be one. When the split had occurred, Forgiveness didn't know, but it was quite obvious now. Lody, the boy he'd once been, had been a watcher, a mimic. Lody spoke like his Pa because his Pa was all Lody knew. After his pa had died, he'd gone to live at the home, the home where he met a boy, a boy named Scott. The boy with the eyepatch. Scott had been educated, well-spoken, and Lody had taken account of that. What else had Lody taken from Scott?

What else had he *accepted*?

Lody sat on the bed. Forgiveness stood in the center of the room. And the Midnight Man hovered near the hallway.

"It is time." The shadow grinned, and it was a hideous thing.

"Time we pulled ourselves together," Forgiveness said.

"If the bitch wants a battle, we'll give her one," Lody said, not feeling the joy of the impending war, only wanting all this to be over.

"Where's the doll?" the Bastard asked.

Lody, looking morose and dejected, said, "I'll take you to it."

"What about Regret?" Forgiveness asked.

"Let the witchery woman have her. The reaping is at hand."

THE CREATOR

How long had it been since he'd loved? He could not remember. For the life of him,
(Life, what a joke)
he couldn't remember Joy. Somewhere in the stacks of the library of his mind was a volume of text on the subject. There was no card catalog, no fancy computer on which he could search for Joy, but it had existed. Once upon a time, Joy was all there was.

The Creator, cloaked in the visage of the boy with the eyepatch, a child whose name he had long since forgotten, sat beside the ravaged state trooper, the one that refused to die.

Four times since the Creator had come to visit Tom Morgan, nurses had comes in to check that Tom's pulse was still going strong. At some point yesterday, they'd pulled the plug on the man, but his heart continued on.

The Creator held a memory in his hand. This was the memory he'd taken from Nell Morgan, Tom's wife. The memory was represented in this world as memories are usually perceived—as a fog. Inside the sphere of fog hovering above the Creator's small hand, the memory played out again and again. He thought this was Joy. At least a part of it. Humankind had known so much cruelty and regret and forgiveness that they'd forgotten a basic necessity.

Joy.

They sought Joy in drugs and sex and alcohol. They sought Joy in other people's pain. They sought Joy in church. But Joy was none of these things. Joy was companionship, because life, by itself, is not enough.

"In the beginning," the Creator told the comatose man laying in the hospital bed at his side, "there was Joy. And I saw that it was good. So I ate it. Not because I was hungry, but because I was jealous. Jealous of something bigger than me. I had hoped that by consuming it, I would become it. But that's not how it works. Now, an eternity later, Joy is nothing but a memory, and hope is a concept that forever is not accustomed to. Why? Well, Tom, because everything must end. It is the nature of reality. At some point even the Wither and the Roaming will cease to exist. People will stop following religions and these places they know as Heaven and Hell will simply not be any longer. Then, I suppose it will be Death's time. But Death is just a concept, much like cruelty and regret and forgiveness. But, without concepts, you sacks of flesh and blood and bone don't have anything to hold on to. Do you know what it means if the person you've wronged forgives you? Nothing. Not a thing. Do you realize that regret is powerless if you simply forget? Oh, but you men and women cannot forget. Your conscience—isn't that a funny word? Conscience? Con and science put together. Wouldn't those two things cancel each other out. Like 'dislike' or 'irrefutable'? Anyway, your conscience will not let you drop these meaningless concepts because it is the wish of all of mankind to be loved and accepted. This is what gives forgiveness its power. Ah, but what if you had cruelty without the necessity of forgiveness for balance? Therein lies the problem. As long as you people believe that there's something else to life other than living, other than existing, then true contentment, true Joy, will be lost to you. Life's big conundrum. Glad I don't have to deal with that shit.

"But this," he nodded toward the fog in his hand, "this seems to be worth it, you know. It's not, but it seems that way. Love is a concept just like forgiveness and cruelty and regret. Once you stop believing, it stops having control over you. Am I going on too long, Tom? Stop me if I'm boring you."

Tom said nothing. He only slept and existed, if you could call his state *existing*.

"I know you're not in there, Tom. You're with them. I must learn to stop talking to myself." The Creator sighed and continued. "I guess this is goodbye, buddy. You say hello to Nell for me when you see her. I imagine you'll be the only ones left when this is said and done, but who really knows. I'm not the all-seeing, all-knowing fuckabout I once was."

He leaned in and whispered into Tom's ear: "Pat Robertson would be appalled to hear me use such language, wouldn't he? I do so love pissing off that crazy old fuck."

The Creator stood and adjusted his eyepatch. He lifted his hand and blew the fog off his palm. It drifted languidly through the space between Tom Morgan and this eternal being. The fog crept slowly up Tom's nose, into his ears, snaked through his pursed lips, and stabbed into his tear-ducts. It got in where it fit in, and was gone.

"That's it then. See you when I see you, Tom. They're doing wonderful things with prosthetics these days, so chin up. You'll be just fine."

The Creator patted Tom on the thigh and left the room.

Any moment now, the end would begin.

Any moment now...

CRUELTY

RANDY

Randy brought his cruiser to a sliding stop in front of Kerr County Dispatch. He killed the siren and the engine in one fluid motion of his right hand, and popped open his door. He didn't so much as step from the vehicle as he kind of spilled out onto the grass. Nick's patrol car was sitting sideways in the three-car parking lot, so Randy had had to park on the lawn to the side of the building.

He only made it two steps before he heard Matthew calling from inside. "That you, Miser?"

"Yeah, kid, it's me!" Randy called back.

"Get in here, you worthless fuck!"

"Watch your language, young man!"

"Fuck you and your language, you uppity cock-polishing, badge-wearing, vagina-phobe!"

Randy had to give the guy credit for originality. Pain obviously brought out Matthew's creative side.

When the sheriff made it to the open front door, he drew his .357 and swung inward. The hallway, while not empty, was devoid of life. Nick Wuncell lay in a mound of limp appendages, as if someone had stole away with his skeleton. A pool of blood the radius of the Great Lakes surrounded the man, but it was obvious the gore had come from a head wound. The blood around the outside of the pool was beginning to coagulate, but the stuff nearest the back of Nick's head was shiny and fresh. Once Randy was close enough, he could see the ragged exit wound on the back of his deputy's head. He skipped around the puddle and into the adjacent hallway. He glanced right. Nothing. He swung back left. Bingo.

Matthew had crawled into a corner. Randy knew this because there was a not-insubstantial trail of smeared blood leading from the middle of the hallway to where Matthew now sat, clutching his arm like a baby and trembling. He didn't have any pants on, and Randy figured that the blue jeans currently acting as a tourniquet on Matt's leg was the reason for that. For the briefest moment, Randy wondered how the guy had tied his leg off with his arm all shot to hell and back, but figured anything was possible when you were in fear for your life.

"You look like crap, Matt," Randy observed as he approached his friend's son.

"Eat my entire ass." Matt said breathlessly.

"Sorry about this."

"Sorry doesn't get me not shot fulla holes, does it?"

"No, I guess it don't. Can you stand?"

"The fuck does it look like? I know, how about I just do the Charleston out of this motherfucker while you mash potatoes until some real cops show up."

"You sure are mouthy when you've been injured."

"Mortally, fuck twat. Mortally injured. Remember that. I'm about to die here, and you're—"

"I seriously doubt it. The arm looks like a flesh wound."

"I oughta shoot you, you know that. Better yet, I shoulda let you shoot the fucking birds."

"Do you wanna get outta here or not?"

Matthew inhaled and blew out a shaky breath. Sweat trickled down his damp forehead and into his eyes. Strangely enough, Matthew looked stoned. Then Randy recalled that Matthew always looked high, especially in photos where he smiled.

After calming considerably, Matthew asked: "How do you wanna do this?"

"I can either call the hospital and get you an ambulance, or I can try and get you out of here. But getting past that"—Randy hitched his thumb back to the pile of Nick sitting at the hall's junction point—"is gonna be an issue. He's blocking the way, and I doubt you're going to be able to hop over him. I could drag him out of the way, but you'd still slip and slide in all that biohazard. We should really wait on a gurney."

"Fuck. You want me to wait for an ambulance? I'm gonna die after all." Matthew blew an errant hair from his eye. "You really do hate me, don't you?"

"You're not going to die. I know you feel like it, young buck, but you're not even pale yet. You haven't lost enough blood to get out of this the easy way."

"Easy way? Fuck you, Miser. Fuck you in your swollen mangina."

"Remind me to buy a bar of soap when you get better. I plan to wash your mouth out." Randy flipped open his cell phone and dialed the hospital. A female emergency room desk clerk answered, and then relayed his call to the proper people. Less than a minute later, a man with a voice two octaves deeper than Barry White's voice assured Randy that EMTs were on the way.

As soon as Randy hung up, Matthew said, "Remember what dad said when we told him you hadn't shot anything?"

"You talkin' about those darn birds again?"

"Yeah. Do you remember?"

"I believe he said, 'The boy got to you, huh?' "

Matthew nodded. "I never killed anything. Not until..." Matthew trailed off. Instead of finishing his thought, he jerked his chin in Nick's direction and winced in pain. He clutched his arm more firmly and gazed down at his wounded leg. "I've been thinking, you know, while waiting on your slow ass to get here. I've been thinking that it's a bit of balance. I asked you not to shoot the birds and you didn't, but because I'd wasted your little hunting trip, you said I owed you one. Now, in order to pay you back, I had to take a life. I never killed anything, Miser, not even when I was a cop. Did I ever tell you that's why I quit?"

Randy shook his head. He dropped into a catcher's squat beside Matthew and his knees popped. He braced himself on the wall with one palm and continued listening.

Matthew nodded. "It wasn't really Dad's cancer that made me quit. You remember that incident I got into, the one where my partner got shot outside of Farad's 24/7, in Chestnut, back in Ohio? Well, that was my fault. I was leaned over the hood, aiming down the sights at this guy who was holding Mr. Farad's son by the throat—kid pissed himself, Randy; I didn't think people really pissed themselves when they were scared until I saw the front of that kid's jeans, but they do—and when he drew down on Tony—that was my partner's name, Tony Marchescini—I had ample time to pop him in the ear or the forehead or the shoulder. I had a clear shot over that kid's right shoulder, but I didn't take it. You wanna know why?"

"Because killin' ain't easy. Killin' is about the hardest thing a good man can do. I killed a few in 'Nam. I bet ol' Nick over there killed a few in Iraq or Pakistan or wherever he was stationed. That nonsense will change a man. I'd bet there's more than a few brothers out there still killin' people in their dreams. Some of them maybe even hoping they aren't really dreaming."

Matthew stared up at Randy with a look in his eyes that said he'd not expected Randy, good old clean-living Sheriff Randy Miser, to understand the problems associated with taking a life, or choosing not to take one. Randy found that he liked that. He liked that people could look at him and see a man they'd be surprised to learn could kill when he needed to. They'd be even more surprised to find out that, back in the rice fields of an unwinnable war, Randy hadn't minded shooting living things and watching their insides pour from the holes.

There was a part of him that enjoyed that about as much as he'd once loved drinking. Flo had dampened that need a bit, but she hadn't been enough. So he'd killed her to. Only the murder weapon hadn't been a rifle. It had been food. Even so, every time she'd asked for more, he'd pulled the trigger. Until finally she did the right proper thing and died.

Sure, Sheriff Randy Miser didn't cuss. Sure, he frequented church and worshipped the Lord. Sure, he loved his wife, all the way to the end, he'd loved her. But that's just what men do. They love and then they destroy. Randy was no different.

"Are you crying, Randy?"

"Yeah, Matt, I am." Randy swiped tears from his cheeks. "You're ugly enough to make a grown man shed tears, kid."

"Hardy har har, old man." Matthew's face scrunched up as another wave of pain washed over him.

Ten minutes later, the first sirens cleaved the early morning air. By four-thirty that morning, a total of seventeen minutes after Randy had arrived, two EMTs rolled Matthew Pontiff out the front of Kerr County Dispatch, leaving four thin red lines and a matching pair of crimson footprints in their wake. Randy stayed behind. He lingered beside Nick's body where it lay farther down the hall from where the deputy had died. Randy had yanked the dead man out of the way so the EMTs could get to Matthew. He looked down on his deputy with a certain solemnity he hadn't expected to feel. Nick had never been easy to get along with. He'd never gotten any of Randy's jokes, and always seemed just the other side of wrong to the sheriff. Still, the young man had been one of them. An officer of the law. Randy figured that was the saddest part. Randy finally attributed his morose attitude to the fact that Nick had disappointed him and nothing more.

"What I want to know is, what did you do with Shirley, Nick?"

Randy found the woman five minutes later, laying motionless in the single bathroom off the back hallway, less than five feet from where Matthew had been shot. The only thing between them had been the restroom door. What Randy didn't find was a pulse. She didn't seem to have a mark on her aside from track marks on her inner arms, and Randy doubted those had been what shuffled off her mortal coil.

He hadn't know she had been a user. Randy figured everything would lead back to Twon, in one way or another. He knew Nick had been working with him, so—

"God bless it!" Randy hollered, coming out of detective mode like a man fired from a cannon. "Natalie! Crap!"

As Randy hustled back outside (he was mindful of not slipping in the Nick's leftover juices), he chided himself for getting old and forgetful.

CRUELTY

NATALIE & MERLO

Natalie pulled the trigger five times. Two shots went wide, and the other three plinked off the doll's body armor. At least she assumed it was wearing body armor. Hell, the thing could be nothing *but* body armor for all she knew.

A bullet ricocheted off and through one of the house's rear windows. Another whizzed by Natalie's left ear—a lover whispering his intentions. She had no idea where the third one ran off to.

What she did know, and was ashamed to say terrified her, was this:

The fucking thing was still coming. Whatever lived inside this baby doll costume wasn't going to be stopped by mere bullets. Running was her only option.

She didn't like the idea of fleeing this thing. She wanted to kill it. She wanted to end it. But what other choice did she have? It wasn't like she had a magic sword up her sleeve with which she could slay this fearful dragon. She only had fear. So she would use her fear to fuel her escape.

The new lady was running. Merlo thought this was a very good idea and ran with her. He had an awful taste in his mouth, and an even worse scent in his nose. He'd tried licking himself to get the taste out of his mouth, and it had almost worked, but the aroma of dead tree rat still haunted his nasal passageways.

All this seemed awfully familiar, but his poor little doggie brain could not correlate one instance with another. Merlo knew he had run away from something similar not too terribly long ago, but he couldn't remember why. Tree rat was a horrible stench, but it wasn't scary. Not in and of itself. There had been something else. Something he'd sensed. Before rocketing from the backyard, close on the new lady's heels, Merlo was pretty sure he hadn't sensed this something upon previously smelling that awful smell.

He hadn't been this confused since the Mister bought him a furry kitty. Merlo had torn it to pieces one afternoon, and when the Lady came home, she'd hollered and whapped Merlo on the top of his head with her purse. She'd chased Merlo through the house, jabbing fistfuls of white clouds at Merlo and screaming at the top of her lungs.

As terrified as Merlo had been, he'd also wondered why the furry kitty had been stuffed with clouds. That seemed very strange indeed.

Eventually, the Lady had calmed down. She'd found Merlo in a closet sometime later and gave him lovins. When the Mister got home, he gave Merlo bacon and all was better again.

Still, Merlo had been confused, and he didn't think he would ever forget that feeling. Being confused was like being afraid. They both put a horrible, awful, disgusting taste in your mouth.

Merlo thought about dropping to his side and licking himself again, but then he remembered they were running.

So he ran.

Natalie had always thought that one of the biggest mistakes made by any horror movie chick since the dawn of the slasher film was the over-the-shoulder look.

Why would you do such a thing? Why would you take your eyes off where you were going and look back at the thing you were fleeing from? Why?

Well, the answer was quite obvious to her now.

Distance.

You would want to make sure that the distance between you and your pursuer was roughly the same distance as the Grand Canyon was wide. As the Great Wall of China was long.

So she glanced.

And she saw.

It was coming. The baby doll was coming, lumbering along in a rolling gait, tossing its shoulder out and dragging one leg. It was coming slowly, but coming all the same. Oh yes, it was.

She faced forward again just in time to keep from tripping over the curb in front of Walgreens. Without really paying much attention to where she was going, Natalie found it odd that she was heading directly for Kerr County Medical Center. She'd already cut through the parking lot of the Walgreens on the corner and sped past the crippled vehicle that had been stolen from Monlezun Estates. Another fifty yards would put her at the entrance to the medical center's emergency room across the street.

But was that safe? Could the hospital be considered a place of sanctuary?

Or was she leading an unstoppable monster directly into a den of waiting victims.

Fuck.

Fuck!

She cut right and headed for the drive thru set into the side of Walgreens. Merlo followed at her side, his tongue bouncing stupidly from the corner of his mouth. She looped around, ran past the teller's window, and sprinted toward a dumpster enclosure in the rear corner of the property. She stopped at the heavy double doors and glanced around as Merlo ducked under the doors of the enclosure. The doll was nowhere to be found, but she could hear, in the still of the night, the faint shuffle and drag of its approach. She listened closely, matched the shush of the doll's boots on asphalt against her opening the enclosure's door an inch at a time. Sweating and panting, she did this in an attempt to mask the whining noise the heavy door made as she swung it out and open. When the ingress was wide enough, she slid backward into the dumpster enclosure at the exact instant the doll came lumbering around the side of Walgreens and into view.

There was no way she could be sure that she hadn't been seen. She tried to hide all the same. There was enough space for her to squeeze in behind the large green dumpster, which had two plastic wings for lids, but she didn't want to be stuck there if the doll showed up. She had a idea that it would simply shove the dumpster and crush her against the cinder block wall at the back of the enclosure.

The words *Natalie Pâté* flitted into her mind and she almost laughed. Instead of bursting into guffaws, she dropped down into a squat behind a tower of milk crates in the back corner. Here, she was far enough away from the ingress that she could leap for the edge of the cinder block wall and crawl over long before that doll got close enough to graze her, much less rip her apart.

She thought about how Markum had told her someone in a doll's mask had killed John Landover. She thought about how John Landover's arm had been found sticking out of a toilet bowl in a stall at Bob's Bait and Fuel. She wondered if, tomorrow, Randy would find her arm in the dumpster, waving at him from the lip of one of the lids.

She shook off those thoughts. She would survive. She would not end up like her parents.

An eternity passed while she knelt in the half-dark of the dumpster enclosure, the only light the red glow of Walgreens' signage. After a while, she thought she heard voices. Three distinct voices. None of them sounded like the doll.

Her cell phone began to chirp in her pocket, and Natalie shrieked. Even while panting, she managed a scream that would rival Jennifer Love Hewitt in any *I Know What You Did Last Summer* movie.

She didn't mean to answer it; she'd only wanted to silence the thing. Nonetheless, she pressed the device to her ear. If nothing else she could tell the person on the other end where she was and that she needed help. Tell the person on the line that they should call the cops. Maybe even the state troopers—

(HA! funny because I'm a state trooper; State Trooper Natalie Holden, that's me, Bumble Bee!)

—or the National Guard. Get a fucking tank out here and blow this baby doll fuck back to whatever fresh hell it spawned from.

"*Help me!*" was how she answered the phone. Not "Hello?", not "State Trooper Natalie Holden, how may I help you," not "For six-ninety-five a minute, I can be your every desire," but a snake-like hiss of "*Help me!*"

"Nat? Nat, what's wrong? God bless it, I knew I shouldn'ta—"

"Oh, thank fuck. Miser, it's alive. I don't... I don't know how... but that fucking... that fucking *doll* is alive. I saw it... It *spoke* to me." Her words came in stage-whispered staccato bursts. She took several deep breaths. Her vision swam. If she kept this up, she was going to hyperventilate, black out. She had to control her breathing. Her survival depended on it. "*Where are you?*"

"I'm just coming over the Guadalupe. Where are *you?*"

"I'm—"

The enclosure's door began to whine. Natalie gazed through the diamond-patterned walls of the milk crates and watched the door swing outward.

It was time to go.

"*Walgreens*," she hissed, and pressed end. She stuffed the cell back into her pocket even as she was standing, twisting, and using her upward momentum to leap for the edge of the cinder block wall. Behind her, the door banged fully open. She ground her palms into the abrasive stone and shoved herself over.

Her fall wasn't graceful.

Her fall was painful.

She landed on her wrist and it bent a way it wasn't meant to bend. Nothing snapped, but that didn't stop it from hurting like a flaming bitch in a pool of kerosene. Tears sprung from her eyes, blurring her vision.

"She's a sneaky one," said a hissing voice.

"Kill her and let's go," said a much younger voice.

"Yes. Kill 'er and feed," said a third voice.

Something dark loomed over her. This presence bent toward her, haloed in the red glow of the pharmacy's sign. It snatched her by the wrist and squeezed until she screamed. A boot came down on her side and commenced trying to grind her into the pavement. Her arm was yanked upward until her wrist locked and she felt the tendons and muscles give, popping off one by one. She heard herself squealing like a police siren. She kept getting louder and louder. And as her hand became independent of her body she watched thick red ropes being pulled from her arm.

Shock plunged her into darkness.

Merlo burst from the back of the dumpster as the enclosure's doors banged open. He tore off around the side opposite from where Natalie was hiding behind the milk crates, and darted past the thing that smelled of dead tree rat.

He was almost to the road when he heard the woman thump to the ground and scream out in pain.

And for some reason he stopped. He had not stopped the night he lost track of the Lady. He had not thought about Big Gut when he last fled the smell of dead tree rat. But now he did stop. He stopped because he finally realized that there wasn't something missing from the lumbering thing that smelled of death. Not something missing. Something new. A new smell. A smell that gave Merlo courage for the first time in his life.

This smell was the smell of fear.

The monster was afraid, and Merlo liked that very much.

He turned from the road and looked back at the thing looming over the new lady. He watched the thing grab the lady, step on her, and begin to pull, like Merlo sometimes did when he found a rather nasty flea had burrowed into his coat.

Merlo, liking the stench of fear drifting off the monster by the dumpster, saw red. Merlo saw prey. Merlo suddenly wanted to bite something very, very badly. And because Merlo was a dog that followed his gut instincts at all times, he began to sneak back. He planned to snatch the ass off this thing and chew on it for a bit. Who knew, it might smell like dead tree rat, but it could very well taste better than bacon.

As Merlo drew closer, he began to salivate. He was so enthralled that he didn't hear the car coming until it was too late.

CRUELTY

MIA

Wh* hen the film stopped, Mia stood.

Interesting, she thought. *But when did the boy split? And* what *exactly did the Bastard give him?*

She lingered another moment or so, watching the screen. When nothing else played across the canvas, she left the theater using the same hallway by which she'd arrived. Back out in the main corridor, she judged her choices.

Joy seemed to beckon her next. She walked down the hallway and stopped in front of what she thought would be a door. It was not such. A brick wall had been constructed where a door might have been. She placed both hands upon the brickwork and shoved. Absolutely no give. She attempted to pull the wall down brick by brick inside her mind, but it was no use. The Withered was Forgiveness's realm. She was only a visitor. A mostly powerless visitor at that.

She turned toward the door marked **Death** and didn't find a door here either. Nor did she find a brick wall. Here she found a heavy steel door, the kind one might find on a bank vault. She grasped the wheel in the center of the door and tried to spin it. It did not give an inch. Not a centimeter.

She gazed down the hall, back the way she'd come, and considered the doors marked **The Bastard** and **The Creator**. These did not interest her in the least. She felt no draw, no pull from them. In fact, they seemed almost too uninteresting.

She ruminated on the possibility that these two middle doors might lead to important revelations. She thought she knew all she needed to know about both the Creator and his first creation, but she supposed there could always be something of which she wasn't aware.

She approached the Creator's door and tugged it open. A solid nothingness welcomed her. A complete and utter void. No light, no darkness, nothing at all. She'd never seen as much. In all her centuries, since she was birthed of sorrow and greed, she'd never known such an exhaustive emptiness. For a moment, Mia could not move. She was rooted in place as if she stood between a pair of collapsed stars.

The door marked **The Creator** crashed closed, and Mia stumbled backward into **The Bastard**.

If the Creator's door was the absolute absence of all, the Bastard's abode was the center of everything.

Every human emotion washed over her in a torrent of hatred and pain and sadness and happiness and lust and jealousy. She was torn in every direction at once, and perhaps, just for a moment, she understood how Laurette had felt before she came to know the universe on an intimate level.

Mia attempted to clamber back to reality, but couldn't find the way. Everywhere seemed to be everywhere and nowhere at all. She was both ignorant and enlightened. She was alive and dead. Alpha. Omega.

The stars drew out around her, like chalk marks on a blackboard, and she perceived movement. A sucking sensation at her core. If she had to guess, she would have said she was being towed along by some invisible length of rope, which had been tied around her waist.

She broke all barriers: sound, light, thought.

Mia blinked and found herself in the Bastard's lair at the middle of existence.

A bonfire crackled brilliantly in the center of an expansive, domed chamber. The concaved walls held what seemed to be funeral holes, the kind one might find in the catacombs in London. From each dark space came the subtle whispers of thousands.

I'm so sorry...

Please forgive me...

My mother needs your help right now...

The cancer's back...

Why me...

Are you even listening...

"Intruder," came a whispered voice. Even though the utterance was hissed, Mia had no problem hearing the word. She surmised that no matter where she stood in this place of prayer she would hear the minister clearly.

Mia rounded the bonfire and found her preacher standing at its pulpit.

A stone podium sat just beyond the flames. Behind the podium rose a man made of midnight, a thing of such complete darkness that the cold it exuded touched even Mia's ethereal form. And although she was not frightened of this creature, she did respect it.

"You's a big one, *bon ti fi*. Whatchoo been eatin'?"

The ever-shifting shadow that was the Bastard glared at her with his single ruby eye.

"Silence, witch. Why have you come here where you are not welcome?" At first, Mia believed this thing to be hissing, to be spitting its words at her, but that was not so. It's voice was static, mercurial, like a radio dial being rapidly switched between stations. Every channel was playing the same song only by a different artist.

"Was a foolish thing to come, aye. But a mistake it was. Do you see? I open a door, and eternity just kinda plop me down where'er."

The crimson glow brightened considerably, and Mia sensed she had upset the creature.

"No one comes here by accident. You have a purpose. Speak it." The Bastard snapped something in his pitch black claws, popped it into his mouth, and swallowed. Somewhere, a baby cried.

"I seek the Source of Forgiveness's powers, I do. He been runnin' t'ings long enough, seen?" She smiled at this last bit, this little something left over from her time around Twon. "Mayhap you let Mia in on the secret, and then you let her return. I might do somethin' for ye in return, I might. Do you see?"

"Are you truly so terribly stupid?"

"What?" Mia asked, suddenly very confused.

"I gave this one you call Forgiveness nothing. I simply captured and imprisoned one that I could not control."

"I don' believe you."

As if bored, the Bastard began tinkering with something out of sight, behind his podium. Something squealed. Something hissed.

After a moment's silence, the Bastard said, "The truth does not need to be believed for it to be the truth."

RANDY

Natalie's voice came over the phone, quick and breathless: *"Walgreens."*

And then the line went dead.

Out of force of habit, Randy hit the lights, flipped on the wailers, and trounced the gas pedal.

For some reason unknown to Randy, Kerr County's volunteer fire department still hadn't made it to the fire inside Pompeii Café. In all actuality, the café was no longer on fire, but the surrounding businesses sure were. He blew past them without more than a cursory glance. Rocketed through the intersection, just barely missing the hobbled car at the curb, and went sliding sideways into Walgreens' rear parking lot. He jerked the wheel as he tramped the brake, whipped the rear of the car around, and corrected his course. Seemed after all these years he hadn't forgotten any of his defensive driving classes.

He swung the car back to the left, effectively blocking the parking lot's ingress, and threw the transmission into park. He stumbled out, waving his .357 around as if it were nothing more than a peashooter. He felt so alone for the first time in his life. Even after Flo's death, he hadn't had such a sense of utter abandonment as this.

Someone

(Natalie?)

screamed, and Randy tried to follow the sound as it caught an echo's wave and rode it out into the ocean of this dark morning's silence.

A dog howled

(God bless it, is that Merlo?)

and this sound was much easier to follow.

Randy progressed, heading for the rear end of the parking lot, his Depends squishing soggily between his legs. The inside of his legs would be irritated when he finally got these things off, he was sure of it.

He hopped up onto the sidewalk , which ran along the front of the building and ended at the back. Holding his trembling gun arm out in front of him, Randy made it to the end and turned left.

Merlo was creeping slowly forward across what Randy assumed was the employee's parking lot. The dog looked purposeful, intent on stalking a massive black shape moving around by the dumpster. The figure's darkness was cleaved in places by the red signage on the drive thru teller's overhang, and Randy could just make out mostly bald head with patches of black hair hanging here and there.

He heard Natalie's voice stage-whispering in his head.

That fucking doll is alive. I saw it... It spoke to me.

He recalled how the massive doll sitting on the swing set had seemed to have been in a fire recently. Most of its hair had burned away, and the face and exposed scalp had been smudged with soot. He also remembered how those eye holes had been empty. There hadn't been anything in there.

"Freeze!" Randy hollered, and his voice cracked. "Get you hands up."

Merlo didn't seem to hear Randy, and continued to stalk toward the doll. The doll, on the other hand, turned and faced the sheriff. It cocked its head at Randy, was still for a second, and then underhanded something at him.

Had Randy had his finger on the trigger instead of the trigger guard, he might have shot the doll. Hell, maybe he should have shot it then anyway. But, instead of blasting a hole in this walking oddity, Randy simply sidestepped out of the way of the thrown object. Whatever it was thudded down on the blacktop, only five-feet away from him.

Now Merlo was growling deep in his throat. The dog's hackle's rose, and Randy could hear the click of its exposed claws on the asphalt.

The doll finally noticed the dog, and took an unsteady step back.

If Randy was reading the doll's body language correctly—the way it drew its arms up as it hobbled backward away from the beagle—he would have said that this thing was actually scared. Who faces an officer of the law, one with a .357 Magnum trained on their person, and not flinch, but devolves into a fleeing child at the sight of a mid-sized dog?

Randy didn't know, but he found his interest piqued. Curiosity was said to have killed the cat, and if Randy could've found the breath, he might have meowed.

Merlo's shoulders rippled under his coat as he hunkered down, ready to pounce.

"No... *No!*" the doll shrieked. It's voice was high, screechy, like a prepubescent boy's.

Merlo shot forward like a track dog chasing a mechanical rabbit. When he came within five feet of the doll, Merlo launched himself at the thing.

The doll caught the brave beagle around the middle and held Merlo at arm's length. The dog snapped and snarled. Merlo caught a bit of fabric on the doll's arm and tore a swatch free. The doll staggered backward, tripped on its own feet, and crashed down onto its back in front of the dumpster enclosure.

Because his attention was so trapped by the battle currently taking place between the doll and the dog, Randy didn't at first see the balled-up shape laying beside the enclosure. When his peripheral vision caught sight of it, he turned, intent on only sating his curiosity before glancing back to the warring oddity and canine, but when he saw who the balled-up shape was, all concern for himself and Merlo fled.

He jogged across the rear lot, gun trained on the tussling two in front of the enclosure, and reached the growing pool of blood long before he reached Natalie's unconscious form.

Without so much as holstering his gun, Randy dropped to his knees. His joints protested at being ground into the hard blacktop, but he ignored this. He rolled Natalie out of her ball. Her wrist gouted blood at him, and he had just enough time to lean out of the way of the arterial stream.

"Ah, hell," Randy groaned before allowing experience to take over.

Back in 'Nam, he'd come across a brother who'd had his leg blown off by a grenade. The stump started at the knee and hung down in tatters like weeping willow branches. A much younger Randy Miser had slipped off his own belt and tied off the soldier's leg. The belt made an adequate tourniquet, but while carrying the injured to safety, he'd had to keep stopping and pulling his pants up, lest they drop around his ankles and trip him up; all this while bullets zinged around him and mortar fire shook the world.

Because of this experience, Randy yanked off Natalie's belt. He then tore off his own shirt, exposing the sweat-stained tank top he wore under his uniform top. He wrapped the uniform top around Natalie's stump, cinched it closed with the belt, and then tugged the woman up off the blacktop. He got to one knee, tossed her messily over his shoulder, and shoved himself up. He toppled about halfway up. Luckily, the wall of the dumpster enclosure caught him, and he was able to stay upright. He slid up the side of the cinder block wall, leaving a bit of flesh from the outside of his left arm and a dab or two of blood behind on the concrete. He didn't so much as feel a tickle of pain.

Adrenaline was stoking his engine, and the sheriff was firing on all cylinders.

He lurched across the parking lot to the soundtrack of vicious dog and squealing doll. At least, Randy hoped it was the doll that was screaming. It sure wasn't Natalie. She was out. He knew she was still alive because her heart was still pumping blood. Although how much longer she would be among the living Randy did not know.

His heart worked a jackhammer against his ribs, and his lung felt two-sizes too small. He hoped his ticker would last until he got her to the hospital. He said an internal prayer asking as much, and trudged on.

At the car, he dumped her unkindly into the backseat. This was not the time for niceties. He then dumped himself, out of breath and sweating profusely, behind the wheel.

"Hang on, girl. Miser's got this," Randy said as he started the engine, threw the tranny into reverse, and sped across the street to the emergency room.

Back in the employee parking lot of Walgreens in downtown Kerrville, the real battle was just beginning.

MERLO

Fear tastes better than bacon.

CRUELTY

Get this fucking thing off us!

CRUELTY

MIA

Reeling from her encounter with the Bastard, Mia was returned to the theater's hallway. She didn't hesitate, but went right on about her business.

She stepped into **Regret**.

As she moved into the final theater, two things happened at once.

A man in a uniform she was not familiar with, vanished. He'd been standing beside a woman who was seated in the front row. First he was there, then he wasn't. He simply blinked out of existence. Mia did not concern herself with him.

Another man, this one standing closer to the screen, leapt forward and snatched the seated woman out of her chair. He spun and tossed her against the bottom of the screen.

"This is for Dennis!" he shrieked as he began to pummel the dark woman.

This would not do. Mia had been told the dark woman was important, that this Innis Blake person was the battery that ran Regret. Mia's job was simple. Take Regret. Destroy Cruelty. Return order and balance to the world.

Maybe then they could find Joy. At least that was the Bastard's plan. Mia didn't think it was that poor of a plan, either.

"You! Man!" she called.

The man continued to punch and kick at the woman, who was now lying motionless on the floor.

Silly men, Mia thought. *They truly are the stupidest of the species. You cannot physically harm someone here.*

"Fine," Mia said, "have it your way."

She snapped her fingers, and the man in the suit flickered and disappeared.

Mia went to the woman on the floor and helped her up. She really was quite lovely, this Innis Blake. At least her memory of herself was, for that was all a person was in the Withered—a memory of what once was.

"Who are you?" Innis asked drunkenly. The man in the suit had not hurt her, that would have been impossible here, but the dark woman did look stunned.

Oh, no, Mia thought, *not stunned. Drained.*

"Why'd he pick you?" Mia asked.

"Huh?" Innis muttered.

"Why'd he pick someone that was already used up. You're a dyin' battery with a busted cell. Do you see? You're not gonna last long, you ain't. I suggest we get movin', righ'?"

"Whuh?" Innis groaned.

Mia shook her head sadly and sat the dark woman down in the front row again. She cupped one ethereal breast and leaned forward, offering Innis her nipple.

"Here," Mia said, drawing the woman's face forward with her free hand. "Drink of me. Drink of me, and we'll see this through to the end, we will. Good. Nice. Suck... *Suck...*"

MARKUM

F rank snapped awake.

He was face to face with the statue with the fleshy face. He screamed and pressed himself back up against the wall. When he realized he wasn't going to escape in reverse, he scurried sideways. He shoved to standing, and began backing away from the statue, not wanting to take his eyes off it. He bumped into a low structure, wheeled around, and screamed a second time.

On the table, a faceless woman took a shuttering breath.

"What the fuck is going on here!" he hollered to no one in particular. "Where the fuck am I?"

A horrible feeling of Déjà vu stole over him.

He'd been here before. He'd gone through all this *before*.

He slapped himself. Hard.

No clarity came.

A low grinding sound arose. Frank jerked his head around and watched the statue rise from its hunched position. The fleshy face locked gazes with him for only a second before the entire thing started disintegrating. It came apart at the head first, as if it were made of nothing more than sand and a strong wind was blowing through. Down and down the thing dwindled. It looked like something was devouring it from the head down.

The loosened dust, or sand, or whatever this thing was truly made of, snaked through the air in a column of particulates. It headed across the room and up a set of stairs accessed by a framed doorway without a door. Up the steps it went, faster and faster, until the last of it fled and the statue was no more.

"What the fuck was that?" Frank breathed.

"She's off to see the wizard, I would imagine."

Frank twirled at the sound of the voice. On the other side of the table, where the faceless woman laying breathing laboriously, stood a young boy with an eyepatch over one eye.

"Who the fuck are you?"

"It's the eyepatch, isn't it? Stubborn thing always spooks people. Accident with a fork. Well, not really an accident but—never mind. Enough about me. Do you know who this is?" The boy gestured with a slow tilt of his head to the woman on the table.

"Wha? Why the hell should I care—"

"Oh, but you should care. You should care very much, Special Investigator Frank Markum. You should care because she's now in cahoots with the thing that killed your beloved. Your *Dennis*. I know you thought that she—that Innis—was the one who single-handedly murdered dearest Dennis, and I could see how one would come to such a conclusion. Alas, no. But she is *now* working with the one who did. Doesn't that just make you want to—how are the kids putting it these days?—choke a bitch?" The boy smiled a smile that made Frank shiver.

"Who are you?"

"I'm so very tired of that question. Everyone wants to believe that there's something else out there, but then they question when that something is staring them right in the face. I'm nothing. Nothing of importance, anyway. But you, oh, Frank, you can be so much more if you let me help you."

"What the—"

"—fuck am I talking about? My, you are a predictable sack of meat, I swear. I cannot affect this... this world. I can suggest. I can tell you the truth and let you do what you think is right. But before there can be balance, someone must die. And you have to kill them. What do you say?"

"I don't know... Jesus Christ, I'm so fucking confused." Frank said the latter to absolutely no one. He'd gone off the deep end and gotten turned around. Resurfacing seemed an impossibility. All he could do was flounder and drown like some helpless animal.

"*YOU ARE TRYING MY GODDAMN PATIENCE!*" the boy roared, and his voice was unlike what it had been before. This new voice was many. Was legion.

"Look,"—having calmed so quickly it seemed as if he'd never been angered in the first place, the boy carried on—"you know you want to do this. You want revenge, don't you? Kill this woman—she's already dying, so you'll only be speeding along the process—and then we can all go home. What do you say, Frankie Boy?"

Frank's mind reeled. He saw Dennis's bubbling and goopy form crawling across the gravel toward him. He saw Dennis whole and well as they made love in the surveillance trailer's bathroom. He saw their entire relationship: the ups, the downs, the secrets, the lies, the smiles and tears—and Frank began to cry. He'd cheated on the only man he'd ever truly loved, and Dennis had died before he could apologize.

No. He hadn't just died. Dennis had been murdered. Somehow this bitch on the table had poisoned him—

"No. That bit's wrong," the boy with the eyepatch said, as if he'd been able to read Frank's mind. "I cannot let you kill her based on a lie. *She* did not kill Dennis. A witch cursed him. Now, I know that's hard to believe—"

"But she helped?" Frank asked as he swiped snot and tears from his leaking face with the sleeve of his sport coat. "She was part of his death?"

"Well... no, she wasn't, but she is now collaborating with the one who murdered Dennis. That's enough, right?"

Frank began to nod, slow at first, and then faster. "Yeah. Yuh-yeah, that's enough."

"Oh goodie." The boy's grin was wide enough that Frank worried the kid's face was going to split open. "I'll leave you to your work then. Have fun."

When the boy was gone (how he'd gone Frank could not recall), Frank climbed atop the table and laced his fingers around Innis Blake's neck.

CRUELTY

THE WAR

Mia rode the wind with Regret as they sped toward downtown.

Every vehicle needed a power source and a driver. Up until now, Innis had been both. With Forgiveness sucking every ounce of power Regret harvested, Innis's cells had depleted and not had time to recharge. But Mia had had more than enough to share. She'd been storing up energy for so long.

Now, Mia took the driver's seat while Innis fueled the statue with her memories.

In Innis's mind, her brother Gerry died over and over again, and it was always her fault. Always her that had betrayed him by running off with some guy she didn't even know instead of picking him up at after band practice was over. In a way, she had murdered her flesh and blood, had killed her brother, and this regret had its own darkly crushing power.

Regret traveled from the cabin in the woods to downtown Kerrville in less time than it takes a second hand to tick twice. She reformed on the bridge over the Guadalupe.

The fire trucks had finally arrived, and men bustled about in front of Pompeii Café and the surrounding shops. She ignored them, and if any saw the flickering image of a Mother Mary statue floating down the street, they did not show it.

It wasn't until Regret hit the intersection that Mia heard the tussle occurring behind the building. More importantly, she heard the dog.

And, quite suddenly, Mia of the Roaming was very, very afraid.

Merlo tore at the wispy darkness; the tasty, delicious, yummy dark meat, oozing from every crack in the doll's face. He latched on, tugged, swallowed, and sprang forward for another bite. Something inside the doll was shrieking like a toy police car. Shrieking like the neighbor's cat that Merlo had every once in a while chased up a tree.

Hadn't that been why the Mister had brought home that kitty full of cloud for Merlo to *nom nom nom* on?

Perhaps.

Merlo continued his attack. His hunger was insatiable. His desire all consuming. At this rate, he didn't think he'd ever get enough of the goodness coming out of this thing.

And if the thing hadn't finally latched onto the scruff of his neck, Merlo might have devoured it right then and there.

What was happening to them? How had the tables turned so quickly? They were practically gods, and here this mangy mutt was making an all-you-can-eat buffet out of them.

There was barely anything left of the Midnight Man by the time Forgiveness was able to focus and grab the dog by the back of its neck. With the last bit of their combined power, Forgiveness slung the dog askance, as if backhanding a mouthy child. The mutt yelped satisfyingly, and Forgiveness went about trying to get back on their feet.

Cruelty rolled onto its side then its stomach. It pushed up to its knees and then took a kneeling position.

Another shove got it back to both feet. Cruelty staggered forward, stumbled through the open door of the enclosure, and ran face first into the dumpster. It careened backward, almost crashing to the ground again. To an onlooker, the doll might have looked like a member of the Keystone Cops in the middle of a skit.

The dog stopped whimpering and began growling. Cruelty managed to get its not inconsiderable girth turned and ready before the dog attacked again.

This time, the doll had the upper hand. It expected the second rush, so having its arm outstretched and ready to receive the mutt into its embrace was not a problem. It caught the dog around the throat and began to squeeze.

There was no turning back. Mia had made a deal with the Bastard. If she didn't follow through with it, she would have more to fear than a canine.

A dog's power stemmed from their lack of imagination. They saw what the entities of the Wither and the Roaming truly were: personified emotions. And because the little beasts could see, they could attack. They could rend and tear and deconstruct the likes of Mia and the doll and the statue. All of them were in danger. The dog, more so than even Forgiveness and Cruelty, needed to be put to an end.

Still, she was afraid. Laurette had gone on to be one with the stars in the Bastard's world. But she—Mia—would suffer an even worse fate. The nothingness of the Creator. For if she failed, the Bastard would pull his help and she would be left to face the boy in the eyepatch.

I warned Laurette about animals, but I forgot to prepare for the chance of coming across one myself. Ain't that a bitch.

Regret disintegrated and rushed into battle.

Merlo couldn't breathe. He kicked and scratched and snapped at the doll's arm, but could not gain purchase. Its arms were too long. Its grip too crushing. If the fingers closed another inch, Merlo's very throat would burst from the pressure.

"Merlo?" said an all too familiar voice. "Merlo, boy... is that you?"

What was this happy horseshit?

Mia was back in the theater. The last thing she remembered was reforming in the rear parking lot of the Walgreens and then... and then...

And then what, goddamn it?

She glanced around. Something was different. Something was missing. But what? What the fuck was she overlooking?

Nothing. She wasn't overlooking anything because there was nothing to overlook.

The dark woman was gone.

Innis Blake had taken over the statue.

Mia roared. The cacophony crashed into the walls of the theater and shook the entire building. Her rage spilled out tangible gouts of frustration and anger.

"*LET ME BACK IN, YOU BITCH!*"

She thrust herself at the screen. Crashed into the fabric. Bounced off and into the third row. She flung herself forward again, and again the theater's screen held her back.

"*LET ME OUT OF HERE!*"

Somewhere in the distance, someone began to laugh.

"Drop my dog, asshole,"

Innis steered Regret into the doll and charged. She thought, with not a small amount of glee, that the doll's jaundiced eyes widened in surprise, but that might have only been her imagination.

Regret collided with Cruelty and the earth quaked beneath them. Merlo was thrown by the shockwave. He slammed into the wooden fence surrounding Walgreens' back lot, and was still.

Regret drove Cruelty backward into the dumpster enclosure. The dumpster itself was crushed in the collision and shoved halfway through the cinder block wall. Regret pushed off the doll and reared back. She snatched up one of Cruelty's large hands and swung back and out. The doll rocketed through the side wall of the enclosure as if the cinder block was nothing more than a stack of *Jenga* pieces. The doll skipped across the blacktop twice before pitching through the wall next to the pharmacy's teller booth. Regret lost sight of Cruelty after that.

Cruelty came to rest inside cosmetics. Shelving and products rained down over the doll, burying it in a landslide.

Forgiveness swiped foundation and lipstick off the doll's chest and pulled it to its feet.

Only then did he realize he was outside of Cruelty.

This wasn't good.

Not good at all.

"Lody?" Forgiveness said with a voice that wasn't much more than a whisper. "You in there?"

"Yes. There's not enough power left to maintain both of us."

Forgiveness knew this to be true because he could feel it. He could feel how drained he had become. Trying to power Lody, the doll, and himself had proven exhausting. Not to mention all the power that fucking mutt had eaten. That was the worst thing of all, really. If the dog lived, a vast amount of Forgiveness's energy stores would be deposited in a steaming pile come some time tomorrow.

"What do you suggest we do?" Forgiveness asked.

"Die."

"Really funny."

"I'm not trying to be funny. I'm tired. I just want this to be over."

"When did you become such a pussy?"

"When did you become such an asshole?"

Forgiveness took great offense to this. Here this sniveling little weasel was, flaking out on him, threatening their very survival, and he had the audacity to call Forgiveness an asshole. No, sir.

"I kept you alive. I am the reason we've survived all this time. *Me!* I kept us alive while you hid in that fucking doll. I made all those goddamn statues trying to make you happy! I was trying to give you a companion. Some kind of joy! I did it all for you, you ungrateful little fuck. Me! *ME!*"

"You failed me. You failed yourself. We became our father, can't you see that?"

"*SHUT UP!*"

"Dad used us. The Bastard used us. And now you're using me. I'm done. This is over."

"Lody?"

Silence.

"Lody, you get back here."

No answer.

"I am Forgiveness! I am the greatest power in the universe. I cannot exist without you. Together we are everything. Yin and yang. Alpha and omega. You create the pain and I ease it. You cannot abandon me. *YOU CANNOT LEAVE ME!*"

Regret went to the motionless dog by the fence and hovered there, gazing down.

From within Regret, Innis watched Merlo. Watched for breath. After everything that had happened, everything she'd been a part of, she didn't want to have to watch Merlo die.

"Merlo?" she asked in a timid voice. "It's me, boy."

No movement from the beagle.

"Merlo, please..."

Was that movement? Did his side raise a fraction of an inch? Was he breathing?

Oh, please, for the love of God, let him be breathing!

And he was. She could see it clearly now. Her beautiful boy was breathing. The only man that hadn't betrayed her. He was breathing.

But she wasn't. Not any longer.

Back in the basement of the cabin in the woods, inside a place that was only partially of reality, Special Investigator Frank Markum bore down on Innis Blake's faceless form. His fingers tightened around her throat and squeezed. Harder and harder he clenched until he could see the exposed veins in her temple throb with backwashing blood.

Blubbering like a man at his beloved's funeral, Frank whimpered, "Die. Die, you bitch. Please, die."

Innis's eyes snapped open and Frank was able to watch the life as it fled her. She struggled for a bit, but not for long. She was already so weak, had lost so much blood, that her body finally came to know what the boy in the eyepatch had known for some time.

Innis Blake was dead. Her body just hadn't accepted that fact.

"I want Dennis back," Frank muttered as he continued to squeeze. "I want him back, you bitch!"

Frank was unaware of the man who was now standing at the bottom of the stairs. He was unaware that this man had an assault rifle aimed at him. He was unaware that this man was demanding he step off and away from the woman. That Frank should comply or take a bullet in the head. That Frank heard none of this was no surprise. He'd lost his mind long ago, back when he'd not told the truth about his father's death. When he hadn't confessed and told the investigating officers that Papa Markum and he had been fighting when the old man took his tumble. When he failed to call an ambulance after finding no pulse thumping in his father's wrist.

Because killing is hard for good men.

Frank jerked his clasped hands forward and backward, effectively bashing Innis's head against the wooden table.

"I WANT MY DENNIS BACK!"

The man in the doorway regretfully fired his rifle, and Special Investigator Frank Markum wanted for nothing ever again.

Merlo's eyes flickered open and he saw, inches away from him, a statue of maybe six inches tale. It was a lady, he was sure of that, but it was, as far as his little doggie brain could see, not alive. It was too small to be alive. It was barely the size of a strip of bacon.

Speaking of bacon...

When the dog came in, the boy was clutching the doll to his chest. He was once more one person and not three. He was, once more, Lody. There was no more Midnight Man. His father's legacy of cruelty was behind him.

Regret had served its purpose. And now, only forgiveness existed.

Lody petted the doll's hair and cried. Thick tears rolled down his dirty cheeks, and he blinked both wetness and settling plaster dust from his eyes.

Merlo came to him and licked away his tears. The dog sat down beside the boy and leaned his head against the boy's shoulder. No more fear.

In the end, there was only resolution. And resolution trumped forgiveness every time.

The theater was gone. Lody's version of the Withered no longer existed. It would continue on, of course, but in somebody else's mind. In someone else's memory.

Because of this, Mia had nowhere to go but back to the Bastard's lair.

"You failed me," said the Bastard from his pulpit. He tapped forever long fingers against the stone while he awaited his answer.

"Aye," was all Mia said.

"And what do you think I should do with you now? *I* have no use for you."

"Lemme die. I beg of ye, lemme die."

"She asked me the same thing, you know," the Bastard said as he came around his podium and stepped into the light of the bonfire. "The girl you stole. The *child* you stole away from her mother."

"No..."

The Bastard smiled. It was a wicked thing. "Oh, yes."

Mia's shrieking cries echoed down the funeral holes in the walls and played out over forever like organ music.

The Bastard ate, and was full.

The Creator sat upon the porch steps of the cabin in the woods, watching the second DEA team sweep the area. An ambulance carted off Frank Markum's and Innis Blake's corpses. A coroner's van came to collect whatever was left of the first team, the ones Regret had killed the night of the deaf kid's death.

So much had happened in such a small amount of time.

He would need new creations. All of his were now dead.

He considered losing the visage of Scott Fairchild, the boy with the eyepatch, and figured he'd hold on to it for a while yet. It still held a little power. Besides, people can't refuse a kid with an eyepatch. That was a scientific fact.

The Creator, invisible to the bustling bodies running to and fro with their radios squawking and their boss barking orders, stood. He dusted off his front and strode out into the middle of Lody's creations. The uncompleted bull's head piqued his interest, as did Death with his scythe. These guys could come in handy. The pewter gargoyle with the snake in its hands perched on the lip of the porch's overhang didn't interest him in the least. That thing reminded him too much of Joy, what with the apple in the serpent's mouth. Just looking at that thing gave him the willies.

Now, with this war done and over with, the Creator could rest for a while. Perhaps he'd come back out to play when man hit Mars. That would be interesting. He always wondered how it was that none of these nearly-hairless apes had figured out that's where they originally came from. Oh well, it's not like mankind had any idea how this all started anyway.

C'est la vie.

The Creator strolled away, whistling.

RANDY

Matthew got out of surgery just after ten o'clock that morning. He was moved to a room on a med/surg floor shortly before one. Randy was waiting for him when the staff rolled him in.

"Sex change successful, I take it?" Randy asked, and slapped on his biggest "Vote for Miser" smile.

"He needs his rest. Make it short, Sheriff," a pretty middle-aged nurse said. She didn't look amused, but she did vaguely remind Randy of Flo. This was a good thing.

"Yessum." Randy tipped his nonexistent hat at her, and she left with the rest of her crew. He fought his way out of the geri-chair he was stuck in, and went to Matthew's bedside.

"How's my father?"

"I had Moxie run by between carting off bodies. Your old man's in pain, but that's about par for the course these days, right?"

Matthew nodded. "My throat hurts."

"Quit performing fellatio on street bums for crack money and you should recover in no time."

"Listen at you," Matthew gave a laugh mixed with a groan of pain. He attempted to push himself up in bed and failed. "Get everything sorted out?"

"Oh, heck no. But the DEA took over, so I'm free and clear. Everything's on them. I'll have to give statements and testify about this and that, but my work is mostly done. That there was probably the most screwed up thirty-some hours of life."

Truth be told, Randy wasn't one hundred percent positive that things were over. Whatever madness had befallen his town might still be alive and well out there. All he knew was that things were, as of right now, no longer his business. He'd been more than happy to pass it all off to the DEA, who would more than likely pass it off to the FBI, and so on. For now, all was quiet in his little slice of America, and as long as this need to piss persisted and his need of diapers went away, he believed everything was gonna be all right.

"Lucky you," Matthew said, and winced when his most recent bid at getting comfortable ended in him sliding even farther down in the bed. "I hate these things. They go up, down, sideways, and into the fourth dimension, but I'll be damned if anyone can create a hospital bed that doesn't make your ass sore."

"Sit still. I'll get someone." Randy made to walk around the bed, but Matthew grabbed his hand.

"Wait," Matthew said, his voice weak.

"Yeah. Sure, kid. What's the matter."

"He's gonna die, Randy. He's gonna die and I can't do anything about it. How'd you deal with it, man? How'd you *live* with her, knowing she was going to die?"

"Matt, buddy, everything dies. Flo weren't no different than anyone else. When your old man goes, you'll be there for him., and you'll *want* to be there for him. If you're not, *that* is what you'll regret. You will never regret being there. I can promise you that much."

For a time, Matthew cried.

And, for a time, Randy held him.

NELL

Nell Morgan arrived at the hospital that afternoon, expecting the worst. Instead, she found Tom sitting up in bed, reading an issue of *Redbook*.

"Wha-what? How?"

"Hey, baby," Tom said with a smile. She didn't think she'd seen such a beautiful smile in all her days.

"Wh-wh-wh—" She stopped, collected her words, and tried again. "When did you wake up?"

"This morning sometime. Did you know I'm missing a few parts?" he held up his missing hand and smiled.

Nell Morgan fainted dead away.

"Guess you don't want to hear about where I been," Tom said. "That one's a doozy."

He pressed the call button, and when the nurse answered, he asked them to come collect his wife from the floor. When she woke up, he'd tell her about how she was the reason he'd come back. That he'd remembered that time, at the drive–in, and how much he loved her. But that could wait. First thing was first. They had to get her out of the doorway.

Funnily enough, for the first time in his life, Tom Morgan didn't want a cigarette. He was less a few pieces, but complete inside. That was all that really mattered.

CRUELTY

NATALIE

While Tom Morgan was counting his blessings, Natalie Holden was wondering whether or not they'd let her go back to work with only one hand. She gazed down at her bandaged paw and grimaced. She supposed not. Mostly though she was glad it was her left hand. She used her right hand for important shit, like flipping through Netflix on her tablet and wiping her ass.

Just like that, she was laughing. This laughter was stemmed from having survived, from having lived through one of the craziest experiences she was likely ever to have. Like Miser, she worried that the monsters were still around, but deep inside, she knew they were gone. She did not concern herself with the whys of the situation.

She was still cackling like a school girl when her kaku came in, and even though the old woman looked at her like she was crazy, she didn't make Natalie stop. Kaku simply waited. These things took time. Kaku knew that every wound needs the poison sucked out of it, and that's all laughter really was, wasn't it? Poison being evacuated from your body? This thought pleased her, and she sat beside her granddaughter and read Natalie *Wuthering Heights*.

Later she told Natalie about her date with Running with Rabbits. Natalie listened and smiled and laughed at all the right moments and called for medicine when the pain in her hand got too bad. When the drugs kicked in, she promised her grandmother that she'd never miss another shopping date. Kaku told her all right, but knew that children will be children. They all love their parents and grandparents, but even the best ones go astray from time to time. The most important thing to Kaku was that Natalie was happy, that she might find a little joy and hold onto it.

LODY

The desert stretched out before them, welcoming them with expansive arms. Lody thought everything was quite beautiful, from the painted mountains to the rolling dunes to the cacti shimmering and waving in the heat. A smile stretched across his face, and he leaned down to scratch Merlo behind the ear.

Somewhere in the world, a boy and his dog moseyed on down the road.

E. Lorn
Prattville, Alabama
October 2013-April 2015

AFTERWORD

Hello, everybody. E here.

This fever dream disguised as a novel was written and rewritten over the course of eighteen months. Before this project, I had not spent any longer than a month on a novel (*Pennies for the Damned* excluded, but the hard work on that novel didn't start until well after *Cruelty* was in the can).

The cruelty Cruelty deals out over the course of this novel is an extension of the pain I was in while writing it. This pain became so bad that I ended up in the hospital for my fourth back surgery shortly after *Cruelty*'s completion. I used to write in marathon sessions, pouring out eight- to twelve-thousand words per sitting. Nowadays, I've had to train myself to write slower, as I cannot sit for more than thirty to forty-five minutes at a time. I don't like writing in bed, and I don't recommend you do so either. Neck strain is a motherfucker.

Medical bills almost put an end to this series. The first five episodes were live when I went into surgery. The final five were written but unedited. When I got out of the hospital, I had to deal with a slow recovery and a lack of funds. I live off my writing, and at that point I had burned through my savings paying for in-patient physical therapy. Nothing sells better than a new release, and I had nothing new to release because I couldn't afford editing. I was stuck. I didn't think the final five episodes of this serial would ever see the light of day. I posted as much on one of my favorite haunts (Booklikes), and the community responded. I started an

Indiegogo campaign the same day, and the project was funded well before the final week. I cried. A lot. To have so many people invest so much in such a short period of time simply because they believed in my work truly floored me, and I will forever be grateful to anyone who has every done anything to support this project.

Even now as I write this, I have tears in my eyes. These tears are part joyful and part sorrowful. I'm glad this story has final reached you, but knowing I will no longer be working on this project makes me sad.

Oh, and in case you're wondering, the answer is yes. If I had to go through that surgery, my long recovery, and all that pain again simply to be able to start over on this project, I'd do it in a heart beat. What can I say—I'm a glutton for punishment.

Confession time: Twon was one of my favorite characters. Dude was a blast to write. For some reason, the truly awful ones always are.

Merlo, of course, was another favorite. I'm glad he made it. I really am.

Paul Nelson, Matthew Pontiff, Anne-Marie Monlezun, and Sarah Frost are real people. I enjoyed killing the three that died, but only because they asked for it. Literally. They literally asked me to kill them. Cool, right?

Finally, the following people are the reason why you were able to read this:

Shelley Milligan
Mike McBride
Kimberly Yerina
Jeff Brackett
Bill Jones
Erika Croy
Amanda Sulzbach
Diane M. Evans
Paul Cooley
Dixie Pethoud

Matthew Pontiff
Adam Light
Nicole N. Howard
Jason Parent
Jessica Nottingham
Paul Nelson
Autumn Turner
Paul Cardullo
Evans Light
Michael Crane
Scot Leedom
Sarah Frost
Dan Schwent
Anne-Marie Monlezun

Well, that's it then. It's really over. Damn.

Take care of each other,

E.

Made in the USA
San Bernardino, CA
29 August 2019